DOCTOR LEVITIN

DOCTOR LEVITIN

A Novel

David Shrayer-Petrov

Translated from the Russian by Arna B. Bronstein,
Aleksandra I. Fleszar, and Maxim D. Shrayer

Edited and with Notes by
Maxim D. Shrayer

WAYNE STATE UNIVERSITY PRESS
DETROIT

ISBN (paperback) 978-0-8143-4573-3
ISBN (printed case) 978-0-8143-4572-6
ISBN (ebook) 978-0-8143-4574-0

Library of Congress Cataloging number: 2018946849

The translation of this novel was supported by a grant from Boston College.

This is a work of fiction. Names, characters, places, and incidents either are the products of the author's imagination or, if real, are used fictitiously.

Wayne State University Press
Leonard N. Simons Building
4809 Woodward Avenue
Detroit, MI 48201-1309

Visit us online at wsupress.wayne.edu

CONTENTS

A Note on the Translation

This translation follows the text of *Doctor Levitin* as it appears in David Shrayer-Petrov's *Gerbert i Nelli*, the third complete Russian edition, published in 2014 in Moscow by Knizhniki. Detailed information on the text and the history of its publication is found in the back of the volume.

All translations from Russian-language sources, including other Russian literary works and news items, are the work of the novel's translators. All quotations from the Hebrew Bible are from *Tanakh: The Holy Scriptures* (Philadelphia: The Jewish Publication Society, 1988). All quotations from the New Testament are from the King James Bible.

A simplified, and, we hope, reader-friendly version of the Library of Congress system for transliterating the Russian alphabet is used throughout the text of the English translation. Exceptions have been made for some Russian words and geographical and personal names that have gained a common spelling in English, such as Joseph Brodsky instead of "Iosif Brodsky," Osip Mandelstam instead of "Osip Mandelshtam," Babi Yar instead of "Babiy Yar," and so forth.

About the Author

David Shrayer-Petrov was born in 1936 in Leningrad (St. Petersburg), and debuted as a poet in the 1950s. After graduating from medical school in 1959, Shrayer-Petrov served as a military physician in Belarus before returning to Leningrad to pursue both literature and medicine. He married the philologist and translator Emilia Shrayer (née Polyak) in 1962 and moved to his wife's native Moscow in 1964. There, he published a collection of poetry, many literary translations, and two books of essays in the 1960s and 70s. Exploration of Jewish themes put Shrayer-Petrov in conflict with the Soviet authorities, limiting publication of his work and prompting him to emigrate. A Jewish refusenik in 1979–1987, Shrayer-Petrov lived as an outcast in his native country but continued to write prolifically, despite expulsion from the Soviet Writers' Union and persecution by the KGB. He was finally allowed to emigrate in 1987, settling in Providence, Rhode Island, where he was able to continue his academic work as a cancer researcher on the faculty of the Brown University Medical School. Since emigrating, Shrayer-Petrov has published twelve books of poetry, ten novels, six collections of short stories, and four volumes of memoirs. *Doctor Levitin* and *May You Be Cursed, Don't Die*—volumes one and two of Shrayer's trilogy about the Exodus of Jews from the Soviet Union—were written in 1979–84 in Moscow and then smuggled to the West. An incomplete edition of the first volume of the trilogy was published in Israel in 1986, and the first complete edition of volumes one and two came out in post-Soviet Moscow in 1992 and was listed for the Russian Booker Prize. Two other editions of volume one and two of the trilogy have appeared in Russia, in 2006 and 2014. Three collections of Shrayer-Petrov's fiction have appeared in English translation: *Jonah and Sarah: Jewish Stories of Russia and America* (2003); *Autumn in Yalta: A Novel and Three Stories* (2006); and *Dinner with

Stalin and Other Stories (2014 finalist for the Wallant Prize), all three of them edited by his son Maxim D. Shrayer, author and academic. Shrayer-Petrov's works have been listed for a number of other literary prizes and translated into ten foreign languages. Now retired from research, Doctor Shrayer-Petrov lives in Brookline, Massachusetts with his wife of over fifty years, Emilia Shrayer, and devotes himself to full-time writing. Jews and Russians are the "two peoples . . . closest to me in flesh (genes) and spirit (language)," Shrayer-Petrov wrote in 1985, less than two years before emigrating from Russia. In a 2014 interview, Shrayer-Petrov commented on his experience as an immigrant writer: "Most of my recent stories fashion Russian—Jewish-Russian—characters living in America. In this sense, I've become an American writer. . . . I think that I've rooted myself in New England. It has become my second—now my main—habitat."

DOCTOR LEVITIN

PROLOGUE

We know we are Russians;
You consider us Jews.

On the corner of Meshchanskaya Street and some lane, named after God only knows whom, across from a fashionable hair salon located on the ground floor of a concrete-paneled building, there stands an old stately mansion. The mansion is in the last year of its life, even though its fine architecture and location—in the center of Moscow just north of the Garden Ring—should have guaranteed it years of uninterrupted happiness. A long time before the 1917 revolutions, this single-family dwelling with balustrades and adjoining stables used to be taller than its neighbors. The stucco designs, which adorn the cornices and spaces between the roof and upper story windows, spoke to the good taste and prosperity of the mansion's original owners, and also served as a testament to the architect's craft and vision. In the decades following the revolution, the mansion was subdivided into apartments. And now, as Moscow was being readied for the 1980 Olympics, a decision was made to empty the mansion of its inhabitants and renovate it completely. The decision was final, and there was talk that the old residents would be resettled in the city's new sleeping districts.

In this old mansion lived the family of Professor Levitin: Herbert Anatolyevich Levitin himself, his wife Tatyana Vasilyevna and their son Anatoly, and, more recently, Grandfather Vasily Matveyevich, Tatyana's father. For the past twenty years, Professor Herbert Anatolyevich Levitin had been working at the medical school's primary care clinic: first as a young resident having recently returned from two years of medical service in a remote Russian village, then as a young assistant professor, later an associate professor, and, for the last six years, as a full professor of medicine.

The events of the past two years had turned the lives of the Levitins upside down, transmuting them from a successful professorial family with a steady (if not exactly pampered) daily life into a grief-stricken family, and the air itself scraped the soul with something akin to the barbed wire of concentration camps: hopelessness.

But this did not happen all at once. When we first saw this old mansion, when we met the Levitins and began to follow their fate, the plot was just starting to thicken.

Moscow Jews had already been awakened by the wave of Jewish emigration rolling in from the provinces, yet this ever-growing wave had somehow bypassed Doctor Levitin and his family. They had a good enough life, and Doctor Levitin rejected the herd mentality both in social and scientific affairs.

FIRST THIRD

My Slavic soul in a Jewish wrapping . . .

1 t was a blazing, rooster-red Moscow September. The sun was pouring through the yellow, scalloped leaves of the linden trees and the brown, blood-spotted, comblike leaves of the maples. Outside the windows, the Garden Ring boomed like a waterfall. A phone call distracted Doctor Herbert Levitin from reading an article in a British medical journal. He had only managed to get the gist of the author's approach to the regeneration of kidney tissue after a purulent inflammation.

"Herbert, is that you?" a familiar voice said into the receiver.

"Semyon?"

"That's right, you guessed it."

"Any news?" Herbert Anatolyevich asked.

"Only the best. I got permission to leave." Semyon sounded triumphant, like a marathon winner.

At first Herbert Anatolyevich did not believe that Semyon Aizenberg had said those exact words, that he was speaking about a final and complete parting with Russia. Senya Aizenberg was his close childhood friend. They had grown up in the same building and had done watch during the German bombings. In fact they used to do everything together until Senya married and moved to the Novye Cheryomushki district of Moscow—no longer Senya now, but Semyon Isaakovich Aizenberg, head of one of the city's leading construction enterprises. Semyon's voice pulled Herbert Anatolyevich out of his stupor.

"Herbert, can you hear me?"

"Yes, I hear you Senya, it's just that it's all so sudden."

"My dear professor, I didn't want to get you worried before it became final."

"Nobody really knows when the right time is," Herbert Anatolyevich said, not believing his own words.

"But that's not a conversation for the telephone. Galya and I will swing by tonight—say, tenish? We'll say our goodbyes to you and your family, to the old building. For the last time."

There was plenty of time before the Aizenbergs would arrive. Tatyana was sitting and sewing, half listening to the radio, anxious as she was about the changes happening in their home after the illness of the Levitins' son, Anatoly, or Tolya. His admission to the evening division of the medical school where his father worked—essentially a handout. Those conspiratorial glances between her husband and son. And the disapproving groans of Grandfather Vasily Matveyevich, who didn't really understand much of anything, owing both to his lack of education and loss of hearing. Yet he knew that something wasn't right, something had taken a turn of events; he knew and sensed it with his soul, suspicious of his long-nosed Jewish son-in-law, yet loving his grandson. Herbert Anatolyevich went up to his wife and kissed her on the neck, in that cherished spot where he would kiss her after they had been apart or after times of disagreement—wordlessly, to restore their intimate connection. He pushed a strand of hair away from her forehead and then watched as the little spring made of golden straw fell back onto her forehead. This was all part of the Levitins' lovemaking that made Tatyana and Herbert Anatolyevich closer together, a lovemaking not exactly tempestuous, but which always ended in a soul-baring conversation or in intimacy. Tatyana, with her calm, unhurried ways, the kind of person whom the Russian folk imagination would deem an "independent woman," did not immediately respond to these harbingers of foreplay. She had never been able to free herself completely of all the veneration and elated respect she felt for "her professor." And so, each time, Herbert Anatolyevich had to arouse her, to stir up her dormant, bashful passion.

But today all that had a different significance. Herbert Anatolyevich vacillated, then asked her, as if apologizing, "Tanyusha, the Aizenbergs will be coming by around ten tonight. I wonder if you could put something together for supper?"

"Of course. But why so late?"

"They are coming to say goodbye."

"Going on vacation? Where?"

"They're actually leaving for good. That's what's going on, Tanyusha," Herbert Anatolyevich answered.

Tatyana put away her sewing. Anxiety, doubt, alarm—maybe she had lost her ability to understand human speech—all that flickered in her eyes. Herbert Anatolyevich understood that he had to explain immediately, and that this explanation could serve as a link connecting their family issues with the larger issues that so many Jewish families were facing.

"Tanyusha, it seems that they decided, so I was led to believe from their hints. You can't say much on the phone. They decided, it appears, to emigrate. To Israel. Or to America—we'll find out tonight."

Tatyana was looking at Herbert Anatolyevich with fear, as if it weren't the Aizenbergs but their own family that had come to this terrifying threshold. It was as if for the first time she was seeing her husband's elongated cranium with its protruding chin and large ears, his bald patches surrounded by kinky hair, his dark eyes with heavy tortoise eyelids, his beaked nose—all the Semitic characteristic traits, which had not previously given her pause because she loved her husband in his entirety; she loved his quick mind, his passion for work. She loved him and did not ask herself what it was that bound her to him the most. Now, for the first time, she looked at her husband impartially, not with loving eyes, but with the eyes of a Russian woman who was sharing a bed, a home, and food with this long-nosed man. Tatyana even went up to the three-sided mirror and started to look herself over: what if she, too, had grown "their" typical features. Anything could happen, even the most bizarre scenario, if it was happening to their old friend Semyon Aizenberg, the most sociable of their friends, the most Russian of any Jew they knew. Nobody could drink as much, nobody spent as much time at soccer stadiums, nobody was as much of a skirt chaser. And if Semyon was leaving Russia for good, then all sorts of unbelievable transformations could happen to her as well. No, everything had remained as nature had given her: hair, forehead, nose with clearly demarcated nostrils a bit wide at the end, a mouth with fresh and resilient lips, a rounded and dimpled chin. And her breasts were erect; her hips had not spread like it sometimes happens with older Jewish women.

"Is Tolya also going to eat with us tonight?" Tatyana asked, hoping to postpone at least that.

"It would be good for him to know what people are up to these days. Particularly since . . ." Herbert Anatolyevich picked a shiny gold apple, took a bite from its side, and grew silent, hesitant to tell his wife the most important thing of all: their son, too, wished to emigrate. Timidly, like during their first year of marriage, Tatyana leaned toward him. Rubbing her cheek against his chin, she put her arms around his neck, then pressed herself against the length of her husband's body—awkward, Jewish, and yet dear to her. He began to stroke her body, starting at the hips, then to the waist and up. Her breasts tightened, like a bridle strained by an excited horse. Herbert Anatolyevich locked the door from the inside. Tatyana was freeing herself from her robe. She looked like a gymnast, in her turtleneck sweater and tights, only a bit more filled out than the girls that perform on balance beams and gracefully twist on the trapeze. He always asked Tatyana to let her hair down; lying next to his naked wife, he kissed her hair, and she caressed his body: his hairy chest, his stomach, and his Jewish manhood.

And now, when exhausted by their sweetly torturous shudders, they lay there, intertwined, inseparable by anything or by anyone, Tatyana asked very quietly, "There was something you didn't tell me about Tolya. Right?"

Herbert Anatolyevich kissed Tatyana. Then he answered, "It seems to me that Tolya will never forgive them the insult. He's becoming interested in the idea of emigration. I don't want him to do this without us. That would be harder for him and for us, too, Tanyusha darling. You know we can't ever be separated from him."

"And what about my father?"

"He will go with us."

"What are you saying, Herbert? Father will never leave Russia. Never. I understand how you feel because we're connected by blood, we have Tolya. And our whole life is together. But my father won't even understand what we're talking about. That's going to be our misfortune. I don't know how yet, but a misfortune will come to us. I have this feeling, and I'm scared for all of us."

Tatyana rested her head on Herbert Anatolyevich's chest.

Sobs were racking her body, and it was strange how quickly the boundary had been crossed between an insatiable desire, which compressed each one of her cells to the limit before it relaxed totally, and the convulsive quivers of a face involuntarily distorted by grief. A face that even now remained dear, as if it wasn't a woman who had just given him the joy of rejuvenation, but his hurt, ailing child.

WHY DO I write about somebody else and not about myself?

THIS SOMETIMES HAPPENS with passionately monogamous women, who are completely absorbed with their husbands, their own family. They do not have close female friends to whom they can tell their most intimate feelings and emotions, and who in turn reveal theirs—just as powerful yet different, in their texture, or perhaps their coloring. If one has such close female friends, one can teach them something, while also learning how to show more restraint, not to yield so quickly to a husband's caresses before touching on her deepest fantasies or needs; and one might learn from her girlfriends not to bare herself before her husband when in tears, when feeling blue, or in moments of indecision. Tatyana had been deprived of all that because she felt no kinship to the city, and therefore had no close girlfriends here, even though she was naturally sociable and compassionate. She had moved to Moscow from a village and had never quite set roots amid these stones, where trees were planted in crevices between asphalt coverings and did not grow freely. The prisonlike quality of city living had struck Tatyana deeply when she first saw the iron grates on basement windows and ground floors, and iron bars framing even the roots of the linden trees. From under these bars, tree trunks were forced to stretch themselves toward the sun. In Moscow Tatyana hadn't found a soulmate like Masha Teryokhina from her native village of Maryino. For some of these reasons—for all of them—Herbert Anatolyevich became not only her husband but also her best friend. Truthfully, she always harbored the thought that this life she had with Herbert Anatolyevich wasn't real, but invented and fortuitous. As a result a fear resided within her, always hidden but alive, that this life of hers, staged, yet good and stable, would end abruptly, only to be replaced by a real, bad and unwished for life. Each time these burdensome thoughts, unless they came to her in a dream, ended in the same way. She would imagine the poisoned smirk on the face of Pasha Teryokhin, her sweet boyfriend from those birdcherry school years of long ago.

$$\mathscr{J}$$

IT ONLY HAPPENS when you cling to nature with your heart and soul. I know of no greater happiness than walking with my son, fishing rods in hand, across the old Pärnu park toward the jetty. At first only the scattered cobblestones, surrounded by tufts of green grass flattened by shoes, point to the general direction of the jetty—an artificial stone arrow that was shot toward the Baltic Sea a hundred years ago. Then the rushes stand farther apart, and we jump from boulder to boulder. On both sides of the jetty, the lowering sun has set the Pärnu Bay aflame. The water is perfectly still, a tender play of sea and stone. The feminine element is the sea, and the masculine one is the stone. The sun sanctifies their union. We cross from stone to stone amid this harmonious union of sun, sea, and stone. We are happy with nature's happiness. The stone jetty and the sea are one. The sea gives itself to the jetty, and the sun itself performs the triple wedding ceremony of the elements. Sea—jetty—sun. And all the happy people. But it can happen otherwise. Suddenly the wind shifts direction, arises from those unknown evil forces of nature. Shirts fly like sails, and it is hard to hold on to the fishing rods. The sun spills like an egg yolk poured through the clouds, then disappears. The waves thunder and raucously pound against the rocks. Pouring rain, rain with no beginning or end, slices the cold air with cold steel rods. Pelleting the air, the rain drags the sky toward the sea. This discord steals harmony from the relationship of sea, stone, and sun. And people have no place here, because harmony has been destroyed. The disintegration of the elements makes us despondent. We flee in fear.

THE AIZENBERGS ARRIVED a little after ten. Grandfather Vasily Mat- veyevich had his fill of television and went to sleep. The table, set for company, stood in the middle of the living room. Tatyana had never become accustomed to receiving guests in the kitchen—after the urban fashion. Guests should be entertained the living room, just as in her village home celebrations would always be held in the *gornitsa*—the common room. Semyon Aizenberg had burst into the Levitins' apart- ment, bringing along an elixir of self-assuredness and victory, a spirit of departure, of an approaching vacation. When the Levitins kissed Semyon's ruddy freckled cheeks and were poked by his red Cossack mustache, it was as if they also received a dose of this elixir. And when Galya Aizenberg, swishing her leather skirt and squinting her myopic eyes hidden behind the thick round dishes of her lenses, started to jab- ber on about Russian folk crafts' popularity abroad, Tatyana stopped torturing herself and joined the conversation. What will be, will be, she thought to herself. Other people are going, and we won't perish either. After a bit of conversation that distracted her from her thoughts, she fell silent again, thinking about her father. What would happen to him? While they ate and drank, the Aizenbergs told their hosts all about the steps involved in emigrating to Israel. First you get an invitation from a relative. Then you file an application with OVIR, the Visa Section. Then you wait. They did not wait very long, only six months. They were very lucky; Galya's parents had left six months earlier.

"And we didn't even know about it," Tatyana said simply and from the heart.

"People are all different. They react differently. We decided not to spread this around too much," Galya explained.

From the way Herbert Anatolyevich held the shot glass, his hand slightly shaking, Tatyana noticed that he wanted to ask something important.

He finally decided to ask. "You know, Senya, I have an uncle in Tel Aviv. My late father's brother. I'm not sure how to go about this . . ."

"Why that's wonderful. You couldn't ask for anything better. Write to him, old fellow, as soon as possible, and you'll have your invitation on the table."

"Easier said than done. Imagine writing to Israel? I work at a medical school . . ."

"Yes, a professor. Nomenclature," Semyon quipped.

"That's right," Tatyana came to her husband's rescue. "Herbert doesn't want any premature publicity. Doesn't want to put his boss in an awkward position."

"Yeah, yeah, your boss! Treat him with care! And where was this boss of yours when Tolya wasn't accepted to medical school? Cut the crap," Galya broke into the conversation.

"Galya's right, old man. Who cares about all this nonsense," Semyon said.

"I just can't, Semyon. Perhaps you could pass my request on to my uncle in Tel Aviv. But I won't write to him myself. Not quite yet."

Semyon reached into the inside pocket of his sport coat and took out a little notebook. He jotted down the uncle's address and the Levitins' personal information.

"What are you doing about Grandfather Vasily Matveyevich?" he asked.

"I will not leave my father here," Tatyana said sternly.

"So he'll go with you," Galya lit up a cigarette to hide her irritation with Tatyana. "Don't create an issue out of nothing!"

"He won't ever agree to it," Tatyana said.

"I'm almost sure that he won't go," Herbert Anatolyevich said. "He barely tolerates me as is. And over there it's all full of the long-nosed ones like me."

They sat at the table for a long time, drinking wine, then tea. And smoking. What to do with Grandfather Vasily Matveyevich they could not figure out.

Finally Semyon proposed, "I'll ask your uncle to send an invitation for all of you, including Grandfather Vasily Matveyevich. Let's see what happens. Maybe you can break him down. Time is of the essence. Anatoly's position in med school is tenuous at best. Come next autumn, they can draft him into the army. You'd better hurry."

They walked the Aizenbergs partway home, as far as Trubnaya Square. Moscow, illuminated by the flashing sparks of the last trolleys, was turning in for the night. Alone with this huge, quieted city in which they had been born or spent major parts of their lives, melting away in the silence of the night and hiding in the corners of public gardens were all the injustices, insults, long lines, meat-grinding crowds on public transport; the fear of expressing oneself fully and freely; the fear of exposing oneself as an individual who, in essence, had a right to the pursuit of happiness, personal happiness, and not of the collective, mythical, and long-promised prosperity. Like the morning fog displaced by rays of the sun, all of this had drifted to the sidelines in the minute of their communion with nighttime Moscow. Those leaving for good—and those seeing them off—had found themselves alone with Moscow: the mother that was weaning her children.

I WAS DRAWN to the geometry of tree trunks and snowy expanses. I learned how to complete a circuitous ski trail in two hours, no faster and no slower than most people. I blended into the mass of skiers, all of them anticipating the completion of the trail. It was possible to imagine that none of us were moving at all; I did not overtake anybody, and hardly anybody passed me in the course of those 120 minutes of geometric snow time. There were exceptions, when someone refused to trudge patiently along the trail and would go off to the side, pull himself together, rest. Or perhaps the ski trail itself, like some sort of closed loop—an arc bending around the forest's edge, not far from a haystack—this very powerful line of force, which neither I nor any of my friends (I had asked them) had laid out, would refuse to help a particular person in any way. And he would drop out of the race. That's when the others, myself included, would overtake him. But once it happened that they overtook me. Suddenly I found myself off the track. I had become a toppled over and derailed handcar. But there was no crash. To the contrary, it was as if I had seen the light. Instead of the reckless merry-go-around of snow-splattered tree trunks, round bridges of trees bent over the ski track and round tree stumps adorned with rounded snow hats, and oval snow throws draped over fir tree paws, I found myself alone with a family of trees. A birch and a hawthorn. Yes, I had been derailed. Or I had derailed myself, if one considers that it was not we who glided along the track, but rather the track carried us along the geometrically perfect snow panorama. Here was the family of a large old birch tree, with a young birch growing from the side of its trunk and linking the mother birch with the father hawthorn. A holy family. All three were dressed in coarse linen shirts, fastened with narrow dark belts. Somewhere above me, closer to the sky, their branches had intertwined, like fingers of the deaf who did not wish to communicate in front of a stranger. The trees were anxious. They even tried to untangle their branches, agitated by some inner discord. But their trunks, conjoined from birth, could not separate. This was the worst kind of ordeal and punishment. The miserable hawthorn spread out his branches, as if in prayer. There were hardly any sweet crimson berries left on the hawthorn branches, and the birds had abandoned him.

*

Semyon Aizenberg sent them a letter from Haifa. Everything was going well so far. They were learning Hebrew and waiting for their placement. It was still not clear where they would live and work, but as Semyon put it in the letter, "if you have a neck, a harness will always be found." He also said that he had met with Herbert Anatolyevich's uncle and had given him the Levitins' request.

However, before describing the events that took place in the Levitin household after they received the invitation from Israel, we must first return to a time six months before that, because the electric shock that had struck the Levitins would not have stirred them so much had it not been for Anatoly's ill-fated application to medical school.

Professor Levitin's son Anatoly was to graduate from high school in six months, and he had decided to apply to medical school in the field of general and internal medicine. This was a perfectly reasonable decision. A third generation of the Levitins would be entering the field of medicine. Herbert Anatolyevich was well aware of what hardships his son had to face, but did not dissuade him, particularly since the father had never been one to choose the easy path. Right after New Year's 1978, he had a serious talk with Anatoly.

Herbert Anatolyevich's study was bathed in the amber January light. The professor had just returned from the clinic. In the evening he was planning to attend a meeting of the Society of General and Internal Medicine, where Academician Tatishchev was to present a paper. Looking forward to Tatishchev's topic, "Chemotherapy of Pneumonia," Herbert Anatolyevich was in high spirits. Tatyana revered this state of her husband's being.

"Your father is in a state of levitation. So don't contradict him, don't distract him," she instructed Anatoly.

"I actually never contradict anyone, mama. I've simply decided to apply to medical school. I don't want to study anywhere else."

Molten amber had moved from the leather couch to the carpet with a hieroglyphic pattern. The clock had struck three times when Anatoly came up to the desk where his father sat working. Herbert Anatolyevich had eaten his lunch a half hour before, and now he was completing a list of possible questions for Tatishchev along with the speaker's possible answers. Herbert Anatolyevich took special pleasure in this secret method. He had a real talent for predicting the conception, culmination, and outcome of a scientific discussion, how it would flare up after challenging questions were posed to the presenters, and how they would respond—whether correctly or incorrectly, in his opinion. In advance of a presentation at the Society of General and Internal Medicine, Herbert Anatolyevich would create a table of question and answers, so that upon the conclusion of the meeting, he would check his table against the actual discussion, the way a chess player checks the theory of the game against its practice. Anatoly's arrival interrupted the professor's blessed state of levitation, which was not unlike a poet's improvisation.

"Hi, papa! You wanted to see me?"

"Yes, of course, of course, son. Sit down. Just give me one second."

"Been solving your puzzles again?" Anatoly joked, kissing his father.

"Practicing clairvoyance, that's all."

Now that they were sitting across from each other, one could clearly see the strong resemblance between them. The Jewish lineage was dominant in their appearance. Both were tall and lanky, round-shouldered. Herbert Anatolyevich's face was striking in the angularity of its form: nose, chin, structure of the skull, even his glasses—everything had sharp angles. Incredible that within the sharp-edged boundaries of this bellicose-looking being, there lived such a gentle, forgiving, and magnanimous soul. Anatoly looked a lot like his father, but the sharp angles had been rounded out, and the Pskov linen white of Tatyana's skin and hair (the linen white of northwest Russia) had diluted the dark pigmentation of Herbert Anatolyevich's hair and eyes. If the essence of Herbert Anatolyevich's personality could be defined as kindness meeting decisiveness, the fabric of his son's character was woven out of good-naturedness and purity.

Having entered into his table another probable answer of tonight's presenter, Herbert Anatolyevich put his fountain pen aside and stared pensively at his son.

"My dear boy, it's about time to end this uncertainty. Where will you be applying? Mama said to medical school. Is that so?"

"Papa, you yourself wanted me to become a physician. And I want the same thing."

"You see, son, all the pros are there—and only one con."

"What?"

"Will you make the cut?"

"I'll do well on the entrance exams. And the rest will all fall into place."

"The rest. I have never discussed the rest with you: that terrible, unjust situation, where the outcome of any competition, including the one that still lies ahead of you, is influenced not by grades or results, but by something entirely different."

"You mean my Jewish background?"

"Yes, that's exactly what I mean, my boy."

"But I'm listed, registered, as Russian."

"True. We did everything we could to protect you from unavoidable disappointments, although, I must admit, it was demeaning, downright insulting for me. But that was okay. We got through that. Let's just say it's forgotten. But they don't want to forget anything. Particularly now. We know we are Russians; they consider us Jews."

"Who are 'they'? And why particularly now?"

"It's a special department. Let's call it, say, the Committee for Overseeing the Drain of Energy, or the KGB."

"I don't understand, papa. We're honest people, law-abiding citizens. What do you and I, our family and my medical school application, have to do with any of this?"

And thus Herbert Anatolyevich had to tell his son Anatoly that they, too, could end up in the circles of those individuals who are of interest to the agents of the KGB. He told Anatoly that in protest against injustices carried out against Jews, many Jewish families were reconnecting with relatives who had long ago left for the Mandate of Palestine, family connections half-forgotten and erased through decades of separation. That Soviet Jews were now getting invitations from relatives and leaving for Israel. There was so much that Herbert Anatolyevich then told his half-Russian son, and much that Anatoly understood for the first time. Most importantly, for the first time, he felt himself a part of a nation, a nation that had suffered and been persecuted for thousands of years, a nation that was given hope after the 1917 revolutions, a hope that was gradually lost. Anatoly remembered *Uncle Tom's Cabin* and other books depicting the suffering of mulattos and other mixed-race people, who always ended up among the persecuted ones, although they were half or even mostly of the same blood as those who were persecuting them.

"Why then aren't we leaving, papa? If you know all that and you suffer from it? What are we waiting for?" Anatoly asked.

"The time isn't ripe. And it's not going to be all that simple with mama, either. We'll see. Well, all right. I have to leave for the meeting, and you also have things to do. So, what have we resolved?"

"I'm going to apply to medical school," Anatoly answered.

And so, as a result, another knot was tied, later to become a noose around the neck of the Levitin family.

The second knot was Tatyana herself: Tatyana and her father, Tatyana and the Levitins' Russian roots. Herbert Anatolyevich had brought Tatyana out of her native village in the Pskov Province. And now, at age thirty-eight, the blue-eyed and blond-haired Tatyana was still an attractive woman, sporting the kind of naturally fetching look that is particularly valued in blue-eyed and blond-haired Russian women. Blue eyes and blond hair suit German and Estonian women, who also possess a sophisticated nose and chin shape and long legs. Russian beauties, like those noble white boletus mushrooms, enchant with their natural looks and vigor. This statement is meant to bring this writer closer to the naturalist school. We have such a longing for naturalness that we would rather have decisive, resolute realism than the vagueness of speaking in codes. All of this was absolutely true with respect to Tatyana, who had a happy disposition, bubbling over with life's forces.

Twenty years before the current events, the eighteen-year-old Tatyana Pivovarova had a body like a crisp ripe apple—ginger gold at the beginning of August. Tatyana's father, who had commanded a guerilla unit during the war, was chairman of the village council in his native Maryino. All of that took place a little over twenty years before the current events. The main thing here is not to go astray in the chronology, since our principal story line is gaining shape in 1979, while its origins date back to 1956 and to 1978. The young doctor Herbert Anatolyevich Levitin fell in love with Tatyana Pivovarova. One July afternoon they were both returning home to Maryino from the head clinic in the district center. Herbert Anatolyevich dismissed the medical van, and it gleefully raised a trail of dust over the scorched road leading to the village. For a long time now, they had wanted to be alone: Herbert Anatolyevich, a twenty-six-year-old doctor from Moscow, who, for the first time in his three years of doing public service in a rural hospital, decided to free himself from the chains of self-control; and the eighteen-year-old Tatyana, pure milk and honey, joy to the one she chose and envy of all the rest. They walked along the cracked and dusty country road until they became tired. It was not too hard to find a place to rest. There—the freshly gathered haystacks. Step off the road and make yourself comfortable. And so they stepped off and made themselves comfortable. Herbert Anatolyevich just happened to have a bottle of sweet wine with him, Muscat, and a chocolate bar. Tatyana kissed passionately, freeing all the power that was bursting from her body, and at the same time she understood that kisses alone would not free her from the terrible longing that woke her up in her maidenly bed and would not let her get back to sleep. The kisses wouldn't diminish the longing, but only stir it up and intensify it. They drank the Muscat and ate the chocolate. Herbert Anatolyevich and Tatyana. Herbert, the darling Herbert, and Tatyana, the sweet Tanechka, how they kissed to the point of exhaustion. And the haystack was so intoxicatingly aromatic, and the sweet wine so delicious. Finally, from all the heat and tumult, he had to take his suit off and she her little sundress. Herbert Anatolyevich swore to Tatyana that his intentions were honorable and that he would never allow for anything extreme to happen, that he was just helping to free her from her longing, and with that he was allowed to undo the hooks on her bra. And then still more kisses, and new promises. It was already too late to hold back and not drink the sweet nectar of the berries that stood erect right in front of Herbert Anatolyevich's lips. Tatyana herself understood that this was the end, that there was no going back and no holding back. Her eyes were half closed. And when Herbert Anatolyevich threw off the silky fetters of her panties and kissed her quivering lap, Tatyana only managed to moan these words:

"You won't deceive me, will you? You won't leave me, Herbert darling?"

"I won't deceive you, I promise, Tanechka. I love you, you know."

And Herbert Anatolyevich did not deceive Tatyana. He married her and brought her with him to Moscow. Their son Anatoly—Tolik—was born there. He had already grown up. And now his whole future was at stake.

*

IT IS WINTER now. December 31, 1979. Our troops are in Afghanistan. And here in Maleyevka outside Moscow, in the writers' colony, it is New Year's Eve, like in the rest of the world. The writers are preparing to welcome the year 1980. Everyone is wishing everyone else a Happy New Year: Okudzhava to Sidorov, Sidorov to Bushin, Bushin to Karpeko, Karpeko to Kuznetsov, Kuznetsov to Gerasimov, Gerasimov to Okudzhava. I stand alone in this field, like a lonely snow-covered haystack. The ski track is taking me into the forest. Ahead—like a blazing red sun—my wife's red jacket. A flock of village children runs out from around the bend. They are totally different from our writers' children, even if one of the writers had once been such a village boy with his flap hat twisted sideways and his quilted jacket unbuttoned. The children from the village of Glukhovo stare at me. And they do not understand me. We and they are different from each other. This oppresses me deeply, because, more than anything in this world, I would like to be close to these village children. My own son is a total stranger to them, and occasionally this estranges me from him. A long time ago, during the war, we were evacuated from Leningrad, and I was a village boy, just like these boys. During those four wartime years in the village, I got so used to that life that, if a conflict had arisen around the curve of the road between a flock of city boys and a flock of village boys, I would have definitely sided with the villagers. My whole life I have tried to side with them, but they would pull away from me, exchanging bewildered glances, making fun of me to each other and not acknowledging me as one of their own. And so I am left standing, a lonely snow-covered haystack in the middle of a white field, edged with birch trees dressed in icy chain armor, and pine trees wrapped in white down shawls from the tops to the ground. In the village of my childhood, I felt totally at home with the children of the Urals, blue-eyed with high cheekbones, from a mixture of Permyak and Russian blood, pugnacious from the severity of the climate and from the hunter's fervor that lived in every peasant home in the Urals.

Even today I burn with shame at an act of betrayal I committed as a village boy. A new family of evacuees had come to our village. They didn't come right away, with everyone else, but a couple of years later, after what must have been a long perilous journey to our Siva village in the Vereshchagino District of the Molotov (now Perm) Province. I considered myself a local, a Sivan kid. Actually, I didn't consider it at all; I just didn't think about who I was. My Leningrad prewar life seemed like a colorful dream: A July morning, Ladyfinger eating grapes—something fantastic and serendipitous. There was a boy in this newly arrived Jewish family of the evacuees. A dark-haired, swarthy, Middle Eastern looking Jewish boy. I accosted the new boy after classes behind the shed adjacent to the school. There were kids all around us—the locals ones and the evacuees. But these evacuated kids had also bonded to life in the Urals and had made friends with the locals, having already spent two years with them in the fields and vegetable gardens, fishing and running in the woods together.

"Hey you, stinky vacated butt," I said to the new boy, mispronouncing the word "evacuated" after the village fashion. He stood there, silently, staring at me with astonishment, unable to comprehend what it was that I wanted with him.

"Hey, vacated butt, let's fight." There was no stopping me. Flabbergasted by the boy's indifference to my pestering, I pressed on. "Hey you, what are you rolling your slimy eyes for?"

"Just look at yourself," the boy answered quietly. "You're just the same as I am!"

I looked at him, and for the first time, as if in a mirror, I saw myself through the eyes of the boys around me—both the locals and the evacuees. I was just like that Jewish boy, a stranger among them. A wolf cub pulling a dog sled. For me this was a terrible revelation. From that time on, I began to look around and behind my back and to feel like a stranger among both groups. Even though I wanted to belong both to one and to the other. Both were filled with qualities that I held dear: city and village, Europe and Asia. A lonely, snow-covered haystack in the middle of a white field. A symbol of my soul.

AND SO, ANATOLY'S decision to apply to medical school became the first knot in the tragic story of the Levitin family. The second knot had to do with Tatyana's father, Vasily Matveyevich Pivovarov. By this time he was over seventy. Vasily Matveyevich had lived alone and had been weighed down by farm work. He missed his daughter and grandson. Everything had come together. When Tatyana, who worked in the local housing office, found out that their old Moscow building was slated for major renovations, and that its inhabitants would be relocated, she immediately figured out that it was time to invite her father to Moscow. They moved Vasily Matveyevich from his village, registered him as residing with the Levitins, and planned to petition the authorities for a separate apartment allocation for him and Anatoly. All of these machinations and reshufflings annoyed Herbert Anatolyevich, who was by nature a straight shooter averse to scheming. But like other members of the Soviet intelligentsia, he was not trained to fight evil, and preferred not to notice iniquity, or rather to pretend that he didn't notice. Some people consider this pretense a form of cowardice. Others consider it good manners. In Herbert Anatolyevich's case, I consider it to be a type of self-discipline. They would show a person a tasty treat, and every time he would try to eat it, they would crack the whip. Herbert Anatolyevich had taught himself not to get too involved in many such problems, including matters of daily living.

AT THE END of August 1978, Anatoly walked out of the metro at Kropotkinskaya Station. The Boulevard Ring rose like a green collar around the center of Moscow. The green lushness showed spots of rusty brown. September was already around the bend, but the streets were still filled with summer visitors. You could spot them by their timidity in crossing the street and their readiness to talk to strangers. For Anatoly everything in the life of the pre-September capital was irrelevant except for one thing: today he would pass his last exam, physics, and he would be accepted to medical school. The same medical school where his father taught and did research.

A white nylon jacket with red stripes and a cute, balloon-like hood flitted ahead. Anatoly chased after trolleybus No. 15 and jumped in right behind the nylon jacket. The girl wearing it was about seventeen, with an expression of hopeful joy, just like the one on Anatoly's face. They looked at each other and broke into laughter. The girl was not very tall, and next to the long-legged and long-armed Anatoly, she seemed even more petite. She was so good-looking and graceful and so charming, and they talked like old friends all the way to the medical school stop. It turned out that Natasha was applying to the same school, not to the division of clinical medicine but of public health. It was so much fun to ride together along Pirogovka Street, in a trolleybus flashing with sparks and arching its bow toward the sky. To ride to your future school next to a pretty girl sporting short hair and a fetching suede skirt.

They crossed the courtyard, passing the school's custodial offices, and ended up in a building where the admissions office occupied the entire first floor. Natasha saw one of her girlfriends and ran ahead. Anatoly walked up to the bulletin board where the groups and exam room numbers were posted. He glanced at the lists and found his group number: Twenty-one. The luckiest one, as the applicants joked. You could find the most common and the most unusual names among those taking the exams: Kosolapov and Shestipalov, Akhmeteli and Gotua, Sidorov and Nikiforov, many Petrovs and no fewer Smirnovs. Group Twenty-one also had a disproportional number of Jewish names: at least fifteen out of twenty-three applicants. The number of the last names unusual to the Russian ear decreased with each exam, so that for today's exam, the last one, the ratio was more regular: eight native Russian and five Jewish last names. Anatoly noticed all this as if by chance, because statistics was the last thing on his mind, and it was important to maintain the balance that had brought him success: so far only one B, in chemistry, the rest all A's. And on top of that it wasn't all that apparent which category his last name, Levitin, was attributed to—Jewish or Russian. Anatoly walked into the auditorium. He picked up his exam questions and read them. He could have volunteered to answer them right away, but according to the rule, which Herbert Anatolyevich had instilled in him, he sat at a desk, took out a pencil, and began to think through the questions. When it was finally his turn to answer, he forced himself not to appear nervous and to focus on the task at hand: the upcoming exchange with the examiner. In truth he had been surprised by the unusual severity the physics examiner, a short man with a thin, sharp nose, exhibited toward the star of Group Twenty-one, Borya Shapiro. The applicants from their group had no doubt that Borya would get nothing short of an A in physics; he had won the All-Soviet Physics Olympiad. But instead, shorty ran his eyes over Borya's answer sheet, shook his head reproachfully, and barked, "And how about the classical way of solving this problem?" Borya immediately started solving the problem in the traditional way. But something had come apart inside him. He started to crush the chalk, and finally, with a great deal of effort, came up with the answer. The examiner, not even hiding his triumph, dropped him to a C. Shapiro got a C! This could be the fatal blow to his admission prospects.

Nevertheless, Anatoly forced himself not to fall apart and answered the first two questions quite well. Or so he thought. However, the examiner, sliding his glasses down to the tip of his sharp nose, asked him maliciously, and totally off the topic, "Are you perhaps related to Tolstoy's Levin in *Anna Karenina*, young man?"

Anatoly should have figured out where this was going, and either not responded at all or answered so curtly as to cut off any further attempts at a double entendre. But he took the question seriously, thought about it, lost his self-assured tone, and began to babble something like, "I don't believe so, my father's parents, the Levitins, came from Belarus. And they weren't any landowners."

"I thought, pardon my mistake, that you come from the Russian gentry."

"No, we're Jews," Anatoly answered, and sharp-nose shorty tightened up and shot an absurd question at him.

"So, you, Levitin, were talking about photoelectric effect. But you did not provide the first name and the patronymic for Stoletov, neglecting to show respect for our great Russian physicist."

Anatoly thought about it. As luck would have it, Stoletov's first name and patronymic escaped him. He stood there, dazed.

"Why are you mute? And your answers to the first two questions weren't exactly up to snuff. That's not good. You will have wait to enter medical school. A nice little F for you, Levitin."

Anatoly heard a howling and piercing laughter. A flame blinded him. He felt an unbelievable pain crushing his temples. Anatoly could not remember anything else, and when he regained consciousness, he saw a floor lamp decked out with blackberries and partially drawn curtains, and he realized that he was lying on his own daybed. The smell of ether-based heart medication floated in the air, a smell that Anatoly remembered from last year, when his father had an attack of angina pectoris. Anatoly tried to recall and ask himself questions: What's today's date? What happened to me at the admissions office? But he remembered nothing. Instinctively he chased away these oppressing thoughts, like we chase away painful memories imprinted in our minds.

"Sonny, looks like you woke up." Grandfather Vasily Matveyevich stepped quietly into Anatoly's room.

"Hi, Grandpa. What happened to me?"

"Oh, my dear boy. What's done is done and is now all grown over with grass and left in the past. Now you're getting better."

"No, Grandpa, tell me, what happened? Why am I in bed? I was just fine yesterday. I took the trolleybus to med school."

"Tolya, my dear soul. Your plans to study medicine got derailed. They didn't accept you."

"Didn't accept me? But I passed everything just fine. I'll go and get it straightened out. Oh, yes . . . physics."

Anatoly tried to get up, but his strength left him, and he fell back onto the pillow.

"Forget it, son. The hell with them. Looks like this power is not to be conquered. Your dad, Herbert Anatolyevich, even though he's of Jewish stock, isn't too street smart. He's trying to intercede for you. But what's the use of interceding, when it's not to be."

Anatoly loved Grandfather Vasily Matveyevich, although he realized that his grandfather wasn't all that fond of his father. Vasily Matveevich had gotten it into his head that the familial union of the Levitins, successful for twenty years, was a pure coincidence, a fluke. His personal attitude to this could be expressed in an old saying: "A goose isn't the right friend for a pig." The girl got involved with the long-nosed doc. He didn't deceive her, didn't take away what was hers. One should be thankful for that. But Vasily Matveyevich just couldn't love Herbert Anatolyevich, and he had no desire to love him. That is why he sold his village house begrudgingly and moved to his daughter's in Moscow only under the condition that in the new apartment he would live separately from his son-in-law—with his grandson, whom he loved to distraction. An inexplicable phenomenon of human nature expressed itself in this sentiment. Grandfather Vasily Matveyevich did not like the long-nosed doc, but he loved his grandson unconditionally, even though Anatoly had inherited his father's lankiness, and his long Jewish nose, and the Levitins' impetuousness, while inheriting very little from the rounded, unhurried, and docile genes of the village-dwelling Pivovarovs. Only veracity of truth telling was common to both lineages. Anatoly grew up sincere and steadfast.

"An iron-willed guerilla fighter, sailor Zheleznyak no less," Grandfather Vasily Matveyevich would say, proud of his grandson, but already fearing for his future.

In his loose-fitting army shirt that hung on his withering frame, in his navy blue "osiffer's" jodhpurs and tall felt boots, Vasily Matveyevich continued to play the role of an old guerilla commander. His fleshy nose crisscrossed with blue veins, his bluish-grey cheeks overgrown with wild boar's stubble, and his blue eyes under red eyebrows—all that, of course, destroyed the intentionally formidable image of a national avenger. And Grandfather Vasily Matveyevich strictly adhered to his chosen life principles, which completely coincided with the line of the Party and the Soviet government. He believed what the papers and radio said to be sacrosanct. After he moved to Moscow, he continued to watch the daily news with a religious fervor, heeding all discussions and speeches of the political observers. Grandfather Vasily Matveyevich did not doubt the sacred word of *Pravda* and *Izvestia*, or any of the other Soviet papers, which is probably why, when the young Doctor Levitin arrived in Maryino in 1956, he met the doctor with apprehension, suspicion, and dislike. The year 1953, with its affair of the Jewish "doctor-murderers," was still fresh in Vasily Matveyevich's mind. And even though the long-nosed doctor turned out to be a very fine and qualified specialist, a shade of distrust, born from the newspapers and the radio in 1953, was never far from Vasily Matveyevich's mind. As far as the subsequent refutation and dismissal of the charges were concerned, one could surmise many things. It was a real time of troubles—after Stalin's death. As the Russian saying goes, "The first word is more valued than the second." And now, stroking his fleshy nose and trying to comfort his grandson, Grandfather speculated, deep down in his soul, that maybe what happened didn't just happen for no reason, and the lad was paying for the sins of his long-nosed and all-knowing kinsmen.

One would not call Vasily Matveyevich an antisemite. He was not one of those who wished death on this persecuted nation. Yes, it is true, he didn't love Jews. But if he were to be faced with a question, should they live or perish from the face of the earth, he would have unequivocally answered: live. His peasant soul was drawn to life and to the living. But to love? That cannot be taught. You cannot force someone to love. Here Vasily Matveyevich was free before God and the people. An incident that had occurred in the first days of the war bore witness to the fact that Vasily Matveyevich treated Jews not with malice, but perhaps only with pitiful contempt.

Vasily Matveyevich was on patrol on the western bank of the Sorot River. He had a boat. He was supposed to steal to the eastern bank as soon as the Nazis approached. Their guerilla unit was preparing an ambush. Vasily Matveyevich heard the rattle of motorcycles. He jumped into the boat and was about to push off from the shore with a paddle when a barefoot woman, tightly hugging a three- or four-year-old girl, lunged toward the boat. She was wearing a silk dress, green with yellow flowers. The dress, ripped at the breast on the left side, was thrown over her bare body in a hurry, and Vasily Matveyevich caught sight of the woman's perky, olive-skinned breasts, with the little girl tightly holding on to them, and the woman's sturdy hip. Her hair, jet black, fell completely disheveled onto her shoulders. But she had other things to worry about—the guttural German speech and the motorcycles were quite near.

"Save us, for God's sake. We're Jews. They'll shoot us. If you can't take both of us, then take Lilechka with you," the Jewish woman pleaded, as she pulled the crying and clinging little girl from her body.

Vasily Matveyevich knew that with such a load he would be taking a risk and might not be able to escape German bullets. Never mind his own life—he would let his whole unit down. But at the same time, he could not just abandon these unfortunate Jewesses. He could not! By some miracle they were able to cross the Sorot River. One bullet hit the oarlock, ricocheted and slit Vasily Matveyevich's arm. But they managed to jump out onto the bank, crawl to a safe place, catch their breath. The Jewish woman (he never asked her name) ripped off a piece of cloth from the hem of her dress and started to bandage his arm. Her eyes, huge like a cow's when she first runs out into the meadow after a long winter, were right next to Vasily Matveyevich's face. The little girl calmed down; squatting next to her mother's feet, she amused herself with bluebells. The Jewish woman bent down over her savior's arm, and a swarthy breast slipped out of the dress.

"Thank you, my good man. I'm all yours. I have nothing else to give."

"What's the matter with you? Are you crazy? Take the girl and follow me. You'll be taken to a safe place."

And that's what happened.

For a whole week, Anatoly's room with its workbench; his writing table; a daybed and bookshelves that held books, airplane models, and games, looked like a scene from an amateur theater production. First his grandfather would come in, shuffling his felt boots, and then his mother would bring some of Anatoly's favorite treats, and then Herbert Anatolyevich would trot into the room. They decided not to mention Anatoly's future until he got better. Finally, at the beginning of September, after Anatoly had started to go out into the courtyard in front of the house and had even gone with his mother to the Central Farmers' Market to get bell peppers for stuffing, only then did Herbert Anatolyevich revisit the burdensome topic.

Once again they were sitting in his father's study. The September sunlight, filtered through brownish maple leaves, fell onto Herbert Anatolyevich's hands. Holding a Parker pen, the long white fingers of his right hand were shaking.

"Tolik, there is a chance that they'll accept you in the evening division of the medical school. They'll count your exam results. You'll retake physics. This way the losses won't be great."

"So, you too have given up. Made peace with what happened to me."

"No son, I have just chosen a reasonable solution. You have to live and work."

"But that's entering through the back door. All your life you've hated compromise."

Anatoly was getting upset. Herbert Anatolyevich was afraid of another spasm of cerebral vessels, like the one from which he had been taking so long to recover. But at the same time it would be reprehensible to ignore this onerous question.

"Tolik, my darling boy, you know very well that you weren't rejected for your lack of knowledge. You were rejected because they try not to accept our kind into medical schools. Now you are faced with a choice: either you get a job, then the army for two years; or you go now to the evening division and later try to transfer to the day program. You want to be a doctor, swallow your pride."

"Perhaps I should try the School of Biology at Moscow University?" Anatoly asked hopefully.

"The terms of accepting Jews are even stricter there than at medical schools. And besides, the entrance exams are over. All the spots have been taken. The evening division of our medical school is really the best option. At least for the time being."

"For the time being, papa? But these harsh conditions won't change, no matter how much time passes. All my life I will have to compromise."

"Unfortunately you're right."

"Wouldn't it be better for us to leave, papa? You told me about your uncle who had emigrated to Palestine after the Revolution."

"Yes, I did tell you about him."

"So write to him, papa. Ask him to send us an invitation."

❧

I CAME OUT of the winter forest. A panorama of a warm day spanned before me, the kind you encounter only during a wintertime thaw in the country. To me the warmth of the open space expressed the essence of something very meaningful. I sensed this not so much with my mind as with my body. The body grew, unwinding in this sensation and giving it right back to me. I carefully looked around. There wasn't a person in sight, nor an animal, not even a bird. The ski track cut through the belly of the open space, like a scar after a Caesarean. It was a supine woman—the earth. She was sleeping. Her head, actually her face, was not visible. One could divine the outline of her head beyond a distant village. I was standing under the earth's womb, lower than the belly fringed by the circle of the woods. The earth's womb was resting, after giving birth to me. And who am I, born to have caused the suffering of mother-earth, the cause of the scar above her womb. I looked upward toward her snow-clad breasts, toward her powerful hips turned to the sun, and I was lost in angst. In angst because I had lost the language I once had in common with the mother-earth. When did I lose it? Or was I never taught this language? Maybe I am superfluous on this edge of the mother's womb? Maybe she had foreseen my helplessness or even my bothersome futility and cast me out before my time, like an apple tree dropping a green fruit: rotted and turned to ashes, then to disappear for eternity!

❧

No MATTER HOW much Herbert Anatolyevich tried to escape from life's cruelty, circling round Moscow, anxiously treading on his academic and clinical work, life had chased him down, threatening to take away his white coat. Life had stripped him of the distinctions and respect he had earned, removed all the screens behind which he had been hiding from himself for many years, and it put him face to face with the very essence of his values and ideas about homeland, family, camaraderie, and means of survival, as well as his fears for the future and the lives of his loved ones. He wasn't a snob. He could talk for hours with ordinary people without having to choose his words; they just naturally appeared at the right time. As a result, his patients—from many different walks of life and of various ages—loved Professor Levitin and trusted him. Particularly the simple folk from the deepest pockets of Russia. This doesn't mean that he treated the intelligentsia or the non-Russian patients any worse. Not at all. His natural kindness, his intelligence and professional passion for outsmarting and vanquishing an illness—this always belonged to all of his patients alike. Both a general and a cook were for him as equal as they were before God. But most of all he loved simple peasants and dignified retirement-age workers, particularly those that came from afar, where the dialect was different than in Moscow. A Jew himself, he didn't spend too much time in the Jewish milieu. He loved the Russian peasants for their patience and lack of affectation, and also for their tolerance of human frailties. He loved their speech that flowed like rivers through a valley—slow, sinuous, and penetrating to the depths of your soul. That peasant Russian speech is fitted with a multitude of interjections, epithets, prefixes and suffixes, which, like an oven fork, flip a word or a phrase to make the meaning and feeling shine ever more brightly. Maybe Herbert Anatolyevich loved all this so much because he worshiped his Tatyana. She was his link to the Russian soil, and she embodied his spiritual connection to his native land. Tatyana, his one and only, and the most beautiful of all the women on earth. She, who in her maidenhood hadn't discovered the sweet secret of love and later learned more about desire from her husband, he who lured and loved her but never completely figured her out. He understood her like he understood Russia, and this relationship conjoined by love and life, possibly deeper and more important than a blood kinship, was now in danger of being destroyed.

If anyone else had done this, Herbert Anatolyevich would have considered it a terrible act of betrayal. He—a traitor? A violator of the oath of allegiance? Herbert Anatolyevich loved Russia, but not the way this love is experienced, for example, by admirers of ancient churches. In general he shunned sugary banalities, affected Easter greetings and triple kisses in celebration of a risen Christ; all of that reminded him of village idiots, as if people were acting like mummers to cover up their eternal anguish. And that is why, he believed, in Russia vodka goes hand in hand with religiosity. No, this was not the homeland that he revered and loved. It was the purity of the Russian word: Russian prose, Russian verse, being part of the Russian literary and spiritual community. Ties with all this would have to be severed because the wound that had been inflicted on Anatoly would not heal. The wound only closed temporarily, so the boy could survive. But his medical studies, attained at such a price, didn't make Anatoly happy, because it was like a handout from those who had shown that they could also take it away at any moment. Herbert Anatolyevich understood what his son was going though. But what about Tatyana? He was hoping to protect Tatyana himself, and was afraid even to think about possible tragedy. To protect Tatyana, to take her away, that for him was a way to keep his ties with Russia. To lose Tatyana—for him that meant to lose his sense of homeland.

Professor Levitin was a natural Jew. A Jew who knew his ancestors going back four generations, as they survived and lived in the oral family chronicles. He grew up in a Jewish Soviet family that had moved to Moscow in the 1930s, that is, just before Herbert Anatolyevich's birth. His parents had moved to Moscow from Polotsk in Belarus right after getting married, and their parents had fled there from Lithuania, from the bullets of the invading Polish troops. Herbert Anatolyevich's grandfather was a Jewish teacher, a Talmudic scholar, a learned man of the Book for whom the Word was the most important (if not the only) tool in the formation of a family and an individual. He even preferred to communicate with his wife by means of the word, rather than to live in harmony of feelings, hence the many heated family arguments. After having his fill of all this, Herbert Anatolyevich's father decided to break completely with all that religiousness and became an activist of the Blue

Blouse youth movement. Called Abraham at birth, he changed his name to Anatoly after joining MOPR, which stood for the International Organization for the Aid of Revolutionary Fighters. It was at the rehearsals of a Blue Blouse agitprop performance that he fell in love with Tsilya, the daughter of a fellow Litvak, Khayim Ravich. Tsilya, however, had not changed her name.

Herbert Anatolyevich's parents, Anatoly (Abraham) and Tsilya, became true re-settlers into a new world, immigrants to Moscow from the world of the shtetl, people who accepted the ideas of this new world and could no longer confine themselves to the old environment, rife as it was with ornate disputations, doubts, and the odor of mothballs. Tsilya was five months pregnant. Anatoly, the son of a poor Jewish teacher, worked as a hospital orderly at night, and during the day studied medicine at the very same medical school from which his son, Herbert Anatolyevich, would later be graduated, and to which his grandson, Anatoly Levitin, would later fail to gain admission as a daytime student. Herbert Anatolyevich was brought up in a family that, although Jewish by origin, had evolved through its lifestyle and mode of thinking into a family of the Moscow intelligentsia. During the war Herbert Anatolyevich's father, who had graduated from medical school in 1937, served as a division epidemiologist. He was at the front for the four years of the Great Patriotic War, traversing, with the troops of his division, the path from Moscow all the way to Berlin. Before the Nazi invasion and later at the war front, Grandfather Levitin was surrounded by Ukrainians, Russians, Jews, Tatars, by colleagues of many nationalities, by all different types of people—the good and the ordinary.

One cannot say that Herbert Anatolyevich's parents had completely forgotten their Jewishness, or even worse, that they had rejected it. This was not the case—could not be the case—with these conscionable people. Herbert Anatolyevich's father, when tipsy, was known to break into a Freylekhs dance in front of everybody, or to sing "Varnishkes" or perhaps something else in Yiddish that had survived in his soul from childhood. But all of that had, of course, been intertwined with "Ryabina,"

"Suliko," or "Hey Lads, Unharness the Horses . . ." Even louder rang his renditions of "Blue Blouses We Are, Union Members We Are" and other songs from his prewar days in the Young Communist League. That was why, when Anatoly Rafaylovich Levitin, with a certain amount of bewilderment, would come upon the line in applications and forms that asked about one's nationality, he was forced to accept having to fill in the word "Jew." To him the Russian word *evrei* (Jew) sounded archaic, a lot like the word *ierei* (priest).

The first sobering shot was fired in 1949, when Lieutenant Colonel Levitin—Herbert Anatolyevich's father—was suddenly discharged from the medical corps, although his age, health, and service record attested to his ability to remain as chief of the laboratory at a military hospital. In that fateful year for Soviet Jews, the Soviet government had assumed an acutely adversarial position against Israel in the territorial disputes between the Jews and Arabs in the former mandate of Palestine. In 1950 Herbert Anatolyevich Levitin had entered medical school, having graduated from high school with straight A's and the gold medal. In 1953 a storm had thundered over the heads of the Levitin family, as it also did over the heads of many doctors of Jewish origin. The Center for Disease Control of Moscow's Novomaysky district, where Anatoly Rafaylovich Levitin was serving as head epidemiologist, was, out of the blue, visited by a commission consisting of medical personnel and KGB officers. The commission discovered "improper storage" of bacterial test cultures (diphtheria, dysentery, typhoid). The protocol, instead of just citing "improper storage," referred to "malicious absence of vigilance." Anatoly Rafaylovich was arrested. An investigation was under way. While in prison, Herbert Anatolyevich's father fell ill from shame, insult, and fear for the fate of his wife and son. It is hard to believe, in our time, when the virogenetic origin of cancer is a widely understood theory, that a person would develop a new malignancy from sorrow alone. But that's exactly what happened.

After Stalin's death and after the execution of his henchman Beria, after the fabricated charges surrounding Academician Miron Vovsi and his other distinguished colleagues had been dropped and the Jewish doctors exonerated, Anatoly Rafaylovich was transferred from a prison hospital to a military hospital, where he had once been in charge of the lab. By the end of the summer of 1953, he was dead. And three years later, just before Herbert Anatolyevich's assignment to the Maryino rural clinic, his mother, Tsilya Khayimovna Levitina, had also died. So in 1956 the young Doctor Levitin arrived in the Russian village as a true orphan. But that terrible 1953, which hung over the Jews of the USSR like the sword of Damocles, had passed. And Herbert Anatolyevich, like so many other Jews, had breathed with relief.

*

WHAT DOES A writer need? Paper, quill pen, and creative freedom. Actually, the freedom of creative choice, for there is always the option to choose unfreedom. And here I am again in the open field. Two roads, two ski tracks diverge, continuing at an obtuse angle. I set out on the straight ski track. To my right is my double, the snow-covered haystack. Spring is in the air today. I imagine the haystack to be a village hut. Inside there is life. The life of the withering stalks, the life of the rodents, the life of the grass—the grass predestined to feed the animals until summer. I thank this haystack. I am at peace on this white plain, because someone before me laid the tracks here. I choose the path laid out by others. I want truth and peace, and I choose this particular path, through the forest, where everything is geometrically perfect: the rounds of the tree stumps, the cylinders of the trunks, the semicircles of the trees bent over the ski track. I soak in the perfect geometry of this calmness. It is hard to believe that someone, someone akin to me, laid the ski track in such an amazing way; that the black fir tree, its paws drooping down like an old mother bear's, has tenderly hugged this reed pipe of a birch. And suddenly—a dip in the road. I tumble down, a bit terrified that this self-imposed, honey-sweet oblivion will suddenly be cut short. And then a clearing, held by the willows' red hands, and I glide down. I feel good and at peace. I have put everything else out of my mind. I return along the same field, past the same haystack, and tomorrow I will come back to this forest, because I have become accustomed to it, have had time to get accustomed to the fact that someone before me has laid the track through the comforting circle of this forest.

But then, one day, with no warning or signal, a morning will come when I will prefer to wander across the snowy expanse, the snowflakes' swaged bullets digging into my face, my chest burned by the wind. There will be no joy in skiing, only the burdensome duty of making a track. For whom? And for what reason?

HERBERT ANATOLYEVICH WAS totally and completely devoted to medicine. One could definitely say that from the moment of his assignment to Maryino until the days of the disaster that had befallen Anatoly, nothing existed for Professor Levitin besides his family and medicine. It wasn't that Herbert Anatolyevich was entirely detached from his Jewishness. When his parents were still living, he enjoyed having gefilte fish or chicken kishka or numerous Jewish delicacies made from matzo. And when they played a merry Jewish dance tune, disguised in Soviet restaurants as "7:40"—after the arrival time of the legendary Odessa train—his legs would take him right into the circle of other Jews holding onto each others' shoulders and tossing one and then the other leg forward. Herbert Anatolyevich was not religious. Religion had not found a follower in him, and he preferred to discern the world not spiritually, but scientifically and practically. Nevertheless, once a year, usually on his father's yarzeit, August 6, he went to the synagogue. Sometimes he would arrive during prayers; other times he would walk into an empty synagogue. On a morning rich with the hues and smells of a summertime Moscow, he would traverse Dzerzhinsky

Square; leave behind the Children's World department store, Pharmacy
No. 1, and the Polytechnic Museum; then pass the Central Commit-
tee Building with its blood-red flag; and finally find himself on quiet
Arkhipov Street, which flowed down to Solyanka Street. Herbert
Anatolyevich felt that when he would start to descend from Bohdan
Khmelnytsky Street down the slope toward the synagogue, exactly at
the moment when his body changed its spatial orientation, something
would happen to his soul or consciousness—what, he wasn't sure.
In any case he wouldn't call this mood shift a religious experience.
It was more temporary, naturally determined—like the memory of
his parents—his return or reattachment to the notion of Jewishness.
That is, as a member of the Russian intelligentsia, he would suddenly
yet very tangibly rediscover in himself another prominent quality: his
Jewish heritage. And when Professor Levitin approached the granite steps of the temple, built more to resemble a Greek palace than
an Oriental house of worship, he would forget about medicine, the
Russian intelligentsia, his Moscow life. He would be consumed by a
feeling of oneness with this vast temple, scantily lit or brightly illuminated, where there were no pictures, no sculptures—no idols at all,
only the austere, geometrically perfect, Hebrew characters. Herbert
Anatolyevich would cross into the room next to the main sanctuary,
where the synagogue beadle, an old Jew, would search the yellowed
book for the dates in the Jewish calendar to correspond with the dates
of his father's and mother's deaths. And he would light the memorial
candles.

Now, because of his son's inability to bow down his neck, Professor
Herbert Anatolyevich Levitin's entire life had to change dramatically
(though was it just because of Anatoly alone?). Had Herbert Anatolyevich been an easygoing person, capable of altering his life's tenets effort-
lessly, the failure of Anatoly's application to medical school would have
healed by the passage of time and by hard work. And he, Herbert Anatolyevich, having found a way around it, would have calmed down. But
his son was unyielding, refusing to change his convictions.

IN THE EARLY days of November 1978, an envelope showed up in the Levitins' mailbox, an envelope with colorful Israeli stamps, the writing on them in English, Arabic, and Hebrew. The letter was from Tel Aviv, from Uncle Moshe. He wrote about his life in such detail and so openly, as if he had been waiting for his favorite nephew all this time, and now his dream would soon be realized.

At the end of December, the invitation arrived from Israel. Tatyana had just come home from work; her office was a stone's throw from home, conveniently. She worked as an accountant in the housing office located across the courtyard from their building. Herbert Anatolyevich hadn't yet returned from the clinic. The doorbell rang, and the usual postal carrier answered Tatyana's greeting with an unkind smile. She handed her a long light blue envelope with a mica-like window, through which one could peek at their home address and the uncle's return address in Tel Aviv.

"Sign here." The postal carrier had Tatyana sign her office ledger for certified mail, then closed it angrily, as if she were slamming a door. She left without saying a word. Before this Tatyana would have long chats with the postal carrier, who had come to Moscow ten years ago, not from outside Pskov but from the Ryazan Province. "You're one of us villagers! Come in, have some tea," Tatyana would say to the postal carrier. And they would drink tea in the kitchen, sipping it through a Lent milk sugar cube the way they do it in the village. And without fail, Grandfather Vasily Matveyevich would join them. That's the way it used to be, Tatyana thought to herself, and now the postal carrier left abruptly. Like she cut me off or something. She felt bitterness and rejection deep down in her soul, as if she had been orphaned, and the arrival of this white and blue envelope had severed yet another tie that bound her to her village. Tatyana decided not to open the envelope; she waited for Herbert Anatolyevich to come home.

HERBERT ANATOLYEVICH ARRIVED home around six in the evening. He was in high spirits, the way he always was when one of his seriously ill patients would recover. During dinner, quickly scooping up his borsch served with a puff pastry on the side and then delighting in the second course, he talked about a patient he had seen on a house call.

Now in his eighties, Khaim Zusovich Shapiro had retired a long time ago. Until he was sixty-seven Shapiro had worked as an economist. His wife had died ten years ago, and his daughter had married a navy man soon after the victory over Nazi Germany; her husband was now retired, and they lived in Blagoveshchensk in the Far East. The old man didn't feel comfortable living alone in a one-bedroom apartment on Krivokolenny Lane, filled with old carved oak furniture that they had brought with them to Moscow from Zhitomir in the late 1920s. And Khaim Shapiro had felt the need to make a life change. His friends at the synagogue, where he was a regular member, so revered him that every year he was invited to celebrate the Passover Seder to commemorate the Exodus at the same table with the rabbis; and these friends, thank God, had advised him to get married. "What? Why? Who needs that?" old Khaim objected. But life is life, and it made its own arrangements. The friends fixed Khaim up with a widow, also a Muscovite, not bad looking, lively, and a whole eight years younger. When Herbert Anatolyevich began to treat Khaim, he was eighty-six, and his "young wife" was seventy-eight. The old woman had nobody in the world besides a niece who wasn't even that close to her, though close enough for the niece's children to receive annual birthday presents and Hanukah *gelt*.

"So . . . they were married. They lived together for a year. Then for another year. Now five years, in perfect harmony. He contributes his hundred rubles pension, every single kopeck, and she her eighty-three rubles. Not too lavish, but enough to get by. And suddenly old Khaim gets sick. Old age, you know. Back when he was a man in the prime of his life, he didn't use to deprive himself of what his nature demanded. And now—here you go, a severely enlarged prostate. And what do you think happened? They put him in the hospital. But they didn't take out his prostate. They were afraid they would lose the old man. Instead they put a catheter from his bladder to the outside into a urine bag. When

Khaim found out that he would have to carry around a little bottle on his belly for the rest of his life, he became all upset and yelled, 'Operate, for God's sake, I beg you! I'll sign anything. I don't want to go around like a cow with a bell.' But despite his protestations, they discharged him with a urine bag into the old woman's care.

"Right about that time, he receives a letter from his younger sister in Jerusalem. She had found out about his illness and wrote that she was sending him and his wife an invitation to Israel. She claimed there would be surgeons in the Holy Land that wouldn't be afraid to operate on him. And she also mentioned that Shota Rustaveli himself had come to the Holy Land in his old age and died there. For our Khaim, the Georgian classic Shota Rustaveli was the epitome of wisdom and nobility. The thing was that Khaim's mother had come from Georgian Jews. They followed both the Jewish and the Georgian traditions at home."

Herbert Anatolyevich was telling the story, and Tatyana and Grandfather Vasily Matveyevich listened. Tatyana even forgot about their Israeli invitation, and when Herbert Anatolyevich told them about Khaim Shapiro's sister, she stirred, remembering today's mail. But she stopped herself. She didn't want to mention it in front of her father.

"And then what happened to the old man?" Grandfather Vasily Matveyevich suddenly asked.

Tatyana echoed her father's words. "Herbert, please tell us more. And how did you end up with this patient?"

Herbert Anatolyevich sat back, took off his glasses for a minute. Wiped his face with the palm of his hand, sliding it across his forehead as if he were chasing away all the superfluous and irrelevant details.

"The tailor, Hershel Zuskin, asked me to see old Khaim. So, I go to see Khaim Shapiro for the first time. His wife opens the door, a small, wizened old lady. White hair smoothly combed back. Wrapped in an Orenburg down shawl. Her eyes as light blue and clear as a seven-year-old girl's. Quietly, quietly, so the old man wouldn't hear her, she asks me, 'My dear doctor, I beg you, please tell my martyr not to get so upset. He has high blood pressure, you know. How's he supposed to go anywhere now?'

"I walked into the bedroom. You won't believe it, but there's a highlander sitting, propped up on pillows. A grey mustache sticks out like two daggers. A lion's mane like Einstein's. An eagle's head and beak. I can see that the old man has a bad heart. He's short of breath. And of course he shows signs of respiratory distress. Emphysema.

"The old man asks me, 'Get me up and walking, doctor. I must go to Israel. I can't just die carrying around these rattles. I have to stand before God with dignity.'

"So I began to treat Khaim Shapiro and got him better. That was six months ago. The old man received his invitation in the early spring. He called me just before Tolya's finals. I went to see him. The old man was walking around the room. Actually, hobbling. He had trouble moving his feet. How can he go in this condition, I thought. And as if hearing my thoughts, Khaim Shapiro asked, 'Professor, do I have even one chance out of a hundred to make it to Israel alive?'

" 'One chance you do have,' I answered.

" 'Then tomorrow, the old lady and I are taking our documents to the Visa Section. Pray they'll let us out. The state will save two hundred rubles on our pensions. And I won't be taking up hospital beds.'

"We said our goodbyes. There was probably a reason he mentioned hospital beds. When the notification arrived from the Visa Section that they had to submit payment for their exit visas, the old man fell gravely ill. Maybe he overdid it from happiness while packing up their belongings. Or maybe he caught a chill. They took him away with pneumonia. Luckily the old lady managed to reach me, and I got him a bed in our clinic. Imagine the predicament. The old man won't hear of anything else except getting him back onto his feet and then walking onto that plane bound for Vienna. He's been discussing his expatriation problems with his fellow patients on the ward. I wish there was a way of telling him that this puts me in an awkward position."

At this point, Grandfather Vasily Matveyevich coughed nastily, spitefully glanced at his son-in-law, and commented, "What's there to be awkward about, if a man speaks the truth? After all, you, Herbert, aren't planning to move away to Palestine or any such place. And if you aren't planning to go, then why blush from somebody else's shame?"

Herbert Anatolyevich didn't want to contradict his father-in-law. He didn't know how to lie and did not think this was the right time to tell the truth. He saw that Tatyana suddenly went pale, as if she were frightened of something. Herbert Anatolyevich didn't wish to continue with the Khaim Shapiro story, but Grandfather Vasily Matveyevich wouldn't let it go.

"Why don't you tell us more about your holy martyr. Come on, come on! Maybe I'll get to like it yet."

"You'd do better to be quiet, father," Tatyana exploded. "Maybe you should go take a rest. But if you want to listen, then don't interrupt."

"It's all right, Tanyusha, it's fine. Vasily Matveyevich didn't say anything wrong." Herbert Anatolyevich smiled amicably.

"Don't be so clever, professor. Tell us the end of the story. And as far as anything wrong, I'll have something to say about that later. I'm no dimwit. Anatoly mentioned something about your plans. But it's okay, we can talk about that later."

Tatyana noisily put her cup down on her saucer. But she contained herself, calmed by her husband's gentle glance. Herbert Anatolyevich continued.

"And so, I'm treating old Khaim in my clinic. A very difficult case, but luckily we managed to pull him away from the other side. We cured his pneumonia and released the old man. Meantime, the date of his departure is approaching. Things aren't taken care of. Furniture still hasn't been sold. Dishes haven't been packed. And so old man Khaim decides, 'You know, my wife, if such happiness visits me that I'll reach the Holy Land alive, we won't need anything.' They agreed and stopped all the packing." Herbert Anatolyevich took the last sip of his coffee, then picked up the newspaper.

"The old peacock! Yeah, I know this type—it's highlander blood, that's what it is. He'll drop everything just to show off his resolve." Grandfather

Vasily Matveyevich couldn't resist the urge to comment on his son-in-law's story.

"Did they really just leave everything?" Tatyana asked in disbelief.

"Yes, Tanyusha. I wasn't on a house call today, I actually went to say goodbye to the old couple. Tomorrow morning they leave for Vienna, and from there—to Israel."

Upon hearing these words, Grandfather Vasily Matveyevich suddenly stood up and walked out of the kitchen, slamming the door behind him. Tatyana hugged her husband.

"Don't pay any attention to him, sweetheart. We have some news!"

"Tolya passed his anatomy retake test?"

"No. Guess what?"

"A letter from Semyon?"

"You're getting warmer, but that's not it."

"It can't be the invitation?"

"You got it!"

"Hurray!" Herbert Anatolyevich jumped up. It was funny to watch how this awkward, long-legged creature, resembling a giant praying mantis, hopped around the kitchen, happily shouting some unrecognizable words, and spinning around and kissing his wife. On the title page of the official letter, this was printed in Russian and in Hebrew: Permission to enter # 0289/596; date such-and-such; and the following text: "Dear Mr./Mrs . . . , As per your request, I have the honor to inform you, on behalf of the Ministry of Foreign Affairs, that the individuals listed below will be allowed to enter Israel as immigrants. Unless there are medical or other obstacles, your visas will be issued by one of the diplomatic or consular representatives of the state of Israel abroad, or upon your arrival in Israel." Listed then were all their names and dates of birth, including Grandfather Vasily Matveyevich's. On the last page was the typed invitation itself: "I hereby urgently request that the appropriate and authorized offices of the Soviet authorities issue my relatives permission to join me in Israel as permanent residents. My family and I are financially sound and have all the means at our disposal to provide my relatives with everything that is necessary from the day of their arrival. Considering the humane position of the Soviet authorities on the subject of reunification of separated families, I am hopeful for a positive outcome of the request by me and my family, and I thank you in advance for your attention in this matter." Then, once again, were listed the Levitins and Grandfather Vasily Matveyevich, followed by the uncle's name.

Herbert Anatolyevich had waited for the Israeli invitation for so long, and it had often seemed to him that he would never get this charmed sheet of paper, though if he did get the invitation, then everything would go as smooth as silk. Why would it work out for the Aizenbergs and not for them? He had never taken part in any classified research, had never served in the army, had never traveled abroad. And Tatyana—she was just a simple accountant. So the most important thing had now happened. They opened up a bottle of champagne. Grandfather Vasily Matveyevich said he wasn't feeling well and didn't show his face in the kitchen that evening. So they did not reveal anything to him. Anatoly celebrated together with his parents. There were still six months until the fall army draft. Of course they would be able to leave before that.

However, events unraveled according to a scenario of fate that the Levitins could not control.

ソ

ALL OF NOVEMBER I didn't see any stars. And in December, when I would leave the house, the stars would be hidden behind big clouds heavy with swampy waters. I was growing unaccustomed to stars. I forgot that the sky had been created with stars. Yesterday, on New Year's Eve at midnight, I saw the stars once again.

The whole sky was filled with stars. They had reappeared. I had been calling for them; I had been searching for them. And finally, after a month of waiting, I saw my stars. The dippers, Ursa Major and Ursa Minor, were especially bright. The shining molten metal in a purple-black sky enticed me. Suddenly I understood that the appearance of stars to a person like me, lonely and lost among haystacks, snows, and poems, was a form of deceit, a seduction, a promise of something nonexistent. I will go on thinking about the stars and believing that I really need them. Then the stars will have disappeared, and I will ache with losses. Would it be better if the sky just stayed overcast with the muddy autumnal miasma? I learned to breathe the swampy air under this bell jar. I could breathe this way for another twenty years, imagining that I was living a full life. And then I would choke and disappear without a trace. Now I don't want to choke. I push apart the felt curtain of the clouds. I can no longer bear the chloroform of humility that drugs you, taming your imagination and willpower. Lord, if you are omnipotent, let me drink from the air of the universe!

FIRST OF ALL, Herbert Anatolyevich had to disclose his intentions to Academician Baronov, who was Chair of the Department of General and Internal Medicine at the medical school. Herbert Anatolyevich was the other full professor in the same department. He was having trouble deciding how to start the conversation. No matter how he constructed the opening phrases in his head, it all came out forced, unnatural. And Herbert Anatolyevich was incapable of obfuscating and speaking in half-truths. In addition, his boss, as he himself liked to say, could "see through my employees without an X-ray." This was a special type of intuition that for Baronov had become a profession of the utmost importance, and while it remained his main, yet secret, occupation, it also formed the foundation for various other less important activities, which would nevertheless lead to significant, and at times outstanding, achievements of his career. Ivan Ivanovich

Baronov was an individual who, due to that particular professional intuition, had risen to become one of the pillars of Soviet medicine. One can envision several different categories of Soviet medical scientists. First, hereditary intelligentsia, perhaps descendants of the merchant class, clergy, or even gentry, who were able to make it into the ranks and survive during harsh times due to their excellent education, diligence, and inherited talents, and to their ability to act prudently and display loyalty under the most hostile conditions, owing to their proper schooling and upbringing. Then there were tireless physicians, who had earned the right to belong to the ranks of Soviet intelligentsia. They were usually the first in their family lineage to attain higher education—workhorses who had overcome the impediment of insufficient education and who had exhibited personal bravery and toiled under extreme conditions: at war, on research expeditions, and with the most difficult clinical cases. And finally, there were those who had made it to the Academy of Medical Sciences because they were outstanding administrators, because they managed to arrange for the defense of their junior colleagues' dissertations and felt they had the right to call these junior colleagues their disciples. These Academicians from the ranks of the academic administrators placed their disciples in leading clinics and laboratories, and then combined their varied but perfectly respectable results into a single larger project that interested these administrators the most, and those projects would be conventionally called "habilitation dissertations."

But there existed another particular type of member of the Academy of Medical Sciences, one quite disparate from the other types. To this particular type belonged Herbert Anatolyevich's boss, Ivan Ivanovich Baronov. He had been named to the post of Chair of the Department of General and Internal Medicine, vacated after the death of Academician Pushinsky. Baronov did not have to pass the competitive trials of fate. One day he simply appeared in the Department, which Herbert Anatolyevich had been running as the acting chair. The head nurse Klavdiya Petrovna, all out of breath, peeked into Herbert Anatolyevich's office.

"Professor, all employees are to present themselves immediately to the office of the new department chair. I'm off to notify the others."

Herbert Anatolyevich had long been expecting the arrival of a new boss. Deep down he was even looking forward to it; he was weighed down by the countless conferences, meetings, and scientific committees and councils, where he had to represent the department as its acting chair. Now I'll be able to get back to nephrites, Herbert Anatolyevich tried to convince himself, and yet he was anxious. "The top administration could have introduced me to the new department chair. This seems rather hasty." But everything turned out to be much simpler. The new department chair briefly announced himself to his assembled colleagues. He said that his very busy schedule at the Fourth Central Directorate would not afford him much time in the clinic, and that administering the daily tasks of the clinic would again be left to the "respected" Herbert Anatolyevich. And he was gone. He would appear once a week and see Herbert Anatolyevich to get the weekly progress reports. Even the required internal medicine course usually taught by the department chair rested, as before, on Herbert Ana-tolyevich's shoulders. Only the Habilitation Scientific Councils were graced by the presence of Ivan Ivanovich Baronov, and he always asked the same question: "And what's the scientific novelty of your work?" They would only speak about Baronov in whispers. For some reason, when Ivan Iva-novich's shadow entered the conversations, the volume would wane. And so they spoke in whispers about the start of Baronov's medical career in the late 1930s, as chief of a camp hospital somewhere around Saransk, Mordovia.

Later, after the war, he was appointed Chief of General and Internal Medicine at a KGB hospital in Moscow. In that capacity he was granted the rank of full professor. And it was from there that he was transferred to the medical school as Chair of the Department of General and Internal Medicine. Herbert Anatolyevich didn't trust all these stories. He made it a habit not to bother his boss and to solve all the department's scientific and medical problems on his own. Only once, a year or a year and half ago, when Ivan Ivanovich was alone with Herbert Anatolyevich, he wiped his sweating bald head with a napkin, stopped drinking his tea, and suddenly asked, "Did you hear what that bastard Kaufman did? And we trusted him." Herbert Anatolyevich murmured something along the lines of "not a good move" or "he let his coworkers down," but inside he shuddered under the piercing gaze of his boss's beady eyes. Associate Professor Kaufman from the ENT Department had been to see the dean of the medical school and requested a letter confirming his employment—such a letter was required for the Visa Section. He was told to first tender his resignation, and only then did they promise to give him the required letter. Kaufman refused to resign. A battle with the dean ensued. That is, Kaufman was only fighting for the letter, while the administration fought against his presence in the school. Suddenly he had become superfluous: lagging behind in his research, an amoral person, and also a bad colleague. The administration couldn't just fire Kaufman for his desire to go to Israel to be reunified with his relatives. The Visa Section wouldn't accept his application without a letter from his place of employment. It was rumored that Associate Professor Kaufman, a "pesky Jew," had been to see the city Attorney General, but even that didn't help him secure the necessary letter of employment without having to resign his position. Herbert Anatolyevich later heard that the former associate professor had found a job in a neighborhood health center in Zelenograd, outside Moscow, and for about six months he had to endure a two-hour commute to Zelenograd and back, but, thank God, he finally received his exit visa and left the country.

From all these thoughts—and out of fear for Anatoly—Herbert Anatolyevich felt a chill in his heart. Not a cowardly man by nature, but also not a risk-taker, for the first time, he willingly put himself in a critical position.

FLOODED WITH SUNLIGHT, the crisp white expanse glitters with hues of blue, scarlet, and green. Thick ancient pines and vestiges of birches, contorted by the frost, frame this whiteness. Where should I go? Again and again to glide along the horizon's frosty arc until the circle has been closed? Or to rush down toward the hollow, winding between the pines or around the menacing aspen trunks, wound up like athletes before a jump. You can be lucky and bypass the danger, leaving behind the icy scalpel of speed that cleaves the white expanse to red blood; this way you gain confidence and can freely show others how your daring spirit is born. Or, at full speed, you could smash into a fallen deadwood that had once been a living plant, and you will forever lose your taste for risk-taking. You will give up venturing beyond flat surfaces, staying only where the purchased, cheap country fair pleasures have replaced the joy of victory over caution.

RESTRAINT WAS, PERHAPS, Herbert Anatolyevich's main character trait. This trait had served him faithfully and loyally in his duties as a physician, and in family matters. Only once during his village doctoring did he exhibit a lack of restraint, and this had resulted in marriage. But that flight of spirit, enhanced by a call of the flesh, was an exception for Doctor Levitin, and as with any exception, it only served to underscore that main quality which constituted the essence of his nature. Herbert Anatolyevich's outer appearance—sharp facial features, coiled forelocks encasing a half-bald head, legs moving in the manner of a compass—was in stark opposition to his mild bedside manner. He spoke with his patients softly, preferring to use archaic expressions, for example: "my good man," "esteemed friend," "be so kind," "totally in your debt," "much obliged," "all the blessings." And so one expected that Herbert Anatolyevich would also use such terms as "Dear Sir" or "your humble servant" in his speech. However, this passion for archaic language, or rather an affinity for deliberate politeness, drawn from the Russian classics, works Herbert Anatolyevich loved and knew by heart, weren't interpreted as pretentiousness or as a mask. He was as natural in his element as white coats and tall, nun-like nurse's caps are natural in a hospital. Maybe this unflappable politeness, stemming from

Herbert Anatolyevich's intimate understanding of human callousness, irritability, and malice, had a way of irritating people who lacked inner complexity, even if they were honest and simple folk, similar to Vasily Matveyevich's type, or such types as his new boss. Herbert Anatolyevich's natural restraint in interactions with others held him and his boss at a respectful distance, which accorded to each of them a convenient equilibrium that, in the Soviet medical milieu, typified the relationship between a party functionary and a practicing scientist. And now this delicate balance was bound to be upset, owing to Herbert Anatolyevich's actions and initiative. No one can be so punished for violating the harmony between a predator and its victim as the very same careless victim. Herbert Anatolyevich could have existed as a potential victim in a harmonious balance with his boss for many years, perhaps until retirement, while Ivan Ivanovich Baronov would have been content with the equivalent sacrificial offerings in the form of unearned scientific laurels.

Such thoughts tormented Herbert Anatolyevich's soul as he walked along Pirogovka Street toward his second home, his clinic. The sun was just coming up. There were still no students crowding the coatroom. Even the doctors were just starting to gather for the morning rounds. Herbert Anatolyevich shook the coat attendant's hand. Usually Professor Levitin would find this ritual of starting the workday with a handshake in the coatroom stimulating. He was well liked; his egalitarianism was perceived correctly, and it was valued. But today, while liberating himself from his nubby, dark grey wool coat with a silver astrakhan shawl collar, and shaking off droplets of melted snow from his astrakhan fur hat, Herbert Anatolyevich watched the coatroom attendant, as if thinking, could he know about the invitation? Why had the boss's graduate student, a young woman whose work Professor Levitin actually supervised, whizzed pass him without even pausing in the staircase to flirt with him subtly? Why all this? Herbert Anatolyevich looked in the mirrors looming on the landing of the main staircase. Maybe the word INVITATION was branded and blazing on his forehead? No, it's not branded, and it's not blazing, he told himself. Paranoia's setting in.

Herbert Anatolyevich assessed the situation while wondering how many stares he would now have to endure. He, Tatyana, and Tolya. For the first time he was horrified when he looked into the abyss, and they had barely even taken a concrete step yet. He could forget the whole thing. Talk his wife and son out of it. After all, if the KGB agents asked him (and they most likely would since invitations from Israel were all recorded), he could vindicate himself with bewilderment, plead having no knowledge of the person who sent the invitation, state that he had no desire to know any Israeli relatives, and issue other suchlike banalities—and all of this would be, with predetermined readiness, received as his repentance. Today was actually Wednesday, the day that Baronov visited the clinic. Around one o'clock, when the professor's rounds were completed, Herbert Anatolyevich walked into the boss's office with his report. Professor Baronov was sitting behind a black polished wood desk, its surface free of any objects or books; floating on its top, like a yacht on the smooth surface of the bay, was a folder with papers awaiting his signature. Ivan Ivanovich had already had his tea and a snack: a tea glass in a silver holder, a napkin with cheese rinds and the remnants of an apple, and a sugar bowl had been left on the round tea table. Herbert Anatolyevich approached the desk.

"Take a seat. I have been waiting a long time for you," said Ivan Ivanovich, without raising his head from the papers that he was rearranging, reviewing, and signing. Herbert Anatolyevich pulled over a chair and sat across from the boss. Ivan Ivanovich continued looking over the papers. Still without raising his eyes, and only occasionally wiping his sweaty bald spot with a red and green striped handkerchief, he listened to his deputy's report.

"That's all I have to report on the clinic's activities," Herbert Anatolyevich said when he was finished. He took a deep breath. "But besides that, I would like to ask for your advice, Ivan Ivanovich."

"With regard to what?" Ivan Ivanovich asked coolly.

"About a personal matter."

"Haven't you already decided everything?" Ivan Ivanovich asked in a quiet, incensed voice, and Herbert Anatolyevich understood that the boss was fully aware of his second-in-charge's intentions. Nevertheless Herbert Anatolyevich, who had trained himself to be careful and composed in the most troubling of life's circumstances, naively presumed, or rather convinced himself to presume, that his boss was asking him not about emigration, but about Herbert Anatolyevich's old request to be assigned as dissertation advisor to the gifted resident Doctor Shifman, who had come from the Siberian city of Kemerovo. Herbert Anatolyevich had continued to press his request, and this annoyed Ivan Ivanovich to no end. The boss argued that there were already too many dissertations on the docket, and that the Department had already been overextended by the late Academician Pushinsky's research agenda. With that, he cited no other reason.

"Ivan Ivanovich, if you are talking about Shifman, then I again request that you allow him to pursue his dissertation while based in our clinic."

"And I have decided to refuse your request. And you yourself have aided me in making my decision," the boss interrupted.

"I . . . you see, Ivan Ivanovich, I will do whatever is in the best interests of the clinic. I beg you to understand me. As far as Doctor Shifman is concerned, he is totally not at fault here, and he needs to grow as a researcher. In fact his problem and my problem are not at all connected."

"Do you remember Associate Professor Kaufman's case?"

"Yes, of course. That is why I want to assure you of my complete understanding of the situation. I don't want others to suffer because of my decision."

Professor Baronov was silent. Herbert Anatolyevich did not know how to interpret this silence and decided to clarify: "I wouldn't want to cause any trouble for you and for the members of the Department. I would appreciate your advice."

"Go on." Ivan Ivanovich finally finished wiping his sweat and put his handkerchief away. His right hand, now free, fumbled around the table, found his glasses, and began to slide them back and forth. To Herbert Anatolyevich they didn't look like glasses, but like a tank with blazing lights moving toward him in order to crush him, to squash him, a gawky and unarmed member of the home guard. Having finished with him, the tank moves away, only to move forward, demanding more and more victims.

"So, go on, Levitin," the boss reminded him of his bidding.

"My family has decided to move to Israel. There are many reasons for this. Many . . . but not political ones. I therefore request that you give me the opportunity to work in the clinic until I receive a visa. As a regular staff physician, of course."

"This is outrageous," Baronov said. "Didn't you have everything here? I don't think I interfered with your work. I was even ready to tolerate this miserable Shifman for your sake. And you. What sheer ingratitude. Actually, what else could one expect from your kind."

With all his might, Herbert Anatolyevich was trying not to scream from anger, insult, humiliation. Gritting his teeth, he restrained himself: you have to be quiet, you have to endure this. He remembered the poet Tvardovsky's words—that the major character trait of the Russian peasant was the ability to suffer through anything, to take it silently and not humiliate oneself. What does the peasantry have to do with this? Herbert Anatolyevich thought. He imagined himself in a wide and unplowed field, toiling behind a horse, holding on to the plow handles. Restraint. Restraint. Just restrain yourself.

"It's difficult for me to explain all the motives. Particularly since your words kill any predisposition to have a normal conversation."

"Normal?" his boss interrupted. "If only it were normal! But your conduct is abnormal. Both abnormal and amoral."

"I am exercising a right, which is provided to us by the humanitarian position of the Soviet government on the question of unification of families." In a wooden voice Herbert Anatolyevich uttered a phrase well known to all Soviet Jews attempting to emigrate. "This gives Soviet citizens of Jewish nationality the right of voluntary emigration to join their relatives living in Israel. I'm reuniting with my uncle."

"Don't play me for a fool. Uncle. Auntie. A cousin thrice removed! You're nothing but a typical ungrateful Jew, who was given everything here: education, respect, ideas. Even your wife you got from Russia, and now you spit on that which is most holy!"

This last phrase was probably the one that decided the outcome of their argument. Herbert Anatolyevich could no longer restrain himself.

"You think I have forgotten everything else in the world? No, it's you who's sacrilegious. I'm leaving primarily because I . . . I can no longer tolerate you as a professor of medicine. You're as far from the patients as your words are far from the truth. I no longer wish to serve as a smokescreen for such 'scientists' as you. Yes, you are absolutely correct, I am ungrateful. I should have thanked you a long time ago, on behalf of all the patients. You have never come to their bedsides, you have never given thought to their treatment, you have never shown any interest in their lives after discharge. I should have thanked my lucky stars that you entrusted the clinic to me. But that's enough. No more. From me you will never hear either words of gratitude or words of reproach. I only ask one thing: until the question of my emigration is decided, let me stay on as a regular clinician. This is my only profession, the only means of earning my daily bread."

Professor Baronov was silent. His bald head that had shone like a huge ebony ball now began to turn livid from the swelling veins. More and more Baronov's head resembled a colored plaster model from medical school, a model on which Herbert Anatolyevich remembered studying surface head and neck veins in his second-year anatomy lab. Suddenly Ivan Ivanovich uncoiled his back, groped around like an angered boar, grabbed the file with papers, and slammed it down on the gleaming top of the desk. Brimming with indignation and malice, he stood over Herbert Anatolyevich. Doctor Levitin, counting on his boss's well-trained composure, had not expected such a sudden transformation, such a flare of malice.

"You're to tender your resignation immediately, so not one of my people comes into contact with this Zionist pestilence," Professor Baronov shouted over Doctor Levitin's head. And then he repeated slowly, "Im-me-dia-tely."

Herbert Anatolyevich's intellectual civility gave way to despair.

"I will resign after I've finished treating my patients. That's first. And I will resign when I myself see it as necessary. That's second. And finally and most importantly, I have no connection to Zionists, nor any politics for that matter. I am a Jew. My homeland is Russia, but I'm forced to emigrate from here. I'm forced to do so, and I'm exercising a right given to me by the Soviet government. Many different types of Jews live in Israel: those with no political affiliation, Zionists, socialists, Orthodox, and even Communists. Which is why I beg of you not to create a new scandal here at the medical school. The affair of Associate Professor Kaufman was enough."

"You will not get the required letter for the Visa Section until you resign—that's one. Put that in your Jewish pipe and smoke it. And here's one more thing: your son will be kicked out of the medical school right after winter finals. We'll make sure of that. Have you weighed all the consequences, Levitin?"

"Yes."

"And you didn't forget about the autumn military draft?"

Having delivered a mortal blow, Ivan Ivanovich calmed down, plopping himself in the chair like a pool player who has to sink only one more ball while his opponent is not even half finished with his. The boss stared unabashedly into the eyes of his former deputy because the fire in Doctor Levitin's eyes had gone out; they were dead. Herbert Anatolyevich realized that he would be leaving the clinic immediately, that he would agree to endure the rest of his allotted time in this country—to do whatever was necessary—just to deflect the blow from his son.

And so Levitin left behind his life as a professor of medicine, becoming simply rank-and-file physician Doctor Levitin. But there are kind people in this world. Doctor Levitin's reputation and his credentials allowed him to secure a job as a medical consultant at a pay-for-service health center.

*

FIRST BLOW BELOW the belt. First defeat. Could it be that the roots of future defeats and refusals are within us? Should we give up the fight and give the Ivan Ivanovichs the opportunity to blackmail and harass us, to kill our willpower? Perhaps we should work on creating a collective immunity to the Ivan Ivanovichs of the world? After all, people have learned to prevent smallpox. And now there is no smallpox anywhere in the world. We shouldn't dodge Ivan Ivanovich's blows; when we duck, the blows will be transferred to someone who cannot defend him or herself from blackmail, harassment, refusals. We must eradicate from the earth the capacity of the Ivan Ivanovichs to control people's fates. Then the Ivan Ivanovichs of this world will not develop from human children. Today we're not able to alter human genetics, to make everybody kind, happy, wise, and talented. But we're able to construct a social environment, where a phenotype of vileness, obscurantism, sadism, racism—all that humanity has received as Cain's legacy—cannot unfold. I write about all this, and I know that I what I write is true. But when I think of the danger that I myself had brought upon my wife and son—with the mere thought of trying to oppose evil—I cease my well-constructed reasoning. I listen for night sounds. I check the locks and bolts. I put my trust in fate. I fear the refusal.

ANXIOUSNESS, A NEW tenant, had taken residence in the Levitins' home. Conversations became tinged with anxiety; casual phrases took on an anxious character. Anxiety-producing uncertainty now interfered with normal living, even though just the thought of a normal life in this totally abnormal predicament seemed blasphemous. Nevertheless, Anatoly continued with his studies and Tatyana with her work in the accounting branch of the housing office, and Herbert Anatolyevich practiced medicine in a pay-for-service health center. Three weeks had passed since his departure from the medical school and his old academic clinic, and they were almost ready to submit the visa application. And then it turned out that no matter how Herbert Anatolyevich calculated his options, no matter how he drafted his diagrams and tables, he couldn't plan for all the contingencies.

Winter finals began. Anatoly got an F in anatomy and was thrown out of the medical school's evening division. He was without a job, an occupation, and this worried Herbert Anatolyevich. Just over six months remained before the autumn army draft. That which used to seem both impossible and unreal now hung over the Levitin family.

In other areas, though, it seemed they were luckier. Herbert Anatolyevich had talked it over with Tatyana, and they had decided that it would be premature to disclose everything to Grandfather Vasily Matveyevich. When the permission to leave came, they would tell him. They would have to figure out how best to explain this to the old man. Thank God the head of the housing office gave Tatyana the letter she needed for the Visa Section without even mentioning that her resignation would be desirable. And as for the cognac collection that Tatyana had given her boss, that was a completely understandable and accepted way of expressing gratitude to a good man for his kindness and tolerance.

The day came when Herbert Anatolyevich was to take the documents to the district Visa Section. A week before that, Doctor Levitin had stopped by the Visa Section, and they gave him three copies of each application form, one for each family member, including Grandfather Vasily Matveyevich. Things weren't so simple with the old man. Since the day when Herbert Anatolyevich told the story of old Khaim, who had departed for the Promised Land, it was as if Grandfather Vasily had withdrawn into himself. He was uncommunicative and estranged. Tatyana had to get her parents' papers from her hometown village council. She told her father she was attending a three-day training seminar and left for Maryino.

I OPENED THE door to our garret in the second story of a guest cottage in the resort of Maleyevka. My glasses were fogged over from the cold. Before going for a walk in the woods, I opened the ventilation window. There was a fir tree branch spread out between the windowpanes—still there from New Year's. This branch separated the living space from the expanse of the wintry forest outside. Coming inside from the frost, I couldn't see anything except the bright light pouring in from the window. The sun had entered our attic room on the wings of the windows' frosty peacocks. Suddenly I heard a bird's trilling. I wiped my glasses. A tomtit was circling around the room. She was bigger than the others that flew around the cottage, a yellow-green bird with a blackish head and a sharply curved beak with a wide base. The bird was not thrashing in fright, but was slowly circling the room, communicating something important, something I could not comprehend as quickly without the benefit of human language. I rushed to the bird, wanting her to translate its news into Russian, but it was too late. The tomtit prattled some last phrase and bolted past the pine branch and out the window. What news awaits me? Am I hurrying or delaying the hour of its announcement? Was the tomtit really a messenger, or was she but a jingle of a January sunray lost in my garret?

ON A BREATHLESS winter morning, the train arrived at Ostrov Station. From here Tatyana Levitina had to take a bus to get to her home village. Squeezed together with the crowd, she came out onto the train station square. A biting wind, mixed with the bitterness of coal smoke and heavy smells that saturated provincial Russian train stations, stifled her breathing. Ahead was a meeting with the village council; running around to obtain her father's papers; endless conversations. But at this turning point in her life, what could Tatyana talk about with her fellow villagers? By nature she was a candid and open person, not given to cunning and hypocrisy. But she just couldn't share her terrifying plans with her fellow villagers. Would anybody even believe that their own Tatyana was planning to leave for good, and for eternity, and go almost all the way to Africa—to Israel? Tatyana even cackled into her mitten, imagining her dear girlfriend Masha Teryokhina's eyes when she revealed her plans.

The bus to Maryino was leaving at 10:15 in the morning. Tatyana decided to take a walk through town, to see what was available in the stores, although in her bag she had gifts she had bought in Moscow: hard salami, a large tin of herring, halva and other delicacies that were rarely found in the countryside. The same bitterly icy wind was chasing a newspaper along the train station square; it would rise up on its four corners, quivering from the cold and bristling like a mad stray dog. From time to time the wind would subside, and the newspaper would fall on its belly, only to shake its sheets as it roamed from one end of the square to the other with each new gust of wind. Local women wearing short coats made of plush fabrics and quilted vests, and men in green military pea coats, overcoats, or jackets with faded collars, stood around the kiosks still closed for the night. Some of the locals smoked; others shelled sunflower seeds and spat out the shells; yet others were silently biding their time. To Tatyana the square seemed like a huge waiting area full of holes, but what or whom the locals were waiting for they preferred not to say, so as not to tempt fate. Tatyana also surrendered to this collective hypnosis of the silenced truth and strolled the perimeter of this waiting room square, down along the kiosks. Then she found herself on Main Street in the town of Ostrov. Tatyana still remembered how in the summer, after protracted rains, Main Street would be dotted with large deep puddles, which you had to avoid very carefully, or the car would tilt over on its side and get stuck, and you needed a rope and a truck to get it out. Winter would bring cleanness and emptiness. And this time, too, winter had cleansed Main Street of mud and drained its waters. Back in autumn puddles were frozen and covered in snow, and later they got all smudged with winter road sludge that coated the roads like asphalt after it froze. Tatyana recalled how she and Herbert Anatolyevich rode down Main Street in an ambulance. They were going from Maryino to the train station. The new doctor, who had been sent to the rural hospital to replace Herbert Anatolyevich, was seeing them off. An endless autumn rain was coming down. The doctor, a tanned, broad-chested specimen of health, had just arrived from Sochi. "Decided to catch the velvet season by the sea. Look, it's September already, and then off you go to the collective farm to pick potatoes!" The driver, spellbound, getting used to his new boss and giggling at each of the tanned doctor's jokes, drove into one of the puddles that had become a sink hole. They had to pull the car out with a tractor. And the endless rain just poured and poured, until they floated past the station warehouses and past the potato leaves turning black in the signalman's garden.

But back then Tatyana took even the interminable rain as a good omen, a sign of the eternal happiness they would enjoy together. And so it was: for nearly twenty years of living with her husband she was happy, and when she sometimes felt low or experienced loneliness, all she had to do was to think about Ostrov's main street like an island in the endless rain—and the pits, pits, and more pits filled with water, as if the street itself had choked on something very cold, its stiffening jaws opened wide and gaping. These memories would always obliterate her melancholy, like a summer rain beating down the yellow dust of the day. But today, memories of that happy, endless autumn rain did not lift the weight from Tatyana's heart. In vain she walked down the street, stopping in food stores as her heart grew heavier. The sleepy saleswomen in wrinkled smocks and with furrowed faces, already fuming with anger at this morning hour, did not need to guard the fortresses built from little bricks of margarine, towers of canned stuffed cabbage, and cinderblocks of stale dried fruit. Enduring this until ten o'clock, Tatyana went back to the train station square, where the bus schedule to Maryino hung on a post. The closer it was to the time of the bus's departure, the more strained and angry were the faces of those waiting. Even though they all had tickets in hand and knew that they would definitely get on the bus, a kind of anxiety, a feeling of uncertainty, a fear of poor luck, made them form a small crowd, where they were all each other's enemies. Tatyana herself was becoming infected with this negative magnetism, this evil power of distrust. Even though among those waiting for the bus there were several faces she had known since childhood, she didn't feel like making small talk until her place on the bus was conclusively confirmed.

Finally they began to board. The first one on was a tipsy little old man, with a wooden leg polished from years of being an invalid. The little old man jumped up nimbly like a witch flying in its mortar, obnoxiously puffing on his coarse, cheap cigarette, and disappeared inside the bus. Then a Roma woman climbed on with a brood of dirty children, all covered in chocolate, trailing behind her. Where they were going and why, nobody knew. But no matter how resentful and greedy for their own spot the rest of the people were, no one would dare argue with these little devils. Then the doors suddenly closed right in front of everybody's nose, and they all took notice how a Certain Somebody in a thick wool overcoat and a muskrat hat walked up to the driver's side and flashed his ID, and then the crowd parted, the doors opened again, and the Certain Somebody got on and sat in the front seat to the right of the driver and buried his head in the *Village Life* newspaper. Boarding continued, but now without the intensity. The Certain Somebody's back in his thick wool overcoat and his muskrat hat, as well as the rustling of his newspaper, made the boarding more orderly, suppressing the raging instincts. Tatyana was one of the last to get on. Her seat was by the window in the middle of the bus. She put the suitcase with presents next to her in the aisle. Squeaking, the bus doors slammed shut, and the bus was about to leave the stop when suddenly a smiling, broad-shouldered military officer jumped onto the steps.

"Hey, chief, give a soldier on furlough a ride?"

"You're already on," the driver grimly joked, glancing at his neighbor to the right.

The officer got in, looked around, and then went straight toward Tatyana, where there was an empty seat. There was something naggingly familiar in his showy manner of walking, in his roguish way of looking around and suddenly freezing in his tracks. He was like a well-trained hunting dog; it was as if this officer was just about to put his ears up, lift his left front paw, and point. My goodness, Pavel Teryokhin, Pasha—can this really be him? She barely had time to think as the lieutenant colonel with paratrooper's insignia came towards her. First he stared at her with his baby blue eyes, then took a deep breath and blurted out her name:

"Tanyusha! Is it really you?"

"Pasha!" Tatyana sighed in answer, and they hugged each other. The village women—and most of the passengers were women—stopped their endless chatter about what they had bought in town and for how much. They even stopped gnashing on sunflower seeds and unceremoniously turned toward Tatyana and Pavel.

"Where did you come from?"

"And you? Where are you stationed?"

And a thousand other questions. And the three-hour trip seemed a quick leap from today's unexpected meeting to the time of their youth.

"I think of you often, Tanyusha."

"Why didn't you let me hear from you?"

"My sister warned me. She'd say, our Tatyana Vasilievna is living a good life, happily married. So why should I meddle?"

"That's true, Pasha. I do have a good life. Actually, I used to." Tatyana fell silent for a moment, but then immediately remembered that her high school flame, Pasha Teryokhin, should not and could not know anything about the implausible family plans, and that she should not share them even with his sister, Tatyana's bosom friend Masha Teryokhina.

"When I came home on furlough, remember that summer, I was going to propose to you. I was just finishing Airborne Academy. And you—poof—and flew away. So, I didn't stay home even one day. Turned around and went to Sochi."

"To drown your sorrows?"

"That's it."

"So how's life treating you now?"

"Now I've settled down. My wife's an independent woman. Five years my senior. A teacher. We have a son and a daughter. All's according to army regulations. And you, Tanyusha?"

Tatyana answered Pavel's questions and asked questions herself, as if unconsciously, while her conscious memory took her back to the old village days, to the spot where an old birch trunk was thrown across the stream. In the village they called this makeshift bridge "soldier's leg," because from afar the birch bark on the trunk looked like a soldier's leg with foot wrappings. The name had survived from the old days. Bittersweet were Tatyana's memories of waiting for Pavel Teryokhin by the "soldier's leg"; hiding behind a blooming bird cherry shrub with puffy flowers; and peeking out at Pasha, who dashed across the bridge and stood in the path, looking around and sniffing the shrubbery. Like a real hunting dog: peering to the right, to the left, forward and then backward, toward his own tracks. Inhaling deeply, his nostrils aquiver. Only now, sitting next to the adult Pavel Teryokhin, Tatyana understood why the nostrils of that seventeen-year-old lad quivered and billowed. She peeked at the lieutenant colonel sitting next to her. Then she imagined herself in such a situation that she immediately cut short these sinful thoughts, recollecting Herbert Anatolyevich's face, always a bit anxious. I should be ashamed, she thought. Daydreaming about such inappropriate things.

In the meantime, the bus had reached Maryino, clanging, its windows throbbing, coming down on "all fours" in every rut on the road, and bobbing up with each bump. Then it just happened that Tatyana, escorted by Pavel, walked to Masha Teryokhina's house. Where else would she stay, if not with her very best friend? While still in Moscow, she had always planned to stay with Masha. Masha's and Pavel's parents had long since passed away. Masha had been married, but it hadn't worked out. Her ex-husband, with whom she had a daughter, had left for the city to find better work. While the daughter was growing up, he would send ten or twenty rubles a month. At least he did that much. Now that the daughter was all grown up, he had disappeared totally. And last summer the daughter took off for Siberia, where they were building the Baikal-Amur Mainline. Her girlfriends from the village who were already there told her that finding a husband there was as easy as cracking a nut, and off she went. When someone would ask Mashka Teryokhina where her daughter was, she would answer candidly: "Maybe she's toiling at the railroad, or maybe sweating in the steam room," and she laughed heartily at her own joke.

At thirty-eight (she and Tatyana were the same age), she understood that you only live once. And Masha was trying to live the life God and her parents had given her as happily and as lightheartedly as she knew how. When she was having a good time at a village party, she would break into song, chanting the lyrics of a popular hit: "Only once a year the flowers bloom, Only once the spring of love arrives. . . . Only once, owowonly once," in her piercing and sweet voice. And despite her passion for partying, Masha was a good homemaker, and her *izba*, built by her parents in the very center of the village, close to the church, was single-handedly well maintained. The carved wooden fence was shiny yellow, and all the boards aligned like perfect baby teeth. After the revolution the church was partly knocked down, partly dismantled for its bricks. And the village council building went up on the other side of the village square. So the Teryokhins were in the middle of things again. Yeast of good luck had always been in her dough, especially now when Masha was left alone to be both the man and the woman of the household. The good condition and tidiness of her *izba* stemmed first of all from the fact that Masha carried on "a friendship and a love affair" (as she herself put it) with the local trade folk: carpenters, painters, drivers. Additionally, it had to do with the nature of Masha Teryokhina's employment; for years now she had worked as an accountant on the collective farm. And where there is an accountant, there are workdays to be counted. And so, in her not so young years, Masha had preserved a vitality of character, a taste for life, and most importantly, an understanding of how to make this life fit her desires.

While still in Moscow, Tatyana had decided that she would stay with Masha. But now, walking side by side with Pavel, she started to wonder whether she should follow this plan or look for a place to stay in another *izba*. What was the big deal? What had changed after meeting Pavel? And her inner voice immediately warned her, everything's changed. Don't do it. But her legs carried her, and on the way to Masha's *izba*, she and Pavel were chatting about all sorts of things as she chased away Herbert Anatolyevich's reproachful stare.

Masha Teryokhina was expecting both of them—her only brother and her close girlfriend; the night before she had received a telegram from each of them. When you wait for the people you love with all your heart, you prepare for the meeting in your mind; you recall the most memorable moments that bind you to those whom you are waiting to see. You tune yourself to that inherent emotional wavelength, characteristic of the guest, because no matter how small and insignificant that person may be to the world, to dear and loved ones he will always be special, even exceptional. Her brother and her close girlfriend. From birth until her marriage, Masha Teryokhina had never been apart from them. If her brother had come separately and her girlfriend separately, Masha would have sat with each of them in endless conversations full of details and minutiae. But it was so strange: they hadn't seen each other for almost twenty years, and all three of them hadn't been together for so long, and now they decided to arrive both at once, as if fate took them by the hand and brought them back to their home village, to Masha's home. What did this sudden change of fortune mean? Masha Teryokhina could not stand ambiguity, like a genuine Russian preferring to cut all the way to the root if you are going to cut at all. Masha employed a tried and true approach. She circled her *izba* with a dance in her step, appearing in the hallway or lifting the cellar door by its ring to disappear into the cellar, or looking in the cupboard. She was getting the table ready for a celebration. Tatyana, now warmed up and more relaxed, was taking out her Moscow gifts.

"Oh my, what delicacies!" Masha exclaimed dramatically with the presentation of each gift: hard salami, pickled herring, chocolates.

Having already given to his sister a suitcase, which must have contained presents that were household items rather than food items, Pavel plopped himself on a bench to the right of the red corner, where he sat smoking and, from time to time, looking out the window and at Tatyana. Good Lord, Pavel was thinking, how many years have gone by, and it feels like yesterday; I look at her and can't get enough. I could just pick her up in my arms, like in those bygone, carefree, sky-blue years, and take her away, God knows where. Good Lord, how did I let my happiness slip away, all my life convincing myself that this was not happiness, that happiness was that which came later with the warmth of a home, children, and a settled life. Even now I would drop everything and follow her, without looking back, if only she asked me to. Such thoughts made Pavel uneasy and prevented him from talking freely, without constraint, with his sister and with Tatyana. And so their conversation was awkward until they sat down at the table to fortify themselves after the trip. And even then, after the first round of drinks, the conversation waned, replete with pauses and interjections. Only later, when the liquor began to wind its way through their veins in a heavy, hot stream, did conversation flow freely, and a song sprang out as if by itself, demanding full attention from all three of them. It was not for naught that they all had the same village roots, had been singing and dancing together since their young days, and if the sounds of music captivated one of them, they would invariably touch the others' hearts. Masha, looking at her girlfriend with oily tenderness, kept slyly agreeing with something; now and then she would disappear somewhere, reappearing to take care of her guests, refilling their glasses, and putting more food on their plates. Pavel sat next to Tatyana. They hadn't sat so close to each other since the time when they had been young and in love. Tatyana understood she was drowning, in a way that people drown in a dream, when they are fully conscious of their dying but unable to pull themselves out of the horrifying, albeit sweet submersion. Tatyana was still trying to fight the sweet whirlpool that was sucking her in. Why did I go to Masha's house—to my own undoing? I could have stayed with Granny Nastya in the clinic. Or better yet, not have come at all and sent the request by certified mail. They do get mail in the village, Tatyana kept on repeating to herself in her head, desperately trying to remember where the village post office was located and who the postmaster was.

"Tatyanka, you haven't changed one bit. I would have recognized you anywhere among thousands of others."

That's Pasha talking, and I should say something back. But what? Tatyana continued to torment herself even as she replied.

"Pashenka, the post office, yes, help me find the post office. And then everything will be cleared up at the post office."

Masha started to flit about the room, filling their glasses and inviting them to have more of her food. Except that Pavel and Tatyana ate nothing, their odd conversation flowing.

"You and I, Tanyusha, will find the kind of post office, the kind that nobody will find, and unseal our letters," Pavel said to Tatyana.

He was not very drunk, just wound up and excited by the liquor; his male ego, bruised long ago, had been reawakened, his hurt passion now demanding a resolution. And his sister's words had been egging him on: "Look, brother dear, Tanyusha is a ripe apple, none the worse for wear. Come on, stick it to that four-eyed prof." These words wound up a spring, dialing up an internal code, and the will of this powered spring communicated a singular purpose and task to Pavel's voice, his hands, the paratrooper's whole pumped-up body. And Tatyana? Like an autumn leaf ripped away from an aspen frowning over water, Tatyana took off, dragged along by the cold and cruel force of instinct. Where will it swim to? Where will it make land? Whether it be to the lakeshore or a swampy haze, she understood nothing, protested nothing. It was all useless. And still some silly little words cooked up jokes and funny catchphrases, as Tatyana still ventured to fend off the inevitable.

"The post office, Pasha. That's like in Pushkin's *Dubrovsky*—remember in middle school. The meeting place. But the oak has been cut down, you know, and that's why there is no hollow to leave a secret note."

Pasha Teryokhin pressed on, unlocking her and unearthing the past.

Yes, it's all true, Tatyana the village girl made excuses to her present self who was married to Doctor Levitin. It was I who hurt my first sweetheart. My very sweet country boy. For old times sake, as a farewell to the village, I'll give my soul some slack. And then—to leave and to forget. This time leave forever. Aren't I saying goodbye forever? And this absolute severing word of final separation—*forever*—reverberated in Tatyana's soul, spinning around together with the table, clinking together with the shot glasses and cups, gamboling and squealing at the heels of Masha's own gambols and squeals. The entire *izba* was moving to and fro, as if it had been put on stilts, like the ones that Masha, Pasha, and Tanya had strutted on around the village when they were kids. Pasha, Pashenka, my dear one, my darling, my one and only. My first love. Whom did you leave me for, and why didn't you come flying on your carpet-airplane; why didn't you parachute down to me, when I, snake that I was, betrayed you, forgot you in a pure virgin field? Tatyana continued to condemn herself, to ruminate, and all the while she spun around together with the table, the *izba*, the entire world. The world was spinning, and the world was crashing. And her legs carried her somewhere. And next to her, on his stilts, strutting proudly through the village, was Pasha in his officer's tunic with his medals and decorations. Peasant women and kids stuck their heads out the windows and stared, seeing her with Pasha-the-officer; the kids whooped. Tatyana and Pasha ran, jumped, darted away from the staring windows and screaming doors. They finally ran up to a haystack in the virgin field; and there was an impossible sweetness and release when they were left alone and the chase and whooping had stopped; and Tatyana became quiet, because she had never known such happiness and such sweetness before.

Then Tatyana became lost in a dream. Her husband, Herbert Anatolyevich, visited in her dream. He was clumsily hunched over, as if he were ashamed to look into Tatyana's eyes, and when she got a good look at her husband, she saw how much he had aged. Grey curly hair edged the deep furrows appearing on his head; his eyes, dark and melancholy like those of an old tortoise, had sunken deeply, and his gaze had dimmed. His skinny humped nose jutted out of this furrowed tortoise face. Good God, look at his pants and jacket, Tatyana thought, horrified. Herbert Anatolyevich's suit was falling off his shoulders and was patched with multicolored rags. A bright yellow band, with a six-pointed star, burned on his left sleeve like an autumn maple leaf. With his right hand, her husband, Herbert Anatolyevich, held onto a small boy's hand. "Tolik," Tatyana screamed out, bursting into tears. Little Tolik was dressed in a child's military uniform, but without shoulder straps. And his little forage cap had no red star on it. Tatyana ran her hands over her son's skinny body, and she broke into a howl of inconsolable weeping. Her son's right sleeve was empty. She physically felt the emptiness; the sleeve was tucked under a thick belt and stuck into the right pocket of his field pants. Tolik looked at her and comforted her, "Don't cry mommy! We've been fighting for you. And now we're together again: you, papa, and me." These words extinguished Tatyana's nightmarish dream. She woke up covered in tears, awakened by Masha Teryokhina shaking her, consoling her, and giving her homebrew to drink from a ladle for her hangover.

"You're so different, Tatyana. A city girl, no less."

Pavel was not in the *izba*. Masha said that at dawn he had left for a distant village to go rabbit hunting with an old pal. Tatyana didn't ask anything about Pavel and in general tried not to think about last night—when their drunken merriment ended, and the dream began. And only the dream's horrible ending plagued Tatyana's soul. It's all punishment for my sin, she thought. But my sin was in a dream, and so the punishment, too, should end with the anguish in the dream, Tatyana soothed herself. But even these soothing thoughts were a form of suffering.

Masha also pulled herself together, as though setting her mind on serious matters. Or was this a change that always happens in the Russian soul: yesterday—all hell let loose, boards pulled out of the fence, the oven shattered with a crowbar. And the next day: contrition, self-deprecation, meekness, prayer.

Tatyana had a quick glass of tea and set off for the village council. She had brought the female bookkeepers candy from Moscow and collected all of her father's papers. And there—Moscow again. There it was, Three Station Square. And over there, the Garden Ring and her own home. Thank God another horrible dream was behind her. Anatoly was healthy, Grandfather Vasily Matveyevich beaming with joy over his daughter's return. Her husband, Herbert Anatolyevich, greeted Tatyana with a bouquet of early mimosa flowers.

❧

A BRIGHT WINTER morning has been given to you. You wake up peaceful, removed from all those minor problems that had been distracting you. You leave the house. With the soles of your shoes, you test the soft, springy matter of the clean, newborn snow. It crunches pleasantly and entices like fresh bread with a crispy crust. You walk on primordial matter—water that has taken on the qualities of crystallized magic. From this magic radiance, from this newborn purity, a decisiveness crystallizes within you. You finally conclude that all the steps you had taken that morning are true and genuine steps, and all the steps that veer off this morning's path, that veer from this crystalline decision, are wrong steps. You make your final choice.

THEY DECIDED TO take the paperwork to the district branch of the Visa Section on the second Thursday of January. All the documents were in order. Herbert Anatolyevich, with his typical academic scrupulousness and with his habit of checking page proofs, read the application materials three times and checked and rechecked all the paperwork. They still had not told Grandfather Vasily Matveyevich what was about to happen. This was, they decided, their transgression, and they would make everything right after receiving the permission to leave. And there was one very unpleasant moment. The passport clerk Raisa Nikolaevna, a tubby know-it-all who had always been jealous of Tatyana's family stability, growled when she was issuing Grandfather Vasily Matveyevich's authorization.

"You just can't stay in one place, can you? First you bring your grandfather to the new house, and now you're dragging him to Israel. You want to snatch some extra living space there too?"

Tatyana kept silent, and the head of the housing office, whose palms she had greased ahead of time, hushed Raisa Nikolaevna: "Don't quibble, Raisa. It's their right as citizens. Did you read about the Helsinki Accords? Leonid Ilyich Brezhnev himself signed it. You're a real ignoramus, Comrade Konotopova."

And this concluded the office debate over the Levitins' departure to Israel.

Thursday came. Herbert Anatolyevich hailed a cab on the Garden Ring, although he didn't have far to go. He entered the local Visa Section at 2:55 in the afternoon. A young couple ahead of him in the queue were discussing some business matters, and Herbert Anatolyevich kept on hearing the words "lacquered boxes," "carved boards," Palekh, Khokhloma, and other birthplaces of famous crafts. He tried not to focus on these words, and yet he couldn't help wondering how, on the threshold of the biggest step in one's life, when a person voluntarily forfeits one's citizenship and decides to take on another, one could talk, and even argue heatedly, about objects that possessed a concrete monetary value. To him this seemed blasphemous. Herbert Anatolyevich took a step back from the young couple, but they didn't pay any attention to him. Their faces were well-groomed and indifferent. Soon the narrow hallway began to fill up. A lady of about seventy-five, breathing heavily, flopped down into a green armchair with brown polished armrests. Herbert Anatolyevich looked the old lady over with an internist's appraising look. She shifted her wheat-brown Orenburg shawl back off her forehead, then straightened it out on her shoulders. Smoothing down her hair, she looked at Herbert Anatolyevich with penetrating blue eyes covered with a web of tiny reddish-brown vessels that gathered on the whites of her eyes around the irises.

"Fate has brought even you, professor, to this establishment."

Herbert Anatolyevich again examined his neighbor's face. Of course, he thought, though he hadn't recognized her right away. So many years had passed since their first acquaintance. This is what happened.

In his first year after coming back from the village, Herbert Anatolyevich, a young attending physician, was taking care of an interesting patient at the clinic. Her case, in a purely medical context, was rather unimpressive: "acute on chronic" pneumonia. But the persona and the fate of his patient were quite remarkable. She immediately attracted attention: lush copper-red hair; a somewhat elongated face with slightly raised cheekbones; "German type" hawk nose with sensual nostrils; full, red lips. And penetrating sky-blue eyes. The patient's last name was Dorfman, Berta Lvovna Dorfman. She had recently returned from the

Siberian town of Shumsk, where she lived in administrative exile. Before Shumsk, as Herbert Anatolyevich learned from her medical record, Berta Lvovna had been an inmate in a high-security correctional labor camp, where she worked as a rate fixer. The work itself was not too hard, but she had to travel to the logging sectors. Hence the resulting constant respiratory infections. "And what kind of treatment does one get in a camp hospital? Aspirin and, in the very best case scenario, streptocide," Berta Lvovna recounted. Then, later, when she got to know Herbert Anatolyevich better, she revealed her story to him.

Berta Lvovna was born in the Volga Region. Her father, an agronomist, worked on a collective farm, where more than half of the residents were ethnic Germans. Although Berta Lvovna's family was a hundred percent Jewish, their continued living alongside the Volga Germans, and also the kinship of Yiddish and German, created an environment in which the Dorfmans didn't feel estranged from these people, who in the eighteenth century had been brought from the distant Germany to the Saratov steppes. The Nazi invasion had drawn a boundary between the Soviet Germans and Soviet citizens of other nationalities. The Volga Germans were forcibly exiled and resettled into Siberia, the Altai region, and Kazakhstan.

The Dorfman family found themselves evacuated to Chelyabinsk, from where Berta, a former student of philology at Saratov University, was drafted into the army. She worked as a translator in the tank division headquarters and would probably have made it with her tank crews all the way to Hitler's lair, had it not been for an event that resulted in her years of camp life and administrative exile. In 1944, while stationed in a small Lithuanian village, Berta and two other girls from the signals corps, Zoya and Natasha, went to the *banya*, a Russian sauna. They had already been sweating for a while when, worn out by the heat and the aroma of the birch besoms, they decided to soap up once more, rinse off, put on their clean underclothes, and go back to their sleeping quarters. They heard shooting, engines rumbling, explosions thundering. The girls dressed hastily and hid quietly in the *banya* entryway. Suddenly five German soldiers and a young officer burst

into the *banya*. The Germans, as Berta found out from their frightened
chatter, were being pursued by the Russians after an unsuccessful German
attack on the headquarters of a Soviet division. The Germans who burst in
were totally baffled by what to do with the Russian girls. Shoot them? That
would expose their location.

One of the soldiers, a red-cheeked specimen of health, offered to finish off these unwitting witnesses. He even took off his belt and showed
the officer how he would do it without making noise. Berta, who understood each word, froze with fear. She suggested to her girlfriends that they
start to negotiate, to pretend they were medical orderlies, to flirt with the
soldiers. Zoya and Natasha agreed. Berta addressed the officer in perfect
German; she was a *Volksdeutche*, she told him, had been hiding this truth
all of her life so that she wouldn't get shipped off to Siberia. All this made
the Germans well disposed toward the girls. There was no more talk of
disposing of them. Then our soldiers surrounded the *banya*. Berta suggested to the officer that they surrender to save his own life and his soldiers' lives. That's the way the ill-started bath day ended, but the affair had
just begun. The investigating officers of the army's Special Section had
their own interpretation of the girls' account. They were harshly inter-
rogated. First all of them together, then individually. It turned out that it
was Berta Dorfman who talked the other girls into going to the *banya*.
She was the one who opened the door for the Germans, thus saving them
from our shots; she was the first one to negotiate with the enemy; and on
top of that, she proposed that Zoya and Natasha should amuse themselves
with the Germans.

The tribunal asked for capital punishment. In the end, execution was
commuted to hard labor in a maximum security prison camp. Then, after
the end of the war and numerous appeals on her part, Berta was released
from the camp. By the way, the same officer who had burst into the *banya*,
and who had surrendered to the Russians as a prisoner of war with Berta's help, played an important role in her acquittal. He even described the
looks of the girl who suggested the surrender. However, being released from
the camp didn't mean that she could return to European Russia. Berta

Lvovna was assigned as a civilian employee to work in a POW camp for German soldiers. Eventually the prisoners were able to return to Germany from Siberia, and Berta Lvovna moved to the Siberian town of Shumsk, where she found work as a teacher of German. She had gotten used to Shumsk and would have stayed there until the end of her days had 1956 not come, and had she not been invited to the local office of the KGB and told that she was now free to leave for any city on the territory of the Soviet Union. Berta Lvovna's desire was to live in Moscow, where one by one her Siberian exile friends were moving. It was then, in the late 1950s, that she became Herbert Anatolyevich's patient. And here they were, both waiting in line, both in front of the same door. The young couple that was first in line spent about twenty minutes in the inspector's office and left the same way, paying no attention to anyone, preoccupied with their own calculations.

"Now it's your turn to enter purgatory," said Berta Lvovna, cheering up Doctor Levitin.

He went in. A young woman with broad cheekbones and dark hair sat behind a desk in the office. Without turning her head toward Herbert Anatolyevich, she took the envelope with the uncle's invitation to Israel, and then the family members' passports from him. Carefully checking the address on the envelope that the invitation came in against the passport information, the woman leaned back in her rectangular high-backed chair, on which hung a police uniform tunic with the insignia of a full lieutenant.

"Your work record." The inspector took the next document and checked it against the exit visa applications.

"So you're dragging him with you," she smirked, when she got to Grandfather Vasily Matveyevich's application form.

When she opened Anatoly's papers, Herbert Anatolyevich tightened up, as if he were concealing something or lying to someone.

"Why isn't your son studying or working?"

"You see, he was accepted to university. And he attended it for a semester. But the finals didn't go well for him."

"I'm asking you, in plain Russian, it seems, is he studying now or working?"

"At the present time no, but he is planning to," Herbert Anatolyevich mumbled in embarrassment, and right away he added: "We obtained the confirmation from the housing association, just in case."

"What do you mean, just in case? We won't accept the application without that confirmation."

"Yes, the confirmation . . ." Herbert Anatolyevich was so upset that at first he couldn't find the necessary written confirmation in the pile of other documents.

"Your confirmation's here." The inspector faultlessly located the necessary document and placed it in Anatoly's file.

"And what's next? Where can we find out about the results?" Herbert Anatolyevich asked, rising from his chair and securing his briefcase.

"You will get a postcard," the lieutenant answered, and her eyes were again looking straight ahead, as if not even noticing Herbert Anatolyevich, who was saying his goodbyes. He went out into the hall, almost unaware of what had just occurred, what a fatal boundary he had just crossed.

Berta Lvovna whispered very quietly, so that the rest of those waiting would not hear them: "Well, doctor. It's done now. The surgery's over. We shall hope that there will be no complications."

"Of course, of course, we shall hope."

"And here's my phone number." Berta Lvovna put a piece of paper in Herbert Anatolyevich's coat pocket, straightened up, and walked into the office with a determined step.

THE LEVITINS' DAILY living had taken on a different character. Before they had filed their papers with the Visa Section, before that momentous January day in 1979, each new day entering their comfortable apartment was marked by something special, something bright: a new article, a fascinating clinical case, visiting friends or having friends over, theater-going, Anatoly's studies. Now their upcoming departure cast a shadow over everything. Tatyana tried to start her accounting duties in the housing office earlier, so she would have a couple of hours in the afternoon to run around the stores. The Levitins entered the circle of those who were leaving. Women in that circle traded information on what to buy to take with you—when you start out and won't have a job yet. And also, what of that which you bought could be sold abroad: in Vienna, in Rome, in Tel Aviv, just to have a little extra to live on. The unknown was a bit frightening. They wanted to prepare themselves, at least a little bit, for entering their new life not as beggars, but as independent people. Luckily Grandfather Vasily Matveyevich was deaf and didn't hear Tatyana's daily conversations with her new girlfriends, or he just didn't understand anything. The Levitins got used to the idea that everything with Grandfather would be all right, would just somehow work itself out by itself, if only the permission to leave would come soon. Herbert Anatolyevich adjusted and grew accustomed to his new job; he ran around Moscow on his long, tireless, and unrelenting legs, running to make house calls or to see patients in his new clinic. He had forced himself to forget his former research plans—including his recent obsession with the question of kidney tissue regeneration following abscess formation. The main thing now was to get through this.

One day he got a call from a Zhora Driz, a medical school classmate: "Old man, we got our permission. Come see us off." And the three of them—Tatyana, Herbert Anatolyevich, and Anatoly—went to Zhora's house to say goodbye. In the old days they would have definitely taken a cab. Now, it's trolleybus "B" to Mayakovskaya metro station, from there on the metro to Sokol station, then a bus to the depopulated area of Pokrovskoye-Streshnevo.

Zhora Driz lived in a wooden cottage, one of the few that remained in what was once a near suburb of Moscow. Everything around the cottage—the jagged fence, lopsided and spread open like a fan; lilac bushes overgrown with wild elderberry shrubs; empty boxes and crates scattered along the path—all spoke of neglect and abandonment. One could see that the owners couldn't be bothered to fix the rotted steps, falling in like the bridge of a syphilitic nose. Driz's parents had purchased the cottage before the war from the relatives of a family that had perished in the terror of 1937. And now, in just a week, the house where Zhora had spent his entire life was to be abandoned forever. For Herbert Anatolyevch, this house evoked memories of his first, agonizing love, when he and Zhora were in their fourth year of medical school. Zhora, a convivial and witty fellow, tossed his thick head of hair and said to Herbert Anatolyevich, "Come over tonight at 8:00. My parents are going out. A Passover supper or something. We'll have fun."

More than twenty years had passed since that day, and Herbert Anatolyevich still remembered the April dusk gently floating into the living room from the frozen bare garden. Heavy carved oak furniture that cluttered the sitting room is sinking into semidarkness. In that semidarkness, a bottle of wine is standing on an antique table. A long-legged female being is there in the living room, and by some strange coincidence, it's called Katya, except that he, Herbert Anatolyevich, left there alone with this female being, is unable to call her by a plain, ordinary human name.

Katya was a friend of Zhora's girlfriend. Even though Zhora had forewarned Herbert Anatolyevich that "easy girls" would be invited, he was totally incapable of crossing the line of illicitness that lay between him and Katya. Perhaps this timidity, common to many Jewish boys, has remained in the hereditary memory as a heavy yoke, forced upon their genes back in the days of ghettos and Pale of Settlement.

Katya pulled down the curtains and shut the door. There was no key, and so she said, very businesslike: "Move this armchair to block the door. Just in case they suddenly feel an urge to hang out with us." Herbert Anatolyevich moved the armchair over automatically, watching Katya's every move and falling in love with her even more. They say that totally uninhibited girls can elicit a feeling of aversion, something like a mutiny against this nudity—a nudity bordering on shamelessness. Herbert Anatolyevich experienced nothing of the sort. Katya first brought out only a feeling of veneration in him, and blindly he succumbed to the wishes of this long-legged, exciting being. They each had another sip of wine, and Katya put her arms around Herbert Anatolyevich, leaning closely towards his chest. Then Katya took Herbert Anatolyevich's hands and put them under her sweater, putting his fingers on her straining nipples. Herbert Anatolyevich touched these velvety, lustrous nipples, and their tenderness reminded him of rose petals that he had once touched in the long-faded garden of days.

"Katenka, Katyusha," Herbert Anatolyevich repeated over and over, wanting so much to feel with the palms of his hands her entire body and that tantalizing part of her back, hidden under a short skirt.

"Oh you, my silly four eyes," Katya was repeating as she drew Herbert Anatolyevich toward the sofa bed, undressing and giving herself to this awkward Jewish boy she hardly knew.

"Katyusha, Katenka, now! Help me. Where are you?" Herbert Anatolyevich mumbled, barely able to contain that force ripping him from within, and seeking a speedy exit.

"Just be careful," Katya whispered.

Sinking into a bliss that enveloped him as it sucked out his entire soul, Herbert Anatolyevich felt a rapidly nearing happiness that was beyond any words, a levitation over a blossoming meadow, a return to the primordial past when he was but a creature clambering along a bamboo stalk and reaching for the honeyed fruits. Lightening struck, and then a wild scream of an approaching pain that turned into ecstasy; he had taken a bite of the fruit and spilled the sweet sticky juice. Spent, Herbert Anatolyevich lowered his head onto Katya's clavicle. He was so ecstatic with what had just happened to him for the first time in his life that he did not immediately grasp the cause of the anger and revulsion in Katya's eyes. He wanted to kiss her hand, but Katya pushed Herbert Anatolyevich away, as if he were a disgusting and useless animal.

"You moron! What was your hurry? What have you done? Don't they teach you anything in med school?"

She jumped off the sofa bed, rummaged for something in her purse, threw some clothes on, and ran out of the living room. Herbert Anatolyevich heard water running in the bathroom, then excited voices. He got dressed, yet continued to sit in the living room, still infused with joy and delight, and refusing to believe that this unbelievable happiness was broken, turned into disgrace. Zhora came in, looked at his friend with scorn and compassion, collected Katya's things, and, seeing that Herbert Anatolyevich wanted to follow him, interceded.

"Don't go in there; Katya's furious. She's afraid she'll get pregnant. You doofus, why didn't you use protection?"

Herbert Anatolyevich didn't leave the living room until he heard the front door slam, heels clatter on the front steps, and the garden gate rattle. "It's all over. It's all over," he kept on repeating, as if keeping time with the tram carrying him in the direction of Sokol. This rocking reminded him of the repenting and rocking of worshipers in the synagogue, when they repent for their infantile insecurity and indecisiveness in breaking the straps of circumstances that bind their hands and free will.

Herbert Anatolyevich hadn't seen Katya since then. And Katya had not sent any news of herself. But the happiness and sensation of falling in love that had been given to him so suddenly didn't leave Herbert Anatolyevich for several years—not until his marriage to Tatyana. And now he was walking with his wife and son to bid farewell to Zhora Driz. Herbert Anatolyevich had trouble shaking the flood of memories and at first couldn't quite understand how it was that, instead of the bygone girl passing through like a summer storm, there was his wife walking with him, Tatyana, the woman whom he had fallen in love with forever, she who had given him his son Anatoly. In the living room that still held the exulted memories of first love and of the first fall from grace, there stood a long table made up of sections of several smaller and larger tables. The room was filled with tobacco smoke and noise. No one paid any attention to the Levitins; they just made room for the new arrivals and continued with their endless conversations. One could readily distinguish between "oldtimers" and "newbies" among those waiting for their exit visas because the former commanded greater knowledge and practicality. One of Zhora's relatives, a hairdresser from Vostryakovo outside Moscow, gleefully described how he managed to obtain a letter from work.

"Where will they ever find such a master of women's coiffures?" And he answered his own question: "Nowhere!

"So, what do you think happened? I decided to involve my coiffed little ladies . . ."

With his long story, told at the table heavy with vodka and finger foods, the hairdresser had the group's attention. Herbert Anatolyevich was sitting by himself. His wife had moved over to join a group of women, plunging into their spirited discussion of emigration-related tasks and errands. Anatoly found himself in another room, where Zhora's children, a son and a daughter, were entertaining their peers.

The guests were telling jokes at the table. Spring was around the corner. Every day the newspapers talked about the preparations for the SALT II Treaty. The Chinese were planning on sending a delegation to Moscow. From the other end of the table could be heard: "It's safe to go to Israel now. Sadat and Begin have decided to be friends. Maybe they'll make peace with the Palestinians."

"How can one trust those swarthy ones?"

"How? Very simply. Because nobody wants war."

"Let's drink!"

"Let's drink! L'Chaim!"

New guests kept on arriving, bringing cakes, vodka, champagne. Zhora and his wife, Liza, circled among their guests with a mixture of happiness and exhaustion written all over their faces. This farewell party made Herbert Anatolyevich think simultaneously of a wake and a wedding, mourning a life lived in Russia and celebrating a newlywed life in Israel.

"Just think, old man." Finally Zhora found a minute for Herbert Anatolyevich. "What can I say, I'm just a simple rank-and-file internist. Still I'm not afraid; I'll pick up Hebrew somehow. And I'll start working. But you, with your brain—you'll become an Academy Member there. For sure! Academician Levitin!" And Zhora went over to talk to another guest.

Good Lord, Herbert Anatolyevich thought, Why is it that even here, among Jewish people, my own flesh and blood, I feel so alone? Could this all be my accursed character trait? Won't this torturous passion for self-analysis let me be, at least now, after the decision has been made? People are sitting, drinking, having a good time. Waiting for their turn.

But I'm tormenting myself and those close to me. Incredible that Tatyana puts up with me.

The doorbell chimed its melody. Liza ran out into the hallway and led the new arrivals into the sitting room. She searched around the table for empty chairs and for suitable conversationalists for the newly arrived guests. There were three of them. A stocky mustached man with a vibrant, animated face, whose expressions were so lively that you couldn't tell if his jerking his right arm and shoulder and gesticulating were a formed habit or the result of a nervous tick. He was accompanied by a tall, slender woman, Tatyana's age, and by a girl of seventeen or eighteen. The girl was athletic and pretty, having taken after her father with her lively body language, and after her mother with flashes of daring in her eyes and soft blonde hair. Liza called her son over, and he led the girl to where the young people were.

"Herbert, I want to introduce you to my colleague." (Before they submitted the application to the Visa Section, Driz's wife had worked as a sound designer at Popular Science Studios.) "This is Evgeny Leyn, the famous film historian."

"More like a famous film custodian, Liza!"

"Oh, don't listen to him. Zhenya Leyn is our star," Liza said, pouring vodka for her new guests.

"A star that shines over permafrost," his wife commented as if in passing. She looked at Herbert Anatolyevich, and he was burned with the ice of her steely eyes.

"Katya, is it really you?" Herbert Anatolyevich asked her, having trouble making sense of this meeting—and especially under such circumstances.

"Astounding! Leyn darling, imagine, this esteemed professor with one foot out of the country is that inexperienced medical student from my wild, stormy youth."

And both of them, Katya and her husband, broke into happy laughter, drank a toast to the health of the Driz family, and forgot about Herbert Anatolyevich for the rest of the evening.

♪

WHEN DID IT finally happen? This break, this tearing away from the placenta through which my endlessly growing love for Russia had been nourished. Now I'm separated and rejected once and for all—a child of incidental passion. Or maybe a child of purchased love? How did it happen that my forefathers came to love this land? Did she love them back? And now, rejected, I bleed profusely; and Russia bleeds, having rejected me, because we share the same bloodstream. Maybe the rejection began in post-siege Leningrad, when we—eternally hungry boys from the Vyborg side of the city—conjured up another way of procuring food. The bread factory across the street from our buildings worked round the clock. The rich aroma of bread intoxicated us. All day we would dream about bread. Particularly in the summer, when there was nothing else to do but roam around and think about food. For us the factory chimney with its dark grey billow of smoke was a symbol of complete happiness. We concocted astonishingly brave and ingenious plans of procuring the bread loaves that we could see through the open factory windows: golden loaves, hot, blazing with sweetness and abundance. And one day one of us figured out how to get these loaves. We found metal rods and twisted them into long hooks. It was hot in the bread factory; we noticed this because the women bakers wore smocks over their naked bodies, and when the smocks would open up, the pink, well-fed bodies of the female employees enticed us, just as the golden bodies of the bread loaves enticed us. It was hot, and the women opened the windows from the inside; on the outside of the windows there were metal grates made of the same material as our iron hooks. On purpose—or by chance—the female workers would put the freshly baked loaves on the window-sills. They probably did it not for our hungry bunch but for themselves, because you couldn't eat the bread when it was steaming hot, and they had to cool it by the open windows protected by the metal grates. And this was when one of us, whose turn it was to procure our daily bread, would saunter up to the open windows, shove the hook through a square opening of the grate, pierce and hook a loaf of bread, pull its golden body out with a swift movement, and dash across the road to the park with the bread hidden under his jacket. There we divided the spoils. Like the other guys, I stole the bread when it was my turn. We were having such great luck that it was starting to look like the women bakers were opening up the windows and intentionally putting the bread out there for us. But once, when I dropped the hook in through the bars and was poking a loaf, I felt a tug. Someone had grabbed ahold of the hook and was dragging me to the window. I peered inside. A full-bodied young woman was standing by the windowsill. Her red hair was tucked under a gauze kerchief, but its fiery redness burst out, forming a golden halo around the kerchief. The redhead was dressed in a white sleeveless smock; the right side of the smock had slipped down—from the strain of the struggle for my hook, and her breast was popping out through the gap, an armpit aflame with scorching red hair. I dropped the hook and stared, wide-eyed, at this wondrous sight. Too bad the other rouges weren't there to see it. They were waiting for me in the park.

"And what do you think you're doing?" the redhead uttered. "Our Russian people, you know, are always hungry. But you kikes, don't you have enough to buy your bread?"

I stood there silent, dispirited.

"Here, little Jewboy, eat. I don't begrudge you. It's government bread."

The redhead shoved the muzzle of the bread loaf through the square of the grate, and then she pushed my metal hook out onto the street. I was only nine years old at that time. Most likely I still hadn't learned to make the right decision on the spot. Or maybe I hadn't yet learned to relate my instinctive actions to the defined rules of the game. Actually, to this day, I still haven't learned to do this. At that time I had no such thoughts. I grabbed the loaf, hid it under my jacket just in case a cop happened to be nearby, and dashed over to the park. In a clearing at the foot of a huge oak tree, the other boys from our courtyard were waiting for my return. We divided the bread and started to eat. Suddenly I felt nauseous. A heaviness loomed in my chest and my stomach, my temples began to pound, and I ran off into the hawthorn bushes and vomited.

A feeling of morose exceptionality began to haunt me. It appears that I hadn't noticed this before, like a girl who doesn't notice her unattractiveness until she finds herself in the field of vision of people who don't know her and who are making a choice. They didn't choose her. Or, just the opposite, they chose her to exclude her from the game. They began to single me out from among the other boys. Probably as I matured, I began to look more and more Jewish. Often Jews are blond and blue-eyed in childhood. It's often hard to tell a Jewish child from a European child. Only later, when the children reach puberty, do the Semitic (Mediterranean) facial features appear. Perhaps this has to do with the origins of our nation: the original northern Nordic type had been conjoined with the nomadic tribes of Arabia. I began to take heed of casual conversations: in school, in a tram, in a store. Even a slight allusion to my non-Russian lineage wounded my self-esteem. I was taking on the role of the persecuted. This would engender a poignant feeling of compassion for others who were victimized: invalids, prisoners of war, convicts, holy fools, and orphanage kids. I would seek out the friendship of those peers who also had some kind of deformity: in the family, in the body, in the soul. I developed an aggressiveness toward the successful and the affluent. Together with my friend, the illegitimate son of a Jewish man and a Russian village girl, who had come to Leningrad from the Luga region before the war to find work, we scoured the outlying streets and decaying parks of the Vyborg side. We craved fistfights, so that the pain and the blood would wash away the shame of our torturous otherness. We feared no one. Our poor mothers . . . Yet little by little, everything fell into place. The other kids around us no longer talked about our Jewishness. We had scorched that pestilence out of our land. And we began to forget old wrongs. After all, we were still half-children.

Once, in the 7th or 8th grade, we went to a party at an all-girls' school. In those years boys and girls went to separate schools. I believe it was in

January—a belated New Year's celebration. The girls' school was three tram stops from our house, toward the center, past the Forestry Academy Park. We put on clean shirts, bell-bottomed pants, and jackets with geometric inserts made of dark cloth, pulled on our overcoats and hats. The tram moved ever so slowly, and our souls were straining to fly to that special place inhabited by nimble, smiling creations with incredible forms that you could lean into while dancing. And so we danced, went to smoke in the bathroom that was assigned for the visiting boys, and returned to wander around the hall or to stand by the wall, eyeing and identifying the most beautiful among these magical creations known by the word *girls*—chirping and tender like dragonfly wings. We chose one of them and dubbed her "our girl." We even asked her to dance, once or twice. We believed that this girl with a pale, delicate face—slightly olive-skinned and already mature owing to its sharply-defined lips and huge violet eyes—we believed that she, too, thought of herself as "our girl," and we got angry, although not for long and not at her, when she danced with other boys.

But even while dancing, "our girl" managed to scan the hall with her violet-hued glance and to notice us, giving us an almost imperceptible smile. This meant that the game was continuing, and although, according to the rules of the game, we were supposed to part with her, it wasn't for long and the parting wasn't even serious, as with any game. What was serious was the fact that she was "our girl." All the boys in the room saw that and didn't risk asking her to dance more than once during the course of the evening. A feeling of connectedness to this wonderful girl made us happy. In the middle of the evening, when we had concluded that no danger threatened our future friendship with the owner of those violet eyes, my friend nudged me with his elbow. "Look! We're in for a fight." Soplov, the son of some party official, had attached himself to our girl. The record player was playing, the records radiated foxtrots and tangos into the hall, and it was certain that a fight couldn't be avoided. I went up to Soplov, who, even after a second dance, wasn't about to leave our girl's side, and was holding her hand to show that he would ask her again. It seemed to me that our girl looked at me with fear in her eyes. Of course, I thought. She's just afraid of Soplov. It was dangerous to turn down that fellow. They said that he never showed up at parties without his blade.

"Get lost!" I said, quickly and rudely, and my friend nodded in support of my words. Soplov, of course, knew us both, knew of our reputation as reckless fighters and truth-seekers; he knew that many charges had been filed against us at the juvy hall of the local police precinct, and also that we never turned away from an honest fight. But the girl was so wonderful; she looked with such great interest at the boys ready to rip each other apart for her, so that for Soplov to step away, to chicken out, would mean to lose her forever. He was used to never losing anything.

"Take a hike, the both of you, right to your native Palestine," Soplov said loudly, and continued to hold our girl's hand tightly. In those days of the British Mandate, they called Jews "Palestinians" as an insult. We both hit Soplov at the same time. I punched him in his right eye, right in the corner where the tear duct showed its scarlet flesh. My friend hit his left jaw, which was still slightly open, as the last sounds of Soplov's loathsome words slid out with poisonous saliva. We saw Soplov crashing, but just before he hit the ground, blood gushed out of his mouth. We had to make it to the coatroom before they told the teacher on duty, who in turn would call the police. The most important rule for such situations was not to get caught by law enforcement right where the crime had been committed. If that happened—it was court and then juvy. Juvy detention would be a sure thing. For some reason I associated the word "camp" with my grandfather's stories of when his father, my late great-grandfather, fled from czarist authorities who wanted to send him off to a military recruits camp. Some invisible alarm system must have guarded Soplov because as soon as we jumped out onto the street, a "crawfish tail" police car pulled up to the school, howling and roaring right behind us.

"To the park! Hurry up!" my friend shouted. We took off toward the park. It was hard to run. A wet January wind, hardened by the minus

15 F temperature, cut our faces and crushed our lungs. We made our way through courtyards and backyards, down along the Lesnoy Prospect. "Camp . . . Camp . . ." the police sirens howled. We ran up to the railroad bridge. Behind it was the park. But in order to get into the park, we had to cross an intersection, where Lesnoy Prospect crossed First Murinsky. We could hear the dogs barking.

"Those pigs brought their German shepherds!" I shouted to my friend. "Let's cut over to the arboretum!"

Over the tall fence topped with barbed wire, we made our way into the Arboretum of the Forestry Academy. We could hear the chase go off to the right, along the street that turned into a park alley.

It was late at night when I returned home. My mother, all in tears, said that the police had been there. They were looking for me and my friend. We lived in the same apartment building, off the same entrance. But my mother and Aunt Lyuba, my friend's mother, wrote up a statement that we had left for her father's village outside of Luga, well before New Year's. And our neighbors also signed this statement. I remember how we fled from Leningrad on the 6 AM train. "From juvy detention all the way to Palestine," joked my friend's grandfather, a former St. Petersburg coachman.

One could write a whole book, a story of offenses large and small, inflicted deliberately or by accident—by people we had not been acquainted with or by supposed friends—at work, at the stadium, in the metro or during a dinner party. You do not get used to discrimination, the way a Negro cannot get used to the black shell given to him by God, as punishment for some unknown, nonexistent transgressions. Or, perhaps, as advance payment for transgressions not yet committed. Sometimes I would forget about this. I would find myself among equals, where the same burdens and joys washed away the imperceptible color of my Jewish shell. Then all the more terrifying was the return to the primal, almost forgotten, sense of inferiority.

After graduating from medical school I served in the army. It was the second year of my career as a lieutenant in the medical corps. I had recently returned from furlough; after seeing Leningrad, my mother, and my friends, I was feeling more at peace. One more winter—and then back to free civilian life. And yet, after being on furlough, after unhurried meals, Leningrad theaters, bridges, and embankments, after civilian clothes in which you didn't have to salute every officer who has more stars, the return to military life had been oppressive.

They announced to us that we were going for military exercises. The upcoming change of pace seemed like a breath of fresh air: to get away from the garrison town with its nauseatingly even rows of officer housing and its apothecary boredom. And so it was; before us lay empty, cleared fields of wheat. The final blooms of cornflowers were peaking out from between the gold and ochre straw. Thousands of starlings were feasting in the abandoned fields, pecking the grains that had fallen onto the earth. Our unit broke camp at the edge of the forest between the fields and the village. The officers entertained themselves in the evenings by going to dances held in the village hall and by courting sharp-tongued, Polish-looking girls in this village in western Belarus. During the day there was shooting practice, and toward evening our officers' brotherhood would come up with new forms of entertainment: horseback riding, fishing, playing cards. One of the officers, who served at army headquarters, had brought hunting rifles along to the exercises. He was a real expert in how to party, had a reputation as a ladies' man, and was also too good looking to be trusted. "Fish go into the net by themselves," he would say to us, "and in order to enjoy these village 'fish,' we need a change of diet."

We decided to treat ourselves to game. To do this we went out to distant fields—to shoot starlings. There were three of us: the *shtabnik* (the HQ officer), a tall guy from the Kuban region in the south of Russia, with a wavy, "lacquered" hairdo and a pencil-thin mustache; the chemical corps captain, a forty-something fellow originally from the Tula province, which gave him cause, while inebriated, to hint at being related by blood to Leo Tolstoy; and I, a lieutenant, a doctor. The HQ guy distributed the hunting rifles. We approached a flock of feeding starlings from the side, where the sun was slowly dropping behind the horizon. The HQ guy bared his teeth, squatted a bit, and gave out a sort of brigand's whistle; his Cossack ancestors probably used this whistle to warn their comrades of imminent danger. Small brown bodies of starlings sprung up. The field resonated with the flapping of thousands of wings, with a clamor and with screams.

"Shoot!" the HQ guy shrieked.

First I shot and then did the chemical corps captain. Bodies of the birds, caught mid-flight by deadly pellets, dropped to the ground like stones. The HQ guy, who was in the ferocious heat of hunting, and thirsty for more killing, grabbed the rifle from me and shot at the already thinned-out fleeting flock. And again stones fell from the sky. We rushed to collect the starlings and brought our booty back to the camp. In a couple of hours, our military cook came and called us to supper. The cook was in his first year of service; he had been drafted from some small town outside Vinnitsa—I think Khmelnik or Mytnik. But I do remember that he was terribly shy by nature, and his shyness was exacerbated by the fact that he grunted his *r*'s, misrolling them in the manner associated with a "Jewish accent," and lisped on almost all the Russian consonants. A sweet steam whirled over the cauldron. We pored vodka into the mugs. The cook bent over the cauldron and ladled out the potatoes that had been stewing together with the game.

"So damn tasty," the chemical corps captain commented, as he sucked on the bird's bones with delight. The cook sat down off to the side, and you could hear him panting over his own bowl.

"Listen fellows, and what kind of bird is this?" The HQ guy interrupted our feast. "Get over here, you cretin!"

The cook came over. He still had potato on his mouth, and the brown remains of food on his face commingled with his prominent oily freckles. The cook eyed the officer with fear, blinking his short, pale yellow lashes. I was disgusted and pushed my bowl aside, staring at the HQ guy and at the cook. The HQ guy was holding a baked but unplucked starling by its foot. It was a strange sight, this dead bird that looked taxidermied, next to meat that had long since lost its live form and had been turned into a food product.

"So, you little bastard, this is how you decided to make fools of Russian officers?" The HQ guy stood up. Looking around with his bloodshot eyes, he saw an iron rod, which the soldier had been using as a poker to stir the fire under the cauldron.

"Fohgive me, comhade senioh lieutenant," uttered the terrified cook, stepping back.

We hadn't had a chance to react when the HQ guy skewered the ill-starred starling on the rod and smeared it across the soldier's face.

"You dirty kike. I'll show you how to mock a Russian officer!"

The cook was shaking from fear and insult. The chemical corps officer mumbled while still chewing his dinner, "Please, comrades. All sorts of things can happen. Let's not overreact."

I could not restrain myself any more. It was either run away into the forest, to the river, throw myself under a train barreling in the distance. Or take revenge. I ripped the iron rod out of the hand of the HQ lieutenant. I hit him in the solar plexus with my left hand, and when he doubled over and turned up his face with its pencil thin mustache, his mouth contorted with rage and pain, I slashed him across the cheek with the rod, the way Cossacks during the pogroms used to slash defenseless Jews with their sabers and ramrods, the way his own grandfathers slashed unarmed students and workers.

"You want a court marshal? You defender of Jews?" wheezed the HQ guy, hunched over, clutching the deep wound on his cheek.

But for some reason the affair was hushed up, and soon I was honorably discharged to the reserves.

SECOND THIRD

Something snapped inside of me like a string . . .

Grandfather Vasily Matveyevich was greeting a city spring. He would go out in the courtyard, where the pre-revolution granite tiles freed themselves of their icy scabs and dried out earlier than the other paving stones. He would go out into the courtyard in his village felt boots, shuffling along the dried granite tiles, and settle down on a bench alongside the other old men and women. They talked about the upcoming move to a new apartment building, to a new district of Moscow. Where to? They all tried to guess.

"To the Clucking Hills," mumbled Vasily Matveyevich's bench neighbor, and then she added, "There will be fresh air instead."

"And what about the neighborhood amenities?"

"Yes, no one knows about that," the rest of them sighed. But there was nothing to be done. They couldn't change anything with their sighs and idle talk, so they would sigh and grumble and then go their separate ways. Vasily Matveyevich just couldn't come to terms with being at the mercy of circumstances. He, a former guerilla fighter and a peasant leader, that is, a man who was used to being in charge of people and crops, just couldn't imagine that there would come a day that they would get into a moving truck and go who knows where. Would there be a river or a forest near by? Maybe a ravine with a trash dump? How can a person move to a place that he himself did not choose to live in, if that person was a free man and not a shackled convict? And so Vasily Matveyevich decided to take independent action. Sneaking behind Tatyana's back, he found the housing director's office hours on the door. On Tuesdays the director received visitors after four o'clock. Vasily Matveyevich knew that at that time Tatyana would be leaving work, either to go straight home or to do her shopping. The next Tuesday Grandfather Vasily Matveyevich donned his suit jacket with his wartime Order of the Red Star and other regalia won in battle, as well as commemorative medals. He shaved clean and rubbed his face red with Triple Cologne.

"You planning on going far, Vasily Matveyevich?" his son-in-law asked, looking warily at Grandfather's preparations.

Something had snapped, changed, in Herbert Anatolyevich's personality. He wasn't among the ten bravest to begin with, and yet he used to derive pleasure from relating to a lot of people—both friends and strangers. But after filing with the Visa Section, he clammed up, became suspicious. He went from his new clinic back to his apartment, closer to the telephone: what if they were to call suddenly? Invite him to visit a private patient? In his strained mind, where the thought of getting out before the time of Anatoly's draft dominated everything, any unusual movement engendered suspicion, irritation, or discontent. Most of all, nowadays, Herbert Anatolyevich valued order and routine. Anatoly, who had found a job in a metal repair shop right in their neighborhood, was supposed to come home at 7:30 without fail. Tatyana, around three. And Grandfather Vasily Matveyevich was supposed to be a permanent stay-at-home. Therefore, Grandfather's preparations for some official visit beyond the limits of their apartment building raised suspicion for Herbert Anatolyevich. He felt guilty before Grandfather, and the fact that his father-in-law silently continued to stuff his body into the old-fashioned, thick overcoat probably purchased years ago for his wedding worried Herbert Anatolyevich even more.

"What are you all dressed up for?"

"It's spring, sonny. Easter is coming. Maybe I'll set out for the nearest church."

"Enjoy your walk."

The housing office was located in a one-story outbuilding inside their courtyard; it used to be some courtyard addition: a storage room or a laundry facility. Grandfather Vasily Matveyevich walked into the housing director's office, the very same person to whom Tatyana had slipped a gift set of three cognac bottles, after which he issued her all the necessary papers for the Visa Section. The director was not a tall man; he had an amicable and crafty looking face that was particularly enhanced by a wide Zaporozhian Cossack mustache, which the director stroked in moments of joy or pondering. The director looked up at Vasily Matveyevich.

"Sit down, Grandfather. What can I do for you?"

"Thank you. I'm Vasily Matveyevich Pivovarov. Tatyana Vasilyevna's father."

"Oh, it's a pleasure to meet you," the director said, and the solicitous expression on his face disappeared for a second, replaced by confusion. Why the hell had the old man come? But his many years' experience in dealing with people overcame his fear, and the director reiterated, "I would be delighted to be of service to the father of Tatyana Vasilyevna."

"I don't need any service. I just want to get something clear. Where are they planning on moving us: to the woods, to a field, or maybe somewhere in the middle of nowhere?"

By now all traces of affability had left the director's face. He was trying to figure out why the old man cared so much about a new apartment in Moscow if they were going to Israel. What if he knew nothing about their emigration plans? What if Tatyana had obtained all the papers and filed them with the Visa Section without ever telling her father? The director instantly went limp from such terrible thoughts. In his stupor he began to rummage around on his desk, moving a stack of documents from one place to another, and then like a marionette he started bending forward and straightening up, bending forward and straightening up, all the while pondering frantically: What should I do? Which way to go? Finally he decided to pry a bit more information from the old fellow: what does he know and what doesn't he know about their emigration plans. A buttery ray of March sun slinked onto Vasily Matveyevich's face, setting it alight with a special radiance, and the radiance unnerved and frightened the director even more. The dark, clayish, peasant face of Vasily

Matveyevich now looked a lot like the image of St. Nicholas the Wonderworker, which he had once seen on an icon. For the first time in his
life, this flabby little man, crafty and conniving, who had been trotting
through life on short bureaucratic legs that bent under his heavy belly,
for the first time the director realized that he not only must find out the
truth, he must also respond truthfully. And he was about to do just that.

"I understand, I understand, esteemed Vasily Matveyevich. Your
concerns are reasonable. And yet I wonder why you're so worried about
the new apartment building? It seems that you have another trajectory
ahead of you."

"If you're referring to my age, then you got it right. Too late to be worrying about it. Wherever they put me down, there I will be at peace forever.
But what if I do live a little longer? I gave up my house and my village to
move in with my daughter and her family and to reside in a new Moscow
neighborhood. And whatever years God gives me, I'll be grateful for them."

"Well, what you need to do is ask your professor son-in-law about
the future apartment building. He'll tell you what kind of houses they
build there on what rivers. We have the Moscow River, and they have
the Jordan River."

Grandfather Vasily Matveyevich listened closely to the director's
words without comprehending them, even though there was nothing
complicated about his question, and the director should have had no
difficulty at all in answering him.

"It's a simple thing. All I'm asking, comrade director, is where to, to
what part of the city are they going to move us? After all, the building
has been condemned."

The situation was becoming more and more burdensome. It looked
like the old man knew nothing about Tatyana and her Jewish professor's
plans. I've really put my foot in this one, the director mused. Put my foot
in. Between a rock and a hard place. What to do? His recent resolve to be
honest, a flash of purity that had visited the director's soul—all perished,
giving way to reptile fear. I'll be the one to answer for this, he thought.
I'm the one that issued their papers for the Visa Section. But so what if I

issued them. I didn't know, didn't know, I never suspected that Tatyana would lie to me like that. I didn't know anything and didn't take anything from her. And here a brilliant salutary thought came to him. The director pulled the phone over closer and dialed that very special number.

"Yury Sevatyanovich? Shupov here. Yes. I have an interesting case for you. Yes. Any time; I'll be waiting. Now? I'd be pleased."

He looked at Grandfather Vasily Matveyevich, and in a voice once again filled with affection he said, "The district specialist in matters of resettlement will be here any moment. Could you just wait in the hallway?"

Grandfather Vasily Matveyevich sat in a chair outside the director's office and waited. Visitors came and went. Grandfather Vasily Matveyevich knew some of the people. They lived in the same section of the building, and they greeted him as they passed. A car honked somewhere nearby. The front door banged and a smartly dressed young man walked into the housing office, wearing a shearling coat and a muskrat hat. The coat and the fur hat fit him perfectly, like a uniform. The young man knocked, opened the door of the director's office, glanced at Vasily Matveyevich with his bulging lead eyes, and disappeared into the office. In about twenty minutes, the director looked out into the hallway and summoned Grandfather Vasily Matveyevich.

"Citizen Pivovarov, come in!"

Without any introduction, as if they had been long acquainted, the young man in the shearling coat turned to Vasily Matveyevich.

"You were inquiring about the move to a new district, right?"

"That's right, I was."

"To ensure that your wishes be given full consideration, we should probably come up with a letter. A petition, if you will."

The director sat Grandfather Vasily Matveyevich behind his desk and gave him a sheet of white paper and a pen.

"So, write exactly as the district specialist tells you."

Grandfather Vasily Matveyevich brought his hand to the paper and tried to focus so as not to miss a word accidentally. This was no joking matter if the district specialist himself was taking care of it.

The young man in the shearling coat started to dictate: "To the Visa Section of the city of Moscow, from citizen Vasily Matveyevich Pivovarov, residing in Moscow at such and such address. Petition. I hereby request that in the process of assigning us living quarters, you keep in mind that in the next few years, I and the family of my daughter T.V. Levitina have no intention of moving anywhere except within Moscow. And I request that the building to which we will be resettled is located in a green zone. Respectfully yours, Pivovarov, March 17, 1979."

Grandfather Vasily Matveyevich signed his name. The district specialist took the sheet of paper, ran his eyes over the text, and, apparently totally satisfied, put the petition into a leather folder, and the folder into a brown flat briefcase that he locked with a little key. The housing director was smiling, which Grandfather Vasily Matveyevich took for his pleasure at having been able to facilitate a good deed.

"So, Shupov, always call in such cases." The district specialist bid his farewell quickly, buttoned his shearling coat, and then added, half-turning to Vasily Matveyevich, "Until we meet again, citizen Pivovarov."

Outside the window a car rattled, then honked and was gone.

A FEW DAYS after Vasily Matveyevich went to see the housing office director, the Levitins received a postcard with a summons, which requested Herbert Anatolyevich's presence in the Visa Section—but not in Room 24, that frightening place where one formally became a refusenik, but in Room 22. Herbert Anatolyevich hung around the apartment trying to figure out what was hidden behind the boilerplate wording of the summons. Anatoly's upcoming army draft? Something to do with his father-in-law, who hadn't the faintest idea of their portentous developments? On that memorable day, Grandfather Vasily Matveyevich had returned home proud and secretive. During evening tea he mentioned, as if by chance, that some people "will show respect to an old partisan, and they will not resettle him in the boondocks." Puzzled, Tatyana and her husband had just looked at each other.

The apartment was quiet and Herbert Anatolyevich was rereading the postcard for the hundredth time. Tatyana went to see a friend who had received her permission to leave and needed help with packing. Anatoly went to the movies with Natasha Leyn. A strange coincidence: at the farewell party for Zhora Driz, Anatoly had run into Natasha, the girl he had met during the entrance exams to medical school. Natasha turned out to be the daughter of Katya and Evgeny Lvovich Leyn. Anatoly and Natasha had exchanged phone numbers and had been seeing each other.

Grandfather Vasily Matveyevich had gone to bed. Herbert Anatolyevich walked from his study into the hallway, and then into the kitchen. He had some tea with jam. His heart was still heavy. Anxiety was creeping up from somewhere inside, from the very center of his chest, and it scratched and gnawed, not exactly a pain, but it made him want to rip this tormenting feral cat out of his heart. Herbert Anatolyevich looked out the window. There was still some black snow stuck to the edges of the sidewalk. By the elder bush he noticed a black figure with his arm outstretched, like someone giving a speech. The figure turned slowly in the direction of the moving arm. What is this? Herbert Anatolyevich wondered. Am I hallucinating? Then he noticed a dog dragging a person on its leash. That leash, like a mysterious line of force, made him quiver, become alert. How simple everything becomes when you know the cause, he thought with relief.

Herbert Anatolyevich returned to his study. He came up to his son's framed photograph; a five-year-old boy stared at him from under a midshipman's cap. Kindergarten—what a happy time it was, thought Herbert Anatolyevich. And it can be happy again. If we get our visas before next autumn. The political climate seems to be decent. The SALT-II negotiations. The Olympics in Moscow. The desk lamp was on in Anatoly's room; he must have forgotten to turn it off as he hurried to see Natasha. Herbert Anatolyevich sat at his son's desk. There were two tickets under the glass desktop. Anatoly mentioned that soon he would be taking Natasha to a Yugoslav jazz concert. A photo of a girl with Katya's eyes, but whose last name is now Leyn. Herbert Anatolyevich felt a barely perceptible movement, some light shadows floating by in the semidarkness. He lifted up his head. Little red fish, startled by a stranger's presence, glided in the depths of the unlit aquarium.

Herbert Anatolyevich went back to his study, got out his copy of the American *Handbook of Psychiatry,* and concentrated on the reading. He had to figure out one very odd case that he had stumbled upon in his current, not altogether ordinary, practice. It was happening more and more often that patients were turning to him who were already in the process of leaving, or who were waiting for their permission to leave or were planning to file for emigration. He was a good internist, but he wasn't a psychiatrist or a neurologist. But people kept on coming to him, knowing that Doctor Levitin could be trusted with everything, not only with matters of internal medicine. Right now he had a difficult patient who suffered from a combination of bad depression and water-sodium imbalance. All the evidence pointed to a metabolic problem, but the medications he was treated with, which included one of rare earth elements, produced virtually no results. Herbert Anatolyevich strongly urged the patient's wife that they consult a psychiatrist. There was some secret cause hiding at the basis of this ailment, one that labs couldn't detect. But in spite of his urging and advice, this wife of the suffering patient asked Doctor Levitin to see him again. He tried to wave her off by saying that he was busy and not really qualified, but the patient's wife quoted a paragraph about Padre Montanelli's treachery from Voinich's *The Gadfly.* The Khavkins trusted almost no one. Tomorrow I will have to visit the Khavkins, Doctor Levitin was thinking. Around 6:00 p.m. And in the morning—the ill-fated Room 22.

Tatyana came home after visiting a friend. She went straight to the study to see her husband, all fresh from walking outside in the spring air, and full of hope. When you help someone pack, you get infected with the travel bug. It seems any day now happiness will arrive at your doorstep, and you too will be packing up your treasured belongings.

"Maybe everything will turn out fine tomorrow. Well? Why are you so glum?"

"Of course, Tanyusha, it will be just fine."

"Today Rima told me how they too got summoned to Room 22. A copy of some affidavit was missing. And in a month they got their permission to leave."

"The same will happen to us. I've no doubt, Tanyusha. Would you like some tea?"

"I'd like a drink of vermouth. Just imagine, Herbert darling, we're strolling around Rome in the spring. The Coliseum. All that beauty. Remember, together we watched *Girls from the Spanish Steps*?"

"Of course, at the Forum. It was Tolya who got us tickets, and all three of us went, and the ticket lady believed that he was already sixteen."

"You see, my love, how it all used to be—everything in life was going our way."

"And it will work out again. I promise. Now come here."

Herbert Anatolyevich embraced this soft and velvety, tender, comforting woman who was his wife; he ran his palms along Tatyana's back and felt how her body clung to him, froze only to rise up, pulsating, to be filled with primordial strength, to lose oneself in the almighty sensation, which lasts and grows until the very last second—a second that has its own unique duration, a second that bares and empties one out . . . Tatyana fell asleep, spread out on the bed, and Herbert Anatolyevich still lay there for a long time, following the occasional striations of car lights that blinded their nighttime street. He fell asleep only after he heard the key click. Anatoly hung up his coat, slammed the refrigerator door, clinked the dishes, and then went to his room. What will happen to us? thought Herbert Anatolyevich. Good God, what will happen to Anatoly if we become refuseniks? These constant worries about his son and wife punctuated his sleep.

At about ten in the morning, Herbert Anatolyevich entered the Kolpachny Lane building that all the people seeking exit visas knew so well. There was a five-step staircase between the outer door and the door leading inside the office. People were crowding the stairs. On the landing, like a party orator on top of the Lenin Mausoleum, stood an elderly Jew in a fur hat with earflaps. In his hands he held a list, and Herbert Anatolyevich became number seventeen in the queue.

"They'll take you by about noon. I'm number sixteen," a thin-nosed gentleman in an old-fashioned black astrakhan sympathetically explained.

One had to reply casually, so as not to seem too wary or impolite, and so Herbert Anatolyevich just said, "That's what I expected."

They were standing close to each other in groups of two or three. All the while the outside door kept on slamming as more and more people arrived. From scraps of conversation that reached him from different corners of the entryway, Herbert Anatolyevich surmised two things. The first was that people had all been waiting for different lengths of time, that the period from the time of filing with the Visa Section until getting an answer could not be categorized in any way. Even before his summons to the Visa Section, Herbert Anatolyevich had created a chart and placed himself in the third category of difficulty. There were two other categories below his: the fourth, which entailed a very difficult process of obtaining a visa, and the fifth, which indicated an almost hopeless situation. People were convinced (except those who had already been refused, and there were some in this small crowd) that everyone applying to go to Israel would be allowed to leave before the start of the Moscow Olympics, that is before the summer of 1980. As he observed the businesslike faces of the women wrapped in expensive furs, and the confident expressions on the faces of men with expensive glass frames and finely tailored coats, Herbert Anatolyevich calmed down and even joined a conversation about the size of the photos required to obtain public transport passes in Rome and Vienna, a conversation that in his opinion was completely unnecessary, yet quite relevant. Just before 10:00 a.m., the Visa Section employees came through, silently moving aside those waiting in the queue. People recognized some of the visa officers. And this recognition must have also had a familiar, and therefore calming effect. At 10:00 sharp the policeman on duty opened the inner door, and the crowd moved into the waiting room. Herbert Anatolyevich took a chair next to the window and turned to Harold Robbins's novel *Never Love a Stranger*, something he did to practice his English. Social and sexual problems were interspersed in the novel, and Herbert Anatolyevich was struck by the natural manner with which the author shifted his narration from such disparate scenes as the forced dispersal of a workers' demonstration and the murder of the union leader, to a scene in a bordello, where a prostitute demands love from the novel's hero. But we too live in several dimensions at once, thought Herbert Anatolyevich. Here today I'm a pitiful petitioner. And just yesterday, like a twenty-year-old boy, I made love to my Tatyana.

More and more new people poured into the waiting room. Some of them held postcards like the one the Levitins were summoned with, and there was a certain meaningful order in the way the line moved. In the left corner, a group of Jews surrounded a man of about thirty-five. He tugged at his red fox fur hat, taking it off, then putting it back on, and pulling it down over his eyes. He was waiting for his turn to go into Room 24. Everybody knew what this meant—refusenik. And he too knew it, but confusion and dejection on his face would, from time to time, be replaced by an expression of hope, by a stirring of will power, still alive, still uncrushed. And then he went into Room 24 and soon came out. His face showed nothing: it was a stone face with a suicide's glassy eyes.

"Refused. Refused. Refused." These words spiraled across the waiting room.

The refusenik, seeing nothing, made his way toward the exit, and his relatives and friends followed him like in a funeral procession. Herbert Anatolyevich lifted himself from the chair and caught up with the refusenik already at the door.

"Wait, maybe it will all still work out." Herbert Anatolyevich was holding on to the sleeve of the man in the red fox fur hat. The man turned back, slowing down, and looked at Doctor Levitin with dead eyes. Herbert Anatolyevich saw such eyes in condemned cancer patients, who understood the hopelessness of their condition, or in pictures of Auschwitz inmates.

"Nothing will work out. I'm dead," uttered the refusenik, as he left the waiting room.

People didn't feel like talking. An oppressive silence hung in the room. Even the lucky ones who received their appointment cards that listed the amount they had to pay for the exit visas, even they became lost in thought. What if? Were they thinking of their friends and relatives, the ones they were leaving behind in Russia, who may not be spared such terrible blows of fate? Herbert Anatolyevich's former colleague at the medical school, Aleksandr Mikhailovich Rogozhkin, unexpectedly emerged from one of the rooms. He saw Herbert Anatolyevich, and, probably forgetting that Levitin was no longer his coworker, whispered to him excitedly, "Imagine what luck! I'm going to Denmark, to visit my aunt for a whole month. She sent me an invitation."

"You have my most sincere congratulations," Herbert Anatolyevich replied.

But Rogozhkin himself figured out that the former professor was here not as an expectant tourist, and that all of his own excitement was out of place in this alien crowd. The former colleague vanished just as quickly as he had appeared, and a petite, frail woman in a black wool coat and round metal frame glasses sat next to Herbert Anatolyevich. At first they were both occupied with their own affairs: he continued reading, and she was scribbling something on a sheet of paper. When the woman noticed that Herbert Anatolyevich was not reading his book, she said to him with a trusting intonation, "You know, something strange has been happening to me. I've been forgetting all sorts of things. And here I'm so scared that I have no idea what to say. Things are going so badly for me, I don't wish it on anybody. One can lose not only memory, but one's very self."

"What's been happening?" Herbert Anatolyevich queried.

"You have such a prepossessing face," the woman whispered, from time to time fretfully looking around, making sure they weren't eavesdropping on her. "Yes, yes. Right when I saw you, I knew that you were a physician or a man of law."

"You guessed right. I really am a doctor, a physician," Herbert Anatolyevich said.

"There, I knew it. You'll understand me. A week ago my husband, daughter, and I received permission to leave. My mother lives with my brother and his family. She has no intention of leaving. Mother had signed an affidavit that she doesn't object to our leaving. And now, after we have waited almost a year for the permission to leave, haven't been working, have bought some stuff and sold almost all of our household goods, now that we're literally sitting on our suitcases, now a terrible thing has happened. Mother has fallen ill. They X-rayed her. To make a long story short, it's cancer. I feel so miserable."

"So what have you decided?"

"I'm here to ask for an extension on our exit visa, at least until her surgery."

"I don't think they'll refuse you," Herbert Anatolyevich said gently.

"God, I hope not! Oh, God, I hope not!" And the petite woman began to whisper something to herself, rehearsing her conversation with the visa officer.

Finally it was Herbert Anatolyevich's turn. He opened the door and peeked into Room 22.

"Next," a woman with a captain's insignia invited him in, and looking at Herbert Anatolyevich with her listless, fatigued brown eyes, her irises disappearing behind heavy unfolding eyelids, she added, "What's your request?"

"I got this summons." Herbert Anatolyevich showed her the postcard. The visa officer glanced at the card, got up from behind her desk, and dragged a metal drawer with a rectangular handle from a cubbyhole built into the grey metal cabinet made up of many such drawers.

"Last name?" the inspector asked, as if Herbert Anatolyevich's last name weren't listed on the summons.

"Levitin."

The captain ran her fingers along the papers, like a hamster in a wheel, and pulled out an index card.

"Names of all family members emigrating with you?"

"Levitin, my wife and my son. My wife's father, Pivovarov."

"Vasily Matveyevich?"

"Yes, Vasily Matveyevich," Herbert Anatolyevich answered, as a repugnant sensation of fear swished like a mouse somewhere under the heart.

"And your wife's father, does he know you have filed for his emigration?"

"Yes," Herbert Anatolyevich answered vaguely.

"Well, it seems to us that he doesn't know. Or why else would he worry about which region of Moscow you'll be relocating to?"

"I don't understand, please forgive me. There is some kind of misunderstanding." Herbert Anatolyevich tried to say something sensible but felt that his words were slipping and sliding. He had told Tatyana that it would be better to tell Grandfather Vasily Matveyevich the whole truth before filing the papers. She only kept saying, "Father won't agree, and I'm not leaving him here." Now Anatoly will get drafted, without a doubt, ran through Herbert Anatolyevich's head. And that means another seven years of waiting after the army. A total of nine years—nine years erased from science, from active life in society, life in general. I'll be past fifty by then. Some age to start a new life!

In that same voice full of indifference, the visa officer read Vasily Matveyevich's petition, which the district specialist had dictated to him at the housing director's office: "I hereby request that in the process of assigning us living quarters, you keep in mind that in the next few years, I and the family of my daughter T.V. Levitina have no intention of moving anywhere except within Moscow. And I request that the building to which we will be resettled is located in a green zone. Respectfully yours, Pivovarov . . ."

"I don't understand." Herbert Anatolyevich didn't know what to say to the officer, who handed him a sheet of paper, written in Vasily Matveyevich's handwriting, all slanted like rye stalks in the wind.

"You don't understand, but we shall try to find out everything." The visa officer raised her voice, now resonant with harsh, barking tones. She took out a clean sheet of paper, wrote something down, and then said to Herbert Anatolyevich, "Figure out all of your family's wishes and come back next Monday."

Herbert Anatolyevich went out onto the street without even noticing the compassionate looks from the other Jews waiting to be called. We're trapped, Anatoly's doomed, Herbert Anatolyevich kept repeating to himself as he drifted somewhere, treading the black asphalt made bare by the spring sun. Now he understood one thing clearly: they had to confess everything to his father-in-law and try to explain that he and Tatyana had deceived him only for Anatoly's sake. Was it possible that Grandfather wouldn't understand and forgive them? Herbert Anatolyevich walked, paying no attention to the street, and only came to his senses when he hit a downspout with his shoulder. The gutter jingled merrily, and a little beard of icicles fell off. Herbert Anatolyevich looked around and saw an empty cab. In the car, sitting next to the cabby, he groped his chest for the round plastic container of Validol, an anxiolytic. As the tingling sweet coolness melted in his mouth, he began to feel better.

Without stopping at home, Herbert Anatolyevich called Tatyana from a payphone. He didn't want to be seen in the housing office.

"What happened, Herbert? Denied?"

"No. Actually, not yet. But we need to talk immediately."

"I'll be home in ten minutes," Tatyana answered.

"Maybe we'd better talk outside. Without your father."

"Fine. I'll wait for you by the hair salon."

They strolled down the Garden Ring, its boulevards flooded by the midday March sun. They had never talked about this so openly—but now one couldn't hide anything or speak in half-truths. At first Tatyana couldn't grasp everything.

"Where did this ridiculous petition come from? Who talked father into doing this?"

"Whoever talked him into this, we ourselves are guilty before Vasily Matveyevich. We were hiding our intentions. After all, he is a living and thinking human being. This is payback."

"Just the beginning of the payback."

"You mean Anatoly?"

"I'm constantly thinking about him, constantly." Tatyana wiped a tear.

"Don't, Tanyusha. We still have six months. In these six months we must get out. You and I have never had access to anything classified, no clearances. They'll let us go."

"And what about my father?" Tatyana asked.

"We'll tell him the truth."

They crossed Trubnaya Square through the underpass and came out on Tsvetnoy Boulevard. All kinds of people hurried somewhere: unshaven men with mustaches strolled along the façade of the Central Farmers Market; an old van pulled up to the Old Circus (they were unloading cages with monkeys); authors, grandiosely carrying their portfolios stuffed with manuscripts, were walking towards the tall grey building of the *Literary Gazette*. Moscow was coming to life after the winter stupor. Completely oblivious to the torturous problems of the Levitin family, Moscow was now rushing toward the pre-Olympics summer. Herbert Anatolyevich and Tatyana came upon a *shashychnaya* and decided to have lunch.

"How can we tell my father?" Tatyana tried to figure out for the umpteenth time, while Herbert Anatolyevich brought their skewers of *shashlyk* and glasses of fruit compote from the counter.

Suddenly, like she always did when she decided on something definite, Tatyana asked, "Are you busy tonight?"

"Yes, I promised to see Khavkin; he seems to be slipping again. But . . ."

"You should go. And try to stay out as late as possible."

"What have you come up with?"

"I'll talk with him alone. You'll just annoy him for no reason."

"Tanyusha, explain to him that we had no other way out. It's like a judgment."

"And now there's only one way out."

Herbert Anatolyevich walked Tatyana back to work, and then headed to the Central Medical Library. He still had four hours before going to see Khavkin, so he had time to look through the new issues of the medical journals.

THE HOUSING OFFICE director had recently been especially nice to Tatyana, and she was naively happy about it. Friends told stories of their bosses harassing those who had filed for an exit visa, forcing them to resign. In her case, all was well. Of course, Tatyana thought, whatever you say, your own people will always understand and won't hurt you. Our Shupov knows that I have been refashioned from Pivovarova into a Levitina, but my soul is still like his own soul, Russian. By thinking this way, Tatyana calmed herself before the conversation with her father.

Grandfather Vasily Matveyevich was sitting in the kitchen and reading *Pravda*. He had just returned from the bakery and was waiting for the family to come home.

"Darling girl, the bread's so fresh it's still breathing."

"That's good, father. We'll eat soon."

"What about him?"

"Herbert will be late today. He's working."

"All right then."

Grandfather Vasily Matveyevich was pleased to eat with his daughter, just the two of them, so nobody would disturb their heart-to-heart talk. He wanted to reminisce about their village, about her late mother, and all that was near and dear only to the two of them, Pivovarovs by blood and birth. He especially wanted to be alone with his daughter Tatyana since, for a long time, Grandfather Vasily Matveyevich had wanted to tell her about the important petition that he had filed and the important person who helped him file this petition properly. This is why Grandfather Vasily Matveyevich decided to create a ceremonial atmosphere. He opened the ventilation window wider, got out a *papirosa* from his cherished case, and lit up, exhaling the fluffy smoke.

"So Tatyana, believe it or not, your father can still get something accomplished in this life."

"What're you talking about?"

"As if you don't know? What's the biggest fish we have to fry? The move, right?"

"Right. But the question is, father, where to."

"That's what I'm talking about, girl. You two are busy people. Your prof sits up high and looks far in the distance. But he doesn't take care of what is closest to him. And you, even though you work in the housing office, you didn't really learn anything sensible. So, I decided . . ."

"You decided what?"

"I decided to fix everything for you."

Tatyana could barely restrain herself from exploding, from acrimony, from making this foolish, but nevertheless peaceful, conversation into a family squabble. She felt terribly ashamed to speak with her father in the cold voice of someone who sounded like a stranger, when all she really wanted to do was weep, fall on her knees before him, come clean with everything, and tell him that it was all being done for Anatoly's sake. After all he wasn't a stranger; he was Anatoly's own grandfather. How to touch her father's soul, his old man's heart, armored with the indifference of old age, laced with hollow Soviet rhetoric he had been inoculated with during his many years of "leadership work"? Life, Anatoly's life, depended on this sick old man, succumbing to dementia, who nevertheless remained her father, Tatyana was thinking as Vasily Matveyevich was telling his daughter how he went to see the director of the housing office.

"You probably think he doesn't respect war veterans like me? Well, you've got it al wrong. As soon as he saw my medals, Shupov telephoned a district specialist."

Proudful and simple-hearted, Vasily Matveyevich described his conversation with the district specialist, and even summarized his petition.

"Father, I beg you, hear me out. Only try to understand me—as your daughter. After all, who else do you have? Me and Tolya."

"You're all I have, Tatyanochka. But what are you getting at?" Vasily Matveyevich lit up again, which was a true sign of his anxiety. But what am I worrying about, he thought to himself. I did everything right. I even put together a good petition. But was it a good petition?

"Oh father, it's one thing on top of another, as if the walls shifted together, and all of that now threatens to fall on Tolya's head."

"Can you say it more simply, Tatyana, so that I can understand?"

"All of us, Herbert and me for starters, and now you with your petition, we've almost destroyed Tolya."

Grandfather Vasily Matveyevich got up from the table. He ambled around the kitchen, then took a drink of water. From his facial expression one could see that he realized he and his petition, the source of his pride, turned out to be the cause of a misfortune. But what misfortune threatened his grandson? And he couldn't fathom how exactly he brought it upon Anatoly.

"Wait, daughter. You moved me here from the village so we could all live in a new apartment? Right?"

"Right, father."

"And it was for this purpose that I put in that petition, so that they'd assign us to a better location."

"Oh, father dear. We used to think that too, that we'd be moving together with you to a brand new apartment building, on the outskirts of Moscow, closer to the countryside. We thought that Tolya would get into medical school. Later he would get married. That we'd have a good life. But you do know, don't you, what they did to our Tolya?"

"I know, daughter. They mortally wounded my grandson."

"So you see, you've answered all the questions. Now try to understand us, father. When all this happened, Tolya's illness, when he understood that he's not like the others, that they could injure him with impunity, we decided to emigrate to Israel. To Palestine, as it used to be called in the olden days."

"I see," Grandfather Vasily Matveyevich wheezed out, his body drooping, his knees growing weak.

"And, of course, we filed for you together with us. We couldn't leave you here alone. And here you butt in with your petition about moving to a new apartment building. Now do you understand who it was helped you draw up the petition? And where did that petition end up, can you guess?"

Grandfather Vasily Matveyevich didn't reply and only stared at his daughter, as if seeing her for the first time. Was this really his daughter, Tatyana Pivovarova? Was it she that he cared for, cherished, raised without a mother? And now his own daughter, his own flesh and blood, wants to leave her native land and go to the land of a nation that has been cursed by God and by people. And not only does she want to leave for good, having become a traitor, and shaming herself and the Pivovarov kin, but she also wants to take him away, an old guerilla fighter, a *Russian* to the core, to the very bottom of his soul, *Russian* until his dying breath and into the grave, to take him away without even asking for his consent. What was he, a log? A yellowing and crinkled photograph, which could be tossed to the bottom of the trunk? Good God! Whom is he surrounded by! And the housing director? That Shupov. So adroitly he pretended to be compassionate and respectful, calling in the district specialist. While in fact the director was luring him into a trap. They all lured the old fool into a trap. First that Jew caught Tatyana in his trap. Then Tolya was born—a trap for Tatyana. Then they dragged him from his village to Moscow, like an animal in a trap. And now fate is forcing him to drag his only grandson, Anatoly, into a trap. His hands and feet are tied by his own family—and by strangers.

"So this is how it's turned out, daughter. You all sold me out, fooled me. And first and foremost, you're the one who did it."

Grandfather was walking around the room in his felt boots, suffering an unbearable and interminable grief, which squeezed his heart like a red-hot oven fork and wouldn't let him take a deep breath. And he knew that it would be impossible to get used to this grief and to this circle of betrayal. A dull pain was constricting his head. Tatyana went up to her father, and like when she was a child, after her mother's death, when they were left all alone in the whole world, she wanted to put her head on his chest that was now heaving from old-age emphysema, and she wanted to kiss his brick red, furrowed neck of a peasant. But Vasily Matveyevich recoiled from her tenderness, like from a repulsive poison. Tatyana began to cry.

"You don't want to understand anything, father, and you don't care about anyone if you don't want to believe that Herbert and I did this for Anatoly's sake, because of the insult which had been brought down on him."

"Just as your native land will hurt you, she will comfort you like a mother."

"Oh father, father. These are all pretty words, conjured up by poor people to console themselves. And the boy has to live. Live freely. Do you understand? Freely and without constantly fretting about his origins."

"And who is stopping him? Let him not fret. Only cowards fret and look behind their back. And he's living freely now. He chose his job freely. And he chose his girlfriend freely. Next summer he'll apply to another university. Who would ask for more freedom? You can get spoiled by so much freedom."

"Didn't you forget something, father? Come autumn, they'll draft him into the army."

"So, he'll serve two years—and then he'll study. What makes him better than others? That he's a professor's son?"

"Herbert's no longer a professor. They kicked him out of his job. And now they'll throw me out of the housing office as well. How can we suffer all this humiliation? Tell me, father, way down deep, like you would tell a priest, could you take all of this?"

"You can take anything from your mother. From your native land."

"And Anatoly and Herbert considered Russia their native land, too. But the mother turned out to be a mean stepmother. Father, I beg you, for your grandson's sake, please withdraw your petition."

Grandfather Vasily Matveyevich, who until then had been pacing around the room, stopped in front of the window, and staring somewhere into the distance, where a little gold onion dome of a church shone above the roofs, he fell silent, as if looking deep into himself with his bulging old eyes blotched with red coils. As if this were not a room where he was standing, and not Tatyana, his daughter, in front of him, but an anteroom of another world.

"No daughter, I will not go back on my words. God will judge us. Only keep one thing in mind: I'm leaving today to go home to Maryino."

"Come to your senses, father. Where will you live?"

"I'll always find myself a corner. And I do get a pension after all. The good people will not let me perish."

Grandfather Vasily Matveyevich went to his room. Tatyana heard the closet door slam. Then Vasily Matveyevich got dressed and set out for the door.

"Are you going far now, father?"

"I'll just take a walk. Say goodbye to Moscow."

The courtyard of their old building was filled with the inky-blue light of a spring evening. Even the streams that purred at noon, flowing so happy and carefree, now quieted down before the night frost. And the sparrows sat puffed up on the lilac branches. Such an unsettling, perilous time: first sunshine, then cold. Springtime. Grandfather Vasily Matveyevich made his way directly across the courtyard toward the addition where the housing office was located. Someone was sitting outside Shupov's door. Who it was, Vasily Matveyevich didn't really notice. He charged into the office, hunched over and furious, like a bull seeing red, at the thought of Shupov's treachery and deceit. Shupov had the receiver in his left hand as he was lighting his cigarette with a lighter in his right hand. It looked like he was having a pleasant phone conversation, his unctuous face shining and his little eyes squinting with self-satisfaction. He recognized Vasily Matveyevich immediately and half raised himself from the desk, pointing to a chair, but unable to cut short his pleasant conversation, he again waved to Grandfather Vasily Matveyevich, as if to say, "I'm happy to see you, but, as God is my witness, I can't just cut off this conversation." Grandfather Vasily Matveyevich stood there for a minute waiting, then he ripped the receiver out of Shupov's hand and dropped it into the phone cradle.

"That's enough! Now you and I will have a chat!"

Shupov was looking at him, flabbergasted.

"What's the problem, Vasily Matveyevich? That was an important conversation I was having."

"I also have an important conversation," Vasily Matveyevich shot back and continued. "I came here for one thing only: tell me, Judas, how many silver coins did you get from that 'district specialist' for my petition? Or are you both being paid off by some third party?"

"What are you talking about, Vasily Matveyevich? I have no idea what this is all about."

As he dodged the question, Shupov's pancake-like face darkened, and his frightened eyes narrowed.

"Remember, you scum, during the war I shot traitors and *Polizei* like you without any trial or investigation."

"Hey, watch your words. The time for loudmouths and truthsayers has passed."

"Yes, Judas, times are different. Your kind can't be shot or brought to justice. So, here, take a full measure from this old partisan."

Grandfather Vasily Matveyevich spat into that loathsome fat mug.

"And pass it on to your specialist, so he doesn't feel left out."

Having brought up everything that was left in his old bronchial tubes, Vasily Matveyevich spat again. And he walked out in a state of oblivion, not knowing where his legs were taking him. It had already grown dark when Grandfather Vasily Matveyevich found himself in front of a church fence. He followed some people that were going toward the church's main entrance. The parishioners were stopping, raising their heads up toward the icon of Christ above the door, devoutly crossing themselves, and walking into the church. Grandfather Vasily Matveyevich made the sign of the cross three times while looking at the silent image of the Savior and followed the others inside the church. The daily vespers were under way.

Grandfather Vasily Matveyevich looked around, searching with his eyes, and found the Holy Family—the icon of the Mother of God with the baby Jesus and St. Joseph. This was the one he was looking for. Having come nearer to the icon, Vasily Matveyevich peered at their ancient faces, seeing them as if for the first time. The more the old man looked at this strange family, the more clearly and plainly he could see the secret meaning behind this picture. Here is the Mother of God, she who gave the world a Savior, but whose child was fathered by something unfamiliar and otherworldly, by a power that to people seems either divine or wizardly, that is, either beautiful or terrible. Here's Christ, doomed to carry truth and love to people who will not comprehend his unfamiliar origins—godly or wizardly—and who will curse him and his mother, and even curse his truth and love, having no pity for their own salvation in his hands, and killing their own brother and enlightener. And here's Joseph, the holy martyr, the hardworking carpenter, who earned the daily bread for his beloved Mary, whom he met and fell in love with too late for her to love him back and to give him a child conceived through love. But for her inability to give Joseph love, the Virgin Mary kept her purity, and in her innocence gave her poor old husband a baby, Christ. After all, Joseph never had any doubt that Christ was his own son. With his unquestionable faith in Mary's purity, did old Joseph also earn the right to be called holy? Thus thought Vasily Matveyevich as he stood before the image of the Holy Family.

He returned to the entrance, where a sexton was selling candles. He bought three candles, lit them, and carried them over to the Holy Family. Was it the delicate candlelight that helped him, or did it just come to him by itself, fluttering up from the bottom of his soul, but Grandfather Vasily Matveyevich was sure that he recognized his son-in-law's features in the image of St. Joseph. And Christ's eyes, those, of course, are his grandson Anatoly's eyes. And Tatyana, here she is, the full-breasted and quiet Virgin Mary. A sin for the Savior's sake. Dear God, thought Grandfather Vasily Matveyevich. This is really him, his son-in-law, whom Grandfather disliked all of his life and now even started to hate.

It's him, his son-in-law; working hard, without so much as a complaint, he nurtured and raised the son of a strange nation—and that means he raised a strange God. He brought him up, and for his sake he suffered torments, scorn, and mockery. And she was willing to face everything for the sake of her son, like the Holy Mother of God. And now he, Vasily Matveyevich, he betrayed them, betrayed the holy family. Yes, Vasily Matveyevich was thinking, it was he who was a traitor to his daughter and grandson. And he will pay for this a hundredfold.

Dear Lord! Most Holy Mother of God. St. Joseph. Forgive me, sinner that I am. Forgive me. Virgin Mary, help your sister Tatyana on her most difficult path. Our Lord, Jesus Christ, please don't forsake your brother Anatoly. He has already suffered so many tortures of the soul without hurting anyone. And you, St. Joseph, you meek soul, make peace between me, between the memory of me, and my son-in-law, the husband of my daughter Tatyana. Help them. Russian and Jewish people, forgive me, sinner that I am . . .

When the parishioners encircled Grandfather Vasily Matveyevich, he was lying on his back at the feet of the Holy Family. A thin stream of wax had hardened on his temple, as if a secret bullet had killed the old man and left a light trace. Someone knelt before him and put a coat under his head. Grandfather Vasily Matveyevich opened his eyes, looked at the world one last time, and whispered softly, "Forgive me, Tatyana."

ONLY AFTER THE May holidays, after the fortieth day commemoration of Vasily Matveyevich's death, did Tatyana begin to feel a little better. She left her job at the housing office. Shupov had noticeably changed toward her and was only too glad to sign her "voluntary" letter of resignation. Herbert Anatolyevich delivered his father-in-law's death certificate to the Visa Section. Five months had passed since they had applied. Herbert Anatolyevich had grown accustomed to his new job. What had recently been his most active research project, regeneration of kidney tissue after the treatment of purulent processes, now seemed like a distant dream that had floated away. He became tougher and more practical. He eagerly accepted requests for private house calls and didn't say no to payments. In the beginning, during the first couple of months, old colleagues from medical school would telephone him; then the umbilical cord dried up and finally fell off. Only occasionally would someone call, just like that, for no particular reason, and quickly, as if doing their duty before some higher arbiter of social conscience, and then quickly say goodbye.

ONE DAY A call came from a certain Bogush, formerly his doctoral student and now an assistant professor at the old department, who, tripping over his own words, started to profess eternal love and gratitude. But this call was clearly made under the influence of alcohol, and afterwards Herbert Anatolyevich let go and stopped reminiscing about working at the medical school, or rather he taught his mind that it shouldn't reminisce about this. Anatoly had also found a place for himself. There were still four months left until autumn. All around them Moscow in May was turning green, a big clamorous city preparing for the Olympics. At Zhora Driz's farewell party, Anatoly had met Natasha, the girl who was entering the division of public health at the medical school in September. Natasha who turned out to be Katya Leyn's daughter. Today Anatoly asked Ashot, his boss at the metal repair shop, to let him off early. Watching her son dashing across the apartment, tossing shirts and trying on ties ("None seem to be the right color, mama; I can't wear something that's so out of style!"), Tatyana was thinking, Good God, is this really the same Tolya who just three years ago would get into our bed on Sundays and frolic like a first grader? Jealous as she was of her son's attention, at the same time she secretly hoped that this first love would protect him from a horrible uncertainty. Russian by blood and Russian Orthodox by worldview, Tatyana inherently believed in the protective guidance of the feminine, believed in womanhood and motherhood as the beginning of all creation. Not only the Mother of God but also Mary Magdalene were to Tatyana the principal forces capable of guarding and protecting her son. She supported Anatoly in his infatuation with Natasha and wasn't sure why this girl made Herbert Anatolyevich apprehensive. Tatyana even came up with a subterfuge common among Russian wives, in whose character domestic hospitality is coalesced with a desire to enter yet deeper into the Jewish milieu, which used to be so foreign to them, but now is forever a part of their own lives. Tatyana suggested they invite the Leyns to dinner.

"It's not right, Herbert. Our boy goes to their house, and we behave as though we don't like that and show no interest in them."

Herbert Anatolyevich at first didn't answer, and then mumbled something to the effect of Anatoly's uncertain position. They could suddenly have to leave the country, and the Leyns' own plans for the future weren't clear at all. On the one hand, Katya and Evgeny Lvovich kept in touch with many departees, and rumor even had it that they had received an affidavit from Israel. But on the other hand, Evgeny Lvovich continued to work at the magazine *Cinematography*, was a member of the editorial board there, and in the summer Natasha was planning to go on a propaganda trip with her student theater.

Anatoly took an alleyway down to the Garden Ring. He looked at his watch. There was half an hour before the screening at the House of Cinema, and he still had to pick up Natasha on Malaya Bronnaya Street. She lived in a new apartment building overlooking Patriarch's Ponds, a brick edifice with balconies, walls thick as a castle tower, and concierges that stood guard around the clock inside the front entrance. A cab darted out from the direction of Kolkhoznaya Square. Anatoly hailed it, and the cab lurched forward onto the overpass as he began to think about Natasha. There she is, looking out the window. Waiting for him. He took out a pack of Stolichnye cigarettes and lit one. They crossed through a tunnel under Mayakovskaya Square. Two streams of cars, huffing and puffing, throwing air into a vortex, disturbing the most important proportionality in life—the surroundings in which people breathe, think, love. Two streams of cars were rushing at each other, paying no notice to Anatoly's small, pliable body that was barely protected by a thin sheet of metal. Suddenly Anatoly became physically aware of his nakedness before the element of the cars' ironclad order, before the metal that can kill and kill, if it escapes human control. And what if this metal, these cars, were aimed to kill? What if a stream of metal ordered by human design has already come out of garages, car depots, hangers, secret arsenals, and is rushing here to separate him forever from Natasha, the girl in whose presence he becomes muddled and dares not even touch, never mind kiss, her? Boys in school told stories of their love conquests, real and imagined. Anatoly did not play the prude; he listened to their stories, even imagined how this would some day also happen to him. But in front of Natasha he became timid, and she, feeling his timidity, enflamed Anatoly even more, as if it were her life's aim to confuse him.

The many-wheeled column drove over to the other side of Mayakovskaya Square; the cab driver made a U-turn and they veered off onto Malaya Bronnaya, circled around Patriarch's Ponds, and stopped in front of Natasha's apartment building.

"Keep it, chief," Anatoly said casually, as he diverted the cabbie's hand containing the change.

The driver's bulldog face opened its powerful yellow fangs: "Good luck to you!"

Anatoly went into the entryway, and the concierge asked monotonously, "Whom are you visiting, young man?" ripping her eyes away from the newspaper.

"The Leyns."

"Fifth floor, on the left," the automaton's answer rang out.

"Thank you, I know."

Natasha heard the clanking of the elevator and was waiting by the door. There was a time Anatoly poked fun at what he used to think were amusingly naïve, coquettish descriptions of women as flowers, stars, and all the rest of this window dressing. Herbert Anatolyevich brought him up in the spirit of pragmatic materialism: fact always trumps a word. In this Herbert Anatolyevich considered Turgenev's nihilistic hero Bazarov as a role model to be followed. A real doctor, he believed, must base his thinking on an analysis of numerous facts—facts obtained during a conversation with a patient, during an exam, and on the basis of meticulously ordered labs. Anatoly was always in sync with his father. Preparing himself for the life and service of a physician, he didn't want to waste his time on parties, pointless evenings filled with musical dalliances and strumming guitars. Anatoly even considered his current job of necessity at the metal repair shop as a form of training to prepare him for working with complex medical equipment. In any case, that's the way he and his father had resolved to think of it. And now he—a materialist, antiromantic, future medical scientist—stares at this girl in a blue airy dress with all sorts of unimaginable frills, gussets, and recessed zippers, and he can't do anything with himself. He falls into idealism, romanticism, and all that malarkey he used to make fun of. Natasha was standing in the doorway, and the light streaming from behind her back framed her figure in such a way that Anatoly thought of a stem with a blue corolla. Even her slightly parted lips reminded him of the opening petals on a wild flower.

"And I've been waiting for you since 6:30, my Enchanter."

Natasha started calling him Enchanter after she had seen him working in the shop. Anatoly was standing over a grinder. From under a skate, blade sparks were flying like gold fireworks. Anatoly was wearing a black shop coat, and his hands and face were covered in soot. And this blackness of his, contrasted to his white teeth and the golden sparks, reminded Natasha of something from medieval tales.

"And I've been galloping to you since 6:30, Bluebell."

"When did you come up with Bluebell?"

"Just now, looking at you. You are like a bluebell in this dress."

"Do you like it?"

"Very much."

"So you like my dress." Natasha looked at Anatoly with a sly smile, and then suddenly suggested, "If you like, we don't have to go out tonight."

"You mean we stay home?"

"Well, yes. Tonight—we stay in. My parents went to Vilnius for a couple of days, some kind of celebration for a famous Lithuanian film director. Let's stay at home and celebrate being freed from parental supervision."

"Then I'll go pick up some champagne."

"It won't take long?"

"Of course not, Bluebell. Fifteen minutes tops, and the champagne is on the table!"

When Anatoly returned with a bottle of champagne and a bouquet of bluebells, Natasha was setting the table: two champagne flutes, two plates, and a tin of caviar. Anatoly lit up a cigarette, inhaled deeply, and suddenly, either due to his excitement or the effect of nicotine, he saw Natasha differently, in a way she had never before been revealed to him. Her arms were slipping out of the deep sleeves like two tender living creatures, whose names he did not know, but whom he wanted to stroke, caress, and kiss. And her neck seemed lost in the opening of her dress, but from time to time the dress would open up, and her neck would flow down into her enticing small breasts. Or suddenly Anatoly would see her legs in their secret and unattainable space defined by a girl's firm thighs that stretched the downward-pleated dress just so slightly. Natasha bent over the table when she was serving the salad, and the triangle between her thighs and her spine was more sharply delineated. Anatoly embraced her, and the girl clung to him so tightly that Anatoly felt her tenderly tempting body with every fiber of his being. Her lips were slightly parted, and when Anatoly kissed Natasha, he felt that he was falling into an inviting bottomless expanse.

They sat at the table, and Anatoly poured the champagne.

"To you, Bluebell!"

"Thank you, my Enchanter. Be happy!"

"I am happy, just being with you."

Natasha turned on the tape player, and silver syncopations and tender sighing chords of the black pianist burst into the room. Anatoly had never felt as good as he did now. Music and champagne cleansed his soul of the poisonous residues left from this painful year, when for the first time in his life he felt an impossible, irreparable sorrow. First the medical school fiasco, then Grandfather Vasily Matveyevich's death.

Natasha was next to him on the couch, leaning against a pillow embroidered in a cruciform pattern.

"What are you thinking about?" she asked.

"About you."

"What about me?"

"How beautiful you are."

"Really? So you like me? Tell me what specifically."

Anatoly laughed, remembering how his mother used to ask him when he was a young boy, what specifically do we love mommy for?

"You're fun."

"What else?"

"Unpretentious."

"What else?"

"You look like a Bluebell."

"So I knew it. You just like the idea of me. Not specifically me. Any nice-looking girl could be in my place, and you would like her as much."

"Natashenka, I swear! You, just you, are the most beautiful one in the world. And I can prove it to you, not in general, but in specific terms. Let's do this systematically."

"How do you mean?" Natasha was enjoying this game that allowed them to cross the invisible line separating teenage lighthearted bravado and the attraction that was consuming them. Anatoly poured them more champagne. They drank it. He offered Natasha a cigarette. She inhaled, coughed a bit, but bravely continued to smoke.

"Well, you still haven't answered, my Enchanter. How do you plan to prove to me that I'm not like all the others?"

"You know, Natasha, there are such cases—wonders of nature, as it were—when one doesn't need to prove anything. Like the sun, the sea, or the trees. You are all over special, wondrous. For example, let's take your eyes. I'd never seen such eyes before."

Anatoly kissed the corners of her eyes and felt the quivering of her eyelashes with his lips.

"And what else?"

"Your lips. No other girl has such a beautiful mouth."

"One would think that you . . ."

Natasha didn't finish, because they started to kiss.

"My Enchanter, I could suffocate, and on top of that, summer is just beginning. No one will believe that I ate too many blueberries. You're a real champion kisser. Tell me honestly, have you kissed many girls?"

"Two or three. After school parties."

"Were you in love with them or was it just curiosity?"

"Just curiosity."

"Thank God. That means you're a natural. I was worried that you had been practicing with another girl."

"Never before you have I loved anybody, Bluebell. How about you?"

"What about me?"

"Have you kissed anybody before?"

"You won't fall out of love with me if you find out the truth?"

"Because you tell the truth, no. I'll never fall out of love with you."

Natasha moved over to an armchair. Her eyes became focused, distant, as if she was remembering something—but not for Anatoly, just for herself.

"Mother and I vacationed in Gagry on the Black Sea. I was going—it was last summer—to be a senior in high school. The family of a prominent diplomat was also staying at the Artists' House. Actually, I didn't really know then who they were. I just had fun hanging out with this guy, his name was Vadim, and later it turned out that he was the son of a diplomat, an ambassador to some Arab country or something like that. Vadim's father came back to the USSR for vacation, and their whole family was vacationing in Gagry. Vadim was a student at the Institute of International Relations. We went to restaurants together, spent all of our time with each other. And then . . . it just happened between us."

Natasha took a sip of champagne and continued. "Vadim kept saying that when I turned eighteen, we'd get married. Mother knew nothing about our intimacy, or maybe she didn't want to get in the way of such a glamorous plan. Are you listening, Enchanter? Is it terrible that I'm telling you all of this?"

"Terrible. But I'll live. Whom else can you tell everything, if not me?"

"I believed Vadim, although sometimes I did sense a certain estrangement between us. I mean I felt this estrangement, but Vadim, it seems, suspected nothing. Or he just pretended not to feel it. After all he was a diplomat's son and a future diplomat himself."

"I don't understand, Natasha, what kind of estrangement was this?"

"For example, suddenly he would start telling me all about his plans. Like his own father, Vadim hoped to work in the Near East. In his dreams Vadim moved Arab regimes around and deposed the government of Israel, like they were chess pieces. He wouldn't even bother to think that Arabs and Jews live there—people like ourselves, people tied by will of fate into a single cruel knot of contradictions. He daydreamed, playing and dreaming of a future game in real life. Once we were out sunbathing, and Vadim made a map of the Near East out of pebbles. Then he found a larger rock and dropped it between Lebanon, Syria, and Egypt. 'We'll drop a hydrogen bomb here, and this pesky country will be finished. We'll destroy it, like the Temple in Jerusalem was once destroyed.'"

"And you could stand to listen to this?"

"At first I didn't understand what Vadim had actually said. 'It will be finished,' he repeated, picking up the rock and again dropping it on Israel. 'Why do you want to destroy Israel?' I asked him. 'People live there, people like you and me.'"

"And what did your diplomat answer?"

"He said that wherever Jews go, they incite people, parties, social classes, countries. He was convinced that there would be no peace in the world as long as Jews lived as equals to others." Natasha's voice quivered. "Can you imagine what he revealed to me?"

"Scumbag."

"I felt I was coming apart, that I'd burst into tears, and by doing so humiliate myself in front of him. I took hold of myself and told him, 'And you, Vadim, do you know that you've been spending all this time with a Jewess, that you wanted to marry her, that your children could have had Jewish blood?' He was dumbfounded. At first he thought that I was joking; he started to giggle, to clown around. Then he understood that I was telling the truth and started to apologize. 'That's just pure theorizing,' he said. 'It has no relation to individual cases, and consequently, for you and me nothing changes.'"

"And then?"

"Mother and I left the next day. We ran as if from a concentration camp. I was haunted by this feeling, as if I had breached a barbed wire fence and escaped. That's about all I learned about kissing."

"I'm so sorry, my darling. My Bluebell."

Anatoly pulled Natasha to him, kissed her in the dimple between her cheek and nose, in the space where a tear had just slid. But he was too late, and a teardrop plunged down toward her lips. Natasha leaned back against the couch, and her head dropped onto the embroidered pillow. Anatoly was kissing Natasha's chin, her neck, and she kept on repeating, "I love you, my Enchanter. Tell me, do you love me?"

"Yes, Natashenka. Forget what happened. I will never give you up to anyone."

"Really, Anatoly?"

"Really. I love you."

He stroked her chest and in turn kissed her raspberry nipples, then kissed her belly lower, and she quivered from the touch of his lips. At first Natasha's body was afraid of his impatient and clumsy hands, but then suddenly it clung to Anatoly's body with each of its curves, with all of its soft girlish contours. He stroked her legs that lived as if a separate and clandestine life, not ruled even by the girl's own body. Her legs at first did not heed his requests, didn't even succumb to Natasha's own will, and then they accepted Anatoly, trusted him, and didn't want to let him go until he lost himself in the all-emptying rapture that flashed through him like lightning.

ɟ

DISTRICT COURT OF JERUSALEM

Criminal case No. 40/61

Before His Honor Judge Moshe Landau (Presiding)

His Honor Judge Benjamin Halevi

His Honor Judge Yitzchak Raveh

For the Prosecution: Gideon Hausner, Attorney General of Israel

The accused: Adolf Eichmann

Jerusalem, 1961

From the opening speech by the Attorney General of Israel at the Eichmann Trial:

With me at this hour are six million accusers. . . . [their] ashes are piled high on the hills of Auschwitz and the fields of Treblinka and scattered in the forests of Poland. Their graves are strewn about the length and breadth of Europe. Their blood cries out, but their voice cannot be heard. Therefore I will speak for them, and in their name I will submit this terrible indictment . . . Yet only in our generation has an entire state apparatus taken up arms against a peaceful and defenseless population, men, women, the elderly, children and infants, imprisoned them in concentration camps, surrounded them with walls, fenced in by electric barbed wire, having resolved to destroy them all completely. . . . Then began the campaign of fraud. It was "proven" that Jesus Christ was an Aryan, and that in his veins there was not a single drop of Jewish blood. . . . The Jews found themselves at the bottom of the ladder. Still lower were the Roma and the Negroes . . . Hitler had other objects of hate: Marxists and Communists were regular targets of his violent attacks. But there was a difference: the latter could reform by disavowing their former beliefs and in such a way be accepted into the bosom of National Socialism. The Jew, however, was the eternal scapegoat. There was no way out; the Jew could never escape the storm of hate. . . . For the purposes of the internal politics of Hitler's Germany, the Jew was a convenient object of hatred; he was defenseless, and when he was persecuted, the outside world was silent or contented itself with verbal reactions that had little effect. . . . On this point we shall find the accused himself saying: "The Jewish question was a welcome maneuver to divert attention from other difficulties. If any difficulties of another sort arose, they turned at this time to the Jewish question and in this way attention was diverted." . . . Thus a series of new laws excluded Jews from a number of professions: law, medicine, and teaching were closed to them. . . . Having broken the morale of their victims, they would select a few or grant them special duties, and for show grant them certain rights. The program of total extermination was kept secret; as a result, it was possible to make secret promises to some of them or drop hints, that if they took upon themselves specific functions or became informers, for this they would save not only their own life, but also the lives of their families. . . . I do not think that today we can establish a moral code for the proper behavior of a victim, finding himself in a predator's talons, that we can say today how this or that Jewish leader in Warsaw, Budapest, Prague or Vienna should have acted; whether he should have tried to save what he could, or to incite an uprising, or to cling to every straw of hope for deliverance even against all odds. . . . In Vienna the process was organized like an assembly line. A man came into the office still a citizen with full rights, with a status in society, a job, property, occupation, and a roof over his head, and, after passing through all the stages of being "processed," he came out an emigrant, without his property, which was partially confiscated and partially placed by government order in a bank account as frozen currency of little value; his apartment was registered for confiscation, he himself was dismissed from work, his children were expelled from public schools, and the only thing in his possession was a travel document marked *Jude*, which granted him permission to leave Austria by a certain date, never to return. . . . Trading in Jewish freedom was from that time onward the official policy of the Reich.

BACK THEN, IN February 1953, it was early spring outside, just like it is now, when I write these lines. Tomtits were strumming in the birch trees, like little balalaikas. And all of us, high school seniors, were in the middle of logic class. Our logic teacher, a bald pedantic man with a cheek that twitched with a tick, looked like the psychic Wolf Messing and Mahatma Gandhi at the same time. Of course it was purely an external resemblance. We disliked Kiss-Kiss (Konstantin Konstantinovich) because he tortured us with idiotic puzzles comprised of premises and proofs. Unfortunately for me, I always solved these puzzles with ease, and couldn't just plead ignorance and give myself to reading Pilnyak or Bely, the Russian writers who at that time fascinated me terribly. Kiss-Kiss used my logical Jewish mind as insurance against the other students' indecision or failure. But on that day, Kiss-Kiss didn't torture my classmates with his puzzles. He unclicked the lock of his briefcase, took out a newspaper, and proceeded to read one of the many antisemitic anecdotes that was offered in the form of a feuilleton and took up an entire page. This was the nefarious campaign, which had culminated with the so-called Doctors' Plot, and which choked itself in infamy following Stalin's death on March 5, 1953. But the denunciation of the Jewish doctors' accuser Lidia Timashuk (whose praises had been sung by the venal journalist Olga Chechyotkina); the execution of Deputy Minister of State Security Ryumin; and the arrest and downfall of the then all-powerful Minister of Internal Affairs, Beria, would not happen until after Stalin's death.

Back then, during that ill-fated logic class in February 1953, Kiss-Kiss read a newspaper feuilleton out loud. In his repulsive metal-drilling voice, he recited lines from the newspaper and commented on the text. I didn't know what this reading would lead to and how this antisemitic campaign, having already been blazing for more than an entire year, would end, and I sat there curled up into a ball from insult and shame, and from not knowing what to do. Mother made me promise that I wouldn't utter a sound, no matter what they said in front of me about Jews. She was afraid for me; I had the reputation of a brazen fighter. But I had promised mother I would be silent, and silent I was, although I was shaking feverishly from Kiss-Kiss's words. I kept silent because our lives were hanging in the balance: I was graduating from high school and applying to university, and only a year before that, my mother had lived though an unjust dismissal from work and a trial, which ended with her being reinstated in her position as a branch accountant at a large factory. The court could not rule against my mother because all the employees of her factory branch showed up at the hearing. The workers could have cared less about Zionism, antisemitism, or any other "isms." For these people, the most important thing was to come out in support of Bella Vladimirovna, who always tried to maintain decent pay rates for the workers.

I had promised my mother, and so I clammed up and kept silent. Kiss-Kiss finished reading the newspaper article. There was dead silence in the classroom. I was surrounded by my classmates, kids with whom I had been in the same class since second grade, since 1944, when I returned to Leningrad after the siege was broken and started going to this school on Bolotnaya Street, not far from the Kalinin Museum. We studied together, and together we roamed around our Lesnoye working class district—always looking for food. Together we found ourselves in juvy hall at the local precinct, together we performed in the school theater, and together we fought for in-district hockey and soccer championships. We felt a strong kinship with each other, like brothers or orphanage kids, but we were neither brothers nor fellow orphans. The terrible war and everything that happened after the war had formed our bonds: destruction, hunger, family tragedies. We probably did love each other, or else why would our entire class spend all their time together, both in school and after school. And now all of them, my comrades, almost brothers, sat there silently, too ashamed to lift their eyes because they couldn't believe that I was a bad person just because I was a Jew, but at the same time they didn't dare doubt what was written in the newspaper. It was a real torment, a civilized version of torture: to sit silently staring at the top of the desk, and then "Hunchy," Volodya Petrov, the first among hoodlums and fighters, endowed with incredible audacity and strength hidden in his chest that was blown up with a huge deformity, suddenly let out with longing in his voice, "Dudes, wouldn't it be nice to have a smoke now?" The class broke out into uncontrollable nervous laughter that turned into a cough, a cackle, inhuman sounds and convulsions, which only quieted down in the bathroom after a smoke and a drink of water from the tap. I neither laughed nor cried. I was silent. I was also silent another time, again for my mother's sake, when our neighbor, a retired schoolteacher, who had received a medal from the hands of Kalinin himself at the Kremlin, said as she was stirring the soup in her pot in our communal kitchen, "I wish they'd exile all these Jews to Birobidzhan soon." I was silent, because mother bit her pillow at night, so I wouldn't hear her sobs. We were both silent, as were all the other Soviet Jews in those days. And nowadays I bite my pillow at night, so my son doesn't hear my own tears. We continue our silent fight for the right to remain human. I had gotten so used to being silent, that I was silent even during that beautiful March morning when the Soviet Jews saw a deliverance from the shame that had been forced upon them by the Doctors' Plot. After Stalin's death and funeral (oh, how we feared that it would become even worse, how we still believed that he alone had the strength to hold back that evil power that was ready to rip Jews to shreds), they announced on the radio about the exoneration of the falsely accused Jewish doctors. I was silent, afraid to believe in such happiness. I took an oath then: in honor of this event, I would also become a doctor. I remember when Auntie Dusya, our old neighbor from the prewar peaceful years, knocked at our door. She lived across the hallway from us, Auntie Dusya, a retired employee of the Svetlana vacuum tubes factory. Auntie Dusya carried her elephant legs, swollen from the time of the siege of Leningrad, over the threshold. Weeping, she embraced me and said, "Thank God! Thank God you're all of you not guilty. I was so afraid they'd exile you far away from here. I prayed so hard for you to St. Nicholas the Wonderworker. Now he heard my prayers!" May she rest in the heavenly kingdom, our Auntie Dusya! Memory eternal to you, dear Auntie Dusya!

᪥

ANATOLY STILL WASN'T back from Natasha Leyn's house. In his study Herbert Anatolyevich was poring over his medical books. The dreadful outcome of Khavkin's illness wouldn't let him be. It seemed as though all the troubles had fallen onto the head of this poor Jewish fellow. An imbalance of electrolytes was somehow affecting his psychological well-being. Severe depression developed, which in turn was aggravated by a difficult situation at home. Khavkin's mother had, at the last minute, changed her mind about emigrating to Israel together with her son's family. No matter how much he pleaded with his mother, a cutter in a woman's tailor shop, to quit her job, live quietly on her pension until they received their exit visas, and then go with them to Israel, she remained undeterred: "Here I have a job, a guaranteed pension. I have my own room and only two other families in the communal apartment. I raised you alone, without a father, on one salary. Now I want to live without any cares. No! I have made my final decision. I ain't going!" Khavkin lacked the determination to heed to his wife's arguments and apply without his mother. His wife insisted on emigration: "Why should I suffer all because of her? We made the decision, so we should go. Or you can stay with your precious mama, and I'll take Sashenka, and you'll write us letters."

Khavkin couldn't imagine being separated from his son either. And so he dashed back and forth between Sokolniki, where his mother lived in an old two-story annex among other neighbors, and his own apartment in Tushino, on the opposite end of Moscow. No matter how much Doctor Levitin tried to convince Khavkin himself and his wife that the situation was critical, that he needed to see a psychiatrist, and, at least for a while, terminate all discussion of emigration, nothing changed in this family. And so two weeks ago Khavkin told his wife that he was going to the synagogue. Some of their acquaintants saw him there outside the synagogue. In such a crowd, you couldn't tell where he went after the services. Nobody really suspected anything. The Khavkins were very private people, and nobody except Doctor Levitin knew about their family drama. Khavkin didn't come home from the synagogue. His wife Roza waited for him late into the night. "He's probably gone to his mother's," she tried to calm herself. But Khavkin didn't call and didn't come home in the morning. Her mother-in-law had no phone line at the apartment, and so Roza took Sashenka and went by taxi to the apartment of Khavkin's mother. "Something happen to Ilya?" The mother-in-law became alarmed. And then her deep-seated hatred of Roza broke through, like a stream of refuse under the rays of the April sun. "You have ruined my son. You've turned his head with your Zionist tricks. A curse on you!"

Roza took Sashenka over to her friend's and went to see Doctor Levitin. Levitin's refusenik friends came and started to comb through all the acquaintances to see if Khavkin hadn't been there. Then they searched all over the city train stations and looked in the places that had any significance for Ilya Khavkin. He had disappeared. Finally, after about five days, the police called and asked that Roza come immediately. Roza and Doctor Levitin went to 38 Petrovka Street, the police headquarters. They were told that a body of an unknown man had been delivered from outside Moscow to the morgue of one of the city hospitals. It was Ilya Khavkin's body, transformed by death, unkempt, blackened. He had been found in the barracks, in the village of Lvovskaya, the very same barracks where he had stayed back in the autumn of the previous year while picking potatoes at a collective farm. There were cots and mattresses left in the barracks from the harvest time, when city folks would be sent to the countryside to work as farmhands, but the door was nailed shut. Ilya had broken in, drank a glass of vodka, and took a fatal dose of Dimedrole. In the Volokolamsk district of the Moscow province, there was frost at night even in April. Ilya Khavkin froze to death in his sleep.

During his wake—which had become the custom of Russian Jews, like many other Russian customs—they remembered the dearly departed with kind words. One of his close colleagues shared a recollection: Ilya had never been as happy in the factory in Moscow as he had been in the village, during his "potato-picking" autumn.

"He wanted to free himself all at once, from me, from his mother, from the emigration problem, and also from not wanting to stay here, from everything that's ripping all of our hearts," Rosa told Herbert Anatolyevich after the wake. Doctor Levitin was devastated by Khavkin's death. This was the second death in the circle of people that were connected to him by the same intent: to go to Israel. Except that Grandfather Vasily Matveyevich's death was primary on Herbert Anatolyevich's conscience; he couldn't forget about it and couldn't forgive himself. If only the others would have enough strength. What awaited Anatoly? Luckily, during this time of gloom, Anatoly met Natasha, as if God had made sure that the boy would forget his sorrows.

Something wasn't right in the Levitin family. It was as if the clock was running, and then suddenly one of the teeth on the time wheel became dull or even broke off. Ever since her father died, Tatyana had been growing distant from Herbert Anatolyevich. And he felt that that now they should be getting even closer to each other. Something had changed inside her. She continued to be friendly with women from the families of those who had applied for exit visas. She bought sweaters and socks for her men, some trinkets for future gifts. Yet this fussing brought her no pleasure and only slightly dulled the encroaching anxiety. Her anxiety grew with each day. Summer was coming, and although the spring draft had passed Anatoly by, autumn was not that far off. And if they didn't managed to emigrate by then, his impending military service would start and their emigration plans would collapse. Herbert Anatolyevich knew all of this, and he now tried to avoid candid conversations with his wife by going to bed late and immediately falling asleep. He passed his days by running around on house calls, seeing patients in the pay-for-service health center, and meeting with fellow Jews who were waiting for an answer from the Visa Section, or who had already been refused and were taking steps toward reversing this horrible decision. He was always seeing some people off, helping them pack, taking care of different matters on their behalf, assisting with the filing of various documents: requests, appeals, petitions. People knew him as an intelligent and upright Jew, one to whom they could always turn for help and entrust with things they wouldn't even tell their closest family. All of these unending social obligations, in the total absence of any Jewish social organizations, could of course end disastrously for Herbert Anatolyevich. He understood it, too, especially when he started to hear a click and a hissing in his tele-phone receiver. But new people kept on coming, friends and acquain-tances of those whom he had already helped, and Herbert Anatolyevich, with the same encouraging smile, would advise them again and again, would write, explain, make introductions, see people off; he encouraged by word and by deed, and not infrequently also with money. All this new social life just fell into place by itself, as a call of the heart and a response to circumstances, and it distanced Herbert Anatolyevich from Tatyana even more. It was now natural for him to be with them, the ones being chased away from her native land. And it was natural for her to want to stay behind in her native land. And they both understood the change that was taking place, and as they probably realized with both mind and heart the root cause of this ensuing disintegration, they still pretended that everything was transpiring as it should be, consistent with their current condition—if one were to accept as normal this most abnormal condition of being estranged from their previous life and not yet rooted into a future life. Their past kept barging into the current life of the house of Doctor Levitin, and although it didn't lead to such tragic consequences as with the late Khavkin, it did continue to gnaw at the soul, like a woman that one had abandoned but not totally forgotten.

And precisely on this day, the past life once again burst into the Levitins' home. Anatoly was at the Leyns'. Tatyana was knitting in front of TV. Herbert Anatolyevich was reading a new issue of *Nature*. The phone rang. It was a lady from their building. It turned out that two of Herbert Anatolyevich's former academic colleagues had mistakenly rang at the wrong apartment looking for the Levitins. They'd had a lot to drink. Before going out for a drink, they probably had no intention of visiting their former professor. They kept drinking and reminiscing about him, and their awakened consciences brought them to the home they used to frequent in order to discuss their research or simply to receive the infusion of ideas and warmth that always emanated from Professor Levitin. Herbert Anatolyevich came out onto the landing as he was, wearing sweat pants and a plaid shirt with a loose open collar. The guests were still making their way up the stairs, slowly shuffling their feet, heavy with liquor, and Herbert Anatolyevich already recognized their voices. Semyon Antipov and Alik Volkovich. Semyon was a burly, forty-year-old fellow, with green eyes that looked so much like gooseberries, and a red face and coarse red hair that looked glued to his head, like on a circus clown, and was sticking out in every direction. Semyon was always wearing a navy blue, belted overcoat made in the People's Republic of China, of the sort that nobody wore any more. He was always wearing something worn out, due to a chronic lack of money. In his hands Semyon Antipov held a briefcase as decrepit as the dissertation materials that for the past fifteen years he had always dragged around with him inside the briefcase. Semyon had no direct connection to the former professor in the Department of General

and Internal Medicine. He was the in charge of the physiotherapy program in that department, and his dissertation adviser was a well-known
specialist from the Rehabilitation Research Institute. However, Semyon
Antipov used to come to Herbert Anatolyevich for regular advice while
he was still employed there. The second visitor, Alik Volkovich, a perfectly well-built man of average height, with a handsome Semitic face,
was the last Jew left in Levitin's old department. And although all of
Moscow knew both Alik's father, Abram Savelyevich Volkovich, a distinguished professor of dermatovenerology, and Alik's mother, the pianist
Gita Yakovlevna Kogan, in Alik's passport he was listed as a "Belorussian," and that took care of the main issue. It was rumored in the department that their new boss liked to repeat, "If you say it, you pray it." In
any case, after Professor Levitin made known his fateful decision, Alik
began to show an outward coolness toward him.

Tatyana came out into the hallway to see what was happening, and
her presence made the late-night guests even more self-conscious. They
stood there and mumbled some awkward phrases.

"You will excuse us please. Just stopping by to say hello."

"Of course. Don't worry. Please, do come in," said Herbert
Anatolyevich.

In the meantime, Semyon was fishing out a bottle from his rusty-
red briefcase. Alik was growing more timid as he understood, even in
his drunkenness, that he was doing something almost dangerous, and
certainly very dubious. Tatyana went to the kitchen, to prepare some
appetizers to go with the bottle, and the guests dropped down onto the
couch in Herbert Anatolyevich's study. The host himself was quiet, as
he didn't want to force opinions on his former colleagues. Alik went
back to the kitchen, feeling a need to help with the preparations, just
for old times' sake. In the old days, when Herbert Anatolyevich invited
colleagues to parties at his home, Alik Volkovich would always be
part of the celebrations. Well-mannered, a connoisseur of cuisine and
music, Alik was always the life and soul of the party. Maybe it was this
popularity and sociability, in conjunction with his official belonging
to the Belorussian nation, that had stopped Professor Ivan Ivanovich

Baronov from blocking Volkovich's candidature during the search for his academic position. Or maybe the elder Volkovich's stature had played a role.

Semyon Antipov leaned his heavy body towards Herbert Anatolyevich and whispered, "You think I don't feel how you despise us? No, dear Herbert Anatolyevich, I feel it! I feel it all, I see it, and I sense it, like a dog that's afraid of a new owner. Because he beat fear into the dog—beat him to the point of blind terror."

"Don't do this, Senya. Let's not wax sentimental now. Everybody has his own mission in life. And don't torment yourself over what happened to me."

"No, how can I not torment myself? I suffer not only because I've lost you. I've lost my sense of purpose. Together we tried to move the treatment of patients forward, at least a small step forward. Remember how we were all fired up about using the deep kidney diathermy in conjunction with electrophoresis? We had some success in the regeneration of kidney tissue in experimental animals, didn't we?"

"And thank God we had success. So go and finish the work, and you'll immediately get your habilitation and become a doctor of science and a professor," the host said, and smiled gently. He liked Semyon, and he knew very well that the words he just heard were not the affectation of a drunk person, but a lamented truth that broke out of his soul.

"Alik will come back any moment now," Semyon was whispering. "Then I won't be able to talk openly about everything. But please know that we're perishing without you. The most important thing is gone—enthusiasm. A vested interest. Or even more than that."

"What more?" Herbert Anatolyevich asked, and his voice quivered.

"The thin thread that connected us doctors with the patients is gone. It's as if we stopped being doctors. We are now medical employees of different categories with different ranks and titles. Patients felt this even before we did. Particularly those from other cities. They call, they write, begging us to help them, to give them appointments with you. You gave so many of their lives back, Herbert Anatolyevich."

"So why don't you give them my home number? Or the number at the health center where I work?"

"Not allowed to. You're not here anymore. Period. You've been sliced off, my dear Herbert Anatolyevich. Severed from Soviet medicine." Semyon said these words, and a huge cloudy tear rolled from his big green eye and fell onto his rusty-red briefcase, which stood next to the couch.

"You shouldn't really, Semyon. Everything will be all right. The patients will get better and forget all about me. And you'll learn to deal with it. One gets used to everything."

Alik Volkovich entered Doctor Levitin's den. Actually, a table with food and glasses rolled in first, followed by Alik and Tatyana. Tatyana was pleased by this unexpected visit. It was good his old friends came. Perhaps Herbert Anatolyevich would lighten up a bit, be distracted from his dark thoughts. Alik opened the vodka, then looked at the light through this transparent liquid imprisoned in a bottle sweating with condensation. "Good stuff!" Gently gurgling, vodka flowed into glasses. They drank to the success of the "affair" the Levitins had embarked on. Tatyana sat with the men for a bit and then left. Alik was silent, crunching on a pickle. He just couldn't get a conversation going with Herbert Anatolyevich. And they used to be good friends. True, Herbert Anatolyevich had been more successful in those old days when he was part of academic medicine; he had become a full professor. But Alik thought this was fully deserved. Both in their old department and beyond the medical school, Levitin was considered to be a rising star, the "hope" of the country's internal medicine. And this was how things had turned out.

As if apologizing for his silence, Volkovich proposed another toast. "Herbert, I'd like to drink to you, my friend. To the star that no longer shines over the Russian horizon."

"To a star, I agree. I'll drink to that all you want," said Semyon. "But I don't agree with the horizons."

"So what is it you don't agree with, Semyon dear?" Alik smiled slyly.

"Esteemed Alik, I don't agree, because the horizons are the same above all humanity. And the biology of *Homo sapiens* is also the same everywhere. And because the same factors influence all humankind, consisting of identical species, medicine should serve all humankind at the same time. And wherever an honest and talented doctor works, he serves not only his own patients, but all humankind, the entire earthly community of people. That's that. And that's why I don't judge Herbert Anatolyevich, I just mourn his departure. I miss him, and I constantly feel his absence in our clinical work."

Former Professor Levitin was silent, thinking about the words spoken by his former colleagues. Of course Alik is being wily, he doesn't wish to speak his mind, thought Herbert Anatolyevich. But why? Hypocrisy has become a life's principle. He felt sorry for Volkovich, the way one felt sorry for a terminally ill person that one had once been close to. Alik lit up a cigarette and inhaled several times. He got up and walked around the room. It was clear that he didn't want to be judged on the basis of his words. He was suffering from the ambivalence of his position, and, above all, from the bifurcation of his soul.

"You are right, of course, Semyon," Volkovich said. "Right in the ideal sense. But I'm not talking about an ideal situation. It's quite realistic to expect that Herbert Anatolyevich will leave, leave for good, so that we won't be able to just stop by and see him more or less on a whim, at least every once in a while, as we did this time, let's say, in a state of boozy euphoria. Only then will we truly understand what we have lost, although this will have no effect on world medicine, since Professor Levitin will surely secure a professorship abroad, wherever he desires to work. And you, my dear Semyon, will be the first one to realize that here you can still visit Herbert Anatolyevich, but there—it might as well be Mars."

Volkovich's voice suddenly faltered. He sat down, coughing from the vodka and emotion. They were all silent. Then they talked for a while about new things in academic medicine and about their children. Semyon started to ask Herbert Anatolyevich questions about his son.

"Anatoly must be a grown man now, yes? And I remember when I was teaching him to play hockey. Any news about the army?"

"If we don't emigrate, he'll be drafted," Herbert Anatolyevich answered.

They sat there for a little bit longer. Some sort of a spring that had previously held together their relationship had snapped. Now, neither shared academic interests nor a table set for a celebration could hold them together. That's why in the hallway they were talking in a forced, unnatural way, as though they were escorting their guests out, rather than seeing them off. This unnaturalness was totally natural; that is, it was at the very core of the Levitin family predicament, and Herbert Anatolyevich's colleagues saw it and weren't upset with him. Herbert Anatolyevich stood there lost in his thoughts, saying goodbye to Semyon Antipov and to Alik Volkovich, telling them they should come again, without waiting for special invitations, and they promised to stop by soon and kissed him goodbye, and through all this they understood that if there should be an occasion to see each other, it would be an unusual occasion, a difficult one, because the normal, natural course of life was forever taking them in different directions. Downstairs the entryway door slammed shut. The Levitins were still standing in their hallway, and they both knew that the day, filled to the brim with words and emotions, wasn't yet over.

"Are you upset?" Tatyana asked her husband.

"About what?"

"About their visit. The conversation."

"The visit—no. And in fact the conversation was perfectly ordinary, trite. Even if I'm a little upset, Tanyusha, it's by the triteness of the conversation. I'm becoming an ordinary conversation partner, with nothing interesting to contribute. Something snapped inside of me like a string."

"But when? Tell me, when did you start feeling this way?"

Herbert Anatolyevich took Tatyana's hand. The clock struck midnight.

"This started right after Grandfather Vasily Matveyevich's funeral. You know, Tanyusha, there wasn't too much love lost between us. But when he lived with us, I knew way deep inside that always present in our home there was something like a conscience incarnate in the flesh and blood of your father. Some kind of a constantly present opponent. For me it was like a benchmark."

"I know this, darling. You're tormenting yourself because you think that you were the one that destroyed this benchmark," said Tatyana quietly, and she timidly stroked her husband's prickly cheek with the back of her hand, as she used to do in happier times. "I understand that feeling. Constant losses, like dues we pay for our past sins or sins we might have committed. My father died. Now I'm constantly worried about Anatoly. I just hope all turns out well for him and Natasha."

"You're right, Tanyusha. Our family's life has moved on into a difficult, still unchartered phase. A period of self-reflection has begun, except now we shouldn't be reflecting, just acting. Time's running out. I'm turning into Chekhov's character Ionych, the old doctor. Look, just today, my friends came over, my colleagues. It seems they valued me for something; they were drawn to me for some reason. But everything that I had done was so imperfect; I never had the leisure to look at myself carefully. Oh how I'd love to work at my fullest capacity now, having seen my way anew.

"Do you want to return to the old department, to the medical school?" Tatyana asked.

"No, of course not. There's no way back there. I want to return to real science, to real medicine, but not to Baronov's shop. I want to return to a place where they don't constantly make note of relationships, states of mind, and correspondences of words allowed and disallowed. Take today's visitors, Semyon and Alik. It would seem that they are both my comrades, that they were once my good friends, but my impression is that they aren't even honest with each other, that they're always on guard. It's not good for a friendship and for working together."

"But still, they are your good friends, ones you can rely on, Herbert."

"That's what you think. But when Alik was in the kitchen with you, Semyon whispered that I should be careful. It seems that Alik has become a KGB informant."

"That's not possible! This way you'll stop trusting the whole world."

"I don't believe it, either. But something else is frightening, Tanyu-sha. And I know you find it hard to believe. Something rotten, some kind of a giant swamp rat, is grating at my soul. Believe it if you want or don't believe it, it's saying, but don't you forget, trust no one."

Herbert Anatolyevich pulled the curtain to the side and opened the window. The building across the street was sleeping. There were lights in only a few windows. On the fifth floor, a girl was standing in the yellow glow of electric light, smoking, automatically bringing the cigarette to her mouth. You could hear some music. Herbert Anatolyevich imagined that the little spirals of smoke coming through the window were singing a melody. Suddenly a telephone rang, a sound both sharp and distant, like a messenger from another world. The girl abruptly threw away her ciga-rette and dissolved into the yellow world of the room. The telephone fell silent. Then Herbert Anatolyevich saw that the girl had returned to the window, hugging the phone to her cheek, and then she closed the window and turned off the light.

Someone was running from the Garden Ring down a lane toward their house. While he ran, his legs were dancing, and his lips were hum-ming a joyful song. It was impossible to hear what exactly the runner was singing, but Herbert Anatolyevich immediately recognized the gait and voice of his son Anatoly. He would sing with such abandon when he was in happy solitude. What could be more joyful than the happiness you feel when you are alone with this happiness, when nothing and no one can prevent you from concentrating on this feeling, from frolicking in the waves of happiness. It's as if you're plunging into the Black Sea in the early morning, when there are only seagulls and crabs on the shore.

Tatyana and Herbert Anatolyevich rushed to the hallway and opened the door even before their son rang the bell—they were dying to see Anatoly. He was coming up the stairs, tap-dancing on the jagged granite steps, and singing, very quietly, so as not to wake anybody: "Tra-ta-ta, ta-ta-ta-ta-ta. Tra-ta-ta, Shalom Aleichem, tara-ta shalom, shalom, Sha-lom Aleichem!" They were waiting for their son on the landing, Tatyana in a brown wool top thrown over her shoulders and Herbert Anatolyevich in his navy sweat suit. Anatoly saw his parents, smiled, hugged them both at once, and shoved them back into the apartment.

"Papa! Mama! Please don't be upset that I'm back so late. I'm so happy. I have never been so happy!"

He kissed Tatyana on the cheek and touched his father's stubble-covered neck with his lips.

"You were at Natasha's?" Tatyana hugged her son and looked deep into his eyes.

"Yes, mama."

"And Natasha, is she as happy as you?"

"Yes, she's happy. We both are the happiest people in the world. So please don't worry. Everything's going to be fine."

He disappeared to his room, and from there he yelled, "Good night, mama, good night, papa!"

THERE EXISTS A saving proportionality in the world. Not a harmony in the high, pantheistic sense, but a proportionality destined to distribute happiness and unhappiness among people. I know this most definitely from my own experience, because a writer has nowhere to learn all of this for certain, except from the depths of his own soul. From where else, if not from those inescapable depths, does a writer gain the knowledge of human beings? Of course experience is important, as are also the powers of observation and imagination. These are all forms into which the energy of the writer's soul is poured. The more active the life of the writer's soul is in both the external and the internal world, the greater are the writer's opportunities to understand his characters, to penetrate along with them into the hidden treasure chambers of their souls, to live with his heroes through their happiest and bitterest moments. The right hand of fate has long been raised over the character's head, and he, unaware of that, lives as though he still has a thousand years of rejoicing and happiness ahead of him.

ꭻ

NATASHA COMPLETED HER spring semester exams. The whole summer lay ahead. And even though she and Anatoly were spending every free moment together, they still wanted more, because each separation—for an hour, a day, a night—was turning into an ordeal for them. Natasha's parents, worldly and liberal people, always assumed that their daughter would act with common sense and good character. Natasha's mother, Katya Leyn, or Ekaterina Nikolaevna, as Anatoly addressed her, came to admire the younger Levitin, and this was, perhaps, her attempt to soothe the guilty feeling that had followed her all her life since that ill-fated encounter with Herbert Anatolyevich at Driz's party. A feeling of guilt before an innocent, uninitiated Jewish boy who had readily opened his heart to her and who couldn't comprehend why she had so cruelly rejected him. And the suave Evgeny Lvovich Leyn himself, he who scorned many conventions as long as these conventions did not interfere with his life, saturated as it was with pleasant and useful activities, looked at his daughter's infatuation as something perfectly natural, like good food or good company, but also transient, like any good food or good company, and therefore not requiring serious thought. Ekaterina Nikolaevna had, on several occasions, tried to speak to her husband about the possible consequences of Natasha's new friendship, but Evgeny Lvovich only dismissed her with carefree laughter and continued to display a lack of concern. However, the friendship grew into an infatuation, and the infatuation into a mutual bond that is universally referred to as love. Natasha didn't hide from her mother her intimacy with Anatoly. It would have been difficult to hide such a thing from Ekaterina Nikolaevna, who was an expert in these matters. As time passed, the Leyns took no measures. Finally Natasha said that she wanted to spend the whole summer with Anatoly.

"And then?" Ekaterina Nikolaevna asked her daughter.

"What do you mean 'then,' Katenka?" Natasha queried, as if she had no idea what was being said. In the Leyn household, everybody called Ekaterina Nikolaevna by diminutives: Katya, Katenka, Katyusha.

"What do you plan on doing after that, Natochka?" Natochka was Ekaterina Nikolaevna's name for her daughter.

"We'll get married."

And here Ekaterina Nikolaevna understood that the time had come for a serious conversation with her daughter. They sat down on the sofa, and, as always in times of full candor, each of them moved to her own corner, with legs tucked underneath. The mother beneath a still life by Pyotr Konchalovsky, and the daughter beneath a photograph of Evgeny Lvovich with Lucchino Visconti. The picture was taken at Cannes about fifteen years ago, when Evgeny Lvovich was writing his art history dissertation on Italian neorealism. In the Leyn household, this photo and the Konchalovsky still life were both sacred objects. Guests who visited the Leyns for the first time were quickly led from the entryway to the living room, directly toward these relics, and were told—quite matter-of-factly and unpretentiously, without false modesty—how Evgeny Lvovich began his friendship with the great Italians. Then the guests were told about the photograph with Visconti and about "mutual enrichment," which was particularly evident in his film *Gruppo di famiglia in un interno*, and how this was hardly surprising if one considered Visconti's indisputable attention to the theory of painterly juxtaposition in cinema, the very theory Evgeny Lvovich had been credited with developing. From here conversations flowed rather naturally to visual arts, and the guests were told about Konchalovsky's painting. And, of course, inevitably, the painter's grandsons were mentioned, not only Andrey Mikhalkov-Konchalovsky but also Nikita Mikhalkov, both of them filmmakers and both of them (the older less than the younger) having been influenced by Leyn's generative theory. Then the guests would hear the fascinating tale of how the Konchalovsky still life had found its way to the Leyn household. The guest, or an entire group of guests, would step onto the escalator of cherished memories, auto-graphed copies, and other such remembrances. And it was impossible to step off this escalator, since all of it was terribly interesting, and was woven into the fabric of the Leyn family history. And so now Ekaterina Nikolaevna and Natasha were sitting on their favorite sofa surrounded by the family's hallowed objects, and they both understood that a very special conversation stood before them, not just a candid talk between two women related in the most intimate way, but an exceptional con-versation, demanding complete candor and deepest soul-searching, and also requiring an absolute intensity of conscience and rigorousness of intellect. Ekaterina Nikolaevna was sitting in her corner of the sofa, lean-ing back, her beautiful naked legs showing from under the open wings of her robe. She lit up a cigarette. Natasha jumped off the sofa and brought over a box of fruit jellies. This is how they liked to have heart-to-heart talks: mother with a cigarette and daughter with sweet treats.

"Let's talk, Natochka. We haven't talked about anything really seri-ous since last summer."

And because Ekaterina Nikolaevna recalled what had not so long ago happened in Gagry, though it seemed like a distant memory, Natasha knew that her mother was alarmed. Natasha told her mother that she loved Anatoly, and that they would like to get married, but they didn't know what to do. The Levitins had filed the papers with the Visa Section, and they couldn't make any changes in the application forms lest the out-come be ruined. If they were to get married now, there would be a stamp in their internal passports, and when the time came to exchange the passports for the exit visas, it would all come out. Anatoly's visa would be terminated, and he would be drafted into the army. Then, after the military service, who knows how long he would have to wait for per-mission to leave, because the authorities are merciless when it comes to ex-servicemen. In Anatoly and Natasha's lot, the cruel conspiracy of circumstances was so enmeshed with the joy of their love, that even

Ekaterina Nikolaevna couldn't figure out what to advise her daughter and how to help the young people.

"All right, Natochka. Fine. Let's look at this logically. Let's assume that this is not you and Anatoly, but pretend figures, sort of like pieces on a chessboard."

"No way, Katenka, no pretend figures."

"All right, then. In the best-case scenario, the Levitins will get their permission and go abroad. What will happen to you? In fact, how can Anatoly leave you—and you be separated from him—if what you have, all of this, is real?"

Natasha moved from her corner closer to her mother and snuggled up against her. Ekaterina Nikolaevna was thinking how much her little girl had changed lately. Not only had she become more mature, more articulate in her words and actions, but a metamorphosis was under way, not only of her spirit, but also of her body. Her thighs filled out and were as if radiant, as if a new type of energy now emanated from them. Her breasts were persistently pushing against the fabric of her dress, under-scoring the final transformation of the daughter into a grown woman. Sensing fear in her mother's gaze, Natasha touched her face with her own lips and whispered, "No, Katenka, not that. Don't worry. That won't hap-pen until we have figured things out. We don't want to risk having a little one while everything is so unstable. But tell me what should I do? How can I figure this out? I can't live a day without him. And he—without me. But we're constantly thinking that at any minute they could separate us. I'll stay on the shore, and he'll sail away. What can we do, Katenka?"

"What can you do? You can wait. If the Levitins emigrate, and if you two still love each other like you do now, then you'll go to join Anatoly."

"But we aren't officially married. How can I leave here? They simply won't let me out, that's for sure. And papa doesn't even want to hear about leaving. He's a player in the Union of Soviet Cinematographers. Here he publishes widely. He lectures around the country. And there, what will he do there? Will he even get a decent job?"

Natasha began to cry. She felt terribly sorry for her father, whose future she was destroying with her egotistical love for Anatoly; sorry for torturing her mother so; and sorry for Anatoly, who could be drafted into the army, and instead of emigration and high hopes for freedom (which Natasha envisioned in shades of white and light blue, like a sail with the fluttering word "Pacific," a sail amid sea and sky), instead of this sail and sea and sky—the drab color of military service and the engulfing years of waiting for a visa after Anatoly's discharge.

Tears bring relief. Natasha cried her heart out and gradually calmed down, because Ekaterina Nikolaevna was not only a loving mother and Natasha's friend, but most importantly she was a Russian woman, who understood the wisdom of the folk formula *vsyo obrazuetsya*, "it will all work out," understood and trusted it. She believed with her inner being that life itself would sweep all the corners and dry all the tears. And that's why she decided to use her time-tested tactic with her daughter, based in the belief that what's pleasing to one's nature never hurts you and never brings evil to others. In addition, or perhaps above all else, Ekaterina Nikolaevna, as a truly Russian woman, believed in fate. And any attempt to force change upon fate, so she deeply believed, would result in punishment. From this reliance upon fate came the Russian women's lightness and pliancy, their approachability. Ekaterina Niko- laevna, a forty-year-old woman in a bathrobe that was flung open to show her beautiful legs and shapely, well-cared for breasts, now remem- bered herself alone with Anatoly's own father—back when she was still a very young woman just starting to taste of the joys of life. And that awkward, accidental lover of long ago, so authentic in his awkwardness and ridiculousness—and so mercilessly forgotten by her after that idiotic party at Zhora Driz's house—had come back to her, but now through his son and her daughter. Herbert Anatolyevich probably would never believe that Ekaterina Nikolaevna had actually remembered him often, and even after she married Evgeny Lvovich, she sometimes wondered if everything had turned out right. And only now did fate decide to reunite them. And was this not proof that there was nothing else to do but wait, patiently wait, for everything to work out?

Gracefully and very lightly, Ekaterina Nikolaevna jumped onto the floor and pulled on Natasha.

"Enough sorrow, child. You two should love while you can love. Let's go, and I'll give you some fresh dumplings with the first cherries of the year."

And while they were running past the soft armchairs and artwork on the walls above them, past the light fixture imperiously jutting out like the Kremlin's own Spasskaya Tower; past the door to Natasha's room, with its white Karelian birch furniture and a black piano (which they all called "café glacé" for its contrast of black and white); past the parents' bedroom with the bed sprawled out on a thick heavy carpet (about this their friends cheerfully would joke that there was always love and spring eternal in their family); past all the objects and groups of objects that were near and dear to Natasha— while she and her mother were running across their entire apartment, decorated and made comfortable through the years, her tears dried up, and a desire to enjoy life returned. Once again she wanted to tell jokes, to eat tasty things, to relax and be carefree without worrying about the cycle of life that had treated her so cruelly at Gagry and had finally brought her happiness. Natasha sat behind a table, its surface icy-white like the snow, and Ekaterina Nikolaevna took out of the fridge a platter of white dumplings that looked like shells and covered them with sour cream. The cold bodies of the dumplings stuffed with sweet and aromatic filling calmed Natasha down even more, and she was now looking out the window toward Patriarch's Ponds. At the green of the leaves and the gold of the sun, and with anticipation of the vacation she would spend alone with Anatoly, without having to hide from their parents. They wouldn't have to make love hurriedly and wait anxiously for each new meeting, every cell of their bodies quivering with anticipation.

And Ekaterina Nikolavena, as if reading her daughter's thoughts, said, "Go on vacation, just the two of you. Why torture yourselves."

"Can we really, Katenka?"

"Of course you can! You're a smart girl, I know you are. You'll be together, just the two of you. Who knows when you'll get another chance like that?"

"Thank you, Katenka. I'll call Tolya, okay?"

"Call him, my dear."

But their departure had to be postponed until the beginning of August. There were many reasons. Anatoly couldn't get vacation time from the metal repair shop. The senior repairmen took their summer vacation in July, and although Moscow's summer life had quieted down, there were still customers stopping in to order a key or to refill a cigarette lighter. Then the film festival began, and Natasha couldn't miss it, because Evgeny Lvovich had gotten them passes to the best movies. During the weeks of the Moscow Film Festival, the Leyns' apartment resembled a den of the "shadow" festival jury. Evgeny Lvovich's colleagues would constantly come and go—people from Moscow and Leningrad, visitors from various Soviet republics, and of course friends from his travels abroad. They had to maintain an "open table," and Natasha barely had time to run to the viewings, help Ekaterina Nikolaevna receive guests, and meet Anatoly every evening without fail.

Herbert Anatolyevich had telephoned the Visa Section and was told the decision in their case wouldn't be made before the autumn. After that Anatoly's parents contacted an Estonian man, the owner of the apartment in Pärnu where they always spent their summer vacations. Once he had confirmed availability, they went to Estonia for a month and left the apartment in their son's care. Several significant events had occurred in the time between Grandfather Vasily Matveyevich's funeral and the Levitins' departure for Estonia. And although these events didn't change their newly ordered way of living, they were imprinted on the Levitins' memory. First of all, Tatyana received a letter from Masha Teryokhina, her village girlfriend. Among other things Masha mentioned that her brother Pasha finally had drawn a lucky number. He was injured in military exercises (indeed there's no joy without sorrow!), his hip didn't heal properly, and that was the end of his service as a paratrooper. But in consideration of his personal bravery and years of service, he, Pavel Ivanovich Teryokhin, was being transferred to serve at the Moscow City Draft Board. So if Tatyana were to see Pasha in Moscow, wouldn't it be nice for her to let bygones be bygones and treat him as a good friend from home? Even though Tatyana immediately understood what implications Pavel Teryokhin's sudden transfer to Moscow could have for Anatoly, she said nothing to her husband. The very thought of asking Pavel to help her son, asking him after all that had transpired during their last meeting in their home village, seemed shameless to Tatyana. But while it was a shameless, repulsive, and even blasphemous thought, it haunted her, because this was, perhaps, the last and only possible way to save her son.

Another new and important development in the Levitins' life was their friendship with the Zeldin family: Wolf Izrailevich, Debora Davidovna, and their children Artyom and Lilya. Wolf Izrailevich, a famous biochemist, had created the first ever method for the early detection of leukemia. This work had been ongoing for more than ten years, since the mid-60s, and although back then Professor Zeldin had firmly decided to emigrate to Israel, he couldn't stop his research already in progress. Practically his entire lab devoted to the biochemistry of malignant tissues was involved, almost thirty people. And when they had already isolated an antigen from the leukemic hemocytoblasts, when they had produced an antiserum, when the trial had been completed, and the diagnostic method was patented and had gone into mass production, then Wolf Izrailevich finally left his lab and filed papers with the Visa Section. And at that point it suddenly turned out that his discovery, originally reported in domestic and international journals, later corroborated in hundreds of publications, and having become textbook material, was a matter of the country's "defense capability," and Professor Zeldin was refused an exit visa for reasons of "national security." No matter how much Wolf Israilevich tried to plead with the Visa Section that his work was no more a matter of national security than the construction of a gas mask (he had, after all, been awarded a Rockefeller University prize for his discovery), the Visa Section administration was adamant, and the Zeldin family request had been denied for the fifth time. Five "resubmissions" at six-month intervals, because you can resubmit only after a half a year had passed, would render lifeless anybody else, but not Professor Zeldin. Some charitable folks at the Food Industry Ministry hired him and Debora Davidovna, an analytical chemist, as consultants. The Ministry was under pressure to design an express method for identifying toxins emitted by microscopic fungi that grew in cereal grass ears. So the Zeldins were, as always, spending their days in the lab (this time a lab affiliated with a small research institute under the ministry's umbrella) and their evenings in the Lenin Library. Their son Artyom worked at home. He was born handicapped; instead of legs, he had odd stumps that looked like seal flippers. From childhood his parents had supported and encouraged his passion for drawing, and he studied at home and in the studios of some of the best artists. Now the twenty-seven-year-old Artyom was considered an exceptionally gifted visual artist.

"We'll survive," Debora Davidovna would often say. "The Grasshopper will feed us."

"Grasshopper" was the Zeldins' household name for Artyom, who would scamper around the apartment on his stumps inserted into a little cart on casters. Always in motion, always devising puns, practical jokes, and games, he was, in a manner of speaking, an axis around which the life of this family turned. And above all else, Grasshopper worked endlessly. He illustrated books, painted in oil and in watercolors. He was working on a book about the life and work of Henri Rousseau, his famous precursor. Artyom counted himself among the primitivists, believing that the artist's task is to harmonize features of living nature and artifice, features that the unsophisticated eye is capable of discerning. A sophisticated eye that craves refinement, the eye of a true artist, not only records nature, but also desires to see it in a specific fashion. In this the primitivists' concept of art differed radially from that of the naturalists, since the naturalists didn't place into the world they depicted that main element of art—the artist's persona. Legless Artyom, he who was deprived of the joys of living, thrust all the passion of his soul into his paintings. Wondrous animals and birds amid phantasmagoric vegetation shouted to the world about the eternal desire for joy and happiness. And harmony, harmony is happiness. Every time that Wolf Izrailevich returned from the Visa Section with a new cruel refusal, his artist-son would immerse himself—with a greater intensity and passion—in the world discovered by Henri Rousseau. In his room doubling as a studio, Artyom had set up taxidermied animals and birds; outlandish reptiles and insects sat frozen in jars filled with alcohol or formaldehyde, and plants exotic for our parts of the world wound themselves along his walls.

"We'll just have to wait it out, father," Artyom would say on those days of refusal. "We'll wait, bear with it, and we'll dream. You with your molecules, and I with my paints and brushes."

"That they can't take away from us. At least while they still need us," Wolf Izrailevich would reply. And the life of the Zeldin family would go on as before, replete with work, discoveries, and hopes.

One day Professor Zeldin said this to Doctor Levitin: "They think all these varieties of discrimination will deter us. Refusals, restrictions, prohibitions. They're deluding themselves. This, after all, isn't a customs tax on lacquer boxes. You pay it, and you take it out of the country. They don't let you take it with you; you leave it here. They can't stop us Jews from exercising the main function of our nation—a desire to think. We shall continue to think, and we shall rouse other nations with our thinking until they've murdered every single one of us. And even after our death, Jewish thought, etched in the Hebrew Bible and in the Gospels, will become the yeast for the future risings of the minds. But it seems that we haven't arrived at that extreme point as of yet," Zeldin concluded.

The friendship with the Zeldins gave Herbert Anatolyevich new strength. Maybe the Levitins wouldn't have left Anatoly in Moscow alone, but the Zeldins asked to go with them to Estonia, and that settled the matter of the summer vacation.

Yes, the Leyns were having quite a bustling summer. Toward the very end of the festival, when the last films of the official selection were showing, an old acquaintance of Evgeny Lvovich appeared in Moscow. Stanley Fisher had flown in from New York to Moscow and called the Leyns from the Sheremetyevo Airport.

"Well, hello there! My sister and I will be staying at the Metropol."

And that evening Evgeny Lvovich and Ekaterina Nikolaevna stopped at the Metropol to see Stanley, uncorked a bottle of champagne they had brought, and then dragged the Americans home with them. Stanley had come to Moscow for six months as part of a US-Soviet academic exchange program. He was going to lecture on the history of American film at the Institute of Cinematography. His psychiatrist sister Anna (or Hannah as Stanley would sometimes call her, so as to underscore their Jewish background) had "escaped" (that's how she put it) from an impatient fiancé, Richard, who, at all costs, wanted to wrap up all the nuptials and set off on an archeological expedition to Nepal. Anna didn't want to be left alone the first month after the wedding. The expedition was to leave for Nepal in the middle of August. And the quick-thinking bride, under the guise of a great opportunity to visit Moscow having suddenly presented itself, had upset her Richard's research agenda. Now that Anna's wedding plans were all set, and his brotherly duties were totally fulfilled, Stanley had no idea what to do in Moscow with his very energetic sister, who was always bubbling with laughter and consuming endless Russian *zakuski*.

Stanley, a thirty-five-year-old handsome man just starting to fill out a bit, with the refined face of an Ashkenazi Jew, and sporting gold-rimmed glasses, a fashionable haircut, and a burgundy velvet suit, strolled absentmindedly about the Leyns' apartment, making brief stops at the Konchalovsky still life and at the photographs, each of which had become a page of film history. It was around eleven at night. Stanley, who wasn't planning on wasting a single moment in Moscow, had only now fully understood what a burden Anna would be to him. She knew not a word of Russian, and in spite of her sense of physical and moral invincibility, she was totally helpless in what was her grandparents' native country. Stanley had been to the Soviet Union before and had stayed here for extensive periods of time. He spoke Russian fluently, although it was amusing to observe how he rolled those Slavic sounds in his mouth as if they were hot dumplings. The guests and hosts were sitting on the sofa and in armchairs around an English coffee table with a black lacquered top decorated with gold peacocks. Evgeny Lvovich poured cognac into their snifters. They toasted their meeting. The conversation gradually shifted from cinema-related topics to the question of Jewish emigration.

"They say," Stanley pronounced in his accented Russian, taking a sip of cognac and sucking on a slice of lemon. "They say, that in all of American history, there's never been such a spoiled group of immigrants as this one. These are doctors, engineers, actors, visual artists, writers. Almost at once they forget the old hurts and only remember what position they occupied in the USSR."

"Good for them. Why should they act inferior?" Evgeny Lvovich demurred.

"You're right, my dear Evgeny. But the level of knowledge and skills that in the Soviet Union allowed them to hold these high positions is totally inadequate for similar jobs in the US. As a result, for the first three to five years, these immigrants need to be patient and work towards American standards. There's no shame in that."

"And what about the arts?" Evgeny Lvovich asked.

"In the arts one observes a fascinating phenomenon." Stanley took another sip and continued. "The current splits into two uneven parts: the craftsmen and the genuine creators. Since the general level of technical competency, and hence the level of technical skill in literature and the arts, is higher in the US than in the USSR, those Soviet literary and artistic craftsmen who come to the US find themselves below the threshold of demand. They are forced to change their profession, and that's tragic. Like it's tragic for a provincial woman, who fancies herself a beauty, to find that in the capital she's just plain ordinary. At the same time, the flights of Jewish-Russian genius that have given birth to Mandelstam, Chagall, Plisetskaya, and Brodsky impart to the other, smaller part of the

Russian émigré art world an almost unattainable attractiveness, even in our spoiled marketplace.

"And these 'chosen ones,' can they count on finding interesting work?" Evgeny Lvovich asked parenthetically.

Stanley answered with an equally perfunctory question, "Might that be of interest to you?"

"At this point only theoretically, but how's one to know, how's one to know," said Evgeny Lvovich, steering the conversation back to the festival program.

Anna was trying to communicate with Ekaterina Nikolaevna Leyn, but their conversation consisted mainly of gestures and smiles. Thank goodness Natasha returned; running into the living room with her quick impulsive steps, she froze upon seeing the guests. She had met Stanley before, but that was three or four years ago, when she differentiated her father's friends primarily by their first names and countries of origin. And now she suddenly froze, noting the American's handsome face and groomed hands, and that confidently benevolent look with which he greeted her. And there was something else that flickered in Stanley's gaze, something like a camera flash that instantly burst and disappeared. But it was enough for both of them to recall that moment later. Anna, who was happily swallowing strawberry pastries, also noticed the spark that had flashed between her brother and Natasha. Ekaterina Nikolaevna was happy Natasha had come home; finally she could have a normal conversation with Anna, since Natasha spoke excellent English. The three of them went to the kitchen, and there they chatted until Stanley and Evgeny Lvovich finished their conversation. When the guests were leaving, Natasha agreed to be Anna's guide during her stay in Moscow. As it turned out Stanley was always hurrying off somewhere, and as he would hand his sister over to Natasha, he barely managed to exchange two words with her. But the spark that had flashed the first evening was enough for Anna to sigh when they were saying farewell at the airport: "My brother should have a wife like you, Natasha." To which Natasha wanted to answer that everything was okay with her, that she had Anatoly, and that there were so many girls in America that Stanley shouldn't burden himself with Russian acquisitions. But she thought this type of answer would be too drawn out, and it would sound like an apology, or at least an explanation, when she didn't feel like apologizing for or explaining anything. In any case, it was doubtful that Anna, even with all of her psychiatry, could understand their circumstances: Anatoly's likely draft, his family's application for emigration, and Natasha's unhinged position. Doubtful she could understand—and pointless to explain. So she and Anna just said their goodbyes, having promised to write each other.

The film festival ended. Natasha had only two weeks left until September. As a result the plan of a trip south had to be scrapped, and they decided to vacation in Palanga and also to make stops in Vilnius and Trakai on the way to the Lithuanian coast. In Vilnius Natasha and Anatoly were met by Mikolas, Evgeny Lvovich's former student, now a Lithuanian film critic. Mikolas brought them to his apartment on Antakalnio Street, where his wife Angele was waiting for them—a lanky Lithuanian woman, with strong legs and full thighs and a young girl's undeveloped chest. Her smile was so welcoming and open that the guests immediately felt a transition from the perpetual Moscow stress to an atmosphere of calm.

The four of them were sitting in the dining room. The doors to the balcony were open wide, and from the apartment building atop a Vilnius hill they enjoyed a wonderful view of the "Jerusalem of the North," as Ashkenazi Jews used to call the city. There was almost nothing left of this poetic name and of the Jews of Vilnius. Only to spite official regulations did the Lithuanian tour guides showing the old city sneak in a view of the site of the former synagogue, where the great Russian actor Vasily Ivanovich Kachalov had been born in one of the small outbuildings. And so they sat there, the four of them, Mikolas, Angele, Anatoly, and Natasha, chatting about everything under the sun: the film festival, fashion, cars, narcotics. Chatting about everything under the sun, as if only thirty-five years ago it wasn't here in Lithuania but somewhere else—God knows where in a faraway land—that Jews were hunted like vile animals, with the Lithuanians themselves helping the Germans in this hunt, sometimes surpassing even the Nazis in their hatred. Who knows, maybe Angele's and Mikolas's parents had participated in this hunt for Jews. And now all this was somehow forgotten because the four of them were young. The table was crowded with good wines, Lithuanian apple brandy and local Palanga schnapps, and fine Lithuanian dishes: smoked ham, potato dumplings, all sorts of sausages and cheeses. Vegetables rose from the platter like rooster tails; aromatic herbs and greens teased the eyes and lips. Angele started to feel hot; she excused herself and came back in a short outfit, suitable either for tennis or for the beach. The sun was glistening on her sinewy legs. Angele and Mikolas were serving their guests, pouring apple brandy and vodka into shot glasses, filling their plates; they were enjoying themselves and feeling unconstrained.

"Now we'll make the whipped cream," Angele announced loudly. "Whipped cream with raspberries," and she burst out laughing.

Just the words "whipped cream with raspberries" alone emitted sweetness and delight. Why didn't they know these happy and sweet words, particularly cute when spoken with a Lithuanian accent? The tape recorder was playing something unfettered and tenderly exciting—just like the words "whipped cream with raspberries." Mikolas was dancing with Natasha, and Angele was looking at them with such joy that it seemed it wasn't her husband that was dancing with a pretty girl, but her beloved brother, who finally had some luck in choosing a bride. Angele cast a smile of approval at the dancing couple and tugged at Anatoly's sleeve.

"Who will help me whip the cream?"

"Of course! With pleasure." Anatoly quickly followed Angele.

The kitchen was done in black and yellow tile. The tabletops, water heater, and cabinets were also yellow, and in the corner there was a narrow couch covered with a black wool cloth. In the corners and in the middle of the couch were round pillows, bright yellow like sunspots or egg yolks. Angele poured the cream from a plastic package into the mixer. She turned it on and it buzzed, forcing the white fleshy mass to dance and gurgle. Don't raspberries and tongue go with whitish semen and whipping cream? And don't we choose what we eat in accordance with our emotions and feelings? Raspberries and cream, semen and the inner depths of the body. Angele lit up a cigarette and sat on the couch. The heavy golden shock of her hair fell onto the pillows, merging with the bright yellow hues. Anatoly was trying hard not to look at this wealth of bright yellow and this golden mess of the hair, not to notice the golden fluff that sprouted on the strong shins of this Lithuanian woman, on the powerful legs that Angele tossed over the couch cover like two big fish—head to head. Angele was smoking. From the living room rhythmical music was flowing in, entwined with Mikolas and Natasha's laughter the way snowflakes entwine with the sharp green rhythm of pine needles. Anatoly transferred the whipped cream from the mixer into a china bowl.

"Now we add the raspberries." Without getting up from the couch, Angele poured the mosaic of melting berries into the bowl. "And now we taste."

She brought to her mouth a silver dessert spoon, filled with the body of snow white, silvery cream, through which the berries showed like nipples. Suddenly all that splendor disappeared inside her scarlet mouth, greedily laughing and insatiable, a mouth living a life of its own. Slightly separated jaws, which formed corners on the sides of her face, were the main organ of this creature that lived as one with Angele to provide pleasure—this mouth that chewed, sucked, made smacking noises from delight and erotic pleasure. Through the rhythm of Angele's mouth, Anatoly was taking in the joyful rhythm of jazz and of Natasha's laughter. When the laughter would die down, Anatoly squirmed from the terrifying thought, the frightful image: a creature just like Angele, except this creature was Mikolas, now pursued his Natasha. Leaning on one elbow, Angele stretched out her other hand toward Anatoly, holding the scarlet and white body of the berries and cream.

"It's sweet, isn't it? We can make it even sweeter," Angele said quietly. And Anatoly suddenly had the feeling that this predatory and ensnaring mouth would devour him like a small berry. Angele leaned all the way back and pulled Anatoly to herself. Her mouth and tongue took possession of his mouth, and her hands groped under his shirt and belt in a hurried attempt to reach his flesh and join it to hers. Angele's bosom was rising. Her eyes were darting wildly.

"What's wrong, Angele? Are you feeling sick?" Anatoly ripped the woman's hands away with difficulty, grabbed a cup, and poured some cold water. "Please have some water. I beg you, please calm down."

She was already getting herself together; she took a sip of water and fixed her hair. Then she laughed as if nothing at all had transpired.

"It's a joke, Anatoly. It's only a joke. Can you hear them? They're having a good time. I figured we too could have some fun."

Anatoly didn't speak. He was thinking, can everything really be so simple? You drink wine with a woman you barely know. You flip off some switches—of conscience or shame, I don't quite know. Some controls of wild barbarianism. You kill them with alcohol and you have a good time, forgetting yourself, drowning yourself in a kingdom of monkeys, forgetting why and with whom you came to this home.

"You're silent. Have I offended you, Anatoly? Forgive me. Although in such instances, a woman should not be asking forgiveness. You're a nice, pure young man. And I'm a spoiled, aging doll."

"Don't say that, Angele. I thought no such thing. It's just that we, Natasha and I . . . in short, we're . . ."

"In short, you love each other. I envy you."

"And you, don't you love Mikolas, and he you? I was under the impression you were happy together."

Angele got up from the couch. Lighting a cigarette, she walked up to the window and pulled the curtain aside to let the smoke flow freely out onto the street.

"Of course we're happy. I have parts in many movies at Lithuanian Film Studios, and I also play leading roles in the theater. Mikolas is a popular film critic. We do all we can to spend less time together. We're happy when we manage to fill and live through another day, to be satiated with work, entertainment, and shopping. Thank God we're too busy to spend time together. We actually don't desire frequent contact. Lithuanians are secretive people. They don't trust each other with their thoughts, even though they are all thinking the same thing. We've gone astray. We're lost. We've sent off our last Jews with much enthusiasm; we didn't put obstacles in their way, but things have not gotten easier. People who're close to us in language, birth, and most importantly in their mindset, have emigrated—we forced them to do it. And so we're left with our prosperity, emptiness, and a lack of direction. That's why our men, particularly creative people, drink heavily. Mikolas also has started to drink. After receptions and drinking parties with friends, he barely makes it into bed. Is that the way to love and enjoy life? I'm guilty before you Anatoly. I drank a bit too much. You're young and strong. I couldn't help myself. And besides . . ."

"And *besides* what?" Anatoly knew he shouldn't interrupt their conversation that had begun under such strange circumstances. Clearly Angele had not finished telling her story.

"It was still before Mikolas. It's already been six years. I was in love with this fellow, Mark Bermanis was his name. One of our own Lithuanian Jews. His parents had come out alive, survived the Germans."

"Or the Lithuanians," Anatoly couldn't help saying.

"Or the Lithuanians is right. It's true that there were those who rescued Jews, and for that they themselves perished. But now the heroic deeds of these lone Lithuanians are forgotten. Jews remember only how Lithuanians betrayed them."

Angele spoke slowly. Each word was hard for her to utter.

"Tell me about Mark."

"Mark's parents didn't want to forget anything. They preferred to emigrate rather than to stay and fight. They didn't even try to understand that there are different Lithuanians."

"Like there are different Jews."

"That's right, Anatoly. Now you're hearing me. Have some whipped cream. You'll eat, and I'll talk." Angele put some dessert into a dish. "Good?"

He could hear sounds of blues wafting in from the other room. Laughter could no longer be heard, but now Anatoly wasn't agitated about anything except Angele's story. He was now drawn to his woman, who was so candid with him, and he couldn't quite explain what he so liked about her.

"Please go on, Angele."

"So Mark's parents decided to emigrate to Israel. At first Mark tried to do something, to change the situation, but we weren't even married. Their papers were filed with the Visa Section, and two months later the Bermanises received permission to leave. At first I still believed that everything would be restored, that Mark would rescue me. But his letters came less and less frequently. And then he wrote that he was getting married to a girl he met in Israel, an immigrant from Poland."

"And you became Mikolas's wife?"

"Yes, my dear Anatoly. I did. One must make one's own nest."

Anatoly felt a pang of acute pity for this pretty Lithuanian woman, with whom he found himself alone almost by accident. She was so open with him, as if he were her brother. He saw a tear roll down Angele's face and fall, like a tiny crystal, onto her chest. Anatoly walked up to her and put his arms around her shoulders.

"Everything will be okay," he said. "I'm sure of it."

"Yes of course. Everything will turn out fine. That's what Mark told me when we said goodbye. You look so much like him. When I was so careless with you, at that moment, it seemed to me that it wasn't you here with me, but him, like it used to be. But it's all gone, like the smoke from the burning leaves in an autumn park. The leaves turned yellow, people marveled at their colors, and then they were burned. Very soon you too will go."

"Where?" Anatoly didn't immediately understand what leaving Angele was talking about.

"Where all of our Lithuanian Jews have gone: to Israel, to America, to Australia. There where your Jewish brothers await you. Drops collect into streams, and streams flow into rivers."

"In Russia not everybody has decided whether or not to go."

"And you?"

"I've decided."

"Together with Natasha?"

"Not at the moment. Natasha will come later."

"If you really love her, don't get separated. Separation is a terrible force, and time coupled with separation is worse than a swamp. From a distance it seems fine, a person can pass through. But when you step into it, it draws you in to your death. All right, enough of my lamentations. Time to bring the dessert to the table."

Angele placed the round dish with raspberries and cream onto a black tray painted with flowers and carried it from the kitchen. She was walking confidently, rhythmically swiveling her springy hips. It was as if Anatoly saw her for the first time—a movie star, a beauty that attracted thousands of excited masculine glances to the screen. And he immediately understood that for the first time in his life he felt envy, was jealous of Mikolas, who could always look at this beautiful woman. And this envy, although filling some previously unknown part of his soul, didn't stop him from loving Natasha as tenderly as before.

"We were having such fun," Natasha said. "Mikolas, as it turns out, has been studying the gestures and facial expressions of famous movie actors, and he does amazing impressions of them. Miki, could you please show us Louis de Funès?"

Mikolas stuck his jaw out. Bug-eyed, he started to walk around the room spasmodically, just like de Funès himself. And yet it seemed to Anatoly that while doing an impression of the famous French comedian, Mikolas was actually making fun of some old neurotic Jew. Anatoly quickly lost any desire to stay there, and he hurried Natasha back to the hotel.

THE MORNING SUN filled Anatoly's room in yellow light. He looked at the clock; it was around nine. Natasha was sleeping, curled up. In her sleep her face looked just like a little girl's. A little girl, smiling in her dream. Yesterday, on their way back from Angele and Mikolas's, they strolled for a long time through the park overlooking the Vilnia, freeing themselves from vaguely alarming premonitions. Evgeny Lvovich had made sure to book them two single rooms. They put Anatoly's suitcase in one and Natasha's valise in the other and decided to draw straws for which room they would actually use. It fell to Anatoly's room. After the evening stroll in the park, they got a table in the hotel restaurant. With metal etchings decorating the walls, the restaurant's decor looked a lot like that of a Georgian restaurant, although there were no dishes from the Caucasus on the menu. A jazz band was playing nice music. They ate juicy, nicely spiced meat and drank fruit soda. "Like two plebeians," said Natasha, but it was in fact all very delicious. Then they returned to their room and ordered a call to Moscow. Natasha talked with Ekaterina Nikolaevna and asked her to tell the Levitins, if they should call from Pärnu, that everything was fine.

There wasn't a sound coming from the hallway, even though they knew that in the adjoining rooms and in those across the hall, there were people—talking, drinking, discussing business, loving. The floor lady on duty didn't get on their nerves; she was simply invisible. After the noisy afternoon at Angele and Mikolas's, with its notes of danger-ous permissiveness, this quietude immediately enveloped Anatoly and Natasha with a warm cloak of serenity. Previously, when Natasha would begin to undress in front of Anatoly, unzipping her pants or pulling off her sweater, he would rush her impatiently, trying to help but actually getting in the way with his awkward, still boyish movements. Today was different. Now sitting in a deep fluffy chair that engulfed his body, he meticulously zoomed in on Natasha's every movement, like a camera-man during filming. A decisive and deeply rooted change had taken place in him. He located a lever inside himself, one that allowed him to shift his desires, to hold them back, or to enhance them, even in the most intense moments. It was only when Natasha came out of the bathroom in her sheer French nightgown that Anatoly embraced her and carried her to bed. His frantic passion used to burst into flame and explode, leaving a sweet and tormenting memory, more like a fleeting recollection of a moment of happiness. How he used to long for that moment of passing through the gates of happiness—not even the sweet release itself, but the aching joy of longing for its arrival. These intoxicatingly tormenting seconds would flit by so quickly that he only managed to catch a glimpse of Natasha's face, which also expressed this aching sensation of longed-for happiness, and then reflected spent joy and exhaustion. Anatoly was so young, and he was brought up in such a puritanical family, that he simply didn't know how, was never taught how, to control himself in such moments. Herbert Anatolyevich avoided talking with his son about sexual matters, assuming that Anatoly, like himself, would reach an understanding with the help of two trusty teachers: life experience and books. But today Anatoly came to know—like he had gradually come to know his arms, legs, head, and secreting glands—that even in the most cherished moments of intimacy, one could and should control one's emotions and one's body. This knowledge, which had come to him not now, but back at Angele's home, suddenly grew to be a controlling power of his self. If previously Anatoly's "love self" was ruled by two feelings, tenderness toward Natasha and desire to quickly free himself from the exploding thirst for fulfillment (and that self, too, was totally human, and not animalistic, because animals don't exhibit the tenderness of adoration and only caress in advance of gratification), then Anatoly's current "love self" was more mature, suffused with an earlier tenderness, with a thirst for fulfillment and a desire to give pleasure to her, his Natasha. Anatoly embraced Natasha, kissing her eyes and neck, stroking her pulsing nipples, and sensing each cell of her being as she immersed her lover inside herself or let him away for a second, only to thirstily take him again. Now Anatoly didn't rush on the arrival of sweet fulfillment. Taking pleasure, simultaneously feeling her last broken breath not only with his body but also his mind, he watched her half closed eyes, was intoxicated by her moans of pleasure. Only when Natasha flung her head back, shouting out and sobbing and laughing, and his belly felt the shuddering of her belly, and the sweet warmth spilled along from her lap onto his groin, did Anatoly cease to think of himself as separate from his beloved, now plunging into the precipice of acute thirst for completion.

Later Natasha told him that for the first time she felt that she was a woman. And now Natasha was sleeping, like a tired but happy little girl who had played her heart out. In Anatoly's world nothing but happiness was embodied in this sleeping girl, all curled up in their bed; there was nothing but sunlight entangled with the ebb tide of her hair; nothing but her lips that he kissed to chase away the last shadows of sleep; nothing but her arms and legs, that through her dreams were craving his arms and legs; nothing but the continuously recurring state of fulfillment from their new intimacy; nothing but the enticing coolness of a river breeze and the coolness of foaming water; nothing but the quiet swish of an elevator that unhurriedly descended; nothing but the high-vaulted lobby filled with tourists and mirrors; nothing but kiosks selling newspapers in all the languages of the world, and amber jewelry for all the lovers on this planet; nothing but the compliant doors of the hotel restaurant and the energizing aroma of strong coffee; nothing but barley beer and marbled ham; nothing but the two of them strolling in the park above the river they had seen from the windows of their hotel room, the river where young Lithuanian boys were fishing, their little silver hooks loaded with grubs—gawky and whitish like embryos; nothing but the Hungarian-made Icarus tour bus taking Anatoly and Natasha away from this hilly, romantic, and very livable city of Vilnius, so medieval and also so ultramodern that it made the Middle Ages seem like a precursor to our century. There was simply no place in the world for unhappiness, doubt, baseness, disappointment. While sitting next to Natasha in the airplane seat of the Icarus, Anatoly remembered that one of the ancients, probably it was the Greek genius Aristotle, had in mind precisely this happiness of love when he mused about the pursuit of happiness as the ultimate purpose of art.

Natasha was reading an American detective novel. Solicitously, Anatoly took her hand.

"Are you happy, Natasha?" he asked.

She didn't answer immediately. In general she had difficulty transitioning from one state of being to another.

"Yes, of course. Especially now, after yesterday." And again she immersed herself in reading.

Together they had come up with the idea of a day trip to Trakai. Back in Moscow they had been to visit Peredelkino, where many writers had their dachas. After paying homage to Pasternak's grave, after strolling down the narrow shady avenues past the writers' dachas tucked away from the summer Sunday heat, they bumped into the fence that surrounded Ilya Selvinsky's dacha. Natasha immediately recognized this fence and this dacha; she had visited the Selvinskys with her father when she was a little girl. She remembered a strapping man with a mustache, who treated them to apples from a wicker basket.

"Just arrived from Yevpatoria," he told her and her father. "These apples, they have the scent of Crimea, my native land."

After Selvinsky's death her father took her to see the poet's widow, Berta Yakovlevna, and his daughters, Tsilya and Tata. Evgeny Lvovich had been friends with the Selvinskys for a long time. They had agreed to collaborate on a film script based on Selvinsky's novel *O My Youth*. Natasha remembered that the film script turned out to be good; it had nearly passed the review at Mosfilm Studios, but then, suddenly, it was axed due to some episodes that had to do with Crimean Tatars, Krymchaks, and Karaites. Evgeny Lvovich explained to Natasha that Krymchaks were Crimea's indigenous Jews, or at least that is what everybody in the world considered them to be, including the Germans, who annihilated the Krymchaks with the same ferociousness as they did the European Jews. But the Karaites, whose language is so close to the Krymchaks' language, survived. Selvinsky died suddenly in 1968, and the film script was buried with him. Natasha remembered about the Karaites with some feeling of vexation, as if they were the cause of her father's failure. And now it turned out that real Karaites still existed; you could see them, talk with them, and figure out who they really were—Jews or non-Jews. Oddly, a gnawing association between the Karaites and some uncertainty also lived in Anatoly, as if an old bullet splinter kept burrowing in the old wound, or maybe the splinters had been removed a long time ago, while the old scars would periodically become inflamed.

They were walking across a field toward a wood grove. Pasternak's dacha was to the left. Straight ahead, over the tall grass, shrubs, and trees, was a church and the poet's grave. They were walking toward the grove, girding the field and surrendering to the curve of the path that made the trip to the train station longer. The end of June and the haying season were approaching, when the ryegrass is green and fragrant, the wild cereals—oats and timothy—aren't yet prickly but only tickle the ankles, and the daisies are intensely yellow in the center and brashly white around the sides. You could almost sense the white and golden sweetness of the flowers with your lips. Anatoly picked a bluebell with a long stem—a whole tabernacle of blue-violet color with a little bifurcated tongue covered in white dust at the tips.

"Hear it ringing? Do you, Natasha?"

"It's the church bell ringing," she answered, laughing.

And if, in turn, Anatoly hadn't shared a story of his own, which had something to do with the Karaites, she would have forgotten, for a long time if not forever, that feeling of vexation that the very word "Karaite" provoked in her. But his story was a reminder. It happened in Crimea. Anatoly had finished the seventh grade and was traveling with his parents. They were en route from Yalta to Odessa and decided to take a break from travels and stop in Sebastopol for a week. They rented a room in the vicinity of Khersones, and every day they would go down to the shore, where between the blue of the sky and sea stood the marble columns of an ancient Greek temple. It seemed that the spirit of Hellas hovered over this section of the Black Sea shore, strewn with pebbles and pieces of maroon pottery. Maybe they were the fragments of ancient amphoras. One day they saw a woman walking along the shore. She carried a wicker basket filled with meat pastries made of phyllo dough.

"Karaite *pirozhki*! *Pirozhki*, try them! Karaite *pirozhki*, three for a ruble!" The woman was shouting in that peculiar mixture of Ukrainian and street Russian, that by dint of some ill fortune became the commonly accepted colloquial form of communication in the south of Russia and Ukrainian regions that bordered the Russian Federation. The woman had dark skin and a big hooked nose. Like two wrinkled stumps of a dwarf pine, her bare feet stuck out from under her wide pleated skirt.

"Papa," Anatoly asked right away. "What does it mean, 'Karaite'? What are Karaite *pirozhki*? Where does it all come from?"

Professor Levitin waited for the woman to be far enough away from them, and then he started to tell the story of this mysterious people, who had settled in Crimea perhaps as far back as after the disintegration of the Khazar Kingdom (Khaganate). The Karaites lived alongside the Crimean Tatars and the Crimean Jews (Krymchaks), speaking a Turkic language closely related to the Crimean Tatar language but also incorporating ancient Hebrew roots. They observed many Tatar customs and practiced a form of Judaism. The Crimean Tatars were deported from Crimea after World War II, having been accused of collaboration with the Nazis. There were very few Krymchaks left; a few managed to survive by evacuating to the Urals or to Central Asia, but the majority of them were murdered during the occupation. "Well, it's also true," added Herbert Anatolyevich, "that the Karaites have largely survived, here in Crimea and in Lithuania, miraculously having been spared during the German occupation." Herbert Anatolyevich didn't know how they managed to survive. This is what the younger Levitin remembered about the Karaites.

During that visit to Peredelkino, Anatoly and Natasha decided to go to Trakai to see the Karaites, ancient, like the relic pines at Pitsunda on the Abkhazian coast of the Black Sea, or the Labrador tea shrubs in Siberia. At that time young people were becoming more interested in Jewishness—in Jewish customs, Jewish questions—and Anatoly and Natasha, children of Jewish fathers and Russian mothers, both felt a particular yearning for that source that had lain dormant in their own families.

ɤ

A GROUP OF chance acquaintances. People that met by chance. Those who are leaving, emigrating. Actually, those waiting for an exit visa. Those waiting for an invitation from Israel. Curiosity seekers gathering information. And those merely observing. Wine hastily purchased at a nearby shop for the occasion is being poured. Conversation keeps rotating around the question of emigration. If there are about two million Jews in the country (including children of mixed marriages and deeply assimilated Jews that resemble the Marranos in Spain during the Inquisition), then even considering an annual departure of twenty thousand, this loss is compensated by a natural increase in the Jewish population (one percent of increase equals approximately twenty thousand). So the planning agencies that be have no reason to worry. The Russian nation is forever assured (based on the genetic stock of the remaining Jews) of the continuous production of new Raikins, Utyosovs, Plisetskayas, Zorins, Dragunskys, Zilbers, Vovsis, Gabriloviches, Zeldoviches, Kaverins, Pasternaks, Mandelstams . . . and, perhaps, even a new Moses, Christ, Marx, Lenin.

Why do the planning agencies care about such a speck as me? I can only be of use to the author in easing the task of story development.

ɤ

ANATOLY AND NATASHA set out for Trakai to see the Karaites. Summer. Love. The looming prospect of separation. But in this kaleidoscope—this ornament weaving together Vilnius and Lithuanian fields, forests, and villages—the Castle of Trakai also betokened the unlikelihood of separation. Of course, the Karaites and Jewry. Of course it was fascinating for them to see all that. But not so important for the author to write about it, since Anatoly and Natasha, their fate, is but a small drop of the shared fate of our people. Let us leave our poor innamorati at the turn of the road to Trakai. Now the author will tell of the Karaites through his own eyes, even though I visited these parts not in the summer of 1979, like Anatoly and Natasha, but in the winter of 1978. And thus: Trakai, its Karaites, their savory pastries; Selvinsky with his early poetic cycle "Bar Kokhba" and his late novel *O My Youth*; scattered knowledge about the Khazars, who tried to convert Prince Vladimir the Great to Judaism; some speculations on the ethnic origins of Khazars by ethnographer Lev Gumilyov. All of this hazy, because I lacked personal experience. And hence an attempt to understand the Karaites by communing with them.

AT ABOUT NINE o'clock on a stormy and dank winter morning in Vilnius, I got on a bus at Station Square. We rode out of the city. The road crossed the endless white fields, and it seemed strange to me that I was in this white snowy desert and not in a vast stretch of sand, white with desert heat. For we are talking about a people of the southern steppes that hailed from God knows where, but certainly not from the tundra and northern latitudes. I don't remember exactly how long it took, an hour or a bit longer, to get to Trakai. And after that? Besides me, on the occasion of this winter blizzard, there were no other tourists on the bus. My fellow travelers were Lithuanians returning from a shopping expedition to the city. They arrived, got off the bus, and melted into the snowy alleys of what looked like summer homes. It was a good thing I managed to ask for directions to the castle. I knew that, since the time of the Grand Duchy of Lithuania, Karaites had been settling around Trakai Island Castle. The Lithuanian ruler Vytautas the Great brought them out of Crimea because they were renowned warriors: brave, honest, incorruptible. Jewish character traits. Karaites served the Prince as guards—the way the Latvian riflemen would later serve Lenin. They (the Karaites) were the rockbed of the Lithuanian throne, the flower of the Lithuanian military, and they entered the life of the country as a monolithic indestructible host, like the Varangians in medieval Rus. But the Karaites did not assimilate (after the Jewish fashion), preserving their own language and faith. An entry in *The Soviet Encyclopedic Dictionary* (1980): "*KARAIMS* [Karaites]: an ethnicity, living in small groups in the Ukrainian and Lithuanian Soviet republics (total population in the USSR 4.6 thousand people, 1970) and also in Poland. *KARAIM LANGUAGE* belongs to the Turkic language family (Kypchag group)."

The frost and the blizzard were getting in the way of my ethnographic observations. I was walking toward the castle down the street where the Karaites lived. Left and right, little houses, blackened with age, jutted out from behind crooked fences. Somewhere on the outskirts of the town lay the frozen Trakai lakes. I met no one along the way. A craven, shrouding silence had seized the Karaite quarter. Suddenly I nearly bumped into a passerby. A broad, strikingly hooked nose stuck out from under his black mouton hat with tied flaps, commonly known as a *pirozhok* hat. The raised collar of his worn-out herringbone coat couldn't possibly protect this stranger from the cold. He was suffering from the bitter frost. The man wasn't wearing a scarf, and his bluish asphyxiac chin jutted out from under his coat. Under his arm the man with the hooked nose held an ochre-colored briefcase, its leather cracked in places.

"Forgive me," I turned to the man with the hooked nose. "You're a Karaite?"

"Yes, but how could you tell? Actually, why do you care to know?" Both surprised and frightened, the man with the hooked nose gripped his briefcase even tighter.

"Not a soul around. You look so much like a Jew. And I knew that Karaites live here."

"Karaites, yes. But not Jews. You're mistaken. We Karaites aren't at all related to Jews. No connection whatsoever!" And the man with the hooked nose scurried away from me in the direction of the bus station.

"Who are you Karaites, if not Jews? No, I'm not mistaken—you look so much like us," I yelled after him.

"We're not Jews. We are Tatars, Turks, anybody but Jews." The voice of the man with the hooked nose reached me from afar, and then he dissolved into the blizzard.

I walked on. The street curved to the right, in the direction of the castle. I don't like dead, uninhabited stones. Especially in winter. What do I care about Lithuanian princes, even if they did at one time conquer half of Europe, from the Baltic to the Black Sea? I've never been one to get transfixed by slavish admiration when hearing about "the grand conquests" of some cannibal. If only I could just stay at home and read books! I circled around the castle made of red stone and bought a collection of postcards and a few souvenir buttons, only to do my duty toward the museum employees who stood there shivering from the cold. But my main business hadn't made a stitch of progress. I still hadn't learned anything concrete about the Karaites. Or maybe I did learn something, and this something made me want to cry from shame and despair. I turned around and slowly walked back along the same Karaite street. A hunched over old woman was hobbling toward me, carrying a round loaf of bread hidden under a tattered shawl. The old woman was so ugly and destitute that she made you want to give her alms. Her face, wrinkled and brown like a dried pear, expressed a complete indifference toward me, and also a desire to slip through the nearby gate, kinked from hanging just on one hinge.

"Granny," I accosted the old witch. "Granny, where's there a synagogue or a museum here? I mean, where can one see something uniquely Karaite?"

"Synagogue?" repeated the old woman, shrieking at the end of the word and jutting out her one and only rotten tooth. "We don't have a synagogue, because we're not Jews. Jews, they have synagogues. And we're not at all related to Jews. We have a mosque or *kenesa*, in the Karaim language. *Kenesa*, not a synagogue."

The old woman's eye darted from side to side, as if my questions, just the questions, contained something forbidden, something that shouldn't be spoken out loud. Only the blizzard heard us. In the wind, the gate squealed like a lapdog. There was no life in that lane. A dead lane.

"Granny," I continued, trying to speak as gently as I could, because a mixture of vexation, pity, and contempt for her destitution, cowardice, and duplicity was pushing me away. "Granny, don't be afraid of me. I'm also a Jew. A Jew from Russia, just like you're Jews who once lived in Crimea. And my grandfather came from Lithuania. He was an old Jewish rebbe. Reb Chaim-Wolf. For him Yiddish was a native tongue, as well as Lithuanian, like for me it's Russian, a Slavic language, and for you a Turkic language. What's happening, then? Why do Karaites hide their kinship with Jews?"

The old woman glanced at me with apprehension and malice. The same way that a famous old writer, a State Prize Laureate, who happened to be a native of Kamenets-Podolsky like my own father, had once looked at me when I asked him something about the life of Kamenets Jews before the Revolution. "You're mistaken. I know nothing about the life of Jews," he said brusquely, and walked away from me.

And so this time in Trakai the old witch stuck out her rotting tooth like a sting and released poison.

"Jews lived here once. They sold fish. The Germans shot them. But the Karaites didn't get shot, because Karaites are not Jews. We're closer to the Turks. Something like Muslims. Our mosque is called a *kenesa* and not a synagogue. And here it is. You're standing right in front of it. It doesn't look anything like a synagogue, does it?"

The old lady snickered and vanished out of sight.

I was now standing before the crisscross boarded-up doors of a relatively low temple structure with a round dome. In the design winding up to the dome, one could make out outlines of a Mogen Dovid—Star of David.

I recalled Pushkin's tomb at the Holy Hills Monastery. There's a cross on the white tombstone, and beneath the cross, a wreath with a Star of David. Pushkin was a Freemason. A hexagram resembling the Star of David was a Masonic symbol. But on his mother's side, Pushkin had descended from Ethiopian (Abyssinian) princes of the Solomonic dynasty—the "Lions of Judah"—that had originated from the Queen of Sheba and King Solomon. Solomon was the son of King David, the very same one whose name was given to the Star (Shield) of David. In Nikolay Ashukin's book *The Living Pushkin* (Moscow, 1934) we read this: "One of the most interesting Pushkinian heirlooms is the 'talisman' that he described in verse, a seal ring with a carnelian. Legend has it that the ring had been a present of Elizaveta Vorontsova. On the octagonal carnelian, set into the ring, there was an inscription in Hebrew, which Vorontsova might have taken for mysterious Cabbalistic signs."

Pushkin wrote in the opening of "Talisman" (1827), "Where the sea is eternally lapping / Over deserted cliffs, / Where the moon's glow is warmer / At the sweet hour of dusk, / Where in seraglios taking pleasure / Moslem men spend whole days / There an enchantress tender, / Gifted me a talisman."

Of course the ring was made in Crimea. And the Hebrew writing on the Crimean carnelian stone is of Karaite origin. Pushkin was the first and virtually the only one in Russian literature of the time who dared to write and think out loud about Jewry, about the great history of Jews and their pitiful state in the poet's day. (After him came Gogol in *Taras Bulba*). There is pride and pain here, despair and vexation, an impotence to change anything, and, above all, a truthfulness in portrayal and imagination. If one is to accept as axiomatic that genes are eternal, then Pushkin received his poetic genes from David and his son Solomon. The ancestors of Pushkin's mother—the Hannibals—descended from the Abyssinian royal dynasty through King Solomon and the Queen of Sheba.

There was another great poet in this passage of genius genes: Jesus Christ. "The book of the generation of Jesus, the son of David, the son of Abraham. . . . So all the generations from Abraham to David are fourteen generations; and from David until the carrying away to Babylon are fourteen generations; and from the carrying away into Babylon unto Christ, fourteen generations" (Matthew 1:1–17). A defined genealogical, and therefore a genetic, lineage may be traced: David—Solomon—Christ—Pushkin. David with his psalms; Solomon with his *Song of Songs*; Christ with his monologues, addressed to humanity's conscience; and Pushkin.

"I'm too familiar with the Bible/ And unaccustomed to flattery," Pushkin stated in a poetic address to Filipp Vigel, sent from Odessa to Kishinev in November 1823. With pride Pushkin carried the heavy cross of Semitic—Abyssinian—heritage. He was repulsed by the treacherous buffoonery of renegades, who not only betrayed their ancestors' faith but also entertained the public with their treachery. Pushkin was harsh on such people; he called them not Jews, but Yids. On 25 September 1832, Pushkin wrote this from Moscow to his wife Natalya: "Nashchyokin is remarkably charming. There are two new faces among his underlings. One's an actor who used to play second-fiddle lovers and is now shattered by paralysis and totally confused, the other a monk, a converted Yid, chains hanging all over him, who does for us an impression of different Yids gathering in their synagogue and also tells us spicy anecdotes about Moscow nuns." Pushkin had an aversion to the cowardice of those Jews who concealed their origins or mocked the memory of their ancestors. In his heart the poet stored a different image, one of the nation of Israel as proud, wise, and unbending to fate even as fate challenged its understanding of God: "When the Assyrian mighty ruler / Punished entire nations with death, / And Holofernes subjugated / Asian expanses for his king; / Tall with humility and patience, / And strong with faith in God's resolve, / Before the troop of arrogant captors, / Israel didn't bend her neck."

The history of the Jewish people—the Hebrew Bible—told Pushkin about the true Jewish character, about the living spirit of the Jewish people. Under the pretext of writing the humorous narrative poem *Gabrieliad*, the poet openly states that behind the character of Mary there stood a real Jewish young woman, she whose beauty he praised with such inspiration. Just as the mother of Christ—the son of the Jewish people—was a real Jewish woman. In Pushkin's satire aimed at diehard reactionaries, there is both light humor and a deep understanding of history—in short, the poem has everything except disdain for the Jewry: "Indeed I so treasure the salvation/ Of the young Jewess's tender soul,/ So come to me, my ethereal angel,/ Come to accept my worldly blessing/ . . . Sixteen years of age, innocent meekness,/ Dark eyebrows, two maidenly mounds/ Heaving under a shirt of fine fabric,/ Legs made for love, a row of pearly teeth,/ Why did you smile, o Jewess, and the blush,/ Why did it run across your face? No, dear/ Believe me, when I say you're mistaken/ I wasn't describing you, but Virgin Mary."

The year was 1821. One can imagine how Alexander Sergeevich Pushkin, having stepped out of the dusty tarantass to rest and to eat something at a roadside inn, was breathlessly enraptured by the sight of the beautiful daughter of the Jewish innkeeper. Years later, after he had already become a family man, he would recall with self-irony his many traveling infatuations, which included Roma, Greek, Kalmyk, and Georgian young women, as well as our sixteen-year-old Jewess who inspired Pushkin to write his *Gabrieliad*. In a letter sent to his wife from the Boldino estate, on 2 October 1833, the poet writes: "I have the honor to report to you that before you I'm innocent, like a newborn babe. On the road I have chased only skirts in their seventies and eighties. I didn't even look at sixteen-year-old little chickies."

And that's the way one can see life through Pushkin's eyes: to see the Karaites, who forced themselves to forget their Jewishness; to see everything as did Pushkin (with both a historical and a contemporary perspective); to think about the fact that today's sixteen-year-old Jews are seeking truth in life and truth in history as they search for their native roots. There's a lot we don't know about Pushkin's secret thoughts. African blood conjoined with Semitic blood gave birth to the Abyssinian (Ethiopian) nation, the nation of the poet's ancestors. Northern, Russian blood diluted the southern, Ethiopian blood of Pushkin's black ancestors. In the six or seven watercolors, drawings, engravings, and oil paintings created in Pushkin's lifetime, we see a

Jewish teenager, then a young Jewish man, a Jew in the prime of his life, and finally a Jewish man lying on his deathbed. Such was the magical power of genes. Why am I writing all this? Pushkin was not a Jew. He didn't write openly about his heritage, about descending from King Solomon and the Queen of Sheba. In "My Genealogy" he only hints at it: "That my black grandfather Hannibal/ Was purchased for a bottle of rum." But let us return to Trakai, to the street where the Karaites lived.

Now I was walking on the right side of the street, as if heading back to the bus station, but in reality I was looking for the Karaite Museum. There wasn't a soul in the museum except for a guide, an elderly woman. I decided not to startle her with the question "Are you a Karaite?" She had a round, pale-skinned face with slightly protruding cheekbones, striated by broken vessels of old age. Her ashen hair was combed smooth and tightly pulled back. Strictly speaking, this guide, pale-skinned and dark-eyed, looked a lot like a Lithuanian Jewish woman. Yes, it's true that Lithuanian Jews mostly have light eyes, but sometimes they do have darker eyes.

Apparently I hadn't examined the exhibit hall very carefully: in the dimly lit space, there were two other people— a lieutenant colonel in a fur hat with ear flaps that he did not take off, like a Jew inside a synagogue, and his wife in a mouton coat. What brought them to Trakai on this miserable and empty day? Perhaps the lieutenant colonel had shed blood in these parts while liberating Lithuania from the Germans. Lithuania is my mother's native land. Her older brother Eyno, his wife, and two sons had been murdered in Panevėžys during the first days of the Nazi invasion.

Finally the lieutenant colonel and his wife had finished viewing all the exhibits and left the museum. I now stood alone amid the display cases with Karaite prayer clothes: striped cloaks not much different from the *tallis* that my late grandfather used to wear during prayer. And the prayer straps looked just like my late maternal grandfather's. The displayed Karaite weapons attested to their past military glory. But household objects, clothing, a Hebrew Bible, photos from the beginning of the twentieth century with the Karaites wearing *tallises*—all this spoke to me, if not of their Jewish ethnic origins, then at least of their Judaism. This had obviously nothing to do with Islam.

I thought the museum guide was casting curious glances at me. It's not that I was one of her own people, the way a Georgian who meets another Georgian in a foreign land is happy to say, in Georgian, "Greetings, brother." No, of course it wasn't that. But there was some kind of trust in her eyes. After all, I wasn't just any accidental visitor to the museum. I carefully examined some of the materials, reading explanations under the exhibits, and to do that I had to bend all the way to the bottom of the display cases. I even asked her to turn on more lights; in a word, I showed interest. She was a museum guide; she must have loved her work, and served, as well as she could, the history of her disappearing people.

"But these shawls, they're *tallises*." I could not hold it in any more.

"Of course they are, and the Bible is just like the one Jews have," she answered, having understood me and giving me a slight smile.

I gathered my courage and asked directly, "And the Karaites, who do they consider themselves to be? Jews or not?"

The guide looked around. Then she went out into the hallway. There was no one behind the door.

She leaned toward me and asked, "Who are you? Why are you stirring up all this?"

"I'm a writer. A Russian writer. A Jew by nationality. I'm from Moscow. My mother was born in Lithuania—in Šiauliai. Our family members were murdered in Panevėžys. I don't understand what's happening in Trakai today. Why are the Karaites hiding their kinship to Jews? Why are they afraid of their heritage?"

"And don't Jews from time to time fear their own origins?"

"Yes, it does happen."

"There, so you see. They have almost no way to hide that, and still they find ways. They change last names: in Russia to Russian ones, in Lithuania to Lithuanian ones. Now, as it happens, there's an honest solution: to emigrate to Israel. And what do we need Jewishness for? It hasn't brought you anything but misfortune. During the war the Germans started out by rounding up all the Jews in the region, killing them or sending them to concentration camps. All of the Jews.

"In the old days they had Passover, and we have Passover. The same matzo. The same gefilte fish. The same holiday. Similar rituals and customs. Even our synagogue is called *kenesa*. This, after all, comes from the Hebrew word for 'assembly.' We used to gather for prayer. Simply gather, like in a social club. When the Germans finished off the Jews, they turned to us, the Karaites. They cordoned off the street. Wouldn't let us leave our houses or move around Trakai. We were, all of us, awaiting the same fate that had befallen the Jews."

"That means you thought of yourselves as Jews?"

"Yes, in the old days we did. And we didn't hide our kinship. During the war we felt it especially acutely. Fear of death made us feel a closer connection with them. Thank God our *Hakham*—spiritual leader—went to see the Reichskommissar of Baltic Lands and proved to him that Karaites are not Jews, but a Turkic people by blood and by language. Descendants of the Khazars. Hitler was indifferent to religion. This saved us from death."

"And since then you decided to separate yourselves from Jews forever?"

"That's the way it turned out," the museum guide said with a guilty sigh. "It's too late now to regret it or to apologize for it. The old people have died. Customs are forgotten. The *kenesa* is in disrepair."

"And the young people?" I asked. "Who do the young Karaites identify as?"

"They're becoming Lithuanians."

Then someone came in and she walked away from me, relieved to end this burdensome conversation.

I returned to Vilnius. I sequestered myself in the hotel room, its windows facing the old city where a decrepit synagogue took shelter among so many Catholic churches and cathedrals. I didn't answer the phone. I didn't want to see anybody. The bottle's neck was level with the red tile roofs. By my side there was no Natasha, she who could wash away all this shame with her tenderness. Of course, I had no more doubts about the Jewishness of the Karaites.

❧

NATASHA WAS THERE by Anatoly's side. A fine summer night in Vilnius helped dispel the anguish, despair, and repulsion that lingered after the trip to Trakai to see the Karaites.

Last Third

"Yes, my Motherland, my mother—Russia," the professor said. "To every Russian, the destitute, barefoot, breadless Russia shrouded with cemeteries has been the greatest sorrow and the greatest joy, in all human feelings and sensations it brought to convulsions; for those Russians who hadn't been in Russia during those years have forgotten one fundamental human quality—a capacity to become accustomed to anything, an ability to accommodate. Russia lice-infested, sectarian, full of Orthodox priests stubborn to the point of fanaticism, having birthed the Third International out into the world and endowing itself with a Bolshevik time of troubles, cannibalism, national destitution."

Boris Pilnyak

"Filya, why so quiet?"
"What is there to say!"

Nikolay Rubtsov

Moscow September like they hadn't seen in years: Warm days and gentle evenings. Continuous guests. Jews awaiting invitations from Israel, exit visas, news from those who had already left. Going-away parties. Chilling early morning trips to Sheremetyevo Airport; cold air and raw nerves. Friends disappearing behind the doors of customs police. Saying goodbye—not forever, just for now. Tears, but not tears of despair, because this was not forever. Tears of joy for the lucky ones taking their leave. September in Moscow, a city getting ready for the Olympics. A September filled with suitcases, watermelons, international packages, Russian souvenirs, peaches, letters with stamps and seals from foreign lands. Everything divided into leaving and not-leaving; and life itself was divided in half: before emigration and after emigration.

LIKE AN AUTUMN leaf, Tatyana was whirling around Moscow, among other women who were also scurrying around the capital, happily preoccupied with all the tasks that had to be accomplished before their approaching departure. They telephoned each other, made plans together, met up somewhere. Herbert Anatolyevich noted with wonder how his once cozy and well-appointed apartment looked more and more like a warehouse. Stored all around the rooms were boxes with electric teapots, samovars, pots and pans, and irons. Painted trays, nestling dolls, and carved wooden cutting boards were spread out on tables and suitcases; boxes of shoes were piled up here and there; colorful fringed shawls were laid out in open suitcases, as were a dozen unbelievably beautiful dress shirts waiting to present their elegantly-attired owner to potential employers. It would have taken at least ten years for all of this stuff to get used in cooking and around the house, displayed, tried on, washed and ironed. Such was the general rhythm of life, and Tatyana surrendered to it, while Herbert Anatolyevich decided not to interfere in her activities, knowing that he might upset his wife with unsolicited advice.

And thus does the autumn, pre-Olympic Moscow enter a concluding phase of our story. Moscow, with its ubiquitous short-legged teddy bear mascots, striped watermelons, and blue and white mailboxes. Post offices, letters, postcards, packages, parcels—all of these signs and objects of communication had been so ensconced in the Levitins' daily living that Herbert Anatolyevich could no longer look at his own mailbox calmly; he had to open it immediately. What if the postcard from the Visa Section suddenly came? Everything that had to do with emigration centered on that postcard from the Visa Section. Everyone who had filed for an exit visa to Israel knew that if one received a postcard specifying the amount to be paid for the visa, that meant a positive decision, and if one got summoned to Room 24, that indicated a rejection, a refusal. But the numbers of those unfortunate ones couldn't compare to the hundreds of lucky ones who received the happy postcards. The few incidents of refusal could be explained by plausible, if fuzzy, reasons, if one looked at it from the point of view of the Visa Section. And even when inexplicable or even totally inconceivable cases would come up, even then Jews awaiting their exit visas somehow managed to calm themselves by thinking that appalling and incongruous cases happened so infrequently that such a fate would definitely bypass them. But the unfair, negative decisions he heard about always made Herbert Anatolyevich grow quiet, listening to the inner voice that often woke him up in those deserted predawn hours, when janitors and building caretakers got the city ready for a new day. A stanza from somebody's poem that he had recently heard at a going away party crowded his thoughts:

The caretaker shovels the street
rehearsing his snowy reverie
dirty Jew dirty Jew
dirty Jew—
In the camps
I'd break your head in two.

Unfair, unfounded, preposterous refusals kept on being issued. Herbert Anatolyevich, like the other Jews, chased away those troubling thoughts on the brink of dawn, because he had no other choice but to hope for the best. Recently, before Anatoly and Natasha's return from Lithuania, he chanced upon a particularly disheartening scenario. That evening Doctor Levitin's heart was unusually heavy, even though the sun was gently gilding the mums that Tatyana had brought home from the Central Farmers Market, and wafting in from the courtyard were the voices of playing children who had returned to Moscow from summer vacations. Then Misha Zinger called, one of the new friends he had made at an emigration-related event. Was it at the Visa Section, the city's central post office, one of the farewell dinners, or Sheremetyevo Airport? Yes, it was at the airport that he and Misha Zinger had met. It was back in June, and they were seeing off the painter Riva Shaferman, who had been Herbert Anatolyevich's patient about ten years ago. And even after that, she would regularly seek his advice. She was going alone, with no family, no baggage, because she had never known the price of family life or material things. The day before the flight, she had checked her two suitcases. Misha came to see Riva off with David Gertsel, her old friend from the time they both had studied at the Stroganov Art Institute. Misha Zinger now worked as a telephone repairman. He was still "ripening," waiting to file the papers with the Visa Section after having been fired from his old engineering job at a radio factory, but he was closely involved in all the emigration-related activities, and, like Doctor Levitin, he was constantly lending somebody a helping hand, seeing somebody off, introducing someone to somebody else.

And now it was Misha who called Herbert Anatolyevich and told him that David Gertsel had become a refusenik. "He had access to 'classified information,' they said. But what kind of classified information could a visual artist possibly possess?" said Misha, and Herbert Anatolyevich heard disbelief in his friend's voice. This disbelief didn't suggest that Misha questioned where matters stood—of course David couldn't have been privy to any "classified information"—but all along Misha had been harboring suspicions that such vague wording might be used in the case of any person who applied for an exit visa. And who could tell how long it would take to remove that stain, vaguely known as "access to information"?

They met in front of the Pushkin Monument, and then crossed Gorky Street through an underpass. The first autumn yellow leaves colored Tverskoy Boulevard. Like Jewish stars, maple leaves spread out on the paths and on the grass. Something theatrical was in the atmosphere of that September evening on Tverskoy Boulevard, where each house, each building reminded Herbert Anatolyevich of something

significant, memorable to the heart. The sculptor Konenkov's studio. The new Moscow Art Theater building; the Telegraph Agency
of the Soviet Union. Hadn't Jews contributed enough to the culture,
scholarship, and commerce of this vast country? Hadn't they done
enough to be allowed to leave Russia without suffering and heavy
losses, without acrimony? Misha Zinger told Herbert Anatolyevich
the story of David Gertsel. David used to work in the "battlefield art
studio." It went without saying that while painting official portraits of
Soviet marshals and generals or depicting famous battlefield scenes
from Russian history or episodes of the Great Patriotic War, David
couldn't have imagined that it would, in any way, impede his emigration to Israel. Misha and fellow "battlefield painters" had no access to
classified information, and why in the world would they need security
clearance? They painted portraits from photographs, and they relied on
materials on display at museums in order to create battlefield scenes.
Really, it would have been inconceivable for David to imagine all of
these problems, when he had disavowed his talent and calling and just
kept churning out commissions as they kept coming from the military.
Immediately after his application was refused, he was excluded from the
Union of Soviet Artists, and with much difficulty he landed a job painting posters and announcements at a third-rate movie theater.

And so the autumn months flew by. Although cases of new refuseniks elicited a morbid and oppressive feeling in Doctor Levitin, he still
thought them to be infrequent, and each an exception. Daily work, seeing off so many friends and acquaintances, and the hope of receiving
their own permission to leave—all of this accelerated the passing of time.
Even Anatoly's approaching draft looked like something improbable,
a pathological departure from the set rhythm of waiting for their permission to leave; and therefore the draft didn't seem natural. Natasha
acted as though she had forgotten that a draft notice would come, if not
today then tomorrow, and Anatoly would put on a soldier's uniform.
It wasn't the approaching draft or the uniform but the real prospect of
the Levitins' emigration—the imminence of their separation—that now

terrified Natasha the most and made her question their relationship. Everyone around them was leaving. And the uncertainty of Natasha's prospects only intensified her fear and anxiety. There is an idea that magnetic fields, biocurrents, and telepathic power lines can change the course of events. I don't know if Natasha could have feared the possibility of Anatoly's emigration to Israel so much that it influenced the course of events. I don't know what could actually influence the Visa Section's decision to grant permission to one particular person or to refuse another. Here the lines of fate converge with the power lines of black magic. But let us not blame Natasha for another impending misfortune of the Levitin family.

As part of a routine that had started back when Anatoly was in grade school and they would do their morning calisthenics together, Doctor Levitin, now alone, ran out of the house on this sunny October morning. Ahead lay the usual path, which he measured out daily with his lean legs. Others may have taken it for fast jogging, but his was actually an unhurried running along Tsvetnoy Boulevard toward Trubnaya Square, which rolled down and crossed over the circle of other boulevards. Then Herbert Anatolyevich would reach Pushkin Square. The area in front of Russia Cinema House would still be empty of people. Without stopping he perused the film posters and then turned onto Chekhov Street, heading toward the city's main artery, the Garden Ring, humming with early morning traffic. And then he turned back home. This time, as always, the route was the same, and the time that it took Herbert Anatolyevich to surmount this route didn't go beyond the usual limits, yet he felt a heaviness squeezing his heart. As he ran past the Obraztsov Puppet Theater, he even thought that the rooster on the clock with moving figures mocked him, by flapping its wings and screeching: Cock-a-doo-dle-doo—to the fool that's you. What kind of supernatural nonsense is this? thought Herbert Anatolyevich, jutting out his pointed knees as his long hands, working like rowing paddles, ripped apart the cool, still unspoiled morning air. He knew that soon he would reach his lane, turn at the corner, and see the old building, his home; then he would dive into the front entrance, open the mailbox with his hand quivering with impatience, and maybe there would be a postcard, the long-coveted postcard, stating the amount to be paid for an exit visa. Or, most likely, there would still be no postcard. It had been delayed en route. Would be here tomorrow or in a day or two. And now Herbert Anatolyevich would just take the letters and newspapers out of the mailbox. His feet pounded on the granite slabs that led to the front entrance, and he dove into the semidarkness of the building and unlocked the mailbox. The jaw of the blue mailbox dropped, and a white postcard darted out. It fell on the ground some distance from his feet, but Herbert Anatolyevich knew for sure that it was official government business. Only an official summons looked like that. But this wasn't a notice from the draft board. Draft notices were typed on thin colored paper—blue, green, pink—and their texture was different from other government notices. This knowledge was spinning in Herbert Anatolyevich's head, while he bent down and fumbled in the entryway's semidarkness, looking for the postcard that had landed in a corner between the door and the wall. Because of the dim light and his nervous excitement, Herbert Anatolyevich couldn't make out what was written on the postcard. But he did see clearly the words "Room 24." Was this a refusal? How could that be? Why had this happened to him? So many times had Herbert Anatolyevich imagined this moment, the flash when he would take out the long-awaited Visa Section postcard from the mailbox. It was not the card he had been waiting for, and yet, all this time as he lay awake at night, succumbing to his fears, he had imagined getting exactly this postcard.

As he slowly made his way up the stairs, Herbert Anatolyevich stopped on the landing between the first and second floor. Light was coming onto the landing through an old window with an arched top. Once again he started to examine the postcard. It was a deathly white color, with a three-kopeck stamp for citywide delivery. Without exactly reading it, he made out something about Room 24, and failed to find anything about a sum of money that was due for an exit visa. It really is a refusal, Herbert Anatolyevich said to himself, finally grasping what amounted to a verdict.

From that moment of recognition, he put aside all of his feelings, desires, and sensations, leaving but one: the need to move across space like a chess piece and to shift all of his decisions and actions in accordance with the rules of some complex game that he had only now begun to fathom. He realized that he was deadly mistaken in hoping the iron tentacles would either loosen their grip or fail to contract in time, and would let him, Tatyana, and Anatoly go freely. He had rooted himself too deeply into the body of this land, and he had waited too long before he decided to separate himself from the Russian soil. Now he wouldn't be able to rip himself away. With a newly given clarity, Herbert Anatolyevich saw that all those permissions to emigrate were an accident, while the refusals were the expected norm. And even though for the time being the "accidental" decisions had been occurring more frequently, they didn't express the true needs of the ironclad machine that stood behind the façade of the Visa Section. Herbert Anatolyevich should have foreseen this simple and clear truth. A brilliant diagnostician, he should have discerned this based on the total presentation of symptoms and typical cases. But he, like so many others, had deliberately refused to acknowledge the obvious, like one refusing to acknowledge infidelity in the family, if this infidelity hadn't been confirmed by physical degradation, publicity, or firsthand knowledge of events. Having understood all of this at once, Herbert Anatolyevich also fathomed and anticipated the subsequent actions of the ironclad machine: the inescapable eventuality of Anatoly's being drafted into the army. But Herbert Anatolyevich had no more strength left to prognosticate.

He climbed up to his third floor and rang the doorbell.

"Did you forget the key, Herbert?" To answer the door, Tatyana had slipped out of the bathroom in a yellow shower cap, a beige terrycloth bathrobe thrown over her wet body.

"I'm sorry, Tanyusha. Now listen, and please try to bear with it. It looks like we have received a refusal."

"What do you mean? What are you saying? No, it can't be! I don't believe it!"

Tatyana was already imbibing the postcard's condemning words, and with each reading, she became further convinced that there was no room for doubt or for any another interpretation of this unequivocal message. And even so, they both started to convince each other that it did sometimes happen that people were summoned to Room 24, and it was only a matter of some missing paperwork needed for a positive decision. They still couldn't admit that the time had come for them for them to be called refuseniks.

They hastily ate breakfast and set out for the Moscow city branch of the Visa Section, located on Kolpachny Lane, where Herbert Anatolyevich had gone after the late Grandfather Vasily Matveyevich had filed his ill-fated housing petition. The Levitins entered the Visa Section at a little after ten in the morning. On Mondays the senior staff would mainly receive refuseniks, so as not to mix the two streams: the lucky ones who got their permission and the misfortunate refuseniks. A few small groups congregated in the waiting area, but they conducted their conversations like in a morgue, in quiet, muffled voices. And if somebody moved from one group to another, conversation would cease, and it wasn't until they had perused the newcomer, asked him who he was and what his business was, and seen his mandate for misfortune—the postcard summons to Room 24—that they would resume their conversation. The Levitins took their place in line behind an old man, who either from decrepitude or from agitation was describing in a loud megaphone voice how he used to travel to the United States every year to visit his sister, and he was planning to go again this year, except they had refused him an exit visa. Why they refused him, he didn't know. Maybe because of his son, who had emigrated last year. Tatyana didn't listen to the old man's revelations, but kept on asking herself what would happen to her Tolik, if this really was a refusal. She threw a hostile look at her husband's face, petrified with some kind of determination or feeling of doom. Even though she immediately squelched the heavy feeling that he was the cause of all of their family's tribulations, chased it away just like they used to chase away an evil eye or a death hex in her native village, Herbert Anatolyevich's aloof stone face still looked foreign and hostile to her. Why am I here? thought Tatyana, looking around the waiting area and seeing alien, angular, and big-nosed faces. Their lives would still be full of grace, she mused, had her husband not come up with the idea of emigrating to Israel. Father would still be alive, Tolik would be in medical school, and *he* wouldn't be running around making house calls. For the first time, even though only in her thoughts, she called her husband *he*.

Herbert Anatolyevich was sitting next to Tatyana, not noticing anybody or anything around him, sifting in his mind through his life's events that would give even the slightest cause for a refusal. But even the most severe scrutiny gave him no explanation. He recalled one incident, an insignificant event in a wide sphere of activities he had been involved in as a well-known specialist in internal medicine. Could it be that? But, no! The Visa Section was a respectable organization. They wouldn't be making things so complicated all because of a trifle. It would be, after all, a waste of their own time. With effort, Herbert Anatolyevich convinced himself that, if this was a refusal, then the cause must be a misunderstanding that could be resolved with a scrupulous review of their file. And for this he must protest the refusal, and do so logically and resolutely.

"Tanya, we will file a petition if this is a refusal. The main thing is to demand a review," Doctor Levitin whispered, leaning over to his wife.

"And what's the use? Won't we only make trouble for Tolik?"

"No, we won't. The most important thing is not to acquiesce to the refusal."

They hadn't noticed how the old man before them went into Room 24 and soon returned to the waiting area. Now he explained for everybody to hear that he was refused because of his son. They don't let you visit your relatives who have emigrated.

"So my Riva was right after all. You want to eat cracklings, buy a goose," the old man announced in a robust voice and went out onto the street.

The Levitins stepped inside Room 24. Sitting at the desk was a lieutenant colonel in round rimless glasses upon a round puffy face. Actually, it would be more accurate to describe him as having a round swollen head with bald patches. The wrinkles on his forehead and the bald patches seemed to be the only unique features of the lieutenant colonel's head. The rest, including his glasses, was characteristically undefined, complaisant, as roundness often tends to be. Speaking in a perfectly polite voice, the lieutenant colonel asked them to sit down. And they took their seats: Herbert Anatolyevich to the left of the official and Tatyana to the right. The green baize cloth on the T-shaped table where they sat echoed the lieutenant colonel's green uniform and the green piece of paper that he handed to Doctor Levitin.

"Sign here. Your request to be granted an exit visa has been refused."

Looking directly into the slits of the lieutenant colonel's eyes that were enlarged by the lenses, Herbert Anatolyevich said, "We won't sign anything until we know the reason why we have been refused an exit visa to Israel."

Tatyana nodded, confirming her husband's words.

The lieutenant colonel was startled. Even his round, overfed head seemed to have hardened, gaining a stiff form. He leaned against the back of his chair and resolutely reached over to a pile of folders. He pulled one of them out of the pile and brought it right up to his face, either so as not to miss anything while reading through it or to protect the dossier from the Levitins' eyes. Slowly, like a judge, the lieutenant colonel read the text; he was having trouble turning his head toward Herbert Anatolyevich.

"Levitin, Herbert Anatolyevich, has been refused an exit visa to Israel due to access to matters of security."

"You'll forgive me, please, but I never worked with classified documents, I never had security clearance. I protest!" Herbert Anatolyevich got up from behind the table.

"Oh wait a minute. You're not the only one here." The lieutenant colonel turned his head toward Tatyana.

"Levitina, Tatyana Vasilyevna, that's you?"

"Yes, I'm Tatyana Vasilyevna Levitina."

"You also," the lieutenant colonel flipped through a few more pages in the file. "You also have been refused an exit visa due to matters of security."

"Me for matters of security?" Tatyana lost her breath from indignation. "That just can't be!"

"Anything can be." The lieutenant colonel put the Levitins' file away.

It looked like his official posture had let up for an instant when faced with such honest indignation and disbelief in what was typed in the file.

"My job is to inform you," he said quietly. "We don't make these decisions. Please sign that you have been informed about the decision of the Visa Section." And again he handed Herbert Anatolyevich the green sheet of paper on which the Visa Section stated its decision.

Herbert Anatolyevich took the paper and wrote in the precise professorial script that he used to employ for entering recommendations in a patient's medical history: "We protest the decision of the Visa Section to refuse us an exit visa to Israel to be reunified with close family members. We have never worked with any classified information."

And he signed it. Tatyana also signed and returned the green sheet of paper to the lieutenant colonel. The Levitins got up and were getting ready to leave when the lieutenant colonel said quietly, as if separating the official part of the appointment from normal human commerce: "Note the date—September 28. Not today's date, but the day the commission made the decision to refuse your exit visa. You can file for emigration again exactly six months from the date of the refusal."

They said goodbye and left Room 24.

"So what happened?" They were immediately attacked by a woman with a comely Jewish face, framed by a head of thick bleached hair.

"Refused," Herbert Anatolyevich replied.

"They'll play the same song for us in a minute," the woman with fluffy hair said despondently.

"You should protest the decision, if you consider it unjust."

"How do you protest?" asked the husband of the bleached blonde.

"How do you protest? It's simple. In the same Russian language they use to write your refusal. State that you do not agree with the Visa Section's decision. We shouldn't act like meek sheep before them. We have no right to look like cowards, no matter how scared we might be."

Herbert Anatolyevich couldn't believe that he wasn't afraid to say such words out loud, words that earlier he would have been afraid to even hear the others say.

"You advise us to protest?" the blonde's husband asked again.

"Absolutely! Maybe it won't help your individual case, but it will definitely advance somebody else's case. That I'm sure of."

"Herbert, let's go." Tatyana pulled her husband by the sleeve.

MOST OF THE month of October was taken up by get-togethers with fellow applicants and refuseniks. It swished by and rang out with telephone conversations, in which words and sometimes entire phrases were naively concealed so as to adhere to all the rules of the game, and the adage "this isn't for a telephone conversation" was invariably repeated. But what could be deemed appropriate or not appropriate for a telephone conversation, when the rustling of the falling leaves and the trembling of the falling branches were followed by a rustling that stole into a telephone conversation? And could all-important conversations ever be separated from frivolous ones? After they became refuseniks Tatyana wilted, and Herbert Anatolyevich found himself in a vacuum. He didn't want to alarm his son; there was no point in darkening the days left before the draft. Actually Anatoly would get home late at night, and before that, after work, he would only quickly stop in to change his clothes. All of his free time he spent with Natasha. This insatiable thirst for spending time with her made their parents both happy and frightened. And then came the week when Evgeny Lvovich took Natasha with him to Yalta, where he traveled to address a seminar of young screenwriters. This week loomed over Natasha and Anatoly as such an ordeal that it was hard to imagine how they would part for a long period of time. But this trip had its own hidden agenda, one that was, for the time being, only understood by Ekaterina Nikolevna and hidden from Evgeny Lvovich, who didn't concern himself with such practical matters. And yet something concordant with Ekaterina Nikolaevna's hidden plan hovered in the air that Evgeny Lvovich was breathing.

One day at the end of September, not long before the trip to Yalta, Evgeny Lvovich was sitting in his study, leaning back in his soft, comfortable armchair, wrapped in his quilted maroon robe with tassels. He was going through new issues of cinema journals that had arrived to the House of Cinema library after the Moscow Film Festival. A New York journal carried an article by Stanley Fisher, in which the author analyzed and compared the correspondence of compositional features and characters in Eisenstein's and Tarkovsky's films. Stanley had come to the conclusion that, first of all, the directors' artistic methods had a common genealogy. This shared genealogy was rooted in a rich layer of literature born in Russia during the first two decades of the twentieth century. Second of all, Tarkovsky's work was akin to Eisenstein's cinema in its understanding of the main goal of art: seeking to portray an individual character within the spirals of history. The close kinship of their artistic method was revealed in Fisher's comparison of Tarkovsky's *Andrei Rublev* and Eisenstein's *Ivan the Terrible*. And finally, what had particularly struck Evgeny Lvovich, since he himself had long arrived at the same idea, but owing to a force of habit developed in Soviet art criticism, he understood it and yet left it unsaid, . . . and it was the "fading" of the Eisensteinian "artistic flame" that Fisher articulated in his article. This "fading" was particularly evident in *Stalker*, Tarkovsky's latest film. An acutely political treatment of the events taking place within a totalitarian regime (the Mongol-Tatar yoke, the time of Ivan the Terrible, the near-death seizures of Muscovy) was so evident in Eisenstein's and in Tarkovsky's early work. But in *Stalker* this previous political lucidity yielded to a diffuse cosmopolitan landscape, the background against which politics were dissolved in the minutiae of daily living, resulting in a deliberate opacity of form and indeterminacy of message. Stanley had hit the mark when, in Tarkovsky's method, he recognized an attempt to lead the fading cinema (of political engagement) out of a dead end by giving priority to layered character investigation. Hence the portrayal of the main character through the film's series of live portraits and monologues, the character's spiritual biography, his conflicts with people and mundane reality, and his escape into nature (an escape into politics was forbidden!). The great Eisenstein never had this. And thus, Stanley Fisher concluded, it had all come full circle; the ivory tower had once again become a refuge for the creators of new cinema—a new wave of art for art's sake.

Evgeny Lvovich even whistled with pleasure. Those paper pushers from the State Committee on Cinematography wouldn't get over such a blow. Especially since Stanley had carried out this task in keeping with all the rules of critical sparring. What remained to be done now was to organize a public discussion and to announce it in the press. Evgeny Lvovich glanced at Ekaterina Nikolaevna with mischief in his eyes, took a sip of coffee from a slender Japanese porcelain cup painted with little multicolored houses, and started to flip through his organizer.

"Oh Stanley! So good, so good," Evgeny Lvovich kept repeating, while smacking his lips with pleasure and even slapping his knees (genetic memory works without failure). Finally he located the number he was looking for and dialed.

"Pavel Vasilyevich? Leyn speaking. Yes, yes. Thank you. I'm calling about the upcoming seminar in Yalta. And what about inviting Stanley Fisher? He can give a paper . . . And we can critique it. Oh, that would be great! . . . He won't last? Of course he won't last under friendly fire. We'll set Metelitsin on him. Imagine what publicity this will bring: a famous American film critic loses a scholarly debate to Soviet film scholars . . . Ciao. Hugs."

Evgeny Lvovich catapulted out of his chair and was literally hopping around the living room, swishing his tasseled belt around as if it weren't a belt but a riding whip. Such was Evgeny Lvovich's character.

"Evgeny, darling, what new scheme have you come up with?" Midflight, Ekaterina Nikolaevna caught her film guru by one of the tassels and pulled him toward her. Freed from the maroon yoke of his bathrobe, Evgeny Lvovich kissed his wife's splendid body, which he always found enticing.

But even before he could lose himself in her, he heard her say, "Why don't you just take Natasha to Yalta. The girl needs some distraction."

And Evgeny Lvovich, while diving in, drowning, then coming back up from that fateful and most life-giving abyss, whispered back, "Well, of course, Katya. Natasha could certainly go. But what about school?"

"I'll get her a doctor's note."

And that's how Natasha Leyn found herself in Yalta.

In the mornings, while the seminar was underway on the premises of the Vacation Home of Cinematographers, she would walk down to the pier, catch a ferryboat, and go to Nikitsky Botanical Garden, or "Nikity," after the name of the coastal Crimean village where it was located. Only now did Natasha realize how good it was to get away from the hustle and bustle of Moscow life, the same way we may feel grateful to a dentist when after torturous fears and doubts, and even a willingness to get accustomed to attacks of pain (which also allows us to experience periods of relief), the dentist's iron hand removes once and for all this source of our suffering. Though, of course, it was not the same thing. Even if Natasha did suffer in Moscow while thinking anguished thoughts about her future with Anatoly, even if she feared the arrival of each lunar month while embracing danger, Natasha would never in a million years agree to be forever deprived of this source of both her torments and her endless happiness. Therefore, the present, forced separation from Anatoly (she convinced herself that it was forced) simultaneously brought her the dolorous pleasure of missing her loved one and a respite that she so needed. The rare visitors to the Nikitsky Botanical Gardens would notice this pretty young girl, sitting on a bench deep inside an alley, a book in her lap. And if a meticulous observer happened to be there, he would notice the occasional tear drop down from her thick, dark-brown eyelashes onto the lines of Anna Akhmatova's poetry or Jacqueline Susann's fiction. When some meditative visitor to Nikity would grow brazen and try to talk to Natasha, she would smile politely and then re-immerse herself in the printed pages or in contemplation of the bamboo grove, or she would wander into the grove, looping amid the stalks, running her sensually delicate fingers over their erect, glossy bodies. She would hear a melody. Was it is the one the musicians played in the Vilnius restaurant the night before she and Anatoly went to visit Trakai? Suddenly Natasha would run to the ferryboat landing and rush back to Yalta, to be there in time for her scheduled phone call with Anatoly. Only once, two or three days before the end of the seminar, was her seclusion disrupted. Breakfast was about to end when Stanley, who was sitting across from Evgeny Lvovich, turned to Natasha: "Please help me find my focus."

"I would be happy to, Stanley, if it's in my power to do so."

"Oh yes, I believe it is. Although I could be mistaken."

"Sure, Natasha, why don't you help Stanley to concentrate. Take him for a long stroll in Nikity," Evgeny Lvovich said, putting away his newspaper for a moment.

"My dear Stanley, it would be my pleasure. We could go right after breakfast. Agreed?"

"Definitely. As long as you're prepared to tolerate my company for three, maybe four, hours."

Natasha looked at her father, then at Stanley.

"I'm ready to suffer for the sake of cinema art," she quipped.

"I'm grateful for your sacrifice," Stanley laughed, buttering a slice of pound cake and spreading apricot jam on top. "Tomorrow, on these very premises, under the direction of your most esteemed father, I shall be placed on the chopping block."

"Stanley, that's enough! It will be a totally civilized discussion, and nothing more." Evgeny Lvovich drummed out a Turkish march with his knife and fork, which was a sign of his being in a great mood.

"Yes, I'll be crucified in order to preserve socialist realism in Soviet cinema. But I'm going along, since it won't hurt me, and my Russian friend and your most esteemed father (Stanley theatrically bowed to Evgeny Lvovich) will be able to retain a balance of power."

They all laughed, knowing full well that this was only playing with words, and that the game of words would not change how they truly valued each other.

"And so I'm being assigned the role of Mary Magdalene comforting Jesus Christ before his execution?"

"The thought alone of such a comforting presence makes one not fear execution. But I truly value the parental trust given to me, and I won't follow any such historical precedents," Stanley said, giggling like a little boy. "It's precisely this idiotic attachment to convention that has turned me into an incurable bachelor. Girls back home in the US don't exactly appreciate repressed guys like me."

"So what is it that I should do for you, for cinema art, and for history?"

"Please, Natalie, just take me for a walk in your famous Nikitsky Gardens. I need to collect my thoughts before the presentation."

And they set off for Nikity.

STANLEY WALKED IN circles around the bench on which Natasha always sat. He would walk a distance away, taking pictures of wondrous flowers and strangely shaped and colored leaves. He imagined the leaves not as the plants' fingers, but as faces that repeated themselves a thousand times. Stanley spread his hands, argued with someone, and lived a life of freedom, as if there were no one in the center of his gyrations. He kept his distance and didn't pester his companion with conversation, but her presence inadvertently charged him with extraordinary surges of energy. Natasha, who at first worried that "handsome Stanley," as she called the American, would disturb her seclusion, had relaxed, getting accustomed to his presence. She was reminded of the magic tale "The Little Scarlet Flower," in which the beast suddenly turned into a young gentleman full of health and in the prime of his years. Just like this American. Just like Count Fyodor Tolstoy, nicknamed "the American," whom Pushkin had been expecting to duel for many years.

And I'm acting like some savage girl, Natasha thought, suddenly feeling hungry.

"Stanley, can you please come closer," she called out. "I wouldn't be opposed to having something to eat."

A little distance from the Mexican hill, all covered over with agave, cactuses, and banana shoots, they found a little restaurant. Stanley didn't try to act like a rich American, and tried not to violate their silent agreement: just a stroll on the eve of tomorrow's presentation. A bottle of light Crimean wine didn't change the tone of their friendly and perfectly restrained conversation.

They walked in the direction of the sea. Branches of plane trees hung low over their heads, forming an endless shaded corridor.

"Natalie, for the first time in my life, I'm strolling with a Russian girl."

"You can make a wish."

"I made it a long time ago, but it's one that can't come true. Do I not seem old-fashioned to you?"

"I like the classics. And, please, Stanley, don't worry about entertaining me. I actually like it that you can entertain yourself. I'm used to coming here by myself."

"So my presence changes nothing?" One could hear sadness in his voice.

"You want me to tell you the truth, Stanley?"

"No, Natalie, not quite yet. The time hasn't come yet for that truth."

"I hope to God that time won't ever come."

Stanley stopped. He turned toward the girl. Then he took her hand. They both understood that all these words rested on the fragile stems of her love and her duty. And his restraint and patience. The worst of it was that Natasha, while continuing to love and be faithful, understood Stanley's truth with some part of her inner existence. However, to destroy these sacred and fragile supports would mean the opposite of drawing nearer to that inner being, ephemeral even in words; it would mean losing the remote hope of ever hearing the truth that each of them needed.

Stanley brought Natasha's small palm to his face, but he didn't kiss it, just rubbed his lips and chin against it, as if he had uttered something cherished, something words couldn't express.

"Thank you, Stanley." Natasha gently pulled away from this benevolent giant, and his nearsighted brown eyes blinked with sadness—as if someone had taken away a long-awaited toy.

"Just a couple of words more. In America people don't usually toss empty words around. So I want you to remember, always, that if things ever get difficult and you need a strong hand, you can count on me. Everything in this world is precarious. And I'm sure that our stroll today wasn't an accident."

They were getting close to the sea. Natasha was still pondering Stanley's words. Of course the idea that it was a complete accident was absurd. But if the accidental is absurd, then the predetermined is just as absurd, she was thinking. After all, things accidental and things predetermined mirror each other. The most predetermined course of events is the sum total of accidental events that fit together like glass pieces in a kaleidoscope. Vadim, Anatoly, Stanley. Each of them appeared in her life entirely by accident. Or just the opposite, in accordance with some naturally predetermined plan. What was happening to her? Was she placing Vadim and Anatoly in the same box? And Anatoly and Stanley? But she was just thinking, musing. Was it a crime to think? Isn't it disingenuous to forbid oneself to think, conjoining what cannot be joined together or dividing what's forever fused together? To yield to the power of circumstances multiplied by social conventions? But she and Anatoly weren't an accident. They fell in love because it couldn't be otherwise. Anything else would've been absurd. Their love was not accidental because they both wanted it, because it wasn't a burden to either one of them. Not a burden? But where did these alarming thoughts come from? After all she was a free person, and she chose Anatoly freely. And before that, didn't she choose Vadim freely? But if this free choosing were to continue, who would be next in line after Anatoly? Or the opposite, what if Vadim hadn't shown his true colors then, but much later, when it would have been impossible for her to meet Anatoly? Or if he had turned out not to be Vadim at all, but a guy with Anatoly's face, personality, body, and habits, and yet with Vadim's mindset? And if so, what was her love for Anatoly, if not an accident that had fallen into a naturally assigned space, like a spare block for other blocks, prepared and stored by nature: for pleasure, companionship, procreation? And this is where forcing ourselves to accept that she or he is the only one in the whole world seems so utterly out of place. So, why couldn't it be Stanley? Hadn't Anatoly, with all of his love, become a prisoner to secret government interests, and wasn't he about to leave her, to leave Natasha in the precarious position of a recruit's girl? She was entitled to have doubts. Stanley was obviously more honest than she, because he reserved the possibility of some day saying the words that convention forbade him to say at this point in her life.

As if reading her mind, Stanley said, "You Russian Jews are too weak-willed, you somehow lack the strength to choose your own path in life. And, simultaneously, you're also unbelievably frivolous. Deeply mindful of everything and yet so frivolous. Such an odd combination, but I think I'm being fair."

"What do you mean, Stanley? You didn't just say that out of nowhere. Is it true that it's somehow connected to our conversation?"

"Both true and not true. A half truth, most likely. I've been thinking about this for some time, and often. But today the thought seems to have crystallized. Probably these aren't Jewish traits, since American Jews, who also came from Russian Jews, have lost these traits. I suppose this is Russia, unbridled, self-doubting, wishing to have it all: the whole world, all of the worldly love and the world's suffering, and as a result, sometimes not even having enough for a slice of bread."

Natasha was observing the American. It was as if he had been transformed. What happened to his all-around calmness, his pitch-perfect discipline, his *joie de vivre*? The things that made her recoil from him, and if not exactly recoil, then at least keep the kind of distance that the soul alone can measure without resorting to units of length or marks of status in society. Stanley's wavy hair, usually combed with deliberate neatness, had become ruffled. He was waving his hands around, ready to throw off his jacket and to fight for his own truth with fists or with a pistol. A real cowboy, that Stanley! Natasha hadn't expected this.

"Stanley, dear, what's the cause of this storm?"

They stood at the edge of the bamboo grove. Completely desiccated shoots and stalks of bamboo—green, brown, and yellow—were like sedge on a meadow by a riverbank. Stanley leaned against a thick bamboo trunk, feeling its ice-cold polished surface with his cheek.

"It's a storm because we, American Jews, suffer every day and every hour, because we cannot really help you Russian Jews. All of our actions—trading Russian Jews for grain, protests in the UN, demonstrations—all of these things are pathetic attempts to dull our own pain, caused by being unable to change your predicament. One thing is clear: the current situation is simply intolerable. It must be changed. How will that happen? Whether through your exodus from Russia, or through suddenly being granted truly equal rights within this country? Or perhaps there will be an optimal solution, one desired by all, which will give you a free choice between emigrating and living as equals in your native land, in Russia. I don't know what will happen. And I doubt that anyone can know for sure. But please understand, Natasha. Just as you're a Jew and at the same time, or maybe even more so, a Russian, I'm not only a Jew, but first and foremost an American. We Americans have been taught to respect traditions, emotions, illusions, beliefs, and in general, the nonmaterial aspects of human nature. But first of all we're people of action. Not all of us are businessmen, but we're all people of action. And that's why, for that reason alone, I will be happy to help at least one Jewish family, at least one Jewish girl. And what if that turns out to be you?"

"Thank you, Stanley. What a strange turn of events. We've known each other, sort of, for quite some time, but we're only now having a real conversation. I really do find myself in a very complicated situation. What will happen to Jewish emigration? What will my parents decide?

And what about Anatoly's draft? These are entrances to a labyrinth, but will there be an exit? But I would give anything in the world—and please understand me, my honest, decisive, and very kind American brother—I would give anything not to become that girl."

Natasha said all of this while looking into the eyes of the American. And probably to soften the last phrase, she traced her fingers along his cheek, pricking herself on the bristles that poked through his delicate skin.

"I'll try to escape with Anatoly. He's my husband, you know. I'm scared even to think of it any other way."

Was it a dark cloud that had suddenly rolled over from behind the Crimean mountaintops and cast a shadow over her soul? Was it water that had been secretly gathering in bamboo cups? Or was it wine that had suddenly bubbled in her blood? Who could tell? Natasha was ashamed to cry, to burst into tears for no reason in front of Stanley, and in the middle of the day—silly to cry and also to turn away from him and hide her tears. But the rain fell onto the earth. They shook the dew off the leaves, and they spilled the wine. At first Natasha wanted to run, to get away from him and calm down alone, but to act like some savage girl sobbing and running away seemed to her even more embarrassing than unbounded tears. Natasha tried to smile at him, as if to say: look, what a fool I am. But her smile shattered, her lips swelled up, and her mascara was running. Stanley dug in the pocket of his exquisite penguin suit, pulled out a huge white handkerchief, and started to wipe her face, as if she were his little sister. That made her feel better, and she calmed down.

The next day Stanley Fisher presented his paper, and a discussion followed. Taking his presentation apart, one piece after the other, the seminar participants drowned the American critic in quotes from authors considered to be part of the canon of Soviet literature, while Fisher himself mainly referred to sources that had never been published in Russia or were long ago forgotten. As far as his concept of "the dimming of the political and the growth of the personal" in Tarkovsky's cinema was concerned, this thesis (the main point of Fisher's paper and his most significant contribution to film theory) was greeted with complete silence. So Stanley was left in a critical "airless space." But the discussion achieved its goal: as always, the truth of Soviet art had triumphed, and the wolves were appeased. Evgeny Lvovich Leyn, who moderated the discussion, celebrated "our erudite American colleague" for his sharp mind and breadth of knowledge, and praised "esteemed Dr. Stanley Fisher's consistent and unwavering interest in the most exhilarating aspects of Soviet film."

After the discussion, during a five o'clock tea, Natasha told Stanley that he was fabulous because he had managed to withstand the "bellowing of those arses" without retching. She had at first called them "blockheads," but Stanley didn't know what this word meant, so she resorted to the cross-cultural expression "arses."

And that was Natasha's only week without Anatoly during that last September before the refusal. Another phase of their life began after they were refused. But in truth, everything that had happened with the Levitins during the past year—Anatoly's disaster at medical school and Herbert Anatolyevich's decision to emigrate to Israel, waiting for the invitation, filing papers with the Visa Section, Herbert Anatolyevich's dismissal from his academic position, Tatyana's trip to her village and her encounter with Pavel, the death of Grandfather Vasily Matveyevich—this fateful year had all been anxiety and pain, as if it somebody kept dragging them through chinks in camp barbed wire. Their lives kept rolling downhill, or rather they were contracting, becoming smaller, like tiny bodies of single-celled animals forming a cyst in order to preserve the mere foundation of life. And now, even this constrained life of their family had reached its final limit, although it hadn't yet died completely (it seemed the life of their family would die if they were refused, or be reborn if they received permission to leave). Bypassing both the cyst stage and necrobiosis, their life began to unfold in keeping with some laws of nature unknown to both biologists and sociologists. The former life could no longer be possible, because all forms of the old life had been destroyed. A new life abroad, its forms having been discovered by their precursors, Jews who had managed to leave before the door slammed shut, was also out of reach. The only thing left was to form their own semblance of existence, to attempt going back to some long lost paths, overgrown with the grass of oblivion. What was left? To transform themselves into a totally new existence, the existence of refuseniks? Thank God, even here, the Levitins weren't alone and starting from scratch. In essence such forms of existence, antithetical to normal life, had already been discovered by their misfortunate precursors, the older refuseniks.

The regime wouldn't spare them its signs of attention. One October evening the doorbell rang at the Levitins' apartment. Apparently they couldn't wait for someone to answer (alone at home, Herbert Anatolyevich had been taking a nap) and started to pound on the door with fists. Doctor Levitin, as was his custom, opened the door without asking who was there. A sergeant from the local precinct walked in, accompanied by the building superintendent.

"Let me see some identification," the sergeant said.

Seryoga, the superintendent, coughed guiltily because he felt the absurdity of the situation. First, everybody in the building had known Levitin since childhood; second, he had treated them all, visiting each patient on their first call; and third, just a few days ago, Seryoga himself had stopped by to borrow five rubles from Tatyana—until payday.

Without objecting, questioning anything, or engaging in any superfluous conversations, Herbert Anatolyevich just brought the passports.

"Here they are."

"Are you citizen Levitin, Herbert Anatolyevich?"

"I'm citizen Levitin, Herbert Anatolyevich."

"Are you employed?"

"Yes."

"Where and in what capacity?"

The precinct sergeant was checking off his questions against a piece of paper he held and noting down Herbert Anatolyevich's answers. He also checked Tatyana's and Anatoly's passports and wrote down their information on the same form.

"Do you, citizen Levitin, have any plans to go anywhere outside of Moscow in the near future?"

"We were planning on it, but we were refused," Herbert Anatolyevich made a joke.

The sergeant didn't want to take a joke. He became all gruff and looked askance at the super, who wasn't following the conversation; in his daydreams, the super floated into the sideboard from which, in the old days, a bottle would be taken out, and he would be treated to a shot of vodka. It was not for naught that people trusted Doctor Levitin. Not for naught. There was something in his face that made you trust him. The sergeant took the super by his elbow.

"Go. I don't need you here any more," said the sergeant.

And when the door closed behind the super, he quietly said to Herbert Anatolyevich, "Don't be cross with me. We're just doing our job. Social orderlies. And the fact that they refused you, well, too much political instability in the world. That's what they told us during a lecture at the academy."

"Are you studying at the academy?"

"In the evening division. I can't spend the rest of my life hanging out with supers in other people's apartments. Here's my advice, Herbert Anatolyevich: don't rock the boat. You can't chop wood with a penknife. Who knows, things may just work themselves out."

And the sergeant left.

Herbert Anatolyevich stood for a long time, pressing his forehead against the cold of the window. He was humiliated, dispirited, defeated. For the first time in his life, they checked his papers in front of a required witness, as if he were a criminal. He was now under surveillance. "Don't rock the boat": the sergeant expressed the official point of view in simple terms. While in the old days, Herbert Anatolyevich would have told Tatyana about the visit by the sergeant accompanied by superintendent Seryoga, would seek her counsel, now he decided not to say anything when she returned. He made his bed in the study. Sleep wouldn't come. He heard his wife open the door, but he didn't stir, succumbing to a desire to keep silent, to hide in the shell of his own feelings. Then Anatoly got home, and Herbert Anatolyevich still couldn't fall asleep. Finally, in the wee hours of the morning, after taking an aspirin, he lost himself in a half sleep that slowly enveloped him in its warmth.

Surprisingly, he woke up with a clear mind and a resolve not to give up, to break out of the repulsive little cocoon his life had become during these months of waiting for a permission, yet fearing a refusal. He had to appeal, to embark on a new life still unknown to him, a life of protest.

Herbert Anatolyevich phoned David Gertsel and learned from him that on that same day, not far from Herzen Street in an empty lot adjacent to the editorial offices of *The Whistle*, there would be a roll call of those who wished to get an appointment with the director of the Visa Section, Dudko, and with his deputy, Aniskina.

"Ask any Jew where the 'Wailing Wall' is—that's where our line forms."

IF ONE WERE to ask a native Muscovite to name the main reference points of the capital city's downtown, Herzen Street would certainly be one of the first to be identified. For Herbert Anatolyevich this street evoked precious memories. The Music Conservatory, where students would be allowed to sit on the steps of the amphitheater in the main hall. The Museum of Natural History, where his late father used to take him, and where Herbert Anatolyevich himself would later instill in little Anatoly an interest for biology. The movie theater where they played old pictures, and the nearby *shashlyk* restaurant, once a famous venue. The Central House of Writers, whose doors used to be open to the Levitins, owing to their friendship with a poet who had since been expelled and banished—all for his desire to go to Israel. Only one landmark on Herzen Street evoked painful memories. The homeopathic pharmacy, which for some reason stood right next to the Music Conservatory. Herbert Anatolyevich used to come here in despair over his inability to help his father, who was dying of cancer. He would come here harboring a secret hope: what if a miracle happened?

At the time an almost Hoffmannesque old woman worked here as a pharmacist. A head garment, something of a cross between a sleeping cap and a nurse's cap, shrouded her yellow wrinkled head. Her lower lids drooped, like half-open mussels. Herbert Anatolyevich could barely stop himself from prescribing for her, instead of her mythical powders, some normal allopathic iron pills, or from recommending that she eat fresh liver, so pallid and livid were the old woman's mucous lids and lips. This livid paleness of her face blended with her jaundiced skin and acquired a deadly color at the very tip of her nose, so that one wondered if the old woman actually used the tip of her nose to make changes in the prescriptions that were delivered here from all over the city. Estranged from everything except her little white balls and ointments, the old pharmacist made Herbert Anatolyevich think of a trained bird. She almost never made any recommendations to anybody. And only occasionally, when with her watery eyes she spied a visitor that for some reason attracted her attention, would the old woman utter a chortle, and the wrinkles in front of her ears and along her chin would stretch like wires, and words of sorcery would clatter out of the livid slit of her mouth onto the counter: "belladonna, dulcamara, pulsatilla . . ."

Herbert Anatolyevich observed how mesmerized provincials would step aside to a table and jot these words down in their notebooks. And then they would speak the old woman's words back to her, and she, in turn, would tense the wires of her wrinkles, bare her small yellow teeth, and place little paper boxes containing tiny magic balls onto the counter and name their price. But was this the real price of sorcery? And the poor country bumpkins would hurry to the cash register and pay for triple or quadruple portions, so that at home, in Cockroachinsk or some other place in the middle of nowhere, they themselves could practice the sorcery of healing, trying to emulate the old woman from the homeopathic pharmacy. Yet today Herbert Anatolyevich was suddenly and powerfully drawn to this unforgettable pharmacist. He understood what he suddenly had a yearning for. And now, like twenty years ago, Muscovites and visitors from the provinces crowded the narrow hall, all of them yearning for a miraculous cure. They pushed their way to the little window in the tinted glass partition, shouting strange, incantation-like names that grated on Herbert Anatolyevich's ears. After all, he had never stopped believing in allopathic medicine.

All these people eventually made their way to the window and obtained their medicines. And when the medicine wasn't available, they would leave, despondent, their heads downcast. And just like twenty years ago, when Herbert Anatolyevich would come secretly dreaming of a miracle, he once again saw the old woman. There could be no doubt it was her: the same cap, starched and yellowed with time, adorned with barely visible thin lace; the same thin ribbons that trimmed the small area around her bilious-yellow cheeks, shriveled like fallen apples. The same livid-grey inner eyelids, flung open and protruding away from the orbits. Now they resembled dead, not living, mussels. The same little irises, faded grey with brown specs—like sparrow eggs. Herbert Anatolyevich pushed his way through a small crowd of out-of-towners, who weren't buying any remedies, but just stood there, transfixed, staring at the old woman, and he got up close to the counter window.

"What do you need?" The old woman asked, looking directly into Doctor Levitin's eyes. Her eyelids contracted for an instant and immediately released her jaundiced eyeballs.

"I'd like . . . I'd like something calming," Herbert Anatolyevich muttered, and he thought he saw a flash of something in the old woman's eyes, a movement that one can see in the eyes of animals endowed with a third lid, a blinking membrane. Pressing herself close to the little window and poking out her jaundiced face like a bird from a birdhouse, the old woman asked Doctor Levitin, "And do you have a PRESCRIPTUS?"

Seeing bewilderment in Herbert Anatolevich's eyes and posture—his hat slid all the way down to his eyebrows and dislodged his glasses, exposing his helpless nearsighted eyes—the old woman said to him, "If they REFUSE to issue you a PRESCRIPTUS again," and she cast a glance to the right and diagonally over Levitin's shoulder, across Herzen Street, where the dead-end Khlynovsky Alley slithered past the building that housed the appeals office of the Visa Section, where Dudko and Aniskina received refuseniks. "If they refuse, then your case is without hope. Homeopathy is powerless."

The old woman lurched and backed up, running her fingers over the tags of the little drawers filled with medicines like an organist playing the keys of her universe, and then she ducked under something, perhaps a secret passage. A certain association, a hunch really, germinated in Herbert Anatolyevich's inflamed imagination, but this flare of insight was quickly extinguished because he hadn't gathered enough evidence to make a conclusive determination. All of that awaited in the future, and his premonition didn't deceive him. It wasn't by chance that the encounter with the old woman preceded his visit to the live queue of refuseniks.

What awaited him was the appeals office, but before that, there was a queue to get in. Across the street stood an old, turn-of-the-century apartment house with an archway. A vacant lot stretched out further down this dead-end alley, apparently resulting from the ongoing demolition of old Moscow's decrepit buildings. From the back, a tall brick wall abutted the vacant lot; the wall's jagged top resembled a prison wall. The prison itself had been neglected and slated for demolition but never torn down, as though it was awaiting renovation instead. Maybe the wall was left standing as a warning for the queue. Whether owing to a twist of fate or to governmental wisdom, the queue wasn't dispersed. Instead, it seemed to enjoy some official patronage, as if the regime wanted to juxtapose it to the disorganized, spontaneous little groups of protesters that occasionally sprouted up here and in other government offices one visited to lodge an appeal.

In the middle of this queue, which, at the time of Herbert Anatolyevich's arrival, numbered between one and two hundred people, there stood a tall man in a Tyrolean hat and an autumn leather coat trimmed with grey faux fur. With a stern and agitated look, he gazed out over the queue, like a shepherd examining the herd that had returned to the village. Everything about the tall man in the Tyrolean hat—his distinctive tanned face with a permanent dark brown shadow of the sunset, his bright blue eyes, a large hump nose that sharply cut through the cheek line—bespoke someone who used to hold a position of high leadership. In the crowd you could hear people say "Izya, Izya, Izya," calling their leader in a tender and familiar way. They all called each other by diminutives: Zhenya, Marik, Tolya, Alik, Dodik. This crowd had turned into a queue, but hadn't yet acquired the characteristics of an organization; it had, however, lost the gutless, consumerist, cheap attributes of a simple and accidental grouping of people. In this queue, a free and democratic spirit ruled, reminiscent of a *veche*—a medieval Slavic popular assembly. There was no power of position, money, or status here. The sole function of this queue, formed beside the Wailing Wall, was to protect and uphold this concord, to preserve a peaceful and legal communication channel between the queue and the appeals office. The channel between the line and the appeals office was the only remaining means for Jews to express their will—both the Jews who had already received a refusal from the Visa Section and those who for a year and a half had waited without receiving an answer. There were also people here who were simply unable to surmount the formalities of filing for an exit visa. Not to depart from the truth of life, it's worth saying that not only Jews were waiting in this queue. One would also come across ethnic Germans, Ukrainians, Russians, and also people of other nationalities.

Herbert Anatolyevich saw a sturdy-looking, not very tall fellow in his thirties, with the face of a kind and devoted bulldog. He wasn't wearing a hat, which he didn't need anyway because he had very thick and coiled kinky hair. The sad, dark eyes of this fellow followed Izya's every movement as he held a briefcase like a tray. Izya put a roster book on this briefcase and started the roll call. Never before had Herbert Anatolyevich heard such a great variety of Jewish last names recited in a row. One could use this list as an ethnographic guide, tracing the history and geography of the Jewish Diaspora. There were truly ancient biblical names here, the sound of which varied with the many tribal suffixes that had stuck to them throughout thousands of years of wandering: Levi, Levin, Levit, Levitin, for instance, or Kogan, Kon, Koen, Kan, Kagan. The Sephardim had contributed the bearers of the names Pérez and Jiménez to this gloomy vacant lot at the Wailing Wall. Germanic last names, German- and Yiddish-derived, dominated on the list: Fleyshman, Abezguaz, Bernshteyn, Shrayer, Rappaport, Bergman, Fisher, Fishbeyn, Soyfer, Shvarts, Shifman, Averbakh, Vaksmakher, Reyn, Nayman, Kushner, Kaufman, and so on, which made sense, given the origins of Russian Jews.

Among these last names belonging to Jews from all over Russia, from the Baltics, Ukraine, and Belarus, there were also conspicuous last names of ethnic Germans from Altai and Kazakhstan, a bunch of whom stood to the side, congregating around their own leader, who went by the name Rudy. Rudy communicated directly with Izya. The Germanic last names were now and then interjected with last names in which Slavic endings and suffixes were conjoined with the roots that represented original Jewish names and words: Khaimovich, Rabinovich, Solomonov, Beylin, Aronov. But there were also typically Russian, Ukrainian, Georgian, or Central Asian last names, and those attested to the assimilation of Jews among the many nations of Russia: Druzhnikov, Biserkin, Chayko, Golovko, Isaakyan, Moshiashvili, Alayev, Avshalumov, and others. Izya would shout out one last name after another, and someone would answer, either for himself or for a friend who couldn't be at the roll call. Sometimes a last name on the list was unclaimed. In that case the queue would fervently discuss what could have happened. Should they cross the name off the list or not? That would mean losing two or three months of waiting in the queue to see Dudko and Aniskina. Or should the name be kept on the list in spite of three skipped roll calls? Sometimes someone from the queue would announce, "They emigrated." And in those moments the whole queue would come alive. It was possible; it could happen to us as well.

From time to time, black glossy sedans would pull out of the driveway near the entrance to the appeals office. They carried the bosses away from Khlynovsky Alley, leaving behind the vacant lot, the reception, the Wailing Wall, the indefatigable queue of refuseniks. The black sedans took the bosses back to their unofficial world of home life, a world that held everything needed for traditional happiness: a wife, children, grand-children, a color TV, provisions obtained at a special dispensary. In this unofficial world, they even socialized with Jewish families that hadn't blemished themselves by their decision to emigrate, and even some-times saw it fit for their daughters and sons to marry boys and girls from Jewish families. One of these limousines carried Dudko away from the grueling atmosphere of the appeals office, and another one carried Ani-skina. They weren't one and the same person, and each was blessed with a genial Russian first name given to them in childhood. People still called them by these names outside of the appeals office. But immediately upon turning at the corner onto Herzen Street, Dudko and Aniskina would force themselves to forget that the Jews who formed the queue also had nice first names they used at home; that they had children whose names they used with tenderness; that they had family members waiting for them in Israel, relatives who longed to see and embrace their Sofochka, Marik, Benchik, Minochka. Dudko and Aniskina would forget all that, or else how would they have been able to find the strength during their visiting hours to listen to the pleas of yet another twenty people, and then to spend a week or even two rummaging through the files of these twenty Jews and non-Jews from the endless queue.

Finally the tall man in a Tyrolean hat finished the roll call. Because among the twenty people Dudko and Aniskina received there was usually some person that was advanced to the head of the queue, Izya, as usual, proposed to include only nineteen names in tomorrow's list. Everyone agreed with him, and that was one of the manifestations of the queue's democratic self-rule. The crowd began to disperse, and Herbert Anatol-yevich noticed David Gertsel standing not far from Izya. They greeted each other, and Gertsel affably patted Doctor Levitin on the shoulder.

"Now you're with us, professor. Be brave. There are many such roll calls ahead."

"I hope not. I'm sure Dudko and Aniskina will figure this out. What's happened is so absurd. I've never been near anything classified."

"Okay. I also talked like that in the beginning. And now I've come to terms with it. I've donned the skin of a refusenik. I've found many new friends here in the queue. Your present condition is like an ungrounded canvas. Come on, professor, I'll introduce you to Izya. He is our backbone—the keeper of the queue."

And Gertsel took Herbert Anatolyevich over to meet Izya.

"Pleased, very pleased to meet you, Professor Levitin. Even though the circumstances that have brought us together aren't the happiest. But you, a doctor, don't have to get used to seeing suffering."

"Nowadays, more and more often, I've had to see my very own suffering."

"Remember the Gospel according to Luke: 'Physician, heal thyself.'"

Herbert Anatolyevich briefly told Izya how he applied for an exit visa and and got refused.

"So you just wrote on the form: 'We protest the decision.' Good for you and your wife. That's a neat formula and a vehicle of protest. Mark, how do you like it?" Izya turned to his helper. "'We protest the decision,' written down on the piece of office paper they use. 'We protest the decision!' Listen, my friend, what if the queue rewards the good professor for his formula by offering him number 20, conditionally, for tomorrow's office hours?"

"Suggestion accepted. The queue will support it. But the chances of being received by Dudko and Aniskina on a conditional number are about twenty-five percent. Will the professor take the risk?" Mark looked at Izya with a question, then shifted his glance onto Herbert Anatolyevich—his disheveled frame, sunken cheeks, dark lenses barely concealing the circles of his hollowed eyes.

The refusal the Visa Section had handed down to them aged Doctor Levitin by ten years. He looked like an old man who could barely carry the burden of despair.

"So will you take the chance, professor?" asked Izya.

"I'll keep trying, even if there's just one in a thousand chance."

"Excellent. We'll place bets on every card."

"Except the marked ones."

"That's exactly the problem. Not only do they not show us the deck before the game, but they don't even tell us who to play with and on what terms. But there's nothing we can do. The dealer holds the cards. See you tomorrow, professor."

"Until then."

WHY AM I writing all this? The circle has closed. Winter has passed. And spring has brought me and my family sorrow and disappointment. I'm a refusenik, a pariah, a disenfranchised citizen. They first deprived me of the natural means of self-expression—to work in my field—and then they took away my writer's identification card. Everything that I write will most probably be lost, disappear. I'm merely wasting the time I must use to earn my daily bread. But I don't have it in me to lead a practical life. I'm writing the life of Doctor Levitin. Beyond a field overgrown with coastal sedge and reeds lies the living and breathing element of the Baltic Sea. Yesterday a plane flew over the Baltic, carrying the writer Vasily Aksyonov away from his native land. Another little thread has been cut. There will come a time when this day, 22 July 1980, will be considered a sad moment in the history of Russian literature. One more Russian talent has been set free. But how dear is this freedom to him away from his homeland? Dear Lord, when will Russia find the courage and strength to let her children live for her sake but not beyond her borders? To live without constantly having to look back, without hysteria; to live according to one's conscience.

It's summer vacation season here in Estonia. Jews come to Pärnu from all over the USSR to feel comfortable just being themselves and being with each other. They come here so that their children won't be embarrassed by their Jewishness and develop a complex of being *unlike* the ethnic Russian children. Estonians are indifferent toward Jewish problems. Here in Pärnu, there's a tradition of publically showing respect for famous, officially recognized Jews. The great chosen used to be the violinist David Oistrakh, and presently it's the poet David Samoylov (Kaufman). The great poet is being driven around in a Mercedes. A gorgeous automobile with wondrous oversized headlights speeds past me. In the window I can see Samoylov's large head, concealed behind the wondrously oversized headlights of his eyeglasses. But the Mercedes doesn't stop. The poet doesn't see me. Actually he's trying not to notice what's happening around him. The great poet is preoccupied with questions of ancient history. I return to writing the life of Doctor Levitin.

From time to time, I go with my son to fish off the stone jetty. I want to keep walking along this stone arrow pointing toward the West. At the end of the jetty, a lighthouse. Farther out, the open sea with coast guard boats and airplanes. My son and I know that, and we stop in the middle of this rocky ridge. We cast our lines and fish. This distracts me from my heavy thoughts. Oh Lord! When will this ever end: endless and pointless conversations that one cannot escape, like burdensome, wearying dreams. Oh, Lord! Why this strip of sand on the Baltic shore and not the free spirit of the Sinai? Why are these garrulous, talented, and weak-willed people waiting their turn at a café or waiting for an exit visa; why are they my brothers? What is it that unites us and makes us kin? Is it only the blood of our slaughtered ancestors?

ﻉ

IT WASN'T EVEN seven in the morning when all the nineteen people from the top of the queue, awaiting a meeting with Dudko and Aniskina, plus the twentieth—Herbert Anatolyevich—stood shoulder to shoulder together near the entrance to the appeals office. A company car from the editorial offices of *The Whistle* passed by those waiting in line. Three dogs were hanging out in the vacant lot right near the Wailing Wall: a German shepherd, an Irish setter, and a boxer. Their owners were yawning and stealing glances at the small group of Jews pressed against each other. Whether it was from the cold (the end of October had brought spells of morning frost) or from stress, Herbert Anatolyevich felt an indomitable thirst for communication with another human being. He struck up a conversation with number 19, a clear-eyed, round-faced young man of about twenty, who stood there with his arms around a girl who looked about eighteen, olive-skinned and silent.

"Were you also refused?" Herbert Anatolyevich asked the round-faced young man.

"Yes. And it's so ludicrous. My other family members, father, mother and sister, left for Israel a year ago. And we," the young man looked at his companion, "we were refused for having 'access to classified materials.' Before retirement my wife's father," again he glanced at the girl, "worked as chief economist at the Ministry of Agriculture. He has no intention of emigrating. And so, what do you know: they refused us an exit visa."

The girl leaned even closer to her husband, as if asking for forgiveness. Izya and Mark stood at the head of the queue. Izya always made sure to be there on the days that Dudko and Aniskina received petitioners. It was important to preserve the order in the queue. Every time some "unorganized" visitors would show up on the visiting days. Their local friends told them to come here from Kazakhstan and the Caucasus, from Ukraine, from Leningrad and Odessa. Visitors from Odessa were especially pushy. They each had their own story, their own truth and hope, their own family, and each thought this was their only chance to persuade Dudko and Aniskina that the Visa Section's decision to refuse them an exit visa to Israel was unfair. These disorderly—"wild"—competitors were a threat to the queue. They would upset the pace. After all, Dudko and Aniskina received exactly twenty people. And that included the out-of-turn visitors, whom they personally summoned into their offices. This is why Izya personally greeted his fretful wards trembling from the morning chill and from nervous tension, and he gave them his last instructions.

"Hold on to each other. Don't let anybody butt in until you've registered for your appointment. Not anybody. Don't let feelings get in your way."

Herbert Anatolyevich was waiting, his shoulder pressed against the back of the round-faced young man, when a woman with disheveled hair sticking out from under her fluffy white head scarf approached the beginning of the queue.

"Have they already registered today's petitioners?" the woman asked a grim old lady standing in the middle of Izya's "team."

"No, they haven't started the registration," answered the old lady, a musician who was the widow of a retired colonel, and she turned away from the woman wearing the fluffy scarf. The old lady had been refused because her late husband allegedly had access to classified information.

"I beg you, please let me into the queue. I could only get away for one day from Leningrad. I have an extreme situation." The woman in the fluffy scarf began to cry, trying to talk to someone, anyone, in the queue.

"We all have extreme situations. And we don't let anybody ahead of the line. Not for anything! My wife ended up in the hospital from the stress," shouted out a short man in a Finnish hat trimmed with lambskin. The hat shifted to the back of his head, and the man was shouting and shouting hysterically, stomping his feet, and becoming more and more incensed.

The woman in the fluffy scarf recoiled from this man and turned instead to a burly guy with a prominent face and hanging jowls, who was standing toward the end of the queue.

"Maybe you'll let me in?"

"Only behind me."

"May I please? May I . . . May I . . ." the woman from Leningrad kept on repeating as she collided with the queue. And like a billiard ball that was hit clumsily against the side, she kept bouncing further and further back toward the end of the queue. With the corners of her fluffy scarf, she kept smearing her tears, so that her eyes looked pasted over—either with the fluff from the scarf or with her running mascara.

"Please, let me in. Have a heart." The woman in the fluffy scarf was bawling next to the round-faced young man and his wife, right in front of Herbert Anatolyevich. But the loving girl held on to her husband even tighter, shielding him from the Leningrad woman.

"Well, maybe you?" the Leningrad woman asked Herbert Anatolyevich without any hope in her voice.

Herbert Anatolyevich's first impulse was to go, leaving this woman in his stead. In fact he had wanted to offer it earlier, when she was in the beginning and then the middle of the queue, but he didn't want to look like an upstart. As it was, he was practically a figurehead. And these doubts (all of his life he had tried not to be conspicuous), these doubts, and the urgent need to help his own son above all else, had at first prevented him from yielding his spot to this despondent woman. Besides, and this partially vindicated Herbert Anatolyevich in his own eyes, he wasn't all that confident of his own status as a bearer of the conditional number 20, so it would've been foolish to volunteer before the others—the ones with the real numbers—and to mislead this woman from Leningrad with his own dubious spot. Without trying to convince anybody or to seek anybody's opinion, Herbert Anatolyevich suffered painful doubts as he silently stood before the woman in the fluffy shawl.

Seeing that he wasn't outright refusing to help her, the woman went up closer to Herbert Anatolyevich and whispered, "I beg you. For the sake of all that's holy. For your son."

How did she know about his son? Herbert Anatolyevich shivered as he stepped out of the queue. But immediately a harsh voice reached him from behind his back. "God damn you all! Not a single dog is getting in ahead of us. There're many of you and only a few of us, and we also want to escape. If you leave the queue, that's your choice. But one of our people will take your place."

These crude, squawking words stabbed him like a bayonet, and he gasped for breath from surprise and outrage. He turned to the person who had shouted. A huge redheaded guy with light blue eyes stood behind him. This giant whopper of a guy stood with his hands in the pockets of his black leather coat and his legs far apart, as if ready for a fistfight. This was Rudy, the leader of the German refuseniks. Rudy was breathing heavily, spit foaming in the corners of his mouth, and his cheeks, with their deep tan the color of red bricks and overgrown with stubble, puffed like those of a ferocious bulldog. A small bunch of people flanked Rudy. The men were dressed in short coats with collars of sheared lamb, the women in jackets of rough velveteen. They looked a great deal like ordinary Russian collective farmers, except for a certain shared resoluteness or wrath directed against something they all understood, a wrath shining in their eyes faded from the sun of Kazakhstan and Altai. Russian peasant faces are kinder, even in utter despair. Or they can become wildly mischievous. But this was a measured and uniform wrath of a people who couldn't find their place in this land, and who had been unjustly ascribed to it. Thank God, Izya came up to them just in time.

"See here, professor, nobody should break the rules of the queue. Otherwise it goes bad for the rest of the people. Calm down, Rudy. Everything will be okay."

Rudy retreated a bit, angrily mumbling curses in German. The woman in the Orenburg fluffy shawl also walked away, having suddenly stopped crying. The mighty frame of a law enforcement officer appeared in the entrance. Like Gulliver regarding noisy Lilliputians, he kept lowering his condescending gaze at these bristling people as he ran his fingers over the metallic studs on his belt and holster, like an accordion player pressing the keys.

Exactly at nine o'clock, the officer stepped back slowly and went up the small inner stairs that led to the appeals office. All twenty people from the top of the queue followed the officer, their hands placed on each others' shoulders so that nobody could sneak up to the registration and information department before them. Besides the petitioners who came in connection with their emigration proceedings, this place was also frequented by ex-cons: embezzlers, prostitutes, burglars, swindlers, robbers, card sharks. They had all served their terms and now wanted to ask "the bosses" about their lot. But their bosses weren't Dudko and Aniskina. It was much easier to get an appointment with their bosses. In general these criminals felt much more uninhibited than the Jews. They immediately figured out that the Jewish queue was foreign, not for their own kind, and they walked around it like it had the plague. And even the law enforcement officer treated them benevolently, eagerly giving them sensible pieces of advice. Several times the officer, for reasons known to him alone, would give a sign to Izya and Mark, and they would move their people, set them up one by one, and count the whole crew. Finally some old woman passed by, shuffling her worn-out shoes, and disappeared behind a partition in the registration and information department, locking the door from the inside.

"The typist is here . . . the typist is here . . . Now they'll start the registration." The words crept down the queue. The Jews perked up and started to go through their pockets, bags, and briefcases, getting passports and petitions ready. The petitions were not to be handed to the typist, but directly to Dudko and Aniskina. Herbert Anatolyevich managed to make out the hunched over figure of the old woman and the contour of her face, jaundiced and pleated with heavy wrinkles, as she flitted through the doorway of the veneer partition covered in cheap varnish, which separated the typist's cubicle from the waiting area. And this hunchbacked typist, the old woman on whose long-awaited arrival everybody pinned their hopes; this yellow, windowless waiting area; the faces filled with suffering—all of this brought Herbert Anatolyevich to a state of jaundiced emptiness and anguish, particularly so when he remembered how they had all refused to help the woman in the fluffy white shawl. And even though he was overcome with such apathy and repulsion to everything, his hands continued to hold on tightly to the shoulders of the round-faced young man standing in front of him. Finally, after everyone formed a line before the typist's window, they took a recount. Holding the list, Izya started to let his Jews proceed toward registration.

Upon seeing Herbert Anatolyevich's upset and bewildered face, Izya called him over and said, under his breath, "You're unbelievably lucky, professor. There are no extras to see Dudko and Aniskina today. So gather your thoughts and concentrate on the language of your petition."

Over and over again, Herbert Anatolyevich kept analyzing the petition he had prepared for Dudko and Aniskina. And again he just couldn't figure out what it was in his or in Tatyana's life that might have given the Visa Section officials cause to refuse their family's emigration request. Was it, perhaps, that senseless story of his late father-in-law's letter? But Vasily Matveyevich was now long deceased, and if he had been the cause, then the refusal would have come earlier in the spring. The Jews were signing in, and Herbert Anatolyevich was already within reach of the typist's window, yet the petitioners would now and then have to yield their turn to the ex-cons, and so it was almost 10:00 a.m. when he finally faced the registration window. The old typist sat sideways to him inside her tiny cubicle. She grabbed Levitin's passport with her right hand, while with her left, she flipped through the files stored in filing drawers.

"Levitin, Herbert Anatolyevich," mumbled the old woman. "Have you been to the appeals office before?"

"No. Only once in the Moscow City Visa Section."

"First time, then." The typist stopped flipping through the index cards, and with her left hand she took out a blank form from the bottom section of her desk. Then she typed Herbert Anatolyevich's passport data into the form.

"What's the nature of your appeal?"

"I'm here with regard to going to Israel," Herbert Anatolyevich answered, and to his horror and shame, he realized that he was becoming frozen with fear. The typist looked exactly like the old woman in the homeopathic pharmacy: the same grey speckled eyes, set in wide-open, livid, tearing lids; slicked back hair under a cap, its yellowed lacy edge peeking from under a head scarf; a jaundiced, ruched neck. And most importantly, a third lid—a blinking membrane—flashed, quivered, and disappeared before Herbert Anatolyevich's eyes. With this quivering, the gaze of the old woman typist—and it was undoubtedly her—became predatory for a moment, like that of a hungry owl poised at some easy prey. But Izya was already hurrying Doctor Levitin along, leading him away from the window and helping him onto a chair.

"So, there you go, professor. The scary part's over. Now, as the rail-road information service tells you when you telephone there: 'Wait. Wait. Wait.' Just like that, and don't hang up."

Herbert Anatolyevich settled into the waiting mode, now trying to concentrate on the contents of the book he brought from home, now listening in to fragments of conversations. A huge fan, suspended from the ceiling and resembling a windmill, was spinning, and Herbert Anatolyevich kept on going over and over his life to the rhythm of the fan's blades—soulless, but equally fair toward all. It was clear to him that the life of his family had come right to the edge of a precipice, and if today he received no help, the fall couldn't be averted, and further struggle would be useless. The only thing left would be to wait for the finale.

This appeals office was, as Herbert Anatolyevich reckoned, the last available option, the final line, a dead zone separating the real life for which he had prepared himself as well as he knew how, and a life controlled by dark, otherworldly powers. Dark powers that were con-ducting a mad and unstoppable spectacle, one they provisionally called real life, but which was actually designed for plywood puppets, not for friends, citizens, people. Suddenly he imagined that the old woman typist and her secret files ensured the boundary between the world of marionettes—real, even though ruled by the laws of acting on stage—and the world of dark secret powers; this was akin to the old woman from the homeopathic pharmacy guarding the boundary between the suffering people and the dark secret powers capable of cur-ing them or letting them perish.

Feeling totally crushed, Herbert Anatolyevich sat there for another two or three hours, talking to no one and taking no interest in what Dudko and Aniskina said to those who already had their interviews. He had come to a final realization that one could draw no analogies and find no common patterns between so-called real life and the will of dark secret powers. This had nothing to do with laws of natural sci-ences or social sciences; no cruel truth of logic here, nor crafty truth of philosophy. Even religiosity—a belief in the supernatural, even idealism and pantheism as its extreme version representing an indifference to the individual fates of the human species—any forms of worshiping of a unified idea were alien and foreign to this bacchanalia of principles and deeds. Even the implacable doctrine of monotheism or the childish nimbleness of pagan beliefs was closer to the human soul, and at least erected temples for communicating with the gods. None of this could be in any way compared to the surrogates of ethics, law and justice, created in the image of the appeals office. While thinking his own thoughts, Herbert Anatolyevich also overheard stories of how Dudko and Aniskina were skeptical about the prospects of emigration for a young married couple, both of them ballet dancers, while they gave that old lady, the musician, some hope. Doctor Levitin understood that all the words the Jews heard from the officials in the appeals office were but a palliative measure, a means of distraction, a way of letting off steam, while the individual fate of each of them depended on the correspondence of the dark secret powers. It was with this feeling that Herbert Anatolyevich stood in the small hallway near the entrance to Dudko and Aniskina's office, clutching the briefcase with his petition inside, the petition that now seemed useless to him. And yet, when a woman in a brown pinafore dress, who he surmised was Aniskina, came out of that office, and when this woman, without looking at Herbert Anatolyevich but only staring at an index card, announced, "Levitin, Herbert Anatolyevich," his heart quivered, he forced himself to think about his case and to have faith in the significance of the upcoming conversation—otherwise his last chance of saving Anatoly from the army would be lost.

The woman in a brown pinafore dress, Svetlana Mikhailovna Aniskina, invited Doctor Levitin into the office with a gesture of the hand free of the index card, then followed him inside, and closed the door. She sat in the corner of her office at a small desk, cluttered with folders and rolodex files, and also some recording devices, and busied herself with something that was neither visible nor audible. From that moment on, Herbert Anatolyevich didn't feel Aniskina's presence. She worked so quietly, it was as if she had nothing to do with his conversation with Dudko. This being so, Herbert Anatolyevich had heard from pundits in the queue that it was she—this modest-looking, unimposing woman with a pleasant, or rather unprepossessing face—who actually prepared refuseniks' files for the appeals board. This way an anesthesiologist, hidden behind a green screen that separates her from the operating area, holds the patient's life in her hands.

"Please have a seat, Herbert Anatolyevich," said the man in an unbuttoned navy blue jacket and a light brown open collar shirt.

Pyotr Isayevich Dudko's entire appearance gave one the impression of a Cossack's slightly coarse camaraderie, but also an essential open-heartedness. A person knocked off his habitual pace by the indifferent bureaucratic ways, and by being yanked from one office to another, could hardly resist the allure of this openheartedness. Pyotr Isayevich's dark hair, peppered with grey, was cavalierly combed back and hanging down over the sides of his powerful Karl-Marxian head. His deeply furrowed wide forehead, his large face with its prominent cheekbones, and his oily brown eyes spoke of willfulness, theatricality, and slyness that was common to those hailing from the south of Russia. Dudko took out a large, pink-checkered handkerchief, and wiped his face and neck. He wiped gently, dabbing rather than swiping off sweat, careful not to rip off the Band-Aid that a surgeon had placed over a lanced furuncle. Doctor Levitin was immediately struck by the contrast between the sickly pale color of Dudko's skin and his powerfully built body and animated eyes. Such sickly pallor is not uncommon among archivists, warehouse managers, and prison guards—those who spend most of their lives in basements and other places hidden below the ground, with artificial light and poor ventilation. Dudko's sweating and constant thirst for water (he kept on pouring himself effervescent Borjomi and drinking it from a glass), and on top of that his furuncles, all told Doctor Levitin that Dudko was seriously ill with diabetes. But here, in the appeals office, it was not a patient and a doctor, but a ruler of fate and a doomed man; well, maybe not a ruler of fate, but certainly a herald of and a liaison to the rules of fate. Herbert Anatolyevich still remained a doomed man who had come to beg to have the verdict reconsidered. No, the doomed one wasn't Pyotr Isayevich Dudko, even though his diabetes was life-threatening, and the role that he was now playing wasn't that of a doomed man. Doomed was Herbert Anatolyevich Levitin, who would normally be treating a sick patient and not dying from fear, shame, and humiliation because he, a physician, was visiting places such as this office instead of helping patients. Conflicts as strange as this one give life its flavor: a gravely ill henchman and his victim, also his potential savior; glutinous shirkers and hungry peasants; a vapid cabaret actress and a genius madly in love with her, selling his verses to fund her pimp's new silk underclothes. Dudko's eyes, small, oily, and perceptive, ran over Doctor Levitin's face and frame and stopped on his briefcase.

"Did you bring the petition?" Dudko asked.

"Yes, of course, here it is."

Herbert Anatolyevich handed Dudko a sheet of paper covered with his clear professorial handwriting. Holding the petition with his left hand, and a ballpoint pen in his right hand, Dudko pored over the text, reading it carefully, going line by line over Herbert Anatolyev-ich's exhaustive explanation that due to the very nature of his work, he couldn't in any way have access to classified information, and his wife Tatyana Vasilyevna all the more so. It was all so logically and systemati-cally presented, complete with references going back to the first articles he published in domestic journals during his student years, and, during his later years as a full professor, in foreign journals still totally accessible to the public, that it must leave not even a shadow of doubt that an error must have been made by the Visa Section. Remembering this, Herbert Anatolyevich suddenly became calm. He certainly appreciated the way Pyotr Isayevich was working with the text of his petition, unhurriedly and carefully, pausing at specific places and underlining them with a thick stroke of the pen, taking an interest in the meaning of what it said. It nearly resembled the work of a demanding but well-wishing editor on a manuscript. Herbert Anatolyevich no longer felt any antipathy toward this sick man who was smart and educated, and who in spite of his serious illness and his job (he occupied a rather senior position) was sitting and diligently working with his papers. Besides the Levitins' petition, Dudko had spread on the table before him Herbert Anatolyevich's index card, a folder with string fasteners, and also some other documents. Dudko was consulting all these materials while reading Doctor Levitin's petition. Finally he finished his perusal. Once again Dudko reviewed the places he had underlined and some of the other papers. He glanced at his assistant, who was diffidently waiting in the corner; shook himself out after a minute of deep contemplation; and then asked, as if nodding to her, "So what is it you want, Herbert Anatolyevich?"

"I request that the decision of the Visa Section be reconsidered. It's unjust. You can see very clearly that my family has had nothing to do with classified information."

"And have you served in the army, Herbert Anatolyevich?"

"No. Never."

"And have you never visited patients in military hospitals?" Dudko screwed up his eyes. On his face there was an expression of excitement and rush, of the kind common to hunters and anglers before they hear the whistle of the game or feel that the fish are about to start biting, and then it was replaced by an expression of concentration and clear purpose.

"I was never employed at a military hospital. But . . ."

"Go ahead, I'm listening."

"But . . . once . . . I was invited to the hospital at Krasnye Kholmy. They wanted me to consult—meet with the staff physicians—on the condition of General Lanskoy. By the way, it was a bad case of diabetes."

Herbert Anatolyevich looked at Dudko and, embarrassed by his inadvertent lack of tact, he lost track of his account and fell silent.

"You were invited to the hospital at Krasnye Kholmy. I understand. And do you remember if they had to issue a special pass for you?"

"I believe so. Actually, at that time it was of no importance to me. I just wanted to get the patient out of a coma and to assign the proper treatment for him."

"Yes, of course. A physician's duty. But do understand, Herbert Anatolyevich, that the people who check documents and get them ready for the Visa Section review board, these people also have a duty. They cannot ignore or fail to account for certain kinds of facts, just like you, Herbert Anatolyevich, cannot ignore the symptoms of an illness or the results of laboratory tests. You have the Hippocratic oath, and we . . . they have an oath of their own."

"Pyotr Isayevich, during that consult I didn't learn anything besides the symptoms and the test results. A standard hospital with a typical corridor. A functioning elevator. A comfortable ward. General Lansky was the only one there. He was in such serious condition that he could barely speak with anyone. What sort of state secrets, good God!"

"Indeed, we are only having a conversation, Herbert Anatolyevich. Together let's find a way out of your situation."

"Yes, you're right. Quite a situation it is. A torturous situation. Not only have I found myself in it, but also my wife and my son. We all had assumed we'd be treated humanely, given the Soviet government's position on reunification of families. We believed in, and we continue to believe in, the Helsinki Accords."

Dudko's face acquired a stern expression.

"Let's stay away from such declarations. I work with facts only, so let's leave declarations for different offices."

By accident or deliberately, Dudko turned around and looked through the window toward a huge sign advertising *The Whistle* newspaper, which loomed large at the far end of the alley.

"How does your wife feel about your plans?"

"She shares my desire to be reunited with my family members."

"But isn't Tatyana Vasilyevna Russian by nationality? Why this desire to leave her native land only for the sake of her husband's relatives, whom not only she, but you, my dear Herbert Anatolyevich, have never seen in person? Don't you find that strange?"

"For a good family it isn't strange."

"Do you think you have a good family?"

"Yes I do. Anyhow, this goes well beyond the limits of the issue at hand. Doesn't it, Pyotr Isayevich?"

"Well, that actually depends. Perhaps we agents of law enforcement aren't as optimistic as you physicians are. Although in a certain way we're colleagues; you treat human illnesses, and we treat society's illnesses. In total this comprises the illnesses of humanity. But don't let me wax poetic. Let's return to our sheep. And what about your son? What does your son think of your plans, Herbert Anatolyevich?"

"My son is a Jew, and he wants to live in a Jewish state."

"Are you sure, Herbert Anatolyevich? In his passport, and the application filed with the Visa Section confirms the passport data, there it says that Anatoly Herbertovich Levitin is Russian by nationality. And according to the laws of the country where your son is hoping to go, it is the custom to define a person's nationality by his mother. Would it be right for a Russian lad to fight for the interests of Israel? And you know, people do get killed in a war. Do you expect us to be indifferent to such a melancholy prospect?"

"Do you mean to say that we were refused because of Anatoly?"

"There you go again, Herbert Anatolyevich, pushing our general conversation onto some specific track. We're merely discussing things, you and I. Looking for ways to resolve your situation. So let's please help each other."

Dudko got up and gave his assistant a weighty look. Herbert Anatolyevich stood up.

"Thank you, Pyotr Isayevich. When may I expect to hear about the result of our conversation and my petition?"

"They will telephone you within two weeks."

LIKE A MAGNET, the telephone constantly attracted the Levitins. Each ring could be the one from the Visa Section. Two weeks went by. Then two more weeks. It was as if Herbert Anatolyevich had never made that visit to the appeals office, and the conversation with Dudko had never taken place. Had the old woman from the homeopathic pharmacy and her double, the typist from the appeals office, been but a dream? All these images had vanished, covered over with irreality, like a calf lost in a marshy swamp. Now the phone no longer pulled them but repelled, elicited an urge to smash into pieces this lifeless plastic muteness.

It was as though Anatoly noticed none of this. Or else he resigned himself to his lot as an army recruit, withdrew and constricted himself to his own—his and Natasha's—issues.

The family had scattered, fallen into disarray, only superficially residing under the same roof. Everyone was deep in their own thoughts, their own moods—and without a plan. Only one question remained: What will happen to us now?

One of those troubled days, when Anatoly was at his repair shop and Herbert Anatolyevich at the clinic, the mail carrier came, Tatyana's old acquaintance who had stopped being friendly after the Levitins had received their invitation from Israel. Now she brought the summons.

"From the Draft Board," said the mail carrier, without even concealing her glee and malice. "Sign here."

Tatyana turned pale. She signed without looking at the mail carrier and took the notice to the kitchen, still afraid to look at it. She sat there for several minutes in a total stupor, as if it they had delivered not a draft notice but a death notification, forcing her to acknowledge this horrible reality by signing her name. In those minutes she turned over in her mind Anatoly's entire life, starting with that bright summer day and the heady haystack where her son was conceived. The whole life of her little boy, whom now they were taking away from her in the name of military duty, brought her back to the terrifying dream she had lived through in Masha Teryokhina's *izba*. Again and again she imagined her little Tolik dressed in a military uniform without shoulder straps and a garrison cap without a red star. Just like then, on that polluted night, Tatyana felt the emptiness of the sleeve instead of her son's right arm. She was so distinctly aware of two simultaneous realities: the empty sleeve of her little boy's military uniform and the emptiness of her soul, as she sat in the kitchen, stared at the draft notice, and understood that something had to be done quickly to wrest her boy from the terrifying dream that was now becoming a reality.

And then Tatyana thought about Pavel. Not that it was the first time she had thought about him after that ill-fated meeting at her friend Masha's house. She never really let go of him; she just kept chasing the memories away. Now she decided that the time had come to save Anatoly, and her old flame was the one to do it, if her husband couldn't manage it with all of his academic titles, degrees, publications, and various accomplishments. She headed directly to the phone in her husband's study, shifting the carpet runner and not putting it straight. Her steps echoed through the deserted apartment like the nighttime hammering of a village watchman's rattle. Tatyana thought that even her husband's desk was looking at her askance, reproachfully and sadly, following her every movement, as if it weren't a desk but a wise old cow that was about to be taken to slaughter. And Herbert Anatolyevich's books, like witnesses, watched her as she dialed 09 and asked for the phone number of the City Draft Board Office. Books were watching her and whispering to each other, their pages rustling and their leather binding squeaking, these old tomes by the famous Russian doctors Zakharin, Filatov, and Herzen—the books from which generations of Russia's doctors learned their craft. Old tomes, bound in leather, from wise old cows who had once lived their lives, only to realize one day they were being taken away to the slaughterhouse.

Tatyana dialed the number of the City Draft Board, and when they answered, she asked to speak to Lieutenant Colonel Pavel Ivanovich Teryokhin. The receiver was banged on the table and grew silent, but some incomprehensible noises and scratches encroached from time to time. One imagined a lonely autumn field lying between orphaned bushes on the edge of a gloomy forest and a country road, also desolate and dark. The leftover rye stalks, weak and hollow, pierce the distended, mosslike air. No one and nothing moves along the road. Only occasionally would the jeep carrying the collective farm's chairman speed by; green and brown lumps, those vestiges of rain and cattle, splattered from under the wheels. And once again the wind howls in the roadside grasses, waning in the blue-grey muteness of the forest. Tatyana heard the wagon crawling along the road, sloshing in the puddles, leaning to one side and then to the other, and squeaking and rattling. Where did this wagon come from? At that moment Pavel Teryokhin's voice popped up.

"Lieutenant Colonel Teryokhin speaking."

"Pavel Ivanovich? Pasha—it's me, Tatyana."

The voice disappeared. But she could no longer hear the sounds of a country road. The wagon wasn't squeaking or rumbling. Maybe it was stuck in a rut. Tatyana could only hear her heart keeping time with her one and only thought: Save Tolik. Rescue Tolik. Free Tolik from the army.

Then Pavel's voice materialized. "I didn't even hope that you would call. And I didn't want to call myself. I think you know why."

"And here I am, calling you. Pasha, I have to see you."

"Yes, me too. Very much so. Did something happen?"

Tanya wanted to open up and tell him about Anatoly, but she was afraid. In their family they'd gotten used to saying, "We'll talk about that later. It's not a conversation for the telephone."

So she didn't say anything, so as to not get Pavel into trouble. One didn't talk about such things over the phone. And on top of that, one didn't start talking about business just like that, straight out of the fire, without first having a heart-to-heart talk like human beings.

"Something happened, but . . . ," Tatyana replied. "And you, Pasha? You don't sound very happy."

"Oh Tatyana." Pavel only sighed and said nothing else.

Probably he didn't want to talk in front of his coworkers. An officer really shouldn't get all emotional on the phone. They agreed to meet later that same day, at 6:30 p.m., in front of the food emporium on Smolenskaya Square.

Tatyana spent the whole day in anticipation of their meeting. She tried on different dresses, high-heeled shoes, foreign-made lingerie, bras, panties, stockings. She went through many things until she was pleased with the way she looked. It was hard living in a strange land without your soulmate. She could really have used Masha Teryokhina here. While she was carefully applying eye shadow and mascara, outlining her eyebrows, putting blush and powder on her cheeks, all along the words rang in her soul: I'm saving Tolik. I'm helping my son. I'm freeing the blood of my blood from being a recruit.

She left a note for her family members, telling them that an old friend from her home village had called and said she was in town for only one day. So Tatyana had to go see her in Biryulevo, and would probably come home late. She felt that the old women sitting on the bench at the entrance to the building glanced at her with suspicion; she was all made up with rosy cheeks, looking like a girl flying off to a date. And the working people, pushing at the accordion-like doors of the trolleybus, gave her looks of distrust and irritation. And a professor type, bent over with the weight of his overstuffed briefcase, looked at her with melancholy, sunken eyes. Hey four eyes, keep writing your dissertations, silly fool, Tatyana wanted to say to him. Drag them manuscripts around, you egghead, like my husband used to; it won't get you anywhere. But mostly she tried not to notice these looks, as she kept on muttering the same thing in her mind: For Tolik. For my boy's sake. And I don't need anything else. Just to free my son.

The trolleybus floated past the American Embassy, and dove into the semidarkness and the rumble of the tunnel. O Lord, Tatyana thought, closing her eyes for a minute and coming to her senses. O Lord! What am I doing? Am I not committing a sin, not just for my son's sake but for the sake of sin itself? Am I not already sinning? Will I, a sinner, help Tolik by my sins? Or will I make it even worse for him? Shouldn't I get off the trolleybus now and go home? Wouldn't it be better to calm down, not to fuss? Not to sin, even in my thoughts, but instead submit to destiny and *bear* it? But she rode to her stop, got off directly across from the tower building where, she'd heard, the foreign minister Gromyko himself had his head office, took the underpass to the other side where the giant tower stood, and then crossed Arbat Street and saw Pavel. He was standing right by the entrance to the food emporium, leaning on a cane.

Wearing his everyday greatcoat and officer's peaked cap and leaning on a cane, Pavel seemed to her older than during their drunken village tryst, and perhaps more severe looking.

"So you came, Tatyana, didn't you. And I've been hanging out here with my stupid stick, like a pauper at the church doors. Do you have some time now?"

"I do, Pasha."

"We can finally talk to each other. No rushing."

"I'm not in a hurry, dear heart."

And again she just couldn't tell him about the draft notice, postponing the conversation until a better moment.

"Then you know what, sweet girl, there's a pretty good eatery nearby. Rioni, Georgian food. You want to go there? See, like a real bachelor, I haven't even had lunch today. After you called, I wanted nothing else but to see you."

"What do you mean, like a real bachelor?"

"I didn't mean anything. Just a phrase that came to mind. My wife and kids haven't moved up here yet. They're staying with my wife's folks in Oryol. And I'm still waiting for an apartment. And in the meantime just renting a room. I lucked out, believe me. My landlord's some sort of actor. He's always on the road with his troupe. So one room he locks up, and the other's mine. Plus the rest of the apartment, with the kitchen, bathroom, and all that stuff."

"Having fun away from your wife, aren't you?"

"Don't say that, Tatyana. God forbid. I'm not like that. And how can I anyways, with this shaft? I'm just happy to crawl home from work and then back to the Draft Board. There's a ton of work these days. The autumn draft's just around the corner. And so much to do."

"Autumn draft, Pasha?"

"That's right. As soon as the ministry's order came out, the wheels started to spin here, nonstop, and this way until January. And your boy, what's his name?"

"Anatoly."

"What year was he born?"

"'Sixty-one. Don't you remember?"

"I remember. Sure," Pavel answered, frowning and turning morose. They walked another twenty or so steps without speaking.

"What month was he born in?" Pavel asked.

"Tolik? In April."

"So he's ours. Autumn draft. He'll be called up. You'll see what a stud he'll be when he comes home after two years in the army. You're going to love it."

Pavel was discussing these things that were as painful to Tatyana as a burning wound, as if this were a natural, ordinary paragraph in a field manual established forever, one that not only couldn't be changed or violated, but was also pointless, even silly to discuss. And once again Tatyana didn't say a word, couldn't get herself to tell Pavel about her big problem, even though she never let this thought out of her mind: "To help Tolik. To free him from this misfortune."

They plunged into the smoky warmth of the Georgian restaurant and found themselves sharing a table with a handsome guy with a horseshoe mustache, who was bearing his soul to a leggy young lady with a woodpecker nose dotted with blackheads and a mouth so bright red and predatory that one feared for her partner's future. Tatyana listened in to their conversation but couldn't make sense of it, because it was conducted in some other language, warped like a piece of tin, that used Russian words but produced incomprehensible sentences, their meaning revealed only to the lady and the handsome guy from the Caucasus. But at this moment Tatyana wouldn't have been able to understand even normal Russian speech, no matter who spoke it, except Pavel. To her everything seemed abnormal, everything except that *main task*, the one that she kept on convincing herself was the principal reason for coming here with Pavel Teryokhin.

If one were to analyze the state Tatyana was in since she had met with Pavel, or actually since her secret phone conversation with him, or perhaps since that moment when she received Anatoly's draft notice and convinced herself that her village beau would rescue her son, it could be said that a split had occurred in her soul. Or rather a damper had slipped off her split soul—already divided, as it is in everybody, into what's imagined, and what's real and usually closed off from imagination. It was as if there were two Tatyanas now: Anatoly's mother, who wanted to defend her son from an impending disaster; and a secret lover, a harlot, a common adulteress that had been dwelling within and now separated herself from the main Tatyana, from the mother. And it was still unclear which Tatyana was now sitting in this dive, permeated with tobacco smoke and wine, eating those poisoned ungodly viands and conversing with Pavel. Why then, if she hadn't been split in two, had she not immediately come to her *main task* and her dread—to her son? And what if the draft notice had arrived so as to make this tryst possible for the second Tatyana, the common adulteress?

"Well, that's how it is now, a life without the paratroopers," Pavel's voice layered over the neighbors' chatter. "Waiting for my wife and children. Living like a bachelor, all alone with my bum leg."

He was savoring his *satsivi*, Georgian chicken stewed with walnuts and garlic, collecting orange islands of sauce with bread and zestfully biting the flesh off the greasy pieces swimming on his plate.

"Why aren't you eating, Tatyana? At least drink something."

"I'll have a drink. Why don't you pour me some."

They both drank some cold white wine that made the glass sweat. It was wonderful to see these tender drops of moisture through the smoky air, as they rolled down when you barely touched the glass with your finger.

"Your husband won't be cross if you come home tipsy?"

"I'm not tipsy. And it's not a problem, Pasha. I left a note that I was going to meet a girlfriend from our village."

"That's good, that they trust you. And my schoolteacher—I come home from a little gathering like this one, and she keeps smelling my breath, smelling my breath, like a fox in a chicken coop. Phew."

Pavel spat at the thought of this agonizing lack of freedom coupled with guilt. He would always feel this way when he came home from drinking sprees with fellow officers or the occasional one night stands with women he barely knew. This persistent feeling of guilt before his unloved wife put more and more of a divide between them, infuriating him, and now giving him the right to luxuriate publically in this little restaurant with the woman he desired more than anything in the world.

"And your professor husband's probably jealous?"

"I don't know. I haven't given him reason to be jealous."

"And what if you had to?"

At this point Tatyana might have vehemently objected, cut short all this talk that kept creeping in the direction of the forbidden. To object and to transition to Anatoly's situation. But again she opted for silence, again she couldn't get herself to cut him short and turn the conversation in a different direction. They had finished their food and wine. It was time to leave, and Tatyana finally made up her mind, forcing herself to speak.

"Pasha, wait, it's about my Anatoly. If you could . . . you know . . . give him a hand? Help him get a deferral?"

Maybe the seasoned paratrooper figured out that their encounter had reached a breaking point. Or maybe, trained and practiced as he was in the art of rapid response to potential snafus behind enemy lines, even in a wine cellar heavy with smoke and revelry, his ears scanned the air like supersensitive trackers and his eyes pierced the space like night vision goggles with built-in cameras. Pavel shook off the alcohol, took point like a young soldier, and led Tatyana out of the restaurant.

"Later, Tatyana, we'll talk about all this later."

But he didn't forget to ask the waiter for another bottle of wine to go.

Pavel was walking a bit ahead of Tatyana, his cane pounding on the Arbat pavement and his injured leg grazing the water in the puddles, their surfaces glistening yellow under the streetlights. They didn't have far to walk. The actor, Pavel's landlord, lived on Kalinin Prospect in a new apartment building that opened like a huge stone book facing the street, a short distance from a little white stone church with emerald onion domes. The church stood on a knoll above Kalinin Prospect, like many churches standing on knolls over high river banks. Once, about ten years ago, Tatyana came to this church with her family. First the three of them went to a pet shop on the Arbat to buy a tank and fish for Tolik. Afterwards they visited a fish-breeding exhibit inside the little church. And even though Tatyana knew perfectly well this wasn't an active church but only a historical structure, and also that the building she and Pavel were about to enter was a modern apartment house with an express elevator, trash shoots, and state-of-the-art bathrooms, in her heart of hearts she believed that the stone Bibles of the buildings spread out to face the stone river and the church itself weren't accidental symbols of the capital city, but attributes of the sacrificial act she was performing for the sake of saving her son.

Pavel pressed for the elevator, and when the obliging doors silently opened and then closed, and breath escaped for a moment because of the quick acceleration, Tatyana and her companion still didn't speak, as if the sounds of their voices could startle or disturb something. The elevator grew quiet and came to a halt on the fifteenth floor. They walked out and found themselves in a small hallway with plush carpet runners. The hallway was softly lit with a pair of ornate branching candelabras. Pavel leaned his cane against the corner wall by his apartment door. Tatyana memorized the number that shone green on the white enameled plate, like the color of the onion domes against the whiteness of the church. And then she immediately forgot it. The key turned in the lock, and they walked into the entryway.

"Come on in, feel at home. This is my room."

"Let's just sit in the kitchen and talk."

"Okay, the kitchen it is."

They went into the kitchen without shoes, so as to not leave any tracks.

"Maybe that's enough, Pasha. We've had plenty of wine," Tatyana said, pointing to the bottle and glasses that Pavel was arranging on the table.

"We can't just sit here. You might as well be hanged for a sheep as for a lamb. Now tell me about your son."

Swallowing the slightly bitter wine, Tatyana poured out her grief about Tolik: how he wasn't cut out for military service; how he used to be a medical student; and also that he was planning to get married, and if he didn't get married, everything between him and his fiancée would fall apart. She was telling the story, unraveling the ball of untruths entwined with threads of truth, marveling at her own ability to weave all this into a single yarn, without chiding herself for her deceit—all of this because her old village beau could never understand the Levitins' Jewish truth, and most of all because he would never forgive her for it. The world of truth had gone somewhere else, had died, leaving a world of lies between her and Pavel. She begged Pavel to help, and he promised to help. But how could the lying eyes discern between lies and not lies in another's eyes, or hear in response to untruths—hear what? Truth or lies? And thus Tatyana talked herself into believing Pavel's promises, believing his eyes and words, his hands that desired only her in the whole wide world. To believe him, who had so hungered for her and only her, who was helping her out of her "emigration dress," undoing hooks and latches, freeing her body from the traps of city lingerie. And even at that very last moment, when she could still slither off the sheets, escape from under his muscular abdomen and reject his flesh from her own body, Tatyana didn't do this. Quite the contrary—when he became momentarily confused from a lack of sophistication, from greediness and fear that it wouldn't happen, she helped him to enter her, to enter the same womb from which she had once released her Anatoly into God's world.

And no longer sensing anything but the sweetness of coming together with that square abdomen sprawled on top of her stomach, where the abdomen of her husband Herbert Anatolyevich used to be sprawled, Tatyana just whispered, "Will you help my Tolik? Will you? Please help me, Pasha. My sweet, my only one."

And he helped her to free herself from the malady that had been tormenting Tatyana for more than a month, from the moment they became refuseniks, when she suddenly became so cold and indifferent toward her husband, and he to her as well. Pavel helped her to free herself, he lightened her load, but just before that he dropped a promise that he wouldn't neglect her son Tolik.

Pavel took Tatyana home by cab and dropped her off at the beauty salon, almost all the way to her house. They agreed that he would call her as soon as possible, particularly if there were some developments in Anatoly's draft deferral. Tatyana ran inside the entryway. Her heart was fluttering, and in this quickened heartbeat, everything was entangled: the joy of having helped her son, the sweetness of intimacy with Pavel, and the fear that everything would come out in the open. She was flying up the stairs, and her heart was hammering out these words: What's happening at home? What should I tell them?

In this beating of the heart and this agitation there was the joy of having committed a sin for her son's sake, and therefore the joy of her own sacrifice. But immediately this joy was overshadowed by a quiver of consciousness that she was a woman who was loved, for whose sake duty could be disregarded. Her intimacy with Pavel had given her a feeling of exhilaration until then quite unknown, unless one considered as real that crazy and drunken dream that had drugged and possessed her at Masha's house. The excitement that she had previously experienced with her husband, even during the best of their times, had been a habitual, planned excitement, in most cases, anyway, like the excitement of hearing a fine record that you can put on or turn off when you feel so disposed. Like a fine dinner, or in the best-case scenario, an outing to a theater or a restaurant. This excitement from being with her husband would burn out like a match. And because there were plenty of matches in the box, and their flame was always the same, such requisite excitement of the burning flame would pass through her almost without leaving a trace. But today she was gripped by passion and by joy. Passion from her intimacy with Pavel, and joy that she was saving her son through this intimacy.

Everything was turning out so well for Tatyana today. Neither Herbert Anatolyevich nor Anatoly had come home yet, although the wall clock was striking ten as she walked into the apartment.

NATASHA HAD JUST woken up. She had no strength to slip out of bed and run down the hallway shouting joyfully because it was Sunday, and the mood was festive, and life seemed like one long holiday. She felt nothing like that today; her throat was parched, her eyes could barely lift their puffy lids, her hands couldn't find a comfortable place under the blanket or behind her head, and her legs felt like somebody else's. She felt queasy. It had been two weeks since she was put on guard by the lateness of the usual. She was pregnant.

Natasha stretched her body, reaching out for a small mirror, and turned on the floor lamp. Peering at her face, which now belonged not only to her, but to someone lurking in the depths of her body, she sang out: "I'm a beauty, yes I am, only I'm poorly dressed." Words of a folk ditty. This is what Natasha would usually do to cheer herself up and to snap out of it. But the ditty didn't work. There wasn't a sound coming from her parents' bedroom. The revelers were still sleeping, Natasha thought, somewhat annoyed, and immediately admonished herself: I'm turning into a fat-bellied grumbler. She dragged herself to the kitchen and opened the refrigerator. Her eyes scanned the shelves. She didn't feel like having anything in the refrigerator. They said you should have cravings for salty things. But just the sight of the wax paper that the smoked salmon was wrapped in almost made Natasha vomit. She wanted some pickled cabbage, she suddenly realized, as she felt its exciting icy and earthen taste and aroma on her teeth, inside her mouth, throat, and stomach. And then she thought of the old peasant women who sold pickled cabbage at the Tishinsky Farmers Market. Once, when she was a little girl, she talked the maid, Markelovna, into taking her along to shop at the farmers' market. Markelovna, who had come from a village in the Ryazan province, immediately found herself at home among the wide-hipped, round-cheeked peasant women in oilcloth aprons. These women would shove their large, red hands into the depths of their massive pickling barrels and pull out stacks of thorny yellow-white cabbage with orange sparks of carrot slivers. They would stuff the clients' plastic bags, cans, and pots with the cabbage, and, using a mug, scoop out the lemon-colored and delightfully aromatic brine and pour it over the cabbage. Most vivid in Natasha's memory was this brine that she got a sip of by having to plead and plead with Markelovna. Natasha felt the sweetness and strength of the cabbage juice so acutely, as if she actually had a gulp of it. But her mouth was foul and dry as a desert. From this emptiness and vileness, her jaws cramped up, and she felt short of breath. Natasha glanced at the Fedoskino painted wall clock with a fairy tale scene depicting a mermaid and weights in the shape of peasant bast shoes. It was still early for a Sunday, only nine o'clock, but she went to the phone and called Anatoly.

"Tolik, good morning. I'm so sorry."

Even though Anatoly picked up immediately and was happy that Natasha called, she could tell that something had gone wrong. But then her thirst again surged over her, and Natasha tried not to take heed of anything that would keep her from having a gulp of this life-saving drink as soon as possible. Without affectation, like she did everything in life, Natasha asked Anatoly to come soon, and on the way to pick up some pickled cabbage at a farmers' market, because without pickled cabbage she would feel wretched all day. "And have them add more brine. Just tell them to splash some more on top!"

Anatoly arrived half an hour later. Natasha's parents still hadn't come out of their bedroom. Natasha drank a half a glass of the brine, chased it with a few crunchy pieces of the pickled cabbage, and felt a bit better. She led Anatoly from the kitchen to her room and started to comb her hair. He sat silently, flipping through the new issue of a film magazine. She noticed a change; something was clearly weighing on him, but she didn't want to pry. And so she waited for him to tell her.

"You know, Bluebell, my draft notice came. In a week's time, I'll be going to the army."

Natasha felt awful, like never before. Helpless and alone. Both things at the same time: the pregnancy and this terrible news. Her life was becoming pointless. But there were still words, words left to question life's pointlessness and inescapability.

"But didn't Herbert Anatolyevich file appeals? Didn't he protest? They haven't given their final decision yet, have they? How can you then take the oath? This is totally absurd. Tolik, you must protest, file your own appeal, otherwise what will happen to me?"

And she started bawling. She told him about her premonitions, which had now became a reality. Silently Anatoly kissed his Natasha, his Bluebell. He wiped her tears, but not only could he not think of a thing to do, he didn't even have the strength to say a word. Finally he forced himself to speak.

"Don't cry, Bluebell. I beg of you. I'll definitely come back in two years. Our little one will be a year and a half. What name shall we give him? And what if it's a girl, imagine, Natashenka?"

But Natasha didn't want to hear anything and kept crying, burying her swollen face, now resembling the face of a plump peasant woman, in his chest. Her tears summoned Ekaterina Nikolaevna, who immediately understood everything. She put Natasha to bed, in the familiar and warm space of her pillows and blanket, thus returning her to the order established in the Leyn household. It turned out that Anatoly, with his draft notice and no suitable plans for their daughter's future, had become superfluous, and as such a source of disturbance. He realized this and left as soon as Natasha dozed off.

Anatoly came home and immediately went to see his father. Herbert Anatolyevich, who had lost more weight and become even more stooped, was sitting over his books with the look of *tzaddik* withdrawn from this world.

WHEN THE GERMANS broke into the house of my maternal grandfather, an old rabbi, he was reading the sacred books, a *tallis* draped over his shoulders, swaying and rocking, like a Bedouin nomad between a camel's humps. A Bedouin nomad reading a sacred book of the desert with verses of the oases, rhythms of water springs, and refrains of sand dunes. The Germans shot the old rabbi, and stomped on and burned the sacred books.

ﬂ

HERBERT ANATOLYEVICH RAISED his melancholy eyes toward his son. No, not melancholy lurked in his glance, but a dejected submission to the inescapable. Did we not inherit from our nomadic ancestors this wisdom of recognizing the inescapability of fate, of knowing that fate absorbs the vanity of individual life the way sands absorb the fleeting happiness of the oases?

"Father, what should I do? I just found out that Natasha is expecting. How will she be without me? We're not even husband and wife. Couldn't something else have been done? Didn't you go to see Dudko and Aniskina?"

Something like a bright sunny thought flittered in Doctor Levitin's eyes. The sands shifted, the desert dunes rolled back, revealing a source of life.

"Tolik, my dear son. That's so wonderful! That's the best thing in the world. A new little person will come into this life for all our suffering. He will definitely make it to freedom. We'll help Natasha, don't worry. Two years will fly by like one day."

Like life just flew by for me, Herbert Anatolyevich wanted to say, but didn't.

"You see, son," he continued. "Dudko and Aniskina have simply deceived us, that's all. They are imagined, made from plywood, crudely painted, they are cutouts made to deceive and to distract, to ensnare Jews in lies. And on top of that, under the guise of compassion, to pry out of us information that allows them to deceive, distract, and ensnare us with even more sophistication than before."

"That means that all of our suffering and sacrifices were for naught," Anatoly said. "We lost a year. You lost your academic department, I a shot at medical school, mother her job. Natasha will become a miserable soldier's woman with a child born out of wedlock. If I had only known that it would all turn out like this!"

"That's the way of the world, son. We knew there was a chance of failure when we started. But once in our souls we accepted the possibility of a new life, we couldn't have lived like before. And you yourself insisted on emigration. You must be brave."

"Oh, papa. How can I be brave for her, when in effect I'm abandoning her?"

"Not everything's lost, Anatoly. We're all alive. Natasha and the little one will wait for your return."

"Alive? What about Grandfather Vasily Matveyevich? Had it not been for our Jewish schemes, he wouldn't have died. We destroyed him."

"Grandfather would have died from missing you and mother if he'd refused to go with us. Grandfather would've died in Israel from missing Russia. Grandfather is dead, and let's not disturb his memory any more. A baby boy will be born in place of Grandfather. If you and Natasha want, we'll name him Vasily."

"And if it's a girl, then what, Vasilisa? Oh father, you're oversimplifying everything."

"I'm not simplifying it, son, I'm straightening it out. That's old age. In old age roads become shorter and straighter. The end of the road is in sight."

"And what if something happens to me during my service? What will happen to Natasha then? And the little one? All of you?"

"What are you saying, Tolik? Why think about such things? It's peacetime. The army is basically a formality. During the two years, the state tries to prepare young lads just in case of possible entanglements, often even using them merely as a work force. But people survive even wars. You shouldn't think about these horrible things. Have mercy on your mother and me. Don't ever say such things again, and most importantly, don't think them."

Tatyana joined their conversation. But what could she tell them? How to comfort her son? Everything that she had done for him (now she knew for sure that everything she had with Pavel was only for the sake of saving her son) turned out to be for naught. A week after her meeting with Pavel, she called him, without waiting for his promised call. The same voice answered and went to get Lieutenant Colonel Teryokhin. Then for a long time nobody came to the phone; she heard cackling, crackling, scraps of words wafting in. Lieutenant Colonel Teryokhin, they finally told her, was out of town on a work assignment. Again and again she tried to reach Pavel. He finally called her back and set a time to meet. They met in the same place as the last time. Except this time he didn't ask her to go anywhere with him; he spoke roughly and angrily, marking words with the knocking of his cane.

"Why did you hide it from me that you were planning to slip away to Israel?"

"I was afraid that you wouldn't speak to me if you knew."

"Afraid? For whom?"

"For Tolik, for myself, and for you as well."

"No! You were afraid for your kike, worried sick for your little kikeling, and you used me like small change. And I . . . I could've ruined my whole life because of you. And still there's no telling how this will all end for me and for my family. You know whom I went to see about your son? Do you know what they told me there? Do you have any idea what I had to do so they would forget I ever asked? You . . . you hid your dirty Jewish tricks from me. I believed you, you know, but how could I ever prove to them I didn't know? You have disgraced me for the rest of my life."

"Pasha, forgive me. I honestly never thought it could possibly hurt you. And besides that, I wanted to see you. I'd missed you, Pasha dear. And here two threads were intertwined, my son and you."

"I don't believe you, that's all. Now I will never believe you. It was your kike who sent you to my bed, just to seal the deal. Shyster. . . ."

He cursed so wildly and brutally that whatever hope she had of changing his mind immediately disappeared. Pavel turned his back on Tatyana so suddenly that his cane made a semicircle, and she was almost sure that he was going to hit her.

"Go ahead, Pasha, hit me. Hit me! You'll feel better."

But instead he spat, and with his heel ground the spittle into the frozen November slush on the sidewalk. From that very moment, from the unfinished semicircle and the strike that hadn't been dealt her, Tatyana was terrified that the punishment for her sin would fall on her son's head.

THANK GOD THEY no longer shaved the draftees' heads.

The day hadn't yet begun, and already small groups began to form outside the district Draft Board Office: the draftees and those seeing them off. Almost everybody had come directly from going-away parties, from farewell bashes with friends, girlfriends, and family members. Two accordions were clanging with abandon, each in its own way but about the same thing. One could immediately tell the draftees from those who were seeing them off by a certain guarded look in their eyes. From time to time, the draftees would form little groups in order to chat and to figure out when and where they would be taken. Anatoly Levitin joined one of these spontaneous groups.

It was already early morning when he and Natasha had come to collect Anatoly's parents, and now the three of them—Natasha, Tatyana Vasilyevna, and Herbert Anatolyevich—stood off to the side of the entryway and waited for Anatoly. He was standing there with the other draftees, looking like the rest of them: a bird about to make its first migration. He had suddenly matured, gaining a new severity and some sort of estrangement—I'm still with you, my loved ones, but I'm already far away—with this belonging to a new entity called the army. He became a cog of the army, a force capable of defending and trampling, and he no longer belonged to his loved ones, to his family, to whom he had been bound by blood. From this day on, he belonged to another community, the army, also related through blood. Of course Anatoly differed from the majority of the young lads. If one were to define this difference in one word, it would have to be "refinement." He stood among husky guys, mostly working class, dressed in clown jackets of quilted nylon, smoking expensive foreign cigarettes for the road.

Anatoly was wearing a navy blue wool suit and a belted light-colored raincoat with shoulder epaulettes. Even now he looked like a student who had accidentally intruded into a group of his working class peers. One of them, a fellow in a checkered cap, à la Oleg Popov, offered Anatoly a cigarette.

"Smoke?"

"Thank you," Anatoly answered, accepting the cigarette.

"Hear what they say," the fellow looked around and whispered. "Looks like they're dispatching our echelon to Central Asia."

"Does it really matter where? I just hope the two years go by quickly!"

The fellow looked at Anatoly with pity, as if he were developmentally delayed.

"You intellectuals! Lucky folks get sent to Germany. What a life there! Fraus, fine clothes, and all that jazz! And you say 'does it really matter?' Or are you leaving a *Frau* here at home?" the guy snickered.

Anatoly tossed the unfinished cigarette and went back to his loved ones. At first Herbert Anatolyevich started to give his son advice in case he got intestinal problems, but stopped short when he realized that no one was listening to him. Tatyana was forcing herself to remain calm, furtively wiping her tears.

By eight o'clock there were so many people there that the entire lane in front of the district Draft Board was jammed with draftees and those seeing them off. Anatoly didn't go up to his future comrades-in-arms again. He stood there, embracing Natasha. She was holding his hand and staring at him, committing him to memory, the redbrick building of the Draft Board that served as a poster backdrop for this singing, wailing, partying crowd of people, and she was overcome with longing. They had talked about everything during their last night together.

Anatoly had gone over to see Natasha in the evening. She wasn't feeling well. She took a small sip of the champagne Anatoly had brought. ("Like that time, remember?") The transistor radio was quietly playing. Natasha's parents said goodbye, hugged Anatoly, and went to bed. Natasha didn't want them going to the district Draft Board in the morning.

Outside a viscous November rain fell onto the window, freezing in jelly-like fatty drops, which resembled drops of wax melting down from a candle. Natasha closed the curtains.

"See how everything turned out, Bluebell. I'm going away, leaving you."

"And the little one?" She took Anatoly's hand and put it on her belly.

His palm felt the live warmth of her body, radiating through the fabric of her nightgown. And nothing else. There was no third one there. That tiny little person, already on the way to them, hadn't yet made himself known to Anatoly. Anatoly was getting his signals through Natasha. She had been joined with this new life for some time already, and he was so fraily and tentatively connected to it, and now that he got called and forced to serve, he was leaving, maybe forever. A strange feeling took hold of Anatoly, that here in the space of the room, dimly lit with a night-light and closed off from the outside world by curtains, a someone else, a third being, was hiding, one who belonged equally to him as to her, but who had entrusted himself and revealed himself for now only to Natasha. And this knowledge gave Anatoly the assurance that he wasn't being separated from this girl, his beloved, that tomorrow's farewell would only be temporary. As temporary as his father's trips for work, when young Anatoly and his mama knew that time would pass, and they would be together again.

"Maybe, Natashenka, it's all for the best? Imagine if we had gotten permission to emigrate, and you would have had to stay here with the little one. And I would be abroad. It's scary even to imagine that."

"I wouldn't have stayed."

"And what would we have done?"

"He wouldn't be born."

"You're saying that you would have decided to kill him?"

"Tolik, why all these exercises in morality? Everything happened as it had to happen. The little one will stay with me. You will serve your two years and come back. And then the three of us will leave together."

"After the army they'll let me out only after five years."

"Just as he's about to start school. He'll go to first grade there. And while we're here, we will be growing up. We'll be learning Russian, not from books but the live language, here in his native land. The most important thing is that we will be. That's more important than anything."

"You are so smart, Bluebell. I figured out that we'll get married on my first furlough. They do give furloughs for excellent service. So I'll earn a furlough."

"No, daddy, we'll come to visit you before that—as soon as we are born, we'll come. Isn't that right, little one?"

They cheered up, distracted by this game. Anatoly had trouble imagining that in the depths of this body he was kissing, that in the body merging with his own body, there lived a new creature, a continuation of his life. A continuation in the same sense as he was a continuation of his grandfather and father. Would the little one continue his father's life? This thought, never having visited before, now wouldn't let him sleep. As if he were drinking water, never imagining that water could cease to flow, and suddenly he heard that the jet of water was being depleted. What if his water was coming to an end, and he wouldn't be able to watch his son or daughter drink of the water, see the sun, live? What if he, Anatoly, was saying goodbye forever to his unborn child?

Anatoly was lying on his back when Natasha came out of the bathroom and kissed him, crawled under the covers, put her palm under her cheek, and fell asleep, but not before she quietly whispered, "Sleep, Enchanter, tomorrow we have to get up sooo early."

But he couldn't sleep. What if this night was his last one with Natasha? What if he never sees her face again; never again hears her light breathing, occasionally interrupted by an incoherent mumbling (maybe she's talking to their little one in her sleep?); never again buries his face in her hair, tossed all over the pillow like meadow grasses, smelling tenderly of chamomile. It can't possibly be that he'll never again stroke her neck and breasts, which peek out of the nightgown that's shifted in her sleep; that he'll never again press his body to her back, a gorgeous line winding all the way down from the back of her head to her toes that doesn't break anywhere, driving him wild. It can't possibly be that he'll never again be able to awaken her with one touch, like he could now, at this moment! But it also cannot be that he'll never again keep vigil, just for the sake of the great tenderness he feels for this girl, staying up but not wresting her from her sweet dreams, because she is sleeping for two, for herself and for the little one, who belongs to her and to him both together. . . .

In the morning Natasha and Anatoly picked up Herbert Anatolyevich and Tatyana Vasilyevna. Now they were all waiting for the signal to say their goodbyes.

Finally, controlled movement began. Someone gave the order. For the last time the draftees joined their mothers, fathers, brothers, sisters, and girlfriends. Then they came back and fell into formation, first an uneven one, but straightening out more and more. The crowd was overcome with the torturous anguish of parting that gnaws at the soul and makes one want to unburden it quickly by shouting, "Forgive-farewell, Forgive-farewell . . ." Looking at the formation of civilian lads, who were before their eyes turning into soldiers, one only wanted them to disappear quickly, to leave, to cut the umbilical cord that connected them to civilian life. Thus out of parting separation is born.

Anatoly embraced his father. He saw Herbert Anatolyevich looking at him with wide-open eyes, his nearsighted pupils now even wider and enlarged in the small magnifying lenses of tears. These captive tears in his father's eyes opened the valve that Anatoly had been trying his damnedest to keep closed, and he broke into a sob, like a young boy who had been mortally offended yet lacked the strength to punish the ones who brought on the offense, which made the pain even sharper and bitterer.

"Father, forgive me! Forgive me, please. All of you are suffering now because of me. I couldn't get over the insult at medical school. To hell with med school! And Grandfather would be alive, and you would still have your professorship, and mother would be happy."

They all tried to console him, saying their own innermost golden words. He calmed down, growing quiet, and even smiling at the end.

The draftees formed an almost even column. A major was walking up and down before the formation and inspecting the lads with his methodical look that failed to notice anything. Anatoly was making his way to the column through a crowd of people. His parents fell back. Natasha was still walking with him, resting her face on his shoulder. At the very last moment, when he about was to step over the line dividing the draftees from the people who came to see them off, Natasha stopped him and asked, almost hanging on his arm, "What will I do if . . ." She didn't finish, but he understood, because this thought had tormented him during the night.

"If something happens to me, take him away from here—for the sake of all that's sacred."

The formation closed, engulfing Anatoly—a drop of rain engulfed by the sea.

An order rang out. A brass band struck up. Some people in the crowd shouted, others wept: "Good luck in the service! Come home soon! We're all waiting for you!" An accordion bellowed. The column turned the corner and flowed in the direction of Three Stations Square.

*

"THE AFGHAN NEWS agency Bakhtar released the following announcement: 'On the 9th of October, the Chairman of the Revolutionary Council, Nur Muhammad Taraki, died as a result of a serious and lengthy illness'" (*Pravda*, 11 October 1979).

"Responding to this situation, the Afghan government has once again urgently appealed to the Soviet Union to offer immediate aid and cooperation in the struggle against foreign aggression. The Soviet Union has decided to respond to this request and has sent to Afghanistan a limited military contingent, which will be utilized exclusively to help repel military aggression from abroad" (*Pravda*, 31 December 1979).

*

TATYANA WAS WALKING home from the bakery when she bumped into the mail carrier right at the entrance to her house, outside the brown door with its layers of peeling ochre paint, right in front of the door that had iced over when a recent thaw turned back to frost. Ever since Anatoly was drafted, and the Levitins began to receive letters from the army with those particular stampless postal markings known to every-body who either had family in the army or in prison, the mail carrier again acknowledged Tatyana as one of her own. She would bring letters up to the Levitins' apartment instead of tossing them indifferently into their mailbox.

"Were you coming to see me, dearie? And I was just at the bak-ery. Got a nice soft pretzel. Come on up, we'll have some tea together," Tatyana happily greeted the mail carrier.

Now everything connected with the mail reminded her of her son. And the mail carrier was the key person between her and Ana-toly. Except this time the mail carrier didn't return Tatyana's greetings as she usually did ("Seven transgressions, same punishment. Tea ain't vodka, you can't drink a lot of it!") The mail carrier just motioned her head toward the wall, where rows of blue mailboxes were attached, and quietly left. That's how friends and acquaintances of a deceased person exit the funeral parlor, leaving the loved ones alone with him. Over-come with a heavy premonition of inescapability, Tatyana threw herself at the navy blue mailboxes; now, for the first time, she saw their flat bodies as little coffins. She had gotten accustomed to receiving Ana-toly's letters with an official postal marking instead of a stamp. Now a quarter piece of paper fell out of the navy blue urn, resembling a draft notice, or an invitation to a meeting of the General and Inter-nal Medicine Society that they used to send to Herbert Anatolyevich. Tatyana shoved the piece of paper into her bag with the pretzel and bread, lamenting the fact that the mail carrier was avoiding her. Who knew what was in people's hearts! Maybe the mail carrier was pregnant again or her husband got fifteen days for drunk and disorderly conduct. And so, mulling over the mail carrier's behavior, and nearly forgetting the piece of paper stuck in the bag amid bread and produce, Tatyana walked up the stairs to her apartment. She stopped in front of the tall, double wide door, one side of which was always blocked by a pig iron hook connecting the outer door with the inner door. Between the doors, Grandfather Vasily Matveyevich would keep jars with saffron milk-caps that he himself foraged and pickled. Remembering her father, Tatyana ran through everything that had happened to them during the past year. Now their apartment was half empty, and the hook protected this emptiness with the unwavering rigidity of pig iron. Tolik will return from the army to a new apartment, Tatyana mused and pondered. By that time we'll surely have moved. Or maybe he'll still come here one time on furlough. She groped for the apartment keys in her leather tote bag, which had originally been purchased "for the big trip." The key chain fell somewhere deep inside and had to be liberated from under a box of loose Georgian tea and a loaf of bread. Tatyana located the ring and pulled out the key chain. But in the process something had sliced her hand slightly. She picked up this very light burden together with the keys, and it rustled like a mouse along the edge of the leather bag and on the skin of her hand. The postcard or summons, which had arrived instead of a letter from her son, now fell onto the stone floor. Tatyana was flipping through her keys, the back of her wrist remembering the sharp, rustling mouselike pain, by which the piece of paper had announced itself. She placed the massive brass key with its great key bit into the hole that resembled the shape of a boot. The lock and key had remained from the old days. Tatyana turned the key once, and the spring inside jingled expectantly. The key had to be turned once more. Tatyana again remembered the piece of paper; she even shivered from the sharp memory and let the key slip out of her fingers. The leather tote bag hung from the ring like a gymnast. Tatyana flung herself to the postcard, its dead face showing white on the stone floor. She bent over the piece of paper, and it whispered to her:

SERVICEMAN A. H. LEVITIN DIED IN THE LINE. . . .

From that day on, Tatyana didn't part with the death notice even for a minute. Herbert Anatolyevich made calls to all the appropriate places, found out everything that he could, and the Levitins arrived in time for the interment. They were told that their son's body would be delivered in a lead coffin to the *kishlak* of N., in a southern outpost of Soviet Central Asia. Due to her health, Natasha stayed in Moscow. All the days before the burial, Tatyana did not believe in the truth of her son's death. She knew of miraculous cases during the war, when the family would receive the death notice, mourn the soldier, say farewell forever, and the war would end, and he would come home, covered with wounds, but alive. She waited for a miracle. But the entire year was turning out to be a year of death for the Levitins.

When they brought Tatyana to the long metallic box with the label "private A. H. Levitin," for the first time she finally understood that her son would be no more. This meant that she had lived her whole life in vain. Now the last fine thread that connected Tatyana to Herbert Anatolyevich had been severed.

After the burial it was as if Tatyana had turned to stone. For several days Herbert Anatolyevich didn't leave her bedside, taking care of his wife. She didn't eat, didn't sleep, lying in a state of semi-consciousness—at least that was how it looked from the outside. But in reality, all this time Tatyana kept on thinking: So what's next? And while the power of her thinking was reaching a depth and clarity she had never experienced before, her physical strength was ebbing, melting away. She almost couldn't speak. Her eyes, opened day and night, followed the man who for so many years had been considered her husband and who, in this senselessly burnt out life, used to be called the father of her dead young son. The camel had been threaded through a needle, pulling behind a fine thread that had kept them together for almost twenty years. From the outset the unnatural passage of the camel would doom the thread to decaying and severing. She was desperately trying to find the first disastrous step of the camel toward the forbidden eye of the needle. Where was the source of the thread's decay, which had led to the death of her son?

Tatyana was lying in the main room that the owners of the house, local Russians of Old Believers stock, had cleared out for the Moscow doctor and his wife. Four days had passed since they had buried the coffin with Anatoly's body in this *kishlak* in the Pamir mountains. And this day was fading. The owners made do with side rooms and the kitchen, so nobody bothered Tatyana. She was lying on a spacious old bed that took up the length of almost the entire right wall adjoining the kitchen. The headboard was diagonal from the red corner, which actually always looked dark because of the dull brownish-black icon with the image of a saint. For a long time now, starting from the first day, Tatyana had been staring into the saint's face shading the icon, but only now, barely feeling the words with her lips, did she ask Herbert Anatolyevich, "Who is he?"

Herbert Anatolyevich raised his exhausted eyes to his wife. "Whom are you asking about, Tanyusha?"

"Who is he?" she repeated.

Tatyana was looking directly at the icon. Now the saint's face was lit up by the quivering flame of the oil lamp, then fell into darkness when the flame was dimmed by the draft. Herbert Anatolyevich walked up to the icon. In the lamp's feeble, shimmering light he read the words "St. Lazarus."

"That's St. Lazarus, Tanyusha. Now I'm going to give you an injection, and then we'll have some tea."

Tatyana didn't respond to her husband's words. She peered into the far corner of the house, whence the image of St. Lazarus appeared and immediately faded away. My God, Herbert Anatolyevich thought, can it be that she's remembering the same thing? Is something like that possible? Can a vatic text possibly relate to our present, our terrifying condition? No, it's just my chance conjecture. A hallucination. He took a syringe, opened up a vial, and waited for the liquid to fill the calibrated glass barrel. The liquid was barely supporting his wife's fading life. It was one of those cases when medicine was powerless to change anything, because all of life's stimuli had abandoned the patient, had been buried together with her son's body. Herbert Anatolyevich understood this and was carrying out his own orders with little hope for recovery. He consulted no one, harbored no hope for a miraculous recovery, yet he no longer despaired, because by that point he had already crossed the threshold of despair. He was safeguarding his wife's last flickers of life, like a grey wolf, taunted by dogs and chased into a thicket, protects the last wail of his mate, the dying she-wolf.

Tatyana raised herself slightly on her elbows, leaning her back against the pillows. Her mysterious thought process must have been conjoined with the chemical power of the medicine. She opened her eyes and again called to her husband, "Come here."

From the day the death notice came, Tatyana stopped calling her husband by name and addressed him impersonally, repulsed even by the intimacy of communication. Herbert Anatolyevich pretended not to notice.

"What Tanyusha? Are you feeling a little better?"

"I will never feel better because I no longer believe in anything. Do you hear me? Not in your terrifying God, nor in my feeble Christ."

She started to suffocate. Pink foam appeared at the corners of her mouth. Herbert Anatolyevich bent over her.

"Don't, my love. Don't say anything. It's better not to say such things now."

With her last strength she reached for him, or maybe for the icon.

"It's a lie. Lazarus never rose from the dead. It's all a fraud. Tolik, my beloved son, I wanted to rescue you, and I sent you to your death."

A convulsion ripped through her jaws and cheeks. Her eyes began to bulge out of their sockets and then retreated back inside. Her eyelids closed and immediately opened up, like shutters on a house whose windowpanes were blown out in a bombing raid. Her eyes opened, wild and vacant from their intense pupils. But the internal thrust was not of the deceased woman but of her thoughts never fully expressed in earthly life—and it forced her to wheeze out through her dead lips,

"I'm a harlot. It was I who betrayed you all and destroyed you."

And there was no more Tatyana in his life. Herbert Anatolyevich put copper coins over the eyes of the deceased. He left the room,

instructed the owners of the house to call a physician's assistant. From
that moment Doctor Levitin, the last survivor of his family, acted
out of absolute necessity of every move. Nothing superfluous, nothing that would distract him from the last step. He was like a marathon runner who had overcome a dreadfully difficult road, while
along the way losing his competitors one by one until he suddenly
noticed he was all alone. He alone was fated to make it to the finish
line. And here it mattered not how you ran or how long it took. It
mattered not what would happen to you after the finish. It was just
important for someone to cover the distance, to close the circle. Herbert Anatolyevich made arrangements for Tatyana to be buried in the
same plot as her son. Without spending any more time in the *kishlak*,
he made his way to the regional center and forced himself to get a plane
ticket back to Moscow.

HERBERT ANATOLYEVICH UNLOCKED the apartment. The light that
Tatyana had left in the kitchen was still on. She had collected and packed
in a bag some food for the road. The light was on, as if waiting for
Tatyana, like a cat locked in an apartment waits for his owner. Without
taking off his coat and dirty boots, Herbert Anatolyevich walked around
the rooms, leaving lumps of dirty snow that immediately melted into
brownish streaks across the parquet floors. As if nothing had happened.
Anatoly's letter is going to arrive, and Tatyana will run to the telephone
to call Natasha. Or else Natasha is going to call and say Tolik asked that
they send some book he absolutely needs to read, and Herbert Anatolyevich will start making calls to the book dealers he knows . . .

He imagined all that, knowing full well that the things he imagined
were a lie. Just like the omnipotence of his God and the mercy of Christ
had turned out to be a lie. Lazarus wasn't raised from the dead. But why did
Tatyana's last words embed themselves so deeply in his soul: "I'm a harlot.
It was I who betrayed you all and destroyed you." Again the thought of the
connection between the prophetic text and his wife's dying words came to
Herbert Anatolyevich's mind. But if she admitted her guilt before death,

accepting punishment for her betrayal, didn't that prove she believed in a higher power, a power that could punish by death and save by resurrection? Except no resurrection occurred. Could her guilt have been so enormous that she had to pay with both her own death and her son's? She betrayed her homeland, her father, and then . . . was it possible that she betrayed him, which also meant Anatoly?

Just as he was, in his coat and silk scarf, Herbert Anatolyevich walked into his son's room. On Anatoly's desk, under the glass top, there was a picture taken in the Crimea. Back then he was still Associate Professor Levitin, a slim and suntanned thirty-five-year old, with a head of wild kinky hair and a long humped nose, down which his eyeglasses with thick lenses and heavy plastic frames, fashionable in the day, repeatedly slipped down. Tatyana was next to him. Her sun-bleached hair, tan skin taut around her cheeks and neck, and her white sundress made her eyes sparkle like snow on a bright, sunny day. Her face was happy because she was awaiting the arrival of an even greater, endless happiness. Between the Levitins, actually on his father's left knee and in the hollow between his mother's thighs and her stomach, there sat a young boy, who just couldn't wait to jump out of this stillness and go chasing a bird perched up on the branch of a pomegranate tree, which hung low over their heads. The shutter clicked, and the bird gave a start but didn't fly away. Now, Herbert Anatolyevich noticed that it was not just any bird but an owl. And this owl had the face of the old woman from the homeopathic pharmacy, or her double, the old typist from the appeals office. Herbert Anatolyevich clearly saw how Tatyana and Anatoly were terrified and ran far away from the tree.

He returned to the hallway, took off his boots, and hung up his coat. Then he remembered that when he was leaving the *kishlak*, he had taken Tatyana's black purse from among the personal things left after her funeral. Many years ago Herbert Anatolyevich bought this purse for his wife in Leningrad. Tatyana never parted with it, even though fashion for purses, as everybody knows, changes quickly and often. Herbert Anatolyevich had never before dared not only to rummage through Tatyana's purse, but to so much as open it, even when he needed cash or perhaps couldn't find keys. Tatyana's purse was, in all likelihood, the only place that was off limits to the rest of the Levitin family. In spite of all of Tatyana's openness and kindness of character, she wouldn't forgive any transgression against her only veto. Once Anatoly, who was then in the eighth grade or thereabouts, had suddenly decided to go to the movies with friends. There was no money in the usual place where the Levitins kept it. Anatoly opened his mother's purse. When he came home from the movies, Tatyana wouldn't acknowledge him. That night they had dinner without her. It took a week for Tatyana to show any interest in her husband and son, while she slowly made peace with the insult. And now Herbert Anatolyevich was holding in his hands this mysterious black rotund purse with two black handles and a yellow brass lock shaped like two halves of a shell. Doctor Levitin, emaciated, unshaven, and hunched over like an old *shames* from a dilapidated cemetery synagogue, was now sitting on a kitchen stool and using both hands, actually using the thumbs and index fingers of both hands, to press on the brass shell of the lock, gradually prying it open. From the bowels of the purse—out of its impenetrable darkness previously confined by the lock—again emerged his wife's last deathbed words: "I'm a harlot. It was I who betrayed you all and destroyed you." He watched the black jaws of the purse open and the brass lips repeat, "I'm a harlot. It was I who betrayed you all and destroyed you." With his wiry fingers covered in long black hairs, Herbert Anatolyevich pressed the brass lips together. The whispering stopped. But he could no longer go on without hearing these deathbed words, couldn't live without them—although to live listening to this nightmarish whispering was unbearable. Again he pressed with both his thumbs the movable bottom half of the lock, and the top lip lifted up and pouted, letting out something like a hoarse whisper: "I'm a harlot. It was I who betrayed you all and destroyed you."

Herbert Anatolyevich could no longer fight this dark obsession. He listened and listened painfully, trying to recall something. Finally he went over to his study, all stooped over, and glanced at the rows of books. Almost without looking, he put his hands on a small volume bound in calico green. Herbert Anatolyevich could feel the texture of the cover so palpably with the tips of his fingers, down to each square of dark green cloth, even though he had difficulty making out these squares in the semidarkness of the murky winter afternoon. He came back to the kitchen and placed the book right next to the purse, from which the same phrase kept on sounding, like a broken record: "I'm a harlot. It was I who betrayed you all and destroyed you." The book opened by itself. Herbert Anatolyevich made out two names, Sonya and Raskolnikov, which were unrecognizable to him in his current state. He started to read and, as he read, the voice from the black cavity quieted down. Herbert Anatolyevich was now reading self-consciously, forcing himself to use his regained focus to identify what exactly the text spoke about. He couldn't follow what was happening in the book, although he knew now that the coincidence was not at all accidental, that his family had been severely punished for some crime, unbeknownst to him. He was already reading another page, wondering why back then, at his wife's side as she was dying before the icon of St. Lazarus, he hadn't remembered this text:

"After that she didn't read and couldn't read, closed the book and swiftly got off the chair. 'It's all about the raising of Lazarus,' she whispered tersely and sternly and then stood still, turning her gaze to the side, not daring and as if ashamed to raise her eyes to him. A feverish shiver still shook her. The end of the candle had long been dying in the crooked candlestick, dimly lighting the murderer and the harlot so strangely gathered in this pauper's room over the reading of the eternal book. Five or more minutes passed."

After he took his eyes off the text and closed the book shut, Herbert Anatolyevich asked, "But who, then, is the murderer and who the harlot?" his loud voice resounding through the kitchen. And immediately the brass lips whispered a reply: "I'm a harlot. It was I who betrayed you all and destroyed you." His face strained, reflecting the terrible life of his consciousness, and his eyes filled with a leaden twilight fire. He unclasped the incessant dark cavity and ripped it open. A crunching sound followed and the whispering stopped.

I killed you, Herbert Anatolyevich thought triumphantly. You croaked, you loathsome cavity. With a ferocity propelled by morbid curiosity, like a fisherman prying open the gills of a fish that swallowed the hook with bait, he turned out the insides of the purse. A little yellow cylinder of lipstick rolled out onto the table; a blush compact twinkled, waving its slender mirror and another matte winglet; then a wax flower fell out—a yellow tea rose with poisonous green leaves. Tatyana brought this rose home from Grandfather Vasily Matveyevich's grave. The death notice fluttered out and danced a funeral processional before it buried itself again into the purse's black cheek. Finally a photo fell out. An old amateur photo, so weathered and yellowed that it looked pierced by a blinding sunlight. Who were these two? Who took the picture? Against the backdrop of a birch stump, half embracing the girl as was the custom for an engaged young couple in the village, there stood a country boy, strongly built, with a triangular torso that widened from the waist up to the head. The country boy was dressed in a shirt with an upright collar, a black jacket, and matching black pants. Next to him stood Tatyana, still a young girl, even younger than the one with whom Hebert Anatoly-evich once fell onto the haystack in the middle of the field emitting the intoxicating summer scents of love.

Herbert Anatolyevich flipped the picture over, now guided by the concrete idea linking his family's disintegration and death with Tatya-na's deathbed words. In a schoolgirl's hand, still unsteady, someone had inscribed on the back of the photo: "TATYANA AND PAVEL 9th grade." The purple school ink had faded like the rest of the photo. But another inscrip-tion, actually a string of numbers, drew Herbert Anatolyevich's sharpened and inflamed attention: "232–56–42." It was apparent that these numbers had been written in ballpoint pen, and recently, because they still glis-tened with the freshly released grease of the paste. At the very bottom of the purse, a letter was hiding. Herbert Anatolyevich devoured line after line, hunting for one name only. Finally the circle was closed. The chain of numbers was joined with the last name and first name, like a chain connecting with a collar on a dog that used to run free. Even if one could imagine that all these minutes of feverish soul-searching and lightning-rod reflection could be taken back, the minutes when Herbert Anatolyevich, the kind Jew prone to philanthropy, growing older and ripping the fruits of his career, would be reincarnated into a predator seeking revenge—even then it would be difficult to imagine how a human brain ravaged by sorrow and nearly destroyed by a crushing defeat of hopes and aspirations would be capable of making decisions with such precision and finality. We don't even know much about the way a healthy person operates, let alone a person thrust into a spiritual frenzy. And what happens to the souls of the unfortunate ones? Such people's actions also submit to their own system, one that flows with its own precision and logic over the riverbed of their condition, as do the thoughts and actions of healthy people functioning in a familiar environment.

Now Herbert Anatolyevich knew exactly what to do. He took off his suit, all wrinkled and splattered with mud from the journey and with fibers that had stuck from the many chairs, couches, beds, and blankets that he had creased during this funereal week. He washed well in the bathtub and shaved with pleasure. He put on clean underclothes and got out his best "emigration" suit, which he had worn only once when he was seeing Anatoly off to the army. There were some unfinished research activities, but he wasn't concerned about that now. He found a carefully hidden vial in the safe and inspected it in the light of the desk lamp. A little colorless container with colorless liquid, each millimeter containing a lethal dosage. Herbert Anatolyevich renewed this vial every year, keeping careful track of the expiration date. Then he returned to the kitchen and opened the doors of the china cabinet; he was about to get the simple, everyday shot glasses, but then changed his mind. There was a sideboard in the living room. With a clink, Herbert Anatolyevich removed two crystal glasses from the glass shelf.

Now it seems everything's ready, he reflected, placing a bottle of cognac next to the crystal glasses. If he doesn't want cognac, there's a bottle of vodka in the refrigerator. Herbert Anatolyevich was so focused, as if he were getting ready for a visit from a close friend. Again he walked around the apartment and then, remembering something, returned to his study and settled at the desk. On a sheet of fancy stationery still left over from his professorial days, which stated his last name and initials, degree, and title, he jotted down a few things and put the note in the safe. Then he took out another sheet like that and wrote a letter to Natasha, letting her know that the apartment keys were under the doormat, his instructions were in the safe, and the key to the safe was in the kitchen cabinet. He sealed the letter, addressed it to the Leyns, and put it in his coat pocket so as not to forget it. It was around four o'clock now. The appeals office closed at six. And there was still the pharmacy. He had to hurry.

Herbert Anatolyevich went to make a phone call. Being a very focused and punctual person under normal circumstances, Herbert Anatolyevich now acquired a pathological ability not to make a single error in any of his movements. On the way to the phone, he went out into the hallway, and in the storage space between the doors he located a ten-liter canister. In the cutlery drawer he found garden shears that they used for carving roasted poultry: chicken, turkey, or duck. He even remembered clearly how the blades of the shears crunched the cartilages, how the hollow cylindrical bones of the dead birds snapped on a platter amid piles of green herbs, potatoes, and marinated plums in the middle of a holiday table. But no matter how hard he tried to imagine one of the birds whose name he spoke out loud—chicken, turkey, duck—he couldn't conjure up the image of any of them. Only an owl lay before him on the platter in the middle of the table: a motionless, speckled, grayish brown heap of owl meat with green cat eyes framed by livid-yellow lids and an old woman's warped, crooked nose. Around the table sat Vasily Matveyevich in his army shirt with wartime medals; Tatyana in a black mourning headscarf; Anatoly in a soldier's tunic; and also Natasha, who could barely fit behind the table with her incredibly big belly. And behind Herbert Anatolyevich's back, while he prepared to carve the owl, there was someone pacing back and forth, someone whom Tatyana was inviting with an unctuous voice unknown to the Levitins: "Pasha, come on, sit with us at the table, you're now almost part of the family."

HERBERT ANATOLYEVICH PUT the canister and the garden shears into an extra-wide bag, one of the items Tatyana had purchased at GUM—the State Department Store—for when she would be shopping abroad. Now everything was ready. Herbert Anatolyevich dialed the number from the backside of the picture.

"May I speak with Teryokhin, please," he asked.

"Teryokhin speaking."

"Pavel Ivanovich, this is the husband of the late Tatyana Vasilyevna. Today, now, is the wake. Please write the address down. I'm waiting for you."

Herbert Anatolyevich didn't doubt for a minute that Pavel would come, that Tatyana's deathbed words were connected specifically to this person, whom he would see for the first time after his son's and wife's death. Only now the entire system of their family life had been revealed. After all, the life of any family, from its origin to its death, is a unique solar system with flares, eclipses, the death of the old and the birth of new planets. Their son was the sun of their solar system. And then an alien body—something like a comet from other worlds—had flown into the perfect planetary system of their family. This alien comet, this deadly missile, must be rendered harmless right now, immediately. He had no doubts or misgivings about that. And even though Herbert Anatolyevich's inflamed mind was fostering the thought that their annihilated family system had not been perfect from the outset, or that it had lost its perfection as it tried to relocate to another universe, he chased these reasonable doubts away, because the cause of their family's collapse was apparent, and this apparent knowledge justified his actions.

The doorbell rang. Herbert Anatolyevich flung himself into the hallway, hovering for a moment over the table with the cognac and crystal glasses. He opened the vial, emptied the colorless liquid into one of the glasses, and threw the empty vial out the ventilation window. After that he answered the door.

A lieutenant colonel wearing a hat with earflaps and leaning on a cane was standing outside the door.

"I'm here to see the Levitins," the lieutenant colonel said.

"Come in. This is the apartment of the late Tatyana Vasilyevna. I'm her husband."

"Teryokhin, Pavel Ivanovich." The lieutenant colonel introduced himself and took off his greatcoat. He put his hat on the table beneath the mirror and smoothed his hair.

"This way, please," Herbert Anatolyevich pointed with his hand toward the living room, where two crystal glasses stood on the table, a bottle of cognac next to them, and between the glasses and the bottle lay the photograph of Pavel and Tatyana embracing each other.

The guest sat on the very side of the table where the glass with a drop of poison was placed.

"I've known Tatyana Vasilyevna a long time. All my life, one could say. What happened?" Pavel asked, looking apprehensively at this strange wake.

Herbert Anatolyevich was silently studying this man, whom he had condemned to death. For the first time in his life, he, a doctor who had saved many hopeless patients, decided to cross the terrifying line. But there was no other choice. Otherwise they would henceforth deceive and seduce with impunity, treating Jews like people of the lowest sort, whom even the law does not protect, not to speak of conscience. What remained was to convince himself finally of Teryokhin's crime.

"Did you see Tatyana Vasilyevna not long before her death?" he asked his guest.

"Well . . . no. Only accidentally." Teryokhin became unnerved by Levitin's direct question and didn't know how much of the truth he actually knew.

"I know almost everything. I have the diary of the deceased in my hands. So don't lie; at least don't besmirch her memory."

"Yes, she was in my home."

"Did she come to ask you for something?"

"About her son. But you have to understand that I couldn't help him. I didn't know you had filed for emigration to Israel, and I found myself in a difficult position. I wanted to help, but it turned out to be beyond my ability."

"And you decided to send him to a certain death, all at once to cut the knot that tied me and my wife together with one strike?"

"Your son was sent there, bypassing me. Surely you know what's going on in Afghanistan."

"But you didn't do anything to prevent it? Tatyana Vasilyevna died of grief. You destroyed her."

Teryokhin was silent. Herbert Anatolyevich opened up the cognac, but the guest went back to the hallway and brought out a bottle of vodka.

"We will remember her the Russian way. With our pure vodka. God will judge us."

Pavel raised the glass with the vodka to his lips, but some secret impulse stopped his hand, and he put the glass back down on the table. Herbert Anatolyevich was watching his guest silently, conscious of nothing except the powerful wish of finishing off this enemy and continuing on his path of revenge. Teryokhin wasn't in a hurry. He looked into Herbert Anatolyevich's eyes hidden behind the lenses of his glasses. Tongues of flame from the candle lit by the host were reflected in the lenses. There was such longing and hopelessness in Teryokhin's eyes that Herbert Anatolyevich reached out his hand to take away his deadly drink. But it was too late. Apparently understanding that everything that happened between him and Tatyana was for life, until the very last minute, Teryokhin again raised the glass.

"May your soul be at peace, Tatyana. Forgive us all. Nothing is anyone's fault. This fucked up life . . . ," Teryokhin said and began to sob, quelling his sobs with sips of vodka, like people quelling their sobs with water.

Without trying to interrupt anything, Herbert Anatolyevich watched his enemy's consciousness swiftly extinguished as Teryokhin's body lost life's powers, slowly slumping to the ground. When he was certain that his guest was dead, Herbert Anatolyevich drank up his vodka, walked out of the living room, and taking the bag with everything that he would need later, he locked the door and left his home.

Now HE FELT better. Having been brought up in a Russian milieu and having absorbed the sanctimonious "thou shall not kill," in reality he always saw how the principle of "eye for eye, tooth for tooth" had command over everything. For the first time he acted according to his conscience, not in keeping with his upbringing but with his blood ties. People guilty of his son's death belonged to the Russian nation, the nation of Orthodoxy, yet they were guided neither by the principle "thou shall not kill," nor by the cruel but honest thesis, "eye for eye, tooth for tooth," but were rather predators who became enraged from the blood they spilled, blood of innocent victims. By killing Teryokhin he had only begun to reinstate an equilibrium that had been disturbed by mysterious forces, forces that were as far from Judaism and Christianity as the Nazis were far removed from ideas of equality, freedom, and brotherhood, even though they may have stitched a little flag of socialism onto their banner of human hatred. Having crossed the line that separated him from the environment he had considered his own, and which had destroyed his family as relentlessly as tanks destroy mud huts where semiliterate Asiatic dwellers live, Herbert Anatolyevich felt a sense of inner freedom. The next step could be taken without burdensome vacillations and doubts that hindered him as he was exacting retribution from Teryokhin. Levitin's brain was working with startling ease. He remembered that there was a gas station not far from there, on one of the godforsaken little streets that linked up to the Garden Ring. As Levitin set off for it, the garden shears were clanging and drumming against the canister in his bag. He waited for a car to leave the gas pump with the number ninety-three on it, and inserted the nozzle into the neck of the canister. Levitin explained to the intrigued woman who collected money for the gasoline, "To get stains out of the carpet. That's what they told my wife to do."

"We don't care if you drown in it. As long as you pay." The woman pulled the wooden tray with the two rubles into her booth.

Levitin went back to the pump, waved to the woman like a regular driver who had come to fill up the tank, and pressed the sliding handle on the nozzle. The gasoline began to flow into the canister. The arrow moved to the line at five and then stopped at the ten-liter line. He handed the nozzle over to the next customer, and then closed the canister, put it inside his bag, and walked down to Tsvetnoy Boulevard. There Levitin hailed a cab. Sitting in the cab, Levitin was holding the bag with the canister and garden shears between his knees, thinking only about one thing: to make it to the appeals office in time. It was almost six in the evening. It started to snow, and the metronomes of the windshield wipers began to tap their doleful rhythm: "Thou-us, thou-us." Levitin watched the road, swallowing each turn, each building, each human shape the taxi left behind. A thaw had followed a January freeze. Keeping time with the windshield wipers, snowflakes fell to the earth, only to be sucked up by black jelly-like puddles.

They turned onto Pushkin Square. There was a snow *tallis* over the head and shoulders of the bronze Pushkin. The Telegraph Agency building loomed ahead on the left. Over by the Nikitskiye Gates, Levitin asked the driver to stop and paid up. He walked briskly along Herzen Street in the direction of the appeals office, even though his bag with a full canister was pulling on his arm. Running the last few steps from the corner of Herzen Street down Khlynovsky Alley, Levitin flew up the stairs. The officer on duty got up from behind the desk.

"Where are you going, citizen?"

"I want to sign up for an appointment."

"Appointments are only until six. You're late."

"And where is the typist?"

"The typist is also gone for the day. Come back tomorrow in the morning."

"But there she is," Levitin dashed to the room where petitioners usually waited to be seen, with the typist's window down at the end. "There she is—the typist!"

An owl that looked uncannily like the old woman typist was circling right under the ceiling, mocking Levitin and grunting with pleasure. Her face was yellow and jaundiced. Livid puffy lids framed her green eyes. From time to time, the old owl-typist would flicker her yellow membrane, which made Levitin think that she delighted in his bewilderment. He grabbed an ashtray and flung it in her direction.

"Citizen, have you lost your mind? Stop this right now, or I'll have to call the patrol. Just look at him, hurling ashtrays around, and not just any place but at the ceiling fan."

The officer pushed Levitin out onto the street and locked the doors of the appeals office.

All the misfortunes that had brought the Levitin family to ruin were now concentrated in the image of the old woman typist, in the old owl who was the keeper of the files. From here stretched the venomous threads of information that had poisoned his family's life; and here the loathsome owl collected her deadly information and stored it in a data bank. "Eye for eye, tooth for tooth," Levitin was mumbling, looking around from side to side, just in case he should see the owl who had vanished from the appeals office. Suddenly right on the corner, just before the intersection with Herzen Street, he noticed a boarded up and painted window with a round ventilation opening. A momentary hunch forced him to stop and watch the hole. Suddenly the spinning of the small iron blades slowed down, seemed to cringe, and a yellowish face with a crooked beak nose poked out of the opening. "The owl . . . ," Levitin shivered and started to look for a large stone or a brick. But it was too late. Flapping her hefty wings, the owl flew amid the heavy snowflakes across Herzen Street and disappeared into the darkness of dusk. "Now you can't escape from me!" Levitin shouted after her, almost in triumph, and crossed the street.

It was rush hour. People were leaving work and heading first to the stores and then home, preoccupied with their evening thoughts of food and rest. Levitin's clumsy body, thin to the point of inanition, impossibly hunched over under the weight of the canister, his pale neck naked without a scarf and his kinky hair snow-spattered, made people stare at him in wonderment, but nobody really cared about one another. Levitin reached the homeopathic pharmacy. The doors of the pharmacy were half open, but the entrance was blocked with a heavy oak chair. On the inside of the door a sign was posted: CLOSED FOR STOCK INVENTORY. Levitin knew that this was one of the old owl's tricks, meant to deter him. She was hoping that he still believed official announcements. He moved the chair aside and stepped inside.

"We're closed!" an old voice croaked from behind the counter.

"I need a consultation with you," Levitin said, ignoring the admonition and peeking in through the little window.

There, behind the partition, the old apothecary shuffled, surrounded by drawers and little boxes. Levitin saw that she was stuffing the boxes not with white balls of medicine, but with thin scraps of cigarette paper, all strewn with secret signs. Muttering curses and damnations, the old woman straightened her spine with great difficulty and came up to the window.

"What is it that you want? Why are you pursuing me?" she shouted, rotating her green eyes framed by livid lids, and her yellowish face became even more ghastly from hate and horror, because she read her death sentence in Levitin's eyes.

"Give me the files, you old owl. Give them to me, so that nobody else will remain under your surveillance."

With her clawlike paws, the old woman very quickly tossed the little boxes with notes into wooden drawers and started spinning the drum. Each rotation of the drum with the drawers was accompanied by a victoriously mocking howl that would escape from the old woman's gullet, packed tight inside her neck, yellowish and wrinkled like a corrugated drainage pipe.

"Ha-ha-ha," she howled. "I'm only an apothecary. I mix microdoses of venoms, and they turn into medicines. I cure people from Plato's four cardinal virtues: wisdom, courage, temperance, and justice. You yourself just fed your enemy a medicine for love. And he—he-ha-ha!—is now forever cured of this illness."

"What do you know about illnesses and cures, old owl?" Levitin asked, trying to get closer to the old woman, but his head wouldn't fit through the little window cut out in the glass partition, and his hand couldn't reach the old woman. She was retreating toward the rotating card file, as if shielding it with herself.

"I know everything about illnesses. And I also know everything about those infected with a longing for freedom. It's a new sickness in our part of the world. I've just made up a formula that can cure these miserable types of longing for freedom. And I've even prepared the first experimental batch of the remedy. That's why they haven't been calling anybody in to the appeals office—they didn't know what to treat them with. Now everything's ready. Even refuseniks such as you will finally be cured, and you will no longer wish to pester the staff of the appeals office with your idiotic petitions."

"Where is this formula? Give it to me. Or I'll kill you. I'll prepare an antiserum. And I'll distribute the antidote to the people, and you won't be able to force us to change our nature."

"Oh, you unfortunate one. You still haven't been initiated. You've gotten into your head that anyone can be saved. But you don't know these people, the ones who have the same illness as you. You don't know them as well as we, the staff of the appeals office, know them. Do you hear me, unfortunate person, you won't ever be able to make an antiserum because I'll never divulge the secret of the new drug."

And the old woman cackled with ferocity and bile, spraying her saliva and prancing on her short claw-like feet. She was so certain that her visitor was indecisive and docile, like most members of the intelligentsia, that she didn't even try to fly out and escape from the pharmacy after Levitin ripped the partition doors off of their hinges, and she stood right next to the diabolical rotating card file. These boxes contained not only the names and addresses of those infected with a longing for freedom, but also the dosages of the new remedy, individually administered for each individual visitor to the appeals office. Hundreds of thousands of names and addresses. Hundreds of thousands of individual packages with little white balls. Levitin got even closer to the old woman. In his right hand he held the garden shears with their gaping metal jaws. He put down the bag with the canister on the floor. The old woman's breath was foul smelling; her eyes rolled around. Her livid yellowish eyelids gaped like the dry shells of dying mussels, and Levitin saw big yellow drops rolling down her parchment cheeks. Steaming like the aqua regia, drops of deadly acid fell down onto the floor, burning black holes in the linoleum.

"You won't dare to kill me, you pathetic Jewish quack!" A threatening croak bolted out of her beak, and her wings spread out, shielding the card file.

The old woman was prepared to die rather than leave her diabolical galley.

"Eye for eye, tooth for tooth. Your life for the thousands of maimed lives!" Levitin shouted into the old woman's face and grabbed her by the wing.

She contorted herself and, jumping up, dug her claws into his left arm. Then, measuring his strike, Levitin stabbed the powerful sharp ends of the shears into the wooden counter with the rotating drum of the card files. The corrugated yellow pipe of the old owl's neck found itself between the blades of the shears. Blood was spurting out from Levitin's left hand, ripped to the bone. Neither one of them was giving up the struggle. With his right hand Levitin was pressing the shears over his enemy's throat. She was making a croaking sound, a death rattle, and the strength of her claws was slowly ebbing. Blood was squirting out more and more powerfully from his ripped brachial artery, and when the owl's claws separated from Levitin's ripped open arm and slipped, he realized that he would surely die from loss of blood. He would perish without ever finding out the secret of her diabolical formula, which, together with the card files, would remain in the service of the appeals office staff. Using the last of his strength, Levitin brought the two blades of the shears together. He heard a throat cartilage snap. The old woman's head twitched and hung down to the left. Levitin felt that he had only minutes left to live. Holding down his bag with his feet, he opened the stopper in the canister with his right hand and splashed the gasoline out onto the old woman's body and onto the card files. Yellow flames swam past his eyes and went out in a dark fog. He lit a match by the feel of his fingers, then another one, and then he collapsed onto the floor. The fire flared up, dissolving the dark fog. Herbert Anatolyevich's last sensation was the joy of revenge.

My life ebbs away:
all my bones are disjointed;
my heart is like wax,
melting within me;
my vigor dries up like a shard;
my tongue cleaves to my palate;
You commit me to the dust of death.
Dogs surround me; a pack of evil ones closes in on me,
like lions they maul my hands and feet.

(from Psalm 22, a Psalm of David)

DURING THE FIRST days of February 1980, when Moscow winter started to turn toward early spring, showing yellow amid frosts and snowstorms, and wakening in people a longing for mimosa flowers, a married couple was going through customs control at Sheremetyevo Airport. Stanley Fisher was returning home to the United States with his young wife. The customs officers treated Natasha with utmost politeness, and her filled-out figure even freed her from a private examination in a gynecology chair. Stanley was a bit nervous, which was totally understandable, if we recall all the events of this most difficult year. There were plenty of reasons for worry up until the moment they announced boarding. Then, for the last time, Natasha turned to look at her parents and followed her husband onto the airplane.

Moscow—Maleyevka—Moscow—Pärnu—Moscow

December 1979–October 1980

ABOUT THE TEXT OF
DOCTOR LEVITIN

MAXIM D. SHRAYER

HISTORY OF THE ORIGINAL'S
COMPOSITION AND PUBLICATION

*I*n January 1979 David Shrayer-Petrov and his family submitted the necessary paperwork to the OVIR (Section of Visas and Permissions; see note to p. 9). At the time of the application, both Shrayer-Petrov and his wife Emilia Shrayer (née Polyak) lost their academic jobs, and soon thereafter Shrayer-Petrov was also expelled from the Union of Soviet Writers and blacklisted. The Shrayers' application for an exit visa was denied and they became refuseniks. In 1979–80, while working at a hospital emergency room lab and driving an illegal cab at night, Shrayer-Petrov conceived of a panoramic novel, eventually to become a trilogy of novels about the exodus of Soviet Jews and the mutilated destinies of refuseniks. The protagonist, Doctor Herbert Anatolyevich Levitin, is a Moscow professor of medicine. His Jewishness evolves in the course of the novel from a prohibitive ethnic garb to a historical and spiritual mission. Levitin is married to Tatyana Levitina (née Pivovarova), a Russian woman of peasant stock from the Pskov Province of Russia. In documenting with anatomical precision the mutually unbreachable contradictions of a mixed Jewish-Russian marriage, Shrayer-Petrov also treats the story of Doctor Levitin as an allegory of Jewish-Russian history.

Doctor Levitin, Part One of Shrayer-Petrov's refusenik saga, ends with the killing of the Letivins' son, Anatoly, in Afghanistan; Tatyana's death of grief; and Doctor Levitin's phantasmogoric revenge. Shrayer-Petrov completed the composition of *Doctor Levitin* in the autumn of 1980, an author-doctor stuck in refusenik limbo, living out the destinies of his own fictional characters. Over the next three years, he completed the second novel about refuseniks. In Part Two of Shrayer-Petrov's trilogy, a novel in its own right titled *Cursed Be You, Just Don't Die*, refusenik activists, Palestinian drug lords, and chess masters share the stage, as Doctor Levitin himself finds transcendent love in his new beloved Nelly Shamova.

In 1984 the manuscript of Part One and Part Two was clandestinely photographed by a trusted photographer, and the negatives were smuggled out of the USSR to the West. Shrayer-Petrov's persecution by the KGB intensified in 1985, when the publication of Part One was announced in Israel. In 1986 an abridged text of Part One appeared in Jerusalem under the title *V otkaze* (*Being a Refusenik*), in a volume of the same title, comprised of writings by and about refuseniks and published by *Biblioteka-Aliya* (*Aliyah Library*). The earliest critical references to Shrayer-Petrov's refusenik trilogy go back to the late 1980s and early 1990s, when it was still known under its provisional title, *Being a Refusenik* (or *Being Refused)*.

The author and his family left the USSR on 7 June 1987, as the sluices of Jewish emigration were starting to reopen. After a summer in Austria and Italy, they settled in Providence, Rhode Island, where Shrayer-Petrov and his wife would spend almost twenty years, both of them professionally affiliated with Brown University. Shrayer-Petrov believed strongly that his novels about refuseniks and the exodus of Soviet Jews should be published in Russia. In 1991, as the USSR was heading towards dissolution, Shrayer-Petrov submitted Part One (*Doctor Levitin*) and Part Two (*Cursed Be You, Just Don't Die*) for publication in Moscow. They were published in the spring of 1992—the first post-Soviet spring—under the same cover, in a single volume titled *Herbert and Nelly*—Herbert after the protagonist, Doctor Herbert Levitin, Nelly after the principal female character of Part Two, Nelly Shamova. When it was published in Moscow, the first edition of *Herbert and Nelly* looked, ironically, like many Soviet-era mass-produced books—white glossy printed cover with red and black design, and grey pages of newsprint. The print run of 50,000 copies, unimaginably large by the standard of today's Russian book market, was quickly sold out.

To this day, Russian readers worldwide, students of Jewish and Russian literature, and historians of Russian Jewry refer to Shrayer-Petrov's refusenik saga as *Herbert and Nelly*. In 2006 Shrayer-Petrov embarked on the third novel, in which Doctor Levitin finally emigrates from the USSR, spends the transit months in Austria and Italy, and then settles in the Boston area. Part 3, the final part of his trilogy, was published in 2009 under the title *Tret'ya zhizn'* (*The Third Life*). As Shrayer-Petrov worked on *The Third Life*, he also revised the text of the first two parts, and it subsequently appeared in two different editions, first in 2009 in St. Petersburg, and then in 2014 in Moscow. The 2014 Moscow edition came out as part of the series "Prose of Jewish Life," an imprint of Knizhniki, the world's leading publisher of Jewish books in the Russian language. It is the hope of the author, editor, and cotranslators of *Doctor Levitin* that Parts Two and Three of this refusenik trilogy will soon appear in English translation.

Russian Names and How They Are Rendered in Translation

In Russian a person is formally known and addressed by their first name, patronymic (derived from the first name of one's father), and last name. The Russian language employs a rich and varied system of first name diminutives—their style, tone, and register ranging from tenderness, affection, and light humor to condescension, derision, contempt, and mockery. For example, to take just the common affectionate diminutives of Tatyana, the wife of Doctor Levitin in the novel, they include Tanya, Tanechka, Tanyusha, Tatochka, Tanyulechka, Tan'ka, Tatyanka, Tatyanushka, and others. Translators have experimented with using corresponding first names, which in both Russian and English possess a spectrum of diminutives—e.g. Nikolay becomes Nicholas, Kolya becomes Nicky etc. This approach could be seen as a bit more productive when it comes to rendering Jewish names, especially in American English, enriched and colored by the heritage of Yiddish. In rendering Izya, a diminutive of Isaak/Isaac, one might, perhaps, suggest Izzie, and so forth. In general, however, shades of meaning encoded in Russian first name derivatives are lost on the English-language readers who are unfamiliar with Russian language and culture. Very rare indeed are such pairs as Elizaveta/Elizabeth or Margarita/Margaret, both names being of non-Slavic origin, which possess almost equally variegated spectrums of diminutives in Russian and in English.

In rendering Russian first names, including Jewish-Russian names, we have taken what may be deemed a pragmatic approach. While retaining some of the diminutives of the characters' first names, we have limited their use to several, usually two or three forms (e.g. Tolya or Tolik for Anatoly). Furthermore, in some cases, we have used only one form of the first name consistently.

One principal exception in the novel is the first name of the protagonist, Herbert Anatolyevich Levitin. To a Russian ear, the first name "Gerbert" immediately stands out because of its markedly foreign, Germanic (and Ashkenazi Jewish) quality. We decided to go with "Herbert" rather than "Gerbert," partly because the name is relatively rare in Russia, but mainly because the first two parts of Shrayer-Petrov's refusenik trilogy are already known in Western criticism as *Herbert and Nelly*. We have also decided not to reproduce the diminutives of the name Herbert (Herb, Herbie, etc.) because they seem wrong in tone and register, and to refer to the protagonist as "Herbert" or "Herbert Anatolyevich."

Notes to the Text

Maxim D. Shrayer

Page 1

We know we are Russians; You consider us Jews: This epigraph is Shrayer-Petrov's own formulation, which reflected, at the time of the novel's composition, the author's view of Jewish-Russian identity and history, and which Doctor Levitin reiterates in the novel.

Meshchanskaya Street (Meshchanskaya Ulitsa): Formerly 4th Meshchanskaya Street in the northern tip of Moscow's historic center, running north from Sadovaya-Sukharevskaya Street (section of the Garden Ring; see note below) to Ulitsa Durova (Durov Street). The Levitin family resides in an old building on Meshchanskaya Street.

The Garden Ring (Sadovoe kol'tso): A beltway-like succession of multilane avenues encircling the center of Moscow and serving as one of the city's principal thoroughfares.

Olympics: The 1980 Olympic Games, which took place in Moscow, USSR, from 19 July–3 August, 1980. The Soviet invasion of Afghanistan in December 1979 led to a US-led international boycott of the Moscow Olympics.

Medical School: In the late Soviet period, there were three medical schools in Moscow. Though the particular medical school mentioned here is fictitious, certain details, including its location on Bol'shaya Pirogovskaya Street, link the place of Doctor Levitin's work with Moscow's First Medical School, named after M. I. Sechenov, now First Moscow Medical University; see also note to p. 21.

Page 2

the wave of Jewish emigration: The official Soviet census data cites the following
numbers for the Jewish population: 2,151 million in 1970, 1,811 million in
1979, 1,449 million in 1989. The attrition owed itself to the Jewish emigration, which had become a mass movement by the early 1970s. All through the
mid-70s, the wave of Jewish emigration rose by tens of thousands, and 1979,
the year Doctor Levitin and his family applied for an exit visa and became
refuseniks, was the peak year for Jewish emigration from the pre-reform
Soviet Union, with over 51,000 leaving. In 1980 almost 20,000 Jews were
allowed to leave as the passage was already closing. Then the numbers quickly
dwindled, and by the middle of the 1980s, Jewish emigration was reduced
to about a thousand per year. Even though the Jackson-Vanik Amendment,
which had been signed into US law in 1975, had made the release of Soviet
Jews an exchange currency on the market of the "most favored nation" status
(the Stevenson Amendment also limited economic relations between the
US and the USSR), it hardly affected the outcome of emigration during
the years 1981–86. Relations with the West would remain openly hostile
until Mikhail Gorbachev's ascent to power in 1985, and a change in the
refuseniks' lot only came in 1987–1988.

Page 3

My Slavic soul in a Jewish wrapping: This is the first line of one of Shrayer-
Petrov's best-known poems, "Moya slavyanskaya dusha" ("My Slavic Soul,"
1975), in which a Russian Jew's "Slavic soul" abandons his body, likened
here to a "Jewish wrapping," and hides in a hayloft.

Novye Cheryomushki: Neighborhood of Moscow southwest of the center; also
the name of a metro station. Novye Cheryomushki was one of the first two
new neighborhoods of Moscow developed in the late 1950s–early 1960s,
during the Khrushchev-era mass construction boom, and characterized by
inexpensive lowrise apartment buildings, often concrete-paneled in structure and socialist-functionalist in style and decorum, usually without eleva-
tors. Known popularly as *khrushchyovki* (literally "Khrushchev's buildings")
or, more pejoratively, *khrushchyoby* ("Khrushchev's tenements"), they were
designed for small, low-ceilinged apartments aimed at moving people out
of overcrowded communal apartments and accommodating the country's
swelling urban population.

Page 7

Why do I write about somebody else and not about myself?: The first in a
series of narrative authorial digressions (or reflections) that constitute both
an indirect authorial commentary on the events of the novel and a major
component of authorial philosophical presence in the novel. By and large,
the authorial reflections focus on anxieties of a dual Jewish-Russian identity
and on the traumatic process of tearing away from Russia.

Page 8

Pärnu . . . Pärnu Bay: Pärnu (in pre-1920s Russian, *Pernov*, in German, *Pernau*)
is a seaside resort on the west coast of Estonia, about a two-hour drive south
from Tallinn, the Estonian capital. By the end of the nineteenth century,
Pärnu became well known as a Baltic *Kurort*. It owed its reputation to the
long strand, the curative mud baths, and its steady and mild microclimate. The
resort opens onto a double gulf, the Pärnu Bay being part of the larger Gulf of
Riga. Still today the vacation capital of Estonia, Pärnu flourished during the
pre-World War II interlude of Estonian independence. Then came the Soviet
annexation in 1940, the Nazi occupation, and finally the Soviet "liberation,"
which lasted until 1991. In the 1960s and early 1970s, Pärnu became the
object of summer pilgrimages by the Soviet intelligentsia, a large percentage
of its summer population being Jews from large Soviet cities. David Shrayer-
Petrov and his family vacationed in Pärnu ever summer from 1972–1986, and
sections of part 1 and part 2 of the refusenik trilogy were composed in Pärnu.

Page 9

First you get an invitation . . . Then you file an application with OVIR: As a
signatory to the Helsinki Accords, the Soviet Union outwardly endorsed
the idea of reunification of families across national boundaries. In order to
petition the Soviet government for an exit visa to Israel, a Soviet Jew needed
a formal invitation (affidavit), known in Russian as *vyzov*, from a direct
relative residing in Israel. (As a historic note, the Soviet Union broke off
diplomatic relations with Israel immediately after Israel's victory in the Six-
Day War of 1967, and there were no direct consular relations between Israel
and USSR.) OVIR is the acronym of the Section of Visas and Invitations
(*Otdel viz i priglashenii*), a government office in charge of both issuing exit
visas to Soviet citizens and registering entrance visas of foreigners visiting
and staying in the USSR. For applicants for exit visas, the process usually

began at a local branch of the OVIR, which is why the Levitins submit their paperwork for emigration to Israel at the Visa Section branch office of the district where they live in Moscow.

Page 11

Trubnaya Square (Trubnaya Ploshchad'): Prominent landmark in Moscow's historic center, connecting Petrovsky Boulevard and Rozhdenstvensky Boulevard. These boulevards are sections of the Boulevard Ring (Bul'varnoe kol'tso), an incomplete semicircular chain of roads encompassing the historic White City of old Moscow.

Page 14

Pskov linen white of Tatyana's skin: Tatyana hails from a village in the Pskov Province of Russia's northwest, situated southwest of the Leningrad (St. Petersburg) Province and southeast of Estonia. Many of the Pskovians with deep roots in the area still look more Scandinavian than Russian, with blond hair and blue eyes; see also p. 57 of the novel.

Page 18

Afghanistan: The events of the novel begin at the end of 1978, and the Levitins attempt to emigrate in 1979, as the situation escalates in Afghanistan, where in April 1978 a Soviet-backed coup, known as the Saur Revolution, was led by Nur Muhammad Taraki. Taraki himself was deposed in September 1979. On 24 December 1979, the Soviet troops entered Afghanistan, soon reached Kabul, and staged another coup, installing Babrak Karmal, a Soviet stalwart. The Soviet occupation, with over 100,000 Soviet troops deployed in Afghanistan in the mid-1980s, was met with harsh resistance by the insurgent groups (the *mujahedeen*), mainly backed and financed by the US and Persian Gulf Arab countries. The bloody Soviet-Afghan War lasted for nine years and ended in February 1989. Having a son drafted and sent to Afghanistan was every Soviet mother's nightmare incarnate. See also two news items from *Pravda* quoted on p. 252.

Maleyevka: The common name of a famous Soviet writers' colony (in Soviet-speak, All-Soviet Writers' House of Creativity), founded in 1927 on the former estate of the merchant Maleyev (subsequently purchased by the publisher and journalist Vukol Lavrov). Maleyevka is located in the village of Glukhovo, some 60 miles west of Moscow. Shrayer-Petrov and his family spent a winter vacation at Maleyevka in late December 1979 and early

January 1980. Having already already applied for an exit visa, Shrayer-Petrov had been fired from his job in academic medicine, but had not yet been expelled from the Union of Soviet Writers and blacklisted; the expulsion took place in the summer of 1980.

Okudzhava to Sidorov, Sidorov to Bushin . . . : Bulat Okudzhava, Evgeny Sidorov, Vladimir Bushin, Vladimir Karpeko, Feliks Kuznetsov, and Iosif Gerasimov. This list of Soviet Russian-language writers includes official liberals, moderates, Russian nationalists and ultranationalists; it also includes an ethnic Georgian and a Jew, all of them celebrating New Year's against the backdrop of the Soviet invasion of Afghanistan, as the author of the novel reflects on his separation from Soviet literary life and also on some of his earliest experiences of Jewish otherness.

Page 19

Permyak . . . Siva: The Permyaks are speakers of the Komi-Permyak language of the Uralic family. The Komi-Permyaks predominantly reside in the northwest of the Perm Region of the Russian Federation, on the western slope of the middle section of the Ural Mountains. In 1941, as the Nazi siege was closing in on Leningrad, Shrayer-Petrov and his mother were evacuated to the remote village of Siva in the Vereshchagino district of the Perm (formerly Molotov) Province, where they stayed until the spring of 1944.

Page 21

Kropotkinskaya: Metro station and the Soviet-era name of Prechistenka Street. Renamed in 1921 after Prince Nikolay Kropotkin (1842–1921), political philosopher and geographer, and founder of Anarcho-Communism, the street was re-renamed in 1990. A major street in the southwest of Moscow's historic center, it runs from Prechistenskiye Vorota (Gates) Square on the Boulevard Ring (and Kropotkinskaya Metro Station and the Pushkin Museum of Fine Arts) to Zubovskaya Square on the Garden Ring. On the way to taking an entrance examination at the medical school, Anatoly rides to Kropotkinskaya metro station and then goes by trolleybus, first along Kropotkinskaya (Prechistenka), and then, after traversing Zubovskaya Square, along Zubovskaya Street and Bol'shaya Pirogovskaya Street (see below).

Pirogovka: Colloquial name of Bol'shaya Pirogovskaya Street, an important Moscow street just west of the historic city center, named so in 1924 after the great Russian surgeon Nikolay Pirogov (1810–1881), one of the founders of battlefield medicine. The M. I. Sechenov First Moscow Medical University (formerly the First Moscow Medical School) is located on Bol'shaya Pirogovskaya Street.

Page 22

Kosolapov and Shestipalov . . . : This list contains some very common Russian last names; two more unusual Russian last names (Kosolapov and Shestipalov); and two last names, Akhmeteli and Gotua, suggesting their carrier's origins in Georgia. Anatoly Levitin's exam group features a disproportionate number of Jewish names, about fifteen out of twenty-three, so as to force Jewish applicants to compete against one another for a very limited number of slots defined by an unofficial, albeit enforced, Jewish quota (numeris clausus).

Page 23

Tolstoy's Levin in *Anna Karenina*: By wondering, a bit absurdly, if Anatoly is related to Konstantin Levin, a wealthy nobleman in Tolstoy's novel *Anna Karenina* and a bearer of a Jewish name, Antoly Levitin's examiner here makes a double-edged antisemitic innuendo: a Jew cannot descend from the Russian nobility; a Russian nobleman cannot be a Jew.

Stoletov: Aleksandr Grigoryevich Stoletov (1839–1896), great Russian physicist, considered a founding father of electrical engineering.

Page 25

sailor Zheleznyak: Anatoly Zheleznyak (1895–1919), known popularly as Sailor Zheleznyak (*matros Zheleznyak*), sailor of the Baltic Fleet, anarchist, and Red Army commander killed in the Civil War and mythologized in Soviet culture, specifically popular song, fiction, and cinema.

Pravda and *Izvestia*: Two principal, mass-produced, Russian-language Soviet newspapers, *Pravda* being the organ of the Central Committee of the Communist Party of the Soviet Union and *Izvestia* being the organ of the Soviet of People's Deputies, the Soviet legislature.

the affair of the Jewish "doctor-murderers" (see also pp. 125–28): The so-called Doctor's Plot (*Delo vrachey*), a notorious fabrication that marked the culmination of the official, state-sponsored anti-Jewish campaign of the late Stalin years. On 13 January 1953, the Soviet media reported the arrests of a group of highly placed and prominent Soviet medical doctors, among them Miron Vovsi, who had consulted on Stalin's health, and Vladimir Vinogradov, Stalin's personal physician. The doctors were accused of being part of a terrorist group conspiring to murder Soviet leaders. Six of the nine doctors originally named in the official campaign were Jews, and they were said to be agents of American imperialism and "Jewish bourgeois nationalism," specifically, of the American Joint Distribution Committee. The Doctors' Plot quickly grew into a nation-wide campaign of vilification of Jews and mass antisemitic hysteria; fabricated charges were brought against other Jewish medical professionals. Soviet Jews feared collective punitive measures, such as mass deportations to remote areas in Siberia and Central Asia or even worse. After Stalin's death on 5 March 1953, the then collective Soviet leadership distanced itself from the plot. The charges against the accused doctors were dropped, and on 31 March 1953, they were officially exonerated. The whole affair was blamed on Deputy Minister of State Security Mikhail Ryumin, who was arrested and subsequently executed.

Page 26

the Sorot River: River in the Pskov Province (see note to p. 37), a tributary of the Velikaya River.

Page 31

Blue Blouse (in Russian, *Sinyaya bluza*): A Soviet agitprop performance group founded in 1923 and touring the country all through the 1920s and early 1930s. The blue-blousers preached an aesthetic of new proletarian simplicity of style, disdaining the bourgeoisie and mocking its cultural accouterments; see also p. 33.

Page 32

MOPR: Acronym of Mezhdynarodnaya organizatsiya pomoshchi bortsam revolyutsii (International Organization for Assistance to the Fighters of Revolutions), created in 1922 by the decision of the 4th Congress of the Communist International (Komintern). MOPR's Soviet branch was disbanded in 1947.

Litvak: A Lithuanian Jew or descendant of Lithuanian Jews.

"Varnishkes": Yiddish folk song; the word *varnishkes* refers to a popular Ashkenazi dish, buckwheat kasha with bowtie-style noodles.

Freylekhs: From the Yiddish adjective for "happy" or "joyful"; Yiddish term for a group of joyful tunes or, perhaps, a subgenre of Klezmer music.

"Ryabina" or "Tonkaya Ryabina" ("Rowanberry Tree" or "Thin Rowanberry Tree"): Popular Russian song, lyrics by the nineteenth-century poet Ivan Surikov, a man of peasant stock; music is said to be folk music.

Page 33

"Suliko": Georgian song, composed in 1895—lyrics by Akaky Tsereteli, music by Varinka Tsereteli—which became hugely popular during the Stalin years as Stalin's reported favorite, and was widely performed to the original tune with lyrics sung in Russian translation. The Georgian word "Suliko" refers to "soul," both male and female.

"Hey, Lads, Unharness the Horses . . ." (Ukrainian "Rozpryagayte, hlopci, koney"): Popular Ukrainian folk song.

Novomaysky: Fictional name of a Moscow city district; probably refers to the former Pervomaysky (originally, Stalinsky) district in the eastern part of Moscow, restructured and renamed in 1991.

"malicious absence of vigilance": Fabricated charges against Dr. Herbert Levitin's father, Dr. Anatoly Levitin, who was arrested in the weeks following the public announcement of the "Doctors' Plot" in January 1953; for details, see note to p. 25.

Page 35

on his father's *yarzeit* . . . he went to the synagogue: On the anniversary of his father's death, Doctor Levitin went to the historic Moscow Choral Synagogue in the city center, one of only two functioning synagogues during the late Soviet period. He traversed the Dzerzhinsky Square, as Lubyanskya (Lubyanka) Square was known in 1927–1990, named so after the first chief of the Soviet secret police, Feliks Dzerzhinsky. This major square, located north of Red Square, was known for the headquarters of the KGB (now Russian FSB), the Children's World (Detsky Mir) department store, and the monument to Dzerzhinsky in the center (which was erected in 1958 and moved in 1991). Doctor Levitin walks down from the northwest side of the square, past the Polytechnic Museum; veers to the left onto Bohdan Khmelnytsky Street (Ulitsa Bogdana Khmel'nitskogo, as Maroseyka Street was known at the time), leaving behind Staraya Ploshchad' (Square), where Building No. 4 used to house the Central Committee of the Communist Party; and finally takes his first right off Bogdana Khmel'nitskogo (Maroseyka) onto Bolshoy Spasoglinishchevsky Lane, at the time known as Ulitsa Arkhipova (Arkhipov Street). On the left side of this short, steep street, which soon thereafter flowed into the larger Solyanka Street, there stood the Moscow Choral Synagogue.

Page 37

Ryazan Province: Ryazan is an old Russian city and provincial capital situated about 120 miles to the southwest of Moscow.

Page 39

Orenburg shawl: Famed Russian shawls knitted from a particularly fine blend of goat down and silk; the craft originated from the city of Orenburg, located on the Ural River close to the border with Kazakhstan.

Shota Rustaveli . . . : The great Georgian poet and statesman Shota Rustaveli (ca. 1160–ca. 1220), commonly considered to be the author of the epic *The Knight in the Panther's Skin*, widely read in Russian translation; legend has it that Rustaveli made a pilgrimage to and died in Jerusalem.

Page 52

Tvardovsky's words—that the major character trait of the Russian peasant . . . : Aleksandr Tvardovsky (1910–1971), Russian Soviet poet of peasant stock, most famous for his long narrative poem *Vasily Tyorkin*, composed and published serially during World War II. The last name of the protagonist, a charismatic Russian peasant turned soldier, comes from the Russian root *teret'* ("to grate"; "to grind") and suggests the special capacity of Russians for bearing it all, for surviving against all odds though life-grinding circumstances, including foreign invasions.

Page 54

a pay-for-service health center (in Russian, *platnaya poliklinika*): Clinics and health centers that charged for services, and offered shorter or no lines and better quality of care, existed in large Soviet cities and stood somewhat apart from the regular, free network of Soviet healthcare.

Page 57

Ostrov Station: The town of Ostrov, from which Tatyana Levitina takes a bus to her native village of Maryino, is a district center in the Pskov Province, 27 miles south of Pskov (see note to p. 14).

Page 64

red corner (in Russian, *krasnyi ugol*): The red corner (also known in English as the icon corner) is a place of worship in a traditional Russian Orthodox household, usually a corner oriented east and adorned with icons and an oil lamp.

Page 66

Pushkin's *Dubrovsky*: Short novel by Aleksandr Pushkin, composed in 1832–1833. Vladimir Dubrovsky, a young Russian officer and nobleman robbed of his father's estate by a rich and powerful neighbor, retired general Troekurov, becomes a Robin Hood-like leader of a band of peasant robbers. Passing himself off as a Frenchman, young Dubrovsky gains employment as a tutor of Troekurov's daughter Masha, who falls in love not with the real Dubrovsky but with the persona of her French tutor.

Izba: Traditional Russian peasant house, often made of logs.

Page 68

Three Station Square (in Russian, Ploshchad' tryokh vokzalov): The unofficial popular name of Komsomolskaya Square (prior to 1933, Kalanchyovskaya Square) in Moscow. This square, located northeast of the historic center, is the location of three major railway stations—Leningradsky, Kazansky, and Yaroslavsky (and as such the city's biggest railway hub)—and also of the Komsomolskaya metro station.

Page 69

Helsinki Accords: See note to p. 9.

Page 70

Palekh, Khokhloma: Palekh, a town in the Ivanovo Province northeast of Moscow, is the historic center of the famous miniature painting school, especially renowned for its lacquered boxes. Khokhloma, or Khokhloma wood painting, is a traditional Russian style of decorating kitchen and household wooden objects, originating in the Nizhny Novgorod Province. Khokhloma wood objects and artifacts are painted with bright red flowers and berries against a black background and gold trim.

Page 71

Ethnic Germans: Two principal groups of ethnic Germans resided in the Russian Empire. The so-called Baltic Germans had been living in Estonia and Latvia since the twelfth–thirteenth centuries, their elite becoming the area's nobility. After the Baltic lands were ceded to the Russian Empire following Sweden's defeat in the Great Norther War (1700–1721), members of the Baltic German nobility actively entered the Russian Imperial service, many of them becoming Russianized and acculturated after the Russian fashion. In 1914, about 160,000 Germans resided in Russia's Baltic lands. Under the terms of the Molotov-Ribbentrop Pact of 1939 and the ensuing population transfers, the vast majority of the Baltic Germans from Latvia and Estonia were resettled to the Reich territories.

The history of the so-called Volga Germans (*nemtsy Povolzh'ya* or *povolzhskiye nemtsy*, sometimes called "Russian Germans") stands in stark contrast to that of the Baltic Germans. Under Catherine the Great, non-Jewish settlers from Europe were invited to move to the Russian Empire and farm its vast lands. In the 1760s the ancestors of the Volga Germans, thousands of them, many of them Mennonites seeking religious protection, moved to the Russian Empire and founded agricultural colonies, mainly along the lower Volga basin, in and south of the Saratov Province. They became part of Russia and regarded Russia as their true home, although they retained their language and traditions much the way the Amish have in the United States. In 1924 the Volga German Autonomous Republic with the capital city Pokrovsk (renamed Engels in 1931) was formed in the lower basin of the Volga; according to the 1939 Soviet census, about 367,000 Volga Germans resided in the autonomous republic. Soon after Nazi Germany invaded the Soviet Union, the ethnic Germans in the USSR were deemed potential collaborators. Over 400,000 Volga Germans were disenfranchised, rounded up, and exiled to Central Asia and Siberia, mainly to Kazakhstan. Perhaps as many as 200,000 of them died en route and during the resettlement in what amounted to a genocidal collective punishment by default.

The Soviet textbooks said nothing about the mass deportation, its closest American parallel being the internment of Japanese Americans during World War II. In the 1970s, the Volga Germans began to apply for exit visas to emigrate to West Germany (which allowed the return of ethnic Germans); Jewish refuseniks encountered Volga Germans in lines outside Visa Section offices.

Saratov: Major Russian city and regional center located in the lower basin of the Volga, about 530 miles southeast of Moscow; capital of the Saratov Province.

Chelyabinsk: Major Russian industrial city located on the southeastern slopes of the Ural Mountains, at the geographical boundary of the Urals and Siberia; capital of the Chelyabinsk Province.

Page 72

Volskdeutche: In Nazi Germany, this term referred to all ethic Germans regardless of their citizenship and country of residence—as opposed to *Reichsdeutsche*, Germans living within the Reich. Thus ethnic Germans living on Soviet territories generally fell under the definition of *Volksdeutche*.

Page 75

Mayakovskaya: Metro station in the center of Moscow at the intersection of Tverskaya Street (formerly Gorky Street) and the Garden Ring on Mayakovskaya (now Triumfal'naya) Square. The station opened in 1938 as part of the Zamoskvoretskaya Line, the second oldest line of the Moscow Metro; named so after the Russian poet Vladimir Mayakovsky (1893–1930), whose status was posthumously elevated to that of a national Soviet classic.

Sokol: Metro station that opened in 1953 in the Sokol district, which was quickly developed in the 1930s–1950, northwest of the city's historic center.

Page 76

Pale of Settlement (in Russian, *cherta osedlosti*): A swath of Russia's northwestern, western, and southwestern territories, including parts of the present-day Lithuania, Latvia, Belarus, Ukraine, Moldova, and western and southern Russia, where Russia's Jews were generally allowed to reside permanently from the late eighteenth century to the February 1917 revolution, after which restrictions based on nationality and confession were abolished.

Page 78

Vostryakovo: A working-class settlement west of Moscow founded in the 1950s; presently a neighborhood within the western outskirts of Moscow. Also the name of a nearby large cemetery with a Jewish section.

Page 79

SALT II Treaty: SALT is an acronym for Strategic Arms Limitation Talks. The bilateral SALT I and SALT II negotiations, conferences, and resulting treaties between the US and the USSR took place in 1969–79 and addressed the issue of nuclear arms control.

Page 81

The Vyborg side (in Russian, Vyborgskaya storona): Named so after the city of Vyborg on the Karelian Isthmus; the Vyborg side constitutes one of the principal geographical parts ("sides") of the city of St. Petersburg (Petrograd; Leningrad). The Neva divides St. Petersburg into three main areas: northern, southern, and eastern. The Vyborg side, traditionally a working-class and industrial area and a Bolshevik stronghold during both 1917 revolutions, makes up the eastern portion of the northern main area of the city, along with Vasilievsky Island and the Petrograd Side, from which the Vyborg Side is separated by the Bolshaya ("Big") Nevka. As opposed to the Vyborg Side, a geographical term, the Vyborg District (Vyborgsky rayon), as an administrative section of the city of St. Petersburg, dates to 1718, and exists in its present borders since 1978; one of the largest districts in the city, and presently the third most populous.

Page 84

The Forestry Academy Park: Forestry Technology Academy (Russ. Lesotekh-nicheskaya Akademiya), formerly Forestry Institute, founded in 1803 and renamed S. M. Kirov Leningrad Forest Technology Academy in 1929, is located in the Vyborg District of St. Petersburg (Leningrad) and surrounded by a large park; its oldest part dates to the 1830s. Shrayer-Petrov grew up in the Lesnoye section of the Vyborg Side in the vicinity of the Forestry Academy and its arboretum.

Page 86

Luga: Town and district center located about 88 miles south of St. Petersburg (Leningrad).

Page 88

Vinnitsa (in Ukrainian, Vinnitsya): Located about 160 miles southwest of Kiev, Vinnitsa is presently the largest city of the historic Podolia region in the southwest of Ukraine; capital of the Vinnitsa Province and formerly a major regional center of Jewish life.

Page 92

Triple Cologne (in Russian, *troynoy odekolon*): Men's cologne developed in Russia in the first third of the nineteenth century. Mass-produced during the Soviet period, it became not only the most commonly used aftershave but also an antiseptic; owing to its high alcohol content (sixty-four percent), it was not infrequently consumed as an alcoholic beverage. The scent of Triple Cologne was part of the stereotype of a Soviet everyman.

Page 93

Zaporozhian Cossack: Cossacks who lived beyond the rapids of the Dnieper in Central Ukraine. In the sixteenth–seventeenth centuries, the semi-autonomous Zaporozhian Cossack Host (in Ukrainian, Zaporiz'ka Sich) constituted a formidable military and political force in the region. It gained special notoriety during the Khmelnytsky Rebellion of 1648–1657. A Zaporozhian Cossack sported a special long lock of hair hanging from a clean-shaven head, known as *chub* or *oseledets*, and a long mustache extending from both sides of the mouth down to the jaw.

Page 96

that frightening place where one formally became a refusenik: Refusenik is a calque of the Russian (Soviet) *otkaznik* (plural *otkazniki*; from the Russian noun *otkaz* "refusal"). The terms refers to the individuals, predominantly of Jewish origin, who applied for an exit visa to emigrate from the USSR but were denied, or *refused*, permission to leave. In English translation, the term "refusenik" has acquired a bit more ambiguity and unintentional irony: the Soviet authorities, not the Jews, were refusing. The refuseniks had only refused the ticket to Soviet paradise.

Page 98

Padre Montanelli . . . Voinich's *The Gadfly*: A novel by the Irish-born Ethel Lilian Voinich (1864–1960), originally published in 1897 in the United States.

The novel's protagonist, Arthur Burton, an activist of the Italian *Risorgimento* movement in the 1840s, eventually comes in conflict with his mentor (and secret biological father), Father Montanelli, a Catholic priest, subsequently a Cardinal. In translation, *The Gadfly* was phenomenally popular in the USSR, enjoyed the status of required reading, and by some accounts sold 2,500,000 copies.

Page 99

Girls from the Spanish Steps (in Russian, *Devushki s ploshchadi Ispanii*): *Le ragazze di Piazza Spagna*, a 1952 Italian comedy directed by Luciano Emmer; released in the US under the title *Three Girls from Rome.*

Kolpachny Lane (in Russian, Kolpachny Pereulok): Street in the northeast of Moscow's historic center, running south from Pokrovka Street to Khokhlovsky Lane. At the time described in the novel, the Moscow city branch of the Visa Section (OVIR) was located in an old mansion at 10 Kolpachny Lane.

Page 100

Never Love a Stranger: The first in a slew of bestselling novels by Harold Robbins (1916–1997), also a movie of the same title. Smuggled into the USSR, Robbins' novels, including *Never Love and Stranger*, *The Dream Merchants* (1949), and *The Carpetbaggers* (1961), enjoyed popularity in the circles of Soviet intelligentsia, and were read as sources of knowledge and information about the United States. See also the note about Jacqueline Susann (p. 196).

Page 106

Trubnaya Square . . . Tsvetnoy Boulevard: See note to p. 11; Tsvetnoy ("Flower") Boulevard runs north from Trubnaya Square (on the Boulevard Ring) to Sadovaya-Sukharevskaya Street (a section of the Garden Ring). Herbert and Tatyana Levitin pass the former Central Farmers Market and the former Old Circus (now the Nikulin Circus) as they walk on the west side of Tsvetnoy Boulevard toward the Garden Ring. They see the editorial offices of *Literary Gazette* (*Literaturnaya gazeta*) on the other side of Tsvetnoy Boulevard. A *shashlychnaya* is a café or restaurant that serves *shashlyk* (skewered meat grilled over hot coals; closely related to Shish kebab).

Page 107

Papirosa: Russian cigarette with a shorter tube filled with tobacco and a longer filterless section that goes into the mouth.

Page 115

May holidays: After May 1, International Workers Day, and May 9, Victory
Day (which celebrates the Soviet victory over Nazi Germany), both of
which were official Soviet holidays.

Page 117

House of Cinema (in Russian, *Dom Kino*): The Central House of Cinema in
Moscow opened in 1934 as a club, screening, and conference space under
the aegis of the Union of Soviet Cinematographers. The current building
on Vasilievskaya Street opened in 1968 and featured the main screening
hall for 1100 people.

Malaya Bronnaya Street . . . Patriarch's Ponds: Malaya Bronnaya is a very pic-
turesque street (and coveted residential area) in the northwest of Moscow's
historic center, which runs from Tverskoy Boulevard on the Boulevard Ring
to where Bol'shaya Sadovaya Street connects with Sadovaya-Kudrinskaya
Street on the Garden Ring. Toward the end of Malaya Bronnaya Street,
closer to the Garden Ring, is an enchanted area encompassing what remains
of the Patriarch's Ponds (named after the residence of a seventeenth-century
Russian Orthodox Patriarch), presently one pond surrounded by a park and
playground. This area is mythologized in Russian literature, including in the
works of Lev Tolstoy and Mikhail Bulgakov.

Kolkhoznaya Square: In 1934 Moscow, Bol'shaya ("Large") Sukharevskaya
Square, a major landmark in the north of the city's historic center, located
east of the intersection of Sretenka Street and the Garden Ring, was expanded
and renamed Kolkhoznaya ("Collective Farm") Square; at the time Moscow's
Malaya ("Small") Sukharevskaya Square, located on the Garden Ring west of
the intersection with Sretenka Street, was made part of the expanded square.
In 1939 Kolkoznaya Square was divided into Malaya ("Small") and Bol'shaya
("Large"), but Muscovites continued to refer to it simply as "Kolkhoznaya
Square." In 1994, the old names of the adjacent squares were restored.

Mayakovskaya Square: See note to p. 75.

Page 118

Bazarov: Evgeny Bazarov, protagonist of Ivan Turgenev's famous novel *Fathers
and Sons* (1862), set in the summer of 1859, on the eve of the emancipation
of Russian peasant serfs (1861). At the end of the novel, Bazarov, a charismatic nihilist training to become a medical doctor, dies of typhus.

Page 119

Bluebell: Anatoly Levitin's affectionate name for Natasha Leyn. The Russian original has *Nezabudka* (Forget-Me-Not, a feminine noun referring to a flower with associations of fidelity and love everlasting). After numerous discussions and in consultation with the author, the translators settled for "Bluebell."

Page 125

District Court of Jerusalem: In referencing the Adolf Eichmann Trial, the novel in original Russian quotes from the authorized Russian translation of Israel's Attorney General Dr. Gideon Hausner's speech at the Eichmann trial, as published in Israel by Aliyah-Library (see Dr. Gideon Hausner, *6 000 000 obvinyayut*, tr. from the Hebrew, Jerusalem: Biblioteka-Aliya, 1974). Karl Adolf Eichmann (1906–1962) was appointed by Hitler as head of the Reich Central Office of Jewish Emigration, and in 1942, following the Wannsee Conference, took charge of the Final Solution. Agents of the Mossad (Israeli secret service) located Eichmann in Argentina, where he had fled after World War II, and abducted him to Israel in 1960. At his trial in Jerusalem (2 April–14 August 1961), Eichmann argued that he was "following orders." Found guilty of crimes against humanity and the Jewish people, and of war crimes, Eichmann was executed on 31 May 1962.

Page 127

Wolf Messing (1899–1974): A Polish-born Jew who escaped to the USSR in 1939, displayed psychic and telepathic powers, and became a famous performer.

Lidia Timashuk (whose praises had been sung by . . . Olga Chechyotkina): On the so-called Doctor's Plot, see note to p. 25. In 1948 Lidia Timashuk, a cardiologist, wrote a letter to the authorities, denouncing the Kremlin physicians, who treated the party's Central Committee Secretary Andrey Zhdanov (1896–1948), and accusing them of overlooking Zhdanov's heart condition and incorrectly treating the Soviet leader. Zhdanov died a month later. As the so-called Doctors' Plot was already in the process of being fabricated in August 1952, Timoshchuk was summoned to the Ministry of State Security and asked to testify. After the Doctors' Plot was officially announced and the anti-Jewish campaign quickly gained speed, Timashuk's testimony was treated as an act of high Soviet patriotism; she was awarded the Order of

Lenin for "helping the Government denounce the doctor-murderers" and was publically praised. In an article published in *Pravda*, the journalist Olga Chechyotkina wrote of Timashuk as a "symbol of Soviet patriotism, high vigilance, ruthless, courageous struggle against the enemies of our Motherland."

Page 128

Bella Vladimirovna: This autobiographical digression refers to the author's mother, Bella Vul'fovna (Russianized patronymic Vladimirovna) Breydo. In the atmosphere of the escalating state-sponsored antisemitic campaign of January–February 1953, she lost her job as an accountant at a Leningrad factory, but was reinstated under pressure from the workers at her factory, who admired her for her fairness and scrupulousness.

Bolotnaya Street . . . Kalinin Museum: Bolotnaya Street is located on the Vyborg Side of St. Petersburg (Leningrad); see note to p. 81. Mikhail Kalinin (1875–1946) was a prominent Bolshevik and Soviet leader, Chairman of the Central Executive Committee (VTSiK; TsiK after 1922) beginning in 1919, and Chairman of the Presidium of the Supreme Soviet, i.e. a titular Soviet head of state, from 1938 until his death. Following the February 1917 revolution, Kalinin was elected to the Petrograd Council (soviet) of Workers' and Soldiers' Representatives (RSD) as a representative of the Vyborg Side. The Museum, presently known as Bolotnaya Street, 13, is located in a two-story mansion, No. 13/17 Bolotnaya Street. It once housed the Lesnoye-Udelnoye district Duma, which Kalinin was chairman of before the October Bolshevik Revolution. On 16 (29) October 1917, the Central Committee of the Bolshevik Party convened in the mansion to discuss the planning of the October coup d'etat.

siege: The Nazi siege (blockade) of Leningrad in 1941–1944, which lasted 872 days.

Page 129

Birobidzhan: An enclave on the Soviet-China border, capital of the Jewish Autonomous Province. In the 1920s the prospect of solving the Jewish question in the USSR through the "Jews on the land" program—and especially through the Birobidzhan project—offered the Soviet leadership a politically advantageous alternative to Zionism. The plan to create a Jewish enclave in the Far East, in the Amur River basin near the Soviet–Manchurian border, was put forth in 1927. The first 654 settlers-pioneers arrived in Birobidzhan in the spring of 1928 to find themselves in severe climactic conditions, surrounded by the taiga (boreal forest), with insufficient logistical and equipment support. The population grew slowly, many Jewish settlers returning after temporary stays. In 1930 a Jewish national district was incorporated, with 2,672 Jews out of the Birobidzhan area's total population of 38,000. By 1934 the Jewish population of the Birobidzhan area was a little over 8,000, instead of the projected 50,000. Yet the Soviet leadership pushed on with its plan, making the area a Jewish Autonomous Province in 1934. Yiddish was given a special status and taught in the enclave's public schools. While the Birobidzhan project initially stirred enthusiasm among Soviet Jews, it existed primarily as an ideological tool of the Soviet leadership, attracting support and even enlisting settlers among Jewish Communists abroad. According to Soviet data for 1959, 14,289 Jews, or about nine percent of the total population, were living in the Birobidzhan area, and fewer than 2,000 people called Yiddish their native language. According to the Soviet data for 1989, 8,887 Jews, or about four percent of the total population, were living in the Birobidzhan area.

Page 131

Sokolniki: Historic district and residential area in the northeast of Moscow, known for its sprawling urban park of the same name; also a metro station.

Tushino: Historic district and residential area in the northwest of Moscow; part of Moscow since 1960. During the so-called Time of Troubles, the impostor tsar False Dmitry II, also known as the "thief of Tushino," had his camp in the village of Tushino in 1608–1610. In the 1930s–1950s, it was the site of a major military airfield. At the time described in the novel, the ride from Sokolniki metro station to Tushinskaya metro station would take under an hour.

38, Petrovka Street: Location of the Moscow Criminal Police on Petrovka Street in the city center.

Page 140

Chekhov's character Ionych: Protagonist of Chekhov's eponymous story of 1898, a doctor who gives up his youthful hopes and aspirations and becomes callous and indifferent to the world.

Page 141

Tra-ta-ta, ta-ta-ta-ta-ta. Tra-ta-ta, Shalom Aleichem: Anatoly is humming and
singing "Shalom Aleichem" (Peace be upon you), a traditional Jewish song.

Page 144

Pyotr Konchalovsky . . . Andrei Mikhalkov-Konchalovsky . . . Nikita Mikhalkov:
Pyotr Konchalovsky (1876–1956) was a prominent Russian and Soviet visual
artist, in his earlier years one of the founders of the Knave of Diamonds
group (1910–1916). The well-known Russian filmmaker Andrei Mikhalkov-
Konchalovsky (b. 1937) is the grandson of Pyotr Konchalovsky, and the
older son of Soviet poet and children's author Sergey Mikhalkov (who co-
authored the lyrics of the Soviet national anthem) and the author Natalya
Konchalovskaya. The famous Russian filmmaker and actor Nikita Mikhalkov
(b. 1945) is the younger brother of Andrei Mikhalkov-Konchalovsky.

Lucchino Visconti (1906–1976): Great Italian film and stage director. Visconti
was a member of the Italian Communist Party, and some of his films were
shown in the USSR. *Gruppo di famiglia in un interno* (*Family Portrait in
an Interior Setting*, 1974) was Visconti's penultimate film, featuring Burt
Lancaster, Claudia Cardinale, and Helmut Berger. Known in English as
Conversation Piece.

Page 151

Lenin Library: The Russian State Library, the country's largest, was called the
V. I. Lenin State Library in 1925–1992. It is located on Vozdvizhenka
Street near the intersection with Mokhovaya Street, a short walk to the
Aleksandrovsky Garden and the Kremlin.

Page 154

Mandelstam, Chagall, Plisetskaya, Brodsky: Jewish-Russian poet and prose
writer Osip Mandelstam (1891–1938); Jewish-Russian visual artist
Marc Chagall (1887–1985); Jewish-Russian ballerina Maya Plisetskaya
(1925–2015); Jewish-Russian poet and essayist Iosif (Joseph) Brodsky
(1940–1996), who in 1972 emigrated to the US.

Page 156

Palanga . . . Trakai: Palanga is a major resort on the Lithuanian Baltic Coast.
Trakai (Polish *Troki*; Yiddish *Trok*) is a historic town located 17 miles west

of the Lithuanian capital of Vilnius. In the fifteenth century, Trakai functioned as a political and administrative capital of the Duchy of Lithuania; best known for its Island Castle and its historic sites related to Lithuania's Karaite (Karaim) community. On Karaites, see below note to p. 166.

Antakalnio Street: One of the principal streets in the city of Vilnius, running from the center to the northeast along the Neris River.

Vasily Ivanovich Kachalov (1875–1948): Russian and Soviet actor of national fame and acclaim, for decades one of the stars of the Moscow Art Theater. Kachalov (real name Shverubovich) was born in Wilno (in Russian, Vil'na; in Yiddish, Vilne; now Vilnius), where, until 1893, his family lived on Didžioji Gatve (Street) next to the Old Synagogue (Vilniaus Didžioji sinagoga), which is no longer standing.

Page 162

Louis de Funès (1914–1983): French actor, renowned for his numerous comedy parts. Dubbed comedies with de Funès, such as *Le Petit Baigneur* (1969), were widely shown in the USSR and other countries of the Soviet Bloc.

Page 165

Icarus: Hungarian bus manufacturer; Icarus buses were fairly common on Soviet streets and highways.

Page 166

Peredelkino . . . Pasternak's grave: A settlement located some 20 miles southwest of Moscow, Peredelkino, in 1934, became the location of dachas (country or summer houses) built for Soviet writers under the auspices of the Literary Fund of the USSR. Also the location of a writers' colony, the House of Creativity at Peredelkino (see also Maleyevka—note to p. 18). The great Jewish-Russian poet Boris Pasternak (1890–1960) lived in Peredelkino from 1936 until his death, and is buried there.

Ilya Selvinsky (1889–1968): Major Jewish-Russian lyrical and epic poet, playwright, and novelist; in the 1920s, leader of the Literary Center of Constructivists. A military journalist and political officer during World War II, Selvinsky became, in early 1942, one of the earliest literary witnesses to the Shoah (Holocaust). Ostracized and denounced in a number of Party resolutions of the 1930s–1940s, through a combination of personal bravery, political navigation, and luck, Selvinsky weathered the storms of Stalin-ism. He remained a proud Jew during the most antisemitic of the Soviet years, 1949–1953. Jewish and Judaic themes figured prominently in Selvin-sky's works, from the early wreath of sonnets "Bar Kokhba" (1920) to his late autobiographical novel *O My Youth* (1966). A native of Crimea and a descendant of both Ashkenazi Jews and Krymchaks (Crimea's indigenous Jews, see below), Selvinsky was born in the Crimean capital Simferopol and grew up on the west coast of the peninsula in Yevpatoria; he died in Moscow. Selvinsky had a dacha in Peredelkino.

Berta Yakovlevna, and his daughters, Tsilya and Tata: Berta Yakovlevna Selvinskaya was Selvinsky's lifelong wife. Tsilya was Tsetsiliya Voskresenskaya, Selvinsky's stepdaughter, professor of theater arts and a memoirist. Tata was Tatyana Selvinskaya, Selvinsky's daughter, a painter, set designer, and poet.

Pages 166–78

Crimean Tatars are an ethnoreligious group, speakers of a Turkic language (Crimean-Tatar) and followers of Sunni Islam, who until the middle of the nineteenth century constituted Crimea's majority population. Following the liberation of Crimea from Nazi occupation in May 1944, the Crimean Tatars were collectively accused of Nazi collaboration and punitively deported from the peninsula to Central Asia in what amounted to an act of genocide and a crime against humanity. About twenty percent of the populated died en route or during the first year of punitive exile. The return of Crimean Tatars to Crimea slowly began in 1967; only in 1989 did the Soviet legislature declare the exile of Crimean Tatars a lawless act. About 240,000 Crimean Tatars presently reside in Crimea.

Krymchaks: Krymchaks are Crimea's indigenous, Rabbinic, non-Ashkenazi Jews, speakers of a Turkic language closely related to the Crimean-Tatar language. Krymchaks have resided in Crimea since as early as the first cen-tury BCE. Some 6,000 Krymchaks (75% of the entire population) were murdered during the Shoah. At the present time, of about 1,500 Krym-chaks, some 600 live in Israel, and some 200 remain in Crimea.

Karaites: Karaite Judaism, a Jewish religious movement, gained its shape in the eighth century in the Near East. Karaite Judaism is distinct from Rabbinic

Judaism (and, in the Crimean context, from the Judaism of Krymchaks). Karaites only recognize the supreme authority of the Torah and reject Oral Law and its codification in the Talmud. In the ninth–twelfth centuries, the Karaite communities, autonomous from Rabbinic Judaism in Muslim lands, enjoyed a period of growth and a flourish. Some estimates suggest that as much as a third of all Judaic communities at the time were adherents of Karaite Judaism. Their numbers subsequently dwindled, and small Karaite communities survived in the Near East, the Ottoman Empire, and the Russian Empire. An estimated 40,000 Karaites reside worldwide, about 35,000 in Israel, about 4,000 in the US, and about 1,000 in Crimea (in Ukraine until 2014; presently in the Russian Federation). Ukraine, Lithuania, and Poland have very small surviving Karaite communities (on Lithuania's Karaite community, the subject of one of the novel's principal authorial digressions, see below).

The ethnic roots of the Crimean Karaites (Karaims), from which Lithuania's Karaite community originated, are debated to this day, some theories linking Crimean Karaites to the vanished Khazars. By the time the Crimean Khanate ceased to exist and the Crimea had been ceded to the Russian Empire by the Ottoman Empire in 1783, the Karaites had been living in Crimea for about six centuries. At the boundary of the nineteenth century, following the partitions of Poland and the annexation of Crimea, the Russian Empire gained long-established Karaite communities, principally in Crimea and in Vilnius and Trakai, but also in parts of modern-day Ukraine, Belarus, and Poland.

The Karaite presence in Lithuania dates to the fourteenth century, when the greatest Lithuanian warrior and conqueror, Grand Duke Vytautas, brought from Crimea about 300 Karaite men with families, settling them in Trakai (Troki), at the time the Lithuanian capital.

The history of Karaites (Karaims) in the Russian Empire is one of setting Karaites aside from Jews—and of Karaites actively seeking not to be regarded as Jews. Karaites in the Russian Empire were not subject to the official anti-Jewish regulations and enjoyed special privileges. According to the Russian census of 1897, about 13,000 Karaites, and about 5,250.000 Rabbinic Jews, resided in the empire. The Karaite leader Seraya Shapshal, who in 1911 became Chief Hakham (Karaite spiritual leader) of the Russian Empire, further sought to distance his community from Judaism by recognizing both Jesus and Muhammad as prophets and insisting on the Turkic origins of Karaites.

The story of the Karaite survival during the Shoah calls for a brief stop. (For a detailed study, see Kiril Feferman, "Nazi Germany and the Karaites in 1938–1944: Between Racial Theory and *Realpolitik*," *Nationalities Papers* 39, no. 2 [2011]: 277–94.) At the start of World War II, about 6,000 Karaites lived in Crimea, about 1,000 in Lithuania and Poland. In 1937–38, in part because a small group of Karaites residing in Nazi Germany lobbied to be exempted from the anti-Jewish legislation stemming from Nuremberg Laws, the Nazi administration began to investigate the Karaite question. In February 1939 the SS ruled that Karaites were to be treated as Jews. However, as historian Kiril Feferman demonstrated, despite an earlier SS ruling, in March 1939, the Reich Kinship Office "stipulated that the Karaites were not to be regarded as a Jewish religious community affected by the Reich citizenship law." At the same time, the Reich Kinship Office did not make a clear-cut ruling as to the Karaites' ethnic origins, opening up the question for further investigation. Based on this ruling and additional investigations by the Nazi authorities, further exceptions were made for the Karaites in Nazi-occupied territories, most notably, for Lithuanian and Crimean Karaites, who were deemed not to be Jews either religiously or "racially," but rather a distinct Turkic tribe with a spoken Turkic language and a faith of its own, which recognized the Old Testament and incorporated other religious traditions. Still, in two most notable cases, at Babi Yar in Kiev and in the southern Russian city of Krasnodar, Karaites were murdered alongside Jews.

After the war, the small Karaite communities in the USSR found themselves dwindling in numbers and self-isolated from both the Soviet and the world Jewish communities. Lithuania's Karaites (or Karaims, as they elect to call themselves) were mainly living in Trakai and Vilnius, and continuing to insist that they were not of the Jews. By the late 1970s, they had dwindled to fewer than 500, only slightly higher than the number of Crimean Karaites that Vytautas had originally brought to Lithuania in the fourteenth century. About 400 Karaites currently live in Lithuania, mostly still in Trakai and Vilnius, and they continue to insist, at least outwardly, that they are not related to Jews. In modern-day Lithuania, they are recognized as an ethnic minority of Turkic origin. Two Karaite prayer houses, called *kenesa* (cf. the Hebrew *Beit Knesset*, a place of worship/assembly; cf. the Knesset, the Parliament of the State of Israel) can be seen in Vilnius and Trakai. In Trakai, one of the main tourist attractions is Karaimu gatve=Karaite Street, with its traditional wooden houses. While revisiting Trakai in the summer of 2003, for the first time since 1977 when he was there with his parents, the editor of this volume was offered the traditional Karaite *pirozhki*, known as *kibinai* (cf. the Arab and Sephardic *kibbeh*) at a restaurant featuring Karaite dishes, but with pork instead of lamb. In this episode of the novel, the author walks around Trakai, querying the dark-haired, swarthy, eagle-nosed Karaims: Aren't you like us? Aren't you Jews? Only one woman acknowledges the group's Jewish roots, while all the others rigorously deny them. The author wonders: What becomes of Jews' descendants when they sever themselves—or are severed—from their Judaic roots?

Khazar Kingdom (Khaganate). . . . Crimean Tatars . . . Krymchaks . . . Karaites . . . : The Khazar Khaganate (Qağanate) was, in the seventh–tenth centuries, a major state extending from the Caspian Sea to the Black Sea; at the peak of its might, it controlled vast territories, from the basins of the Volga and the Don to the Crimean peninsula, and exerted power over Kievan Rus and Khazaria's other neighbors to the north and east. While Khazaria was a polyethnic and polyreligious state, in the eighth century, the Khazarian *khagan* (supreme ruler) and the ruling elites converted to Judaism. The Russian Primary Chronicle (*Povest' vremennykh let*) mentions that in 986, a Khazarian delegation unsuccessfully sought to convince Grand Prince Vladimir of Kiev to convert to Judaism; he chose Orthodox Christianity over other monotheistic religions. After the defeat of Khazaria by Grand Prince Svyatoslav I of Kievan Rus in 965–969, the state disintegrated. What became of Khazars is to this day a contested issue, and various larger and smaller Jewish and non-Jewish groups, including Ashkenazi Jews of Eastern Europe, Crimean Jews, Mountain Jews (of the Caucasus), Bukharan Jews, Don Cossacks, Avars, and Kazakhs, have claimed to have been descended or partially descended from the Khazars.

Page 167

Khersones: Chersoneuses (Russian: Khersones) was an ancient Greek colony on the southwestern tip of the Crimean peninsula. The ruins of the colony's capital, which include a Roman amphitheater and a Greek temple, are located on the outskirts of the city of Sebastopol.

Page 169

If there are around two million Jews in the country: According to official Soviet statistics, there were 2,170,000 Jews in the USSR in 1970; 1,830,000 in 1979; and 1,480,000 in 1989. In 2000 there were 460,000 Jews in the Russian Federation, and in 2017 only about 170,000 remained.

Raikins, Utyosovs . . . Pasternaks, Mandelstams: A list representing prominent authors, cultural figures, scientists, medical professionals, and military leaders of Jewish-Russian origin who have made important contributions to Russian and Soviet civilization: comedian, actor, and director Arkady Raikin (1911–1987); jazz singer, entertainer, and actor Leonid Utyosov (stage name for Leyzer Vaysbein, 1895–1982); ballerina Maya Plisetskaya (1925–2015); playwright, screenwriter, and fiction writer Leonid Zorin (pseydonym of Leonid Zaltsman, b. 1924); twice Hero of the Soviet Union, Lieutenant General David Dragunsky (1910–1992), who chaired the Anti-Zionist Committee of the Soviet Public since its inception in 1977; virologist and immunologist Lev Zilber (1894–1966); prominent physician Miron Vovsi (1897–1960), one of the doctors falsely accused during the Doctors' Plot of 1953 (see note on p. 23); screenwriter, playwright, fiction writer, and memoirist Evgeny Gabrilovich (1899–1993); nuclear physicist Yakov Zeldovich (1914–1987); fiction writer and memoirist Veniamin Kaverin (pseydonym of Veniamin Zilber, 1902–1989), younger brother of Lev Zilber; poet, fiction writer and translator Boris Pasternak (1890–1960); poet and prose writer Osip Mandelstam (1891–1938).

Marx, Lenin: Karl Marx's parents came from prominent German and Dutch Jewish families; as a young man, Marx's father had converted to Lutheranism in order to bypass anti-Jewish restrictions. Vladimir Lenin's ancestors included ethnic Russians, Chuvashs, Kalmyks, Germans, and Jews. His maternal grandfather, Aleksandr Blank, came from a Jewish family from Zhitomir, Ukraine; a physician, he had converted to Russian Orthodoxy as a young man so as to bypass anti-Jewish regulations and quotas.

Page 170

Selvinsky . . . "Bar Kokhba" . . . *O My Youth*: See note to p. 166.

Khazars who tried to convert Prince Vladimir the Great to Judaism: See note to pp. 166–78.

Lev Gumilyov (1912–1992): Prominent Soviet historian and anthropologist; author of influential if controversial ethnogenetic theories; son of Russian poets Anna Akhmatova and Nikolay Gumilyov.

Page 173

Reb Chaim-Wolf: The author's maternal grandfather, Rabbi Chaim-Wolf Broyde (Breydo), had descended from a long line of Litvak rabbis, which may have included the Gaon Rabbi Yitzchok Aizik Broida. A rabbi in Panevėžys, Lithuania, and subsequently a Jewish schoolteacher in the 1920s and 1930s in the Belarusian town of Polotsk, he was murdered during the Shoah.

Kamenets-Podolsky (Kamyanets-Podilsky in Ukrainian): Historic city in southwest Ukraine. Natives of Kamenets-Podolsky lovingly referred to it as "Kamenets." Located on the banks of the Smotrich River close to the border of the Austro-Hungarian Empire, Kamenets-Podolsk had been the capital of the Podolia Province and an important regional center of commerce. Presently a district center in the Khmelnytskyi Province of Ukraine. On the eve of World War I, there were 23,000 Jews, or nearly half of the population, in Kamenets-Podolsk. Both the families of the author's father (the Shrayers) and the author's father-in-law (the Polyaks) hailed from Kamenets-Podolsky and knew each other as children.

Holy Hills Monastery: Founded in 1569 on orders of Russian tsar Ivan the Terrible, the Holy Hills Monastery of the Holy Assumption (in Russian, Svyatogorsky Svyato-Uspensky Monastyr') is located in the town of Pushkinskiye Gory (Pushkin Hills; until 1925, Svyatye Gory=Holy Hills) in the Pskov Province. Along with the ancestral estates of the Gannibal-Pushkin family—Mikhailovskoye and Petrovskoye, and several other adjacent sites—the Holy Hills Monastery is part of the Pushkin Museum Reserve. It is best known in Russian culture as the location of Alexander Pushkin's grave, which, in turn, is part of the Gannibal-Pushkin family crypt. On 29 (10) January 1837, Pushkin died after being mortally wounded in a duel. His body was brought to and buried at the Holy Hills Monastery. In August 1841 an obelisk made of Italian marble, commissioned by Pushkin's widow Natalya Pushkina (née Goncharova; Lanskaya in her second marriage), was placed over his grave. On the front of the top part of the obelisk, there is a relief—a wreath surrounding a six-pointed star. Affixed above the wreath with the six-pointed star is a metal crucifix. The meaning of a six-pointed star is variously interpreted in scholarship: the Star of David (Mogen Dovid), a hexagram (Masonic symbol), the Star of Bethlehem. In the author's version, the Star of David over Pushkin's grave is linked to his Abyssinian—and Afro-Semitic—origins.

Pages 173–74

But on his mother's side, Pushkin had descended from Ethiopian (Abyssinian) princes: Until quite recently the accepted version of Alexander Pushkin's genealogy—and the version Pushkin himself relied on and promoted—linked his mother's ancestry with Abyssinia (Ethiopia). According to this version, Abram (birth name Ibrahim) Gannibal (Hannibal), the grandfather of Pushkin's mother, came from a princely Abyssinian family, was abducted as a child by Ottoman slave traders and taken to Constantinople, and in 1705 was brought to Russia as a present for Peter the Great. Peter took an interest in the African boy, had him baptized, and became his godfather; the boy was subsequently known as Abram Petrovich Gannibal. He became the emperor's personal valet, secretary, and trusted confidant; was educated in mathematics and engineering; and eventually became Russia's chief military engineer. Gannibal distinguished himself during the reign of Peter's daughter, Empress Elizabeth (Elizaveta), in designing and building military fortifications in Russia's Baltic lands. Gannibal retired as a four-star general and died in 1781, having become a member of the Russian nobility and landed gentry. Of Gannibal's eleven children by his second wife, Christina Regina von Sjöberg, a Baltic German noblewoman whom he met while stationed in Pärnu (Pernov), seven lived into adulthood. Pushkin's mother, Nadezhda Gannibal, was the only daughter of Commander Osip Gannibal, one of Abram Gannibal's sons. She married Sergey Pushkin, her distant cousin and a scion of Russian pre-Petrine aristocracy, and Alexander Pushkin (1799–1837) was their eldest son.

In recent decades, a different version of Pushkin's African ancestry has gained acceptance. According to this version, Pushkin's great-grandfather Ibragim Gannibal had come not from Abyssinia but rather from the present-day borderlands of Chad and Cameroon, where the Sultanate of

Logone-Burmi was located, and as a boy was brought to Peter the Great. What is clear in any case is that Pushkin's origins were both African and Russian. The genius poet himself and his contemporaries were fully conscious of his biracial origins and appearance, his otherness, as is reflected both in contemporary accounts and in Pushkin's literary works, including his lyrical poetry and the novel *Blackmoor of Peter the Great*, written in 1827–1828.

In this authorial digression, which is invited by the author's reflections on Karaites in connection with Natasha and Anatoly's visit to Vilnius and Trakai, the author creatively and speculatively reconstructs Pushkin's thinking about Jewishness as a historical, ethnic, and religious identity, but also as a metaphor of otherness.

Page 174

Solomonic dynasty—"Lions of Judah" . . . the Queen of Sheba and King Solomon: The lion is the symbol of the Biblical Tribe of Judah. The *Kebra Negast* (The Glory of the Kings), a fourteenth-century Ethiopian chronicle, depicts the origins of the Solomonic dynasty, going back to the meeting of the Queen Sheba (Queen Mekeda of Ethiopia) and King Solomon, and the subsequent visit of Ethiopian King Menelik I to Jerusalem, to obtain King Solomon's blessing. In Ethiopian history the kings of the Solomonic dynasty are regarded as direct descendants of King Solomon (and of the Tribe of Judah). The last king of the Solomonic dynasty, Hailie Selassie I, who was deposed in 1975, considered himself the 225th king from King David. During his reign four Stars of David were added to the corners of the Ethiopian green, yellow, and red flag, which depicts the Lion of Judah in the center.

Nikolay Ashukin's book *The Living Pushkin:* Nikolay Ashukin (1890–1972): Soviet literary critic.

Elizaveta Vorontsova (née Branitskaya, 1792–1880): Russian aristocrat of Polish origin, wife of Count (later Prince) Mikhail Vorontsov, Governor-General of Novorossiya (New Russia) and Bessarabia, under whom Pushkin served during part of his southern exile of 1820–1824. Pushkin devoted a number of poems to Vorontsova, and to this day, the extent of their intimacy remains a matter of scholarly debate. A seal ring with a Hebrew inscription was Vorontsova's parting gift to Pushkin, which he received from her in 1824. Based on the contents and script of Hebrew inscription, the famous Russian

Orientalist and Judaic scholar Avraam Garkavi (1839–1919) determined the Crimean-Karaite origin of the seal ring.

"Where the sea is eternally lapping . . ." (in Russian, "Tam, gde more vechno pleshchet . . ."): Opening line of "Talisman," Alexander Pushkin's poem of 1827.

Gogol . . . *Taras Bulba*: 1835 short novel by Russian classic author of Ukrainian origin, Nikolay Gogol (Ukrainian Mykola Hohol, 1809–1852). Set during the Bohdan Khmelnytsky Rebellion of 1648–1657, it depicts a number of Jewish characters living in Ukraine and Poland. While Gogol mostly portrays Jews with derision and mockery, he does construct at least one complex and full character, the Jew Yankel.

Page 175

"I'm too familiar with the Bible . . ." (in Russian, "Ia slishkom s bibliei znakom"): This line occurs in the opening, versified, humorous section of Alexander Pushkin's letter to the future memoirist Filipp Vigel. The letter was composed between 22 October and 4 November 1823, in Kishinev, the capital of Bessarabia (now Chișinău, the capital of Moldova), where Pushkin spent almost three years. While in Kishinev, Pushkin for the first time encountered a variety of contemporary Bessarabian (Moldovan) Jews and observed Jewish life in the Pale of Settlement. Pushkin writes of the "Yids" of Kishinev but also implies his esteem for ancient Hebrews of the Bible.

not Jews, but Yids: By the 1860s, in literary Russian, a distinction had crystallized between the normative noun *evrey* (derived etymologically from Hebrew and meaning "Jew") and the pejorative *zhid* (meaning "Yid" or "Kike"). *Zhid* and its cognates had been normatively used in old Russian, and it continued to be used neutrally until the fifteenth century. West Slavic variants, *Żyd* in Polish, *Žid* in Czech, etc., are still used normatively. A separate noun, *iudey* (literally "Judean"), and its cognates, are used in Russian to refer to religion rather then Jewish ethnic, historical, and cultural identity.

Nashchyokin: Pavel Nashchyokin (1801–1854), Russian philanthropist and collector, a close friend of Pushkin and godfather of his oldest son.

"When the Assyrian mighty ruler . . ." (in Russian, "Kogda vladyka assiriiskii . . ."): Alexander Pushkin's poem of 1835, a retelling of chapter 5–7 of the deuterocanonical Book of Judith, in which a beautiful Jewish woman seduces and beheads the Assyrian general Holofernes, whose forces sack her native village of Bethulia, and thus saves her people.

Page 176

inspired Pushkin to write his *Gabrieliad:* A satirical and irreverent long poem (in Russian, *Gavriiliada*) about Mary, the Mother of Jesus, and immaculate conception, created by young Alexander Pushkin in 1821 and originally circulated anonymously.

Page 177

"My Genealogy": a poem by Alexander Pushkin (in Russian, "Moya rodoslovnaya"), dated 1830; in the "Post Scriptum" section of the poem, Pushkin points to his great-grandfather Abram Gannibal, who became one of Peter's associates, and to Gannibal's son, Lieutenant General Ivan Gannibal (1731–1801), Pushkin's great-uncle.

Page 179

Hakham: Spiritual leader of a Karaite community. In speaking of the survival of Karaites during the Shoah, the Karaite woman refers to the controversial figure of Seraya Shapshal (1873–1961), who was then the *Hakham* of the Lithuanian Karaite community; with regard to Karaites and their survival, see note to pp. 166–78.

Page 181

"Yes, my Motherland, my mother—Russia": This epigraph is taken from the novel *Third Capital* (*Tret'ya stolitsa*, 1923), by the prominent Soviet Russian prose writer Boris Pilnyak (pseudonym of Boris Vogau, 1894–1938).

"*Filya, why so quiet? . . .*": The concluding lines of the famous short poem "The Kind Filya" (*Dobryi Filia*, 1960) by Nikolay Rubtsov (1936–1971), a Soviet Russian poet in the peasant vein.

Page 183

"The caretaker shovels the street . . .": The opening stanza of David Shrayer-Petrov's poem "Early Morning in Moscow" (*Rannee utro zimoi*, 1976), which could not be published in the USSR, owing to its Jewish thrust, but circulated in the underground. English translation by Edwin Honig and Maxim D. Shrayer. See also p. 207 for a self-referential detail about a "poet who had since been expelled and banished—all for his desire to go to Israel."

Page 184

Pushkin Monument: Bronze monument to the great Russian writer Alexander Pushkin (1799–1837). This landmark monument by the sculptor Aleksandr Opekushin was unveiled in 1880 and originally stood at the beginning of Tverskoy Boulevard at Pushkin Square (Pushkinskaya Ploshchad'; prior to 1931, Strastnaya Square); in 1950 it was moved to the other side of the square, where it now stands, facing the principal thoroughfare of the historic city center, Tverskaya Street (Gorky Street in 1932–1990).

Tverskoy Boulevard: A section of the Boulevard Ring, it begins at Pushkin Square, where Strastnoy Boulevard ends, and runs south from Tverskaya to Nikitskiye Gates Square at the intersection with Bolshaya Nikitskaya Street (see note to p. 207), where the boulevard changes its name to Nikitsky Boulevard.

Page 185

Konenkov's studio: The renowned Russian sculptor Sergey Konenkov (1874–1971) lived and worked in the United States in 1922–1945. In 1945 Stalin sanctioned Konenkov's return to the USSR. Konenkov enjoyed high official status and had a studio two blocks from Pushkin Square at 17 Gorky (Tverskaya) Street, presently the Konenkov Museum.

Moscow Arts Theater: Founded in 1898 in Moscow by Konstantin Stanislavsky and Vladimir Nemirovich-Danchenko, it became one of Russia's principal theaters and acting conservatories; its earliest history was associated with Chekhov's dramatic works. The novel here refers to the so-called new stage of the Moscow Arts Theater, a modern building that opened in 1973 on Tverskoy Boulevard, while the historic "old stage" in Kamergersky Lane was under renovation.

Telegraph Agency of the Soviet Union: Still known by its Soviet-era name and the acronym TASS, this news agency dates to 1902, and in 1925 was established as the central Soviet news agency. The modern TASS building with a globe over its entrance, which Doctor Levitin notes on his walk, stands at Nikitskiye Gates Square, where Tverskoy Boulevard ends and Nikitsky Boulevard starts.

Great Patriotic War: In Soviet and post-Soviet Russian historiography, the Soviet war against Nazism in 1941–45 is called the "Great Patriotic War."

Page 186

Chekhov Street (Ulitsa Chekhova): The name, from 1944 to 1993, of Malaya Dmitrovka Street in the center of Moscow, running from Pushkin Square to the Garden Ring.

Page 194

Eisenstein: Sergei Eisenstein (1898–1948), visionary Soviet filmmaker, director, and theorist; creator of *Battleship Potemkin* (1925), *Alexander Nevsky* (1938), and other works.

Tarkovsky: Andrey Tarkovsky (1932–1986), one of the most influential Soviet film directors of the post-Stalin period, author of *Andrei Rublev* (1966), *Solaris* (1972), *Mirror* (1975), and other films. After 1982 Tarkovsky lived and worked in Western Europe; he died in Paris. Tarkovsky's father, Arseny Tarkovsky (1907–1989), was a Russian poet and literary translator.

Page 196

Nikitsky Botanical Garden: One of the oldest in Europe, this sprawling botanical garden and research institute is located on Crimea's south shore outside Yalta.

Jacqueline Susann (1918–1974): Smuggled into the USSR, Susann's bestselling novels, such as *Valley of the Dolls* (1966) and *Once Is Not Enough* (1973), enjoyed popularity among members of the Soviet intelligentsia; see also the note on Harold Robbins (p. 100).

Page 198

"Little Scarlet Flower" (in Russian, *Alen'kii tsvetochek*, 1858): Famous fairy tale by the Russian writer Sergey Aksakov (1791–1859), an adaptation of the Beauty and the Beast story.

Count Fyodor Tolstoy (1782-1846): Colorful Russian aristocrat, nicknamed "the American," renowned for his tempestuous nature, numerous duels (including a near-duel with Alexander Pushkin), gambling, and a passion for travel.

Page 207

"Wailing Wall": In the lore of Soviet Jews of the 1970s–1980s, the vacant lot and wall outside the appeals office of the Visa Section in Moscow's Khlynovsky Alley (see below) was ruefully referred to as the Wailing Wall.

Herzen Street (in Russian, Ulitsa Gertsena): This was the name of Bolshaya Nikitskaya Street in 1920–1993. Alexander Herzen (1812–1870), after whom the street was renamed during the Soviet period, was a key figure in the history of Russian socialism, as well as a novelist and memoirist; see also Herzen's grandson, the distinguished Russian and Soviet surgeon Pyotr Herzen (p. 231). Bolshaya Nikitskaya Street (Herzen Street during the events of the novel), a major street in the historic center of Moscow, runs west for just over a mile from the Manezh Square (which is located close to the Kremlin and Red Square) to the Garden Ring. Doctor Levitin identifies a number of memorable sites and landmarks on the street as he walks west from Manezh Square: the Moscow Conservatory, the Museum of Natural History (Zoological Museum) of Moscow State University, Central House of Writers (TsDL; see also a reference to the "poet who had since been expelled and banished—all for his desire to go to Israel"). As Doctor Levitin walks along Herzen Street to the appeal office of the Visa Section, he turns right into Khlynovsky Alley two blocks before the intersection of Herzen Street and the Boulevard Ring (Nikitsky Boulevard and Tverskoy Boulevard). As he approaches Khlynovsky Alley, he passes a homeopathic pharmacy that used to be located on Herzen Street.

Page 208

Hoffmannesque: This refers to the characters and atmosphere created by Ernst Theodor Amadeus Hoffmann (1776–1822), German Romantic author of phantasmagoric tales.

Page 212

Fleyshman, Abezgauz, Bernshteyn, Shrayer . . . : This composite list of typical Germanic Ashkenazi Jewish last names is informed by the last names of real refuseniks the author encountered in 1979–1980, but also points to Jewish-Russian writers whom the author had personally encountered: poet-turned-filmmaker Ilya Averbakh; translator Moris Vaksmakher; poet, translator, and memoirist

Evgeny Reyn; poet, translator, and prose writer Anatoly Nayman; poet and essayist Aleksandr Kushner; poet and literary critic David Samoylov (pseydonym of David Kaufman). None of these authors sought to emigrate, and yet their names on the list of refuseniks underscores the mass character of the Jewish exodus from the Soviet Union, while also highlighting the fragility of the position of Jews in that country.

ethnic Germans: Here, descendants of the Volga Germans; on Russia's ethnic Germans, see note to p. 71.

Druzhnikov, Biserkin, Chayko, Golovko, Isaakyan, Moshiashvili, Alayev, Avshalumov: The list includes Russian, Ukrainian, and Belarusian last names of Ashkenazi Jews; an Armenian last name derived from the Biblical name "Isaac"; a Georgian last name belonging to a Georgian Jew; a Central Asian-sounding last name presumably belonging to a Bukharan (Central Asian) Jew; a last name suggesting that its bearer is a Mountain Jew from the Caucasus. In the list, the last name Druzhnikov suggests Yuri Druzhnikov (pseydonym of Yuri Alperovich, 1933–2008), author, critic, and journalist, subsequently professor at the University of California-Davis.

Page 214

"Physician, heal thyself": See Luke 4:23.

Page 215

Vasily Aksyonov (1932–2009): Prominent Russian fiction writer, one of the leading figures of the so-called 1960s literature (*shestidesyatniki*) to emerge onto the Soviet literary stage during Khrushchev's Thaw of the late 1950s. Son of a Jewish mother and ethnic Russian father, Aksyonov emigrated to the United States, where he lived and taught until 2004. Aksyonov spent the last years of his life in Biarritz and in Moscow, where he died in July 2009.

Page 216

David Oistrakh (1908–1974): Renowned Jewish-Russian violinist; for a number of summers, Oistrakh rented a dacha in the Estonian resort of Pärnu.

David Samoylov: The pseudonym of David Kaufman, a prominent Russian poet and literary translator of Jewish descent (1920–1990) who distanced himself from Jewishness. In 1974 Samoylov bought a house in Pärnu and relocated there with his second wife and children.

The Whistle (in Russian, *Gudok*): Founded in 1917, *The Whistle* was the main newspaper of the Soviet railroads; in 1971 the print run was 700,000 copies. The newspaper is still published today. In the 1920s a number of important Russian authors were contributors, among them Ilya Ilf and Evgeny Petrov, Valentin Kataev, Yuri Olesha, and Konstantin Paustovsky. Ilf and Petrov described the editorial office in their novel *Twelve Chairs* (1927). In 1924–1998, the editorial office was located at 7 Voznesensky Lane (in 1922–1993, known as Stankevich Street-Ulitsa Stankevicha), a street in the historic heart of Moscow, which runs to the northeast from Bolshaya Nikitskaya Street (formerly Herzen Street) to Tverskaya (formerly Gorky) Street. The dead-end Khlynovsky Tupik (Khlynovsky Alley), which runs parallel to Voznesensky Lane just west of it, used to house the appeals office of the Visa Section; see also pp. 210, 213, 269.

Page 225

Borjomi: Naturally carbonated mineral water from a source in the Republic of Georgia; very popular in the USSR.

Page 227

military hospital at Krasnye Kholmy: Fictional name.

Page 231

Zakharin, Filatov, and Herzen: Grigory Zakharin (1829-1898), renowned Russian physician and professor of medicine; Vladimir Filatov (1875–1956), famous Russian and Soviet ophthalmologist; Pyotr Herzen (Gertsen, 1871–1947), distinguished Russian and Soviet surgeon, one of the founders of oncology in the USSR; grandson of the Russian revolutionary and author Alexander Herzen (see p. 207).

Page 232

Smolenskaya Square: of the western section of the Garden Ring, between Smolenskaya-Sennya Square and Novinsky Boulevard. Pavel Teryokhin and Tatyana Levitina meet in front of the well-known Moscow food emporium,

Gastronom Smolensky (presently, Sed'moy Kontinent supermarket), located at the corner of Arbat Street; see also note to p. 237.

Page 233

Biryulevo: Former village south of Moscow, where, starting in the 1960s, a sleeping district was developed on the city's outskirts.

Page 234

Oryol: Major historic Russian city and provincial capital, located about 220 miles southwest of Moscow.

Page 237

Kalinin Prospect . . . the Arbat: Arbat Street (sometimes referred to as Old Arbat=Staryi Arbat) in Moscow's historic center dates to the fifteenth century and is one of the city's oldest streets. This pedestrian street in the heart of a fancy area of Moscow, once the principal road from the Kremlin in the western direction, runs for about 0.7 miles from Arbatskaya Square and Boulevard Ring to Smolenskaya Square and the Garden Ring. In the 1960s the Arbat became a pedestrian area, while a near-parallel road, known in the Soviet years as Kalinin Prospect (its new part now called Novyi Arbat-the New Arbat), was extended and expanded to allow traffic to run from Mokhovaya Street westward toward Garden Road and beyond, to the Novoarbatsky Bridge over the Moskva River. The newer section of Kalinin Prospect was lined with modern high-rise apartment buildings.

Page 242

Fedoskino: Village outside Moscow, home to the so-called Fedoskino miniature painting school of lacquered boxes and decorative objects; see also Palekh on p. 70.

Page 248

Oleg Popov (1930–2016): Nationally famous Soviet circus clown and actor, who used to appear in a signature checkered cap.

Page 252

"The Afghan news agency . . .": On the Soviet war in Afghanistan, see note to p. 18.

Page 255

kishlak: A village in Central Asia and Azerbaijan (also spelled *qishlaq*); the word entered Russian from Turkic languages.

Page 261

"After that she didn't read and couldn't read . . .": This is a seminal passage from Dostoevsky's *Crime and Punishment*, part 4, chapter 4, in which Raskolnikov and Sonia read from John 11.

ACKNOWLEDGMENTS

*T*he translation of this novel has been in the making for many years, and the author and editor are most grateful to Arna B. Bronstein and Aleksandra I. Fleszar for their dedication and commitment.

The editor completed the work on the manuscript in the Spring of 2017 during a sabbatical leave from Boston College. He gratefully acknowledges the support of Boston College.

Polly Rosenwaike copyedited the entire manuscript, and the author and editor would like to thank her for her expert work, her tact, and love of language.

The author and editor thank Kathryn Wildfong, Kristin Harpster, Rachel Ross, Emily Nowak, Kristina Stonehill, and their colleagues at Wayne State University Press for giving *Doctor Levitin* a loving and hospitable home.

Without the love and support of our family—Mila, Karen, Mira, and Tatiana—this publication would have remained a dream.

Thanks to all of you, the English translation of *Doctor Levitin* is now a reality.

D.S.P. and M.D.S.

January 2018
Brookline, Mass.